WHISPERS IN THE KALAHARI

A NOVEL OF LOVE, SECRETS, AND THE AFRICAN BUSH

WINGS OVER AFRICA
BOOK THREE

B. G. NETTELTON

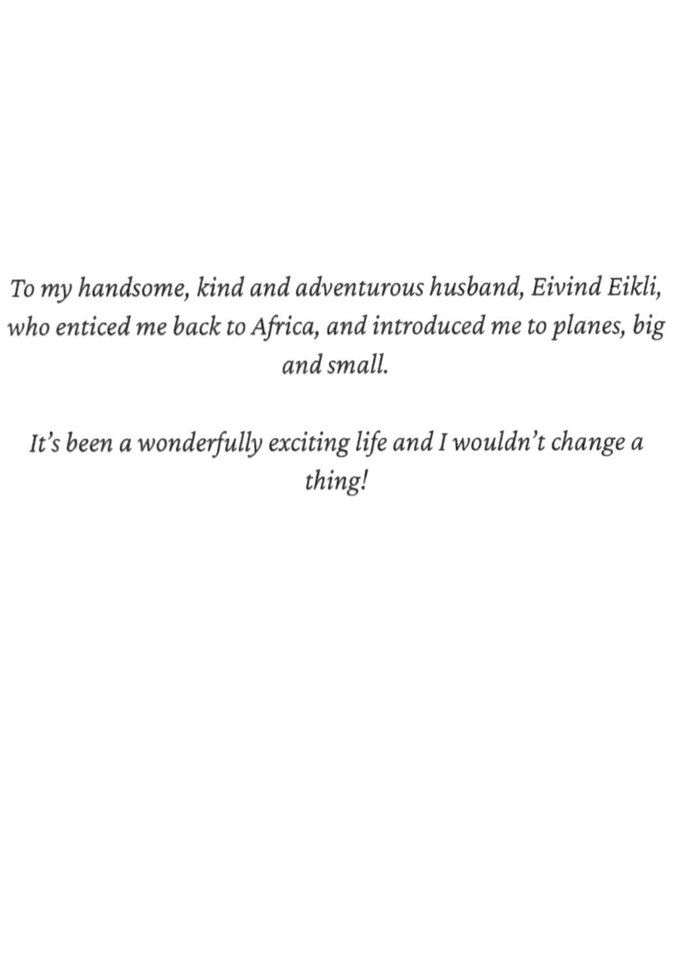

To my handsome, kind and adventurous husband, Eivind Eikli, who enticed me back to Africa, and introduced me to planes, big and small.

It's been a wonderfully exciting life and I wouldn't change a thing!

CHAPTER

ONE

MAUN, BOTSWANA, 1989

Susan sat alone at the bar, nursing her third vodka and lime, wondering what madness had brought her to this Wild West saloon in the middle of Botswana.

It wasn't because she'd seen the writing on the wall at her dreary copywriting job in Johannesburg when James had mentioned there was a position going here.

There were far more salubrious places to further a career than this dorp, with its perpetual dust, its heat haze shimmering above battered Land Cruisers and pickups, and the smell of spilled beer, sweat and avgas drifting in whenever the door swung open.

Catching the appreciative eye of a khaki-clad stranger jostling through the crowd with a handful of Castle Lagers, she sent him a sultry look as she adjusted her cleavage. He wasn't bad-looking. Mid-thirties, perhaps—a little older than herself—dressed in the ubiquitous bush gear that failed to distinguish hunters from safari guides, or the pilots servicing the safari boom, shuttling tourists between camps in the flooded Okavango Delta like a taxi service.

She watched him dispense his alcoholic burden. Sweat darkened the cloth between his shoulder blades. Two days' stubble. Floppy, dirty-blond hair. Funny how she was always attracted to the same type.

She ought to have learned by now.

"Susan?"

She swung around, disappointed. Hunter Dude had looked as though he was heading her way, but someone else had cut in.

"James!" Of course she'd known she'd bump into her cousin within a day of arriving, but his timing was less than perfect. "What a surprise!"

"What are you doing here, Susan? You should have let Verity and me know you were coming!"

"Oh, I'm not visiting. I'm here for good." Susan curved her lips into a secretive smile, not just for James' benefit, for she could still see Hunter Dude from the corner of her eye. And he definitely had his eye on her too.

"The job on the *Okavango Observer* you told me about," she clarified at James's questioning look. "I was already sick of life in the big smoke, and when you mentioned the reporter's job, I acted on a wing and a prayer and decided to come home."

"Impulsive as ever. But Maun has never been home, has it? Not after we were kids in Serowe?"

"No, I meant Botswana in general. I'm a bush girl at heart." Susan picked up her vodka and drained it. "I'm hoping I'll feel the same in a month."

"You and me both. And, of course, I hope so much that Verity will feel the same, soon, too!" said James, looking momentarily stricken as he signalled to the barman for another vodka for her and three beers for himself.

"It'll come back quick smart for you. You grew up here," Susan said. "Verity might be a harder nut to crack. Especially after what happened to Saskia. I wondered if they'd both be on the first plane back to Australia after that ghastly attack. Sorry, I should have asked how Saskia is. God, I'm hopeless." She took another sip, then added, "Though I did know she's okay, otherwise Angie would have told me. I gather the cousins have become firm friends at St Anne's. Of all the coincidences. Who'd have thought?"

"And who'd have thought you were old enough to have a fifteen-year-old daughter at all, much less one going to the same boarding school as Saskia." James looked about to say more when a shout from the back of the bar pulled his attention away. "Sorry, Susan, I've got to get these to the thirsty throng. You okay on your own for now? Waiting for someone?"

Susan smiled. "Always waiting," she said, dressing up the painful truth with a flippant laugh.

Like maybe Hunter Dude next, she thought, as James disappeared into the crowd.

But Hunter Dude had vanished into the jostling mass, so her gaze roamed over what other possibilities this frontier saloon might yield. Overall, the prospects were far more to her liking than the suits who congregated at the bars she used to frequent in Jo'burg.

Her eye settled on the khaki-clad back of a man of decent height, broad-shouldered, sleeves rolled to reveal biceps that made her insides quiver. Dirty-blond hair. No, not Hunter Dude, but—

"Lady's bounty!"

She stilled, poised for him to turn, ready with her best

smile. But he was making a play for some ridiculously young blonde backpacker by the look of her—yes, you could spot them a mile away—brandishing a carved elephant he'd no doubt picked up for a song from one of the traders. In answer to the girl's unintelligible question, as she squealed with delight, he said, "Yes, of course I carved it," accompanying the lie with a theatrical wink.

She should have known it was him by the performance, if not by the words themselves.

Heat flooded her body. Red-hot rage. Shame.

Every emotion under the sun except any that were good.

Goddamn womaniser, Starky Willis.

She should have known she'd bump into him on her first day in this godforsaken dump.

It was why she'd come here, after all.

Not on impulse.

Not on a wing and a prayer.

No.

She'd come here for something far more calculated.

Vengeance.

~

CHAPTER

TWO

CENTRAL KALAHARI, 1974

15 YEARS EARLIER

"Hey, Suze! How'd you like some pretty ostrich feathers to dress up in? Lady's bounty."

Susan swallowed, her throat dry, her palms clammy, her stomach churning with excitement as she forced herself not to leap from her director's chair by the campfire when she saw Starky saunter into camp with his hefty load.

A bloody great ostrich.

"Oh, Starky, what have you done?" she said with a laugh. "You shot it for me?" She flicked a glance at Mike, who'd come back ten minutes earlier. Her brother looked even darker now than when he'd slunk in, glowering at her after she'd teased, playfully, "Not even a guinea fowl for dinner? I'm starving!"

"You shot an ostrich, you bloody idiot!" Mike's voice

was low and tight with barely controlled fury as he flicked a black look between Starky and Phil, who sat nursing both a beer and his rifle between his knees. "What the hell do you think you were doing? You know it's against the law."

Susan knotted her fingers together, shifting from one foot to the other, trying to keep the bright, cheerful look plastered on her face. Uh-oh. It wasn't often her even-tempered brother got so hot under the collar.

Though she longed to say something to restore the peace, perhaps this was not the moment to reveal her feelings for Mike's friend, whom she'd known for years—

But seemed only to have truly noticed for the very first time now.

"Hey, relax, Mike. It was an accident. A *blerry* warthog startled the impala I was about to bag for dinner, and instead this old bugger stumbled into my crosshairs. So— just the feathers for you, Suzie-girl. The rest'll fetch a good price." He looked from Mike to Phil. "Won't it?" he prompted.

As usual, Starky looked as though he couldn't care less about what upset everyone else. It was one of the oh-so-cool things about him. Mike was such a goody-two-shoes, while Phil was—

Well, Phil was the dweebiest, weediest apology for a twenty-one-year-old she'd ever met. He couldn't even look Mike in the eye when Mike wanted backup because… well, perhaps Starky had not been entirely right to break the law.

"I—we'll have rangers handing out fines because Starky violated the Fauna Conservation Act," Phil finally said, staring down at his dusty boots. "But if they do, Starky can just pay it."

"Or face his day in court, where I certainly won't vouch

for him!" Mike all but spat, dropping into a canvas chair with enough force to make the metal frame creak.

"Come on, Mike. What are the chances?" Susan hated it when Mike was in a bad mood. He was usually such a fun big brother, but this whole trip he'd been dark about something, and she was sure it wasn't just her presence. Yes, she'd overheard his objections when her parents had insisted he take along his little sister on their Kalahari camping trip because Granny and Grandpa had decided to join them in Plettenberg Bay for the weekend, and Susan was too young to stay on her own.

Twice now she'd stumbled on Mike and Starky speaking in heated undertones, their conversation cutting off the instant she appeared, as though she'd interrupted something she wasn't meant to hear.

And another reason she didn't want bad blood between Starky and Mike was because who knew where things might lead before the end of their four days in the bush? The way Starky kept looking at her, she was pretty sure she'd be kissing him before midnight. The thought made her stomach flutter with equal parts excitement and apprehension.

"I'm sure it'll be fine," she added for good measure. As the only female, she supposed her role was to play the peacekeeper. Though she couldn't help wondering if that was all she was meant to be. Well, she certainly wasn't going to play cook and mollycoddler.

Right now, among this lot of ill-matched blokes, she wasn't quite sure what her role was.

"Yeah, I'm sure it'll be fine." Phil leaned back in his camp chair and stretched out his long, skinny legs, encased in bell-bottomed jeans. He stared morosely into the fire, his gaze flicking between them all, lingering a fraction too long on Susan before sliding away. In the firelight his eyes looked pale and unreadable.

She shivered. But not the way she did when Starky looked at her.

Really, it didn't look like anyone was enjoying themselves.

Wrinkling her nose at the acrid smell of smoke, she wrapped her arms around herself, suddenly cold despite the day's lingering heat. Beyond the ring of firelight, the bush had turned black, and somewhere out there a hyena laughed—high, cracked, almost human.

She jumped.

Normally, Mike would have laughed at her reaction and teased her for never getting used to the sounds of the bush.

But tonight he seemed to be on another planet, staring into the fire as if he saw something there no one else could.

"Isn't anyone going to offer a lady a drink?" she asked brightly, breaking the silence. The words came out more flirtatious than she'd intended, but she couldn't seem to help herself around Starky.

Starky rose and, with a smile and a flourish that made her heart skip, went to the cooler box. "Coke or..." He winked at her. "Perhaps a Castle Lager?"

"Ooh, that sounds perfect," she said, tipping up her nose at Mike's look and adding defensively, "One beer is hardly going to go to my head." Though the way Starky was looking at her, she already felt intoxicated.

"It's everything else," Mike said, with that uncharacteristically dour expression.

Really, Susan couldn't think what had got into him, but there was no point wondering about what he'd never tell her, because Starky was opening a beer and pouring it into a glass, which he handed to her. And the way he looked at her made everything else seem to fade. She tried to ignore Phil's narrowed gaze following the exchange.

"Not much to cook over the fire tonight, since your brother missed his shot at the impala." Starky grinned as he rested one foot on the rocks encircling their merrily blazing campfire.

"Shut up," Mike said quietly, tapping his fingernails against the side of his can.

Then he stopped.

All at once, every man in the camp seemed to hear it at the same time—the distant growl of an engine.

Mike was on his feet in an instant. "Someone's here! Christ, Starky, what have you done with the ostrich? You've got it bloody draped over the *bakkie* for all the world to see."

Now Starky did look concerned. Susan knew the rangers patrolled the area, and although it wasn't likely they'd stumble upon them, it wasn't beyond the bounds of possibility.

And now someone was here.

The three of them lurched into motion, chairs scraping, dust kicking up. Starky sprinted towards the ostrich, dragging it from the back of the vehicle and flinging it as far as he could into the bush just as a Land Rover roared into camp, headlights slashing white across the clearing. Susan's heart hammered against her ribs. Phil alone remained seated, watching it all unfold with an oddly intent, almost satisfied expression.

Guiltily, the four of them stood waiting for the ranger to leap out and charge them with poaching, or whatever it was Starky was guilty of.

But it wasn't the ranger.

"Jeremy!" Susan cried, too shocked to say anything else.

Her stomach dropped at the sight of her ex-boyfriend's familiar face.

Then Mike stepped forward with a half-smile. "What are you doing here, man? I thought you and Susan had broken up."

Jeremy, good-natured—too good-natured, which was part of the reason Susan had ended things—shrugged with that same bland smile that had begun to irritate her after two weeks of doing nothing more than holding hands and kissing. "We're still old friends, aren't we?"

"Sure!" said Susan, going towards him to give him a sisterly hug, hoping it might make Starky jealous. There were plenty of blokes who thought she was all right. He wasn't the only one. Though she couldn't help noticing how Phil's attention sharpened at Jeremy's arrival, his pale eyes watchful now, calculating.

"But what are you doing here?"

"Your pa told me where you were going. It's one of our favourite camping spots too, so I thought I'd drop in and say hi."

"Want a beer?" asked Mike, looking a bit more relaxed now as he opened the cooler box. "We thought you were the rangers come to check on us."

"Nah." Jeremy gave a short laugh as he took the beer handed to him. "They did stop me on the road a little way back and checked my vehicle, though."

Susan glanced at the three boys. All wore slightly panicked expressions they were trying hard to hide.

"Were they travelling this way?" Mike asked.

As Starky slunk off, Susan at first thought he was going towards the ostrich. Then she realised he was heading for his gun, which for one ghastly moment made her think he might use it if they were confronted by the authorities.

But he merely slung the weapon over his shoulder before disappearing into the bush. Susan realised Starky was the only one carrying a Krieghoff double rifle. Obviously, if the ostrich were discovered, he didn't want the shot traced back to him.

By the time the rest of them were sitting around the fire again, which Phil had stoked higher, the mood had improved—at least on the surface. Starky had got rid of the evidence—the ostrich and his gun—and the rangers hadn't stopped by to ask questions. Even so, something taut seemed to remain beneath the talk, as though one wrong word might snap it all tight again.

By the time Susan was on her third beer, the sun had dipped, and she was feeling happily light-headed. The late-afternoon gold had drained from the sky, leaving the acacias etched dark against a wash of violet dusk. The fire popped and spat. Smoke drifted low. Phil kept throwing her furtive glances that made her skin crawl, though she couldn't have said why.

"What about a photo before we lose the light complete-ly?" she asked, reaching for her Instamatic camera on the camp table. Film was precious out here, and she had only a few frames left on the roll, but she'd been saving them for something special. She'd taken plenty of shots of the land-scape and animals, but none yet of herself with the three boys.

And that would be a prize shot to show the girls at varsity: Susan, on safari, alone with three blokes. No—four, now that Jeremy was here.

"Oh, come on," she cajoled, pushing the camera into Jeremy's hands and pulling Mike to his feet before grabbing Starky's strong, warm hands to do the same.

Longing rippled through her as she smiled up into his

face, and he winked as he squeezed her hand. The look in his eyes promised everything she'd been dreaming of.

She knew she ought to be similarly encouraging to Phil, but the thought of touching Phil's cold, girlish hands for even a moment made her shudder. He was such a poor specimen of a fellow, with his dark hair lank and oily, his chest hairless as far as she could tell, and a complete lack of self-confidence.

"Be a good sport, Jem," she said, smiling at him as he studied the camera. Since someone had to take the shot of Susan with her band of admirers, it might as well be easy-going Jeremy, whom she could cajole into anything. "No hard feelings?"

"Not really," he said. "I did hope—"

"Okay, everyone, get close together," Susan directed, standing in the middle and slipping her arms around Mike's and Starky's waists on either side of her. She felt Starky's muscles tense beneath her touch, and her heart began to race. "Just one good one, Jem. Ma will like it. She'll want to send it to Australia to Auntie Margaret, who can show James what he's missing."

Jeremy took a step back and lifted the camera. "James? Your cousin?" he asked. "I remember him. You were great mates in Serowe. Wasn't he supposed to come on this hunt? All the way from Australia?"

"James and his girlfriend, Verity, booked tickets to see his dad, who's gone back to work at the diamond mine in Orapa, and to go hunting with Mike and me, but then they bailed at the last minute," Susan said cheerfully. "That's why Phil's here, isn't it, Phil?"

She noticed Phil's expression darken, though he quickly masked it.

"Right. Shall I take it now?" Jeremy asked, cutting

across whatever Phil might have said in response—which probably wasn't much, thought Susan, though James said he was brainy.

Which meant nothing if a man wasn't brawny.

Like Starky.

"Wait," she said as they started to break apart. "Everyone grab your rifles. You too, Starky. Aunty Margaret'll want to see you all looking the part. Even though no one's shot anything yet, this *is* a proper hunting expedition, isn't it?"

For the first time, no one moved at once before Starky slunk off to fetch his.

Then the evening light caught the gleam of metal as the men positioned their rifles. Jeremy's Krieghoff looked almost identical to Starky's, though Jeremy's was meticulously maintained while Starky's showed signs of harder use. The contrast was just like the two men: Jeremy, so boringly careful; Starky, so recklessly alive.

Now, what kind of choice was that?

Jeremy raised the camera.

Something stirred in the bushes behind them, and everyone tensed.

But it was only a duiker, slipping silently through the gathering darkness.

CHAPTER

THREE

By the time the sun had dropped below the horizon, painting the sky in bruised shades of crimson and purple, Susan was feeling woozy. That didn't stop her accepting another beer from Starky, their fingers brushing in a way that sent electric shivers all the way up her arm.

To her surprise, Mike didn't seem to notice. Instead, his gaze kept straying to the horizon, as though he were expecting trouble to come out of the dark. She wondered what on earth was eating him.

It served her interests, though. She shifted her camp chair a little closer to Starky, who glanced at her with raised eyebrows, a flicker of desire in his eyes. The campfire seemed to hold everyone else's attention. It fizzled and crackled when Phil laid another acacia branch on the embers, the sharp scent of burning wood mingling with the dry, dusty smell of the Kalahari night. At least Phil was earning his keep by making sure they didn't all freeze. He'd also managed a passable stew from the tinned bully beef Mike had insisted they wouldn't need.

Susan sighed, longing to snuggle into Starky, but knowing it was too soon with weird, weedy Phil watching them from the corner of his eye, and Mike and Jeremy locked in tense conversation nearby.

To her surprise, their voices suddenly rose. Susan had never heard Jeremy sound anything but calm, but he was certainly laying into Mike about something, their words snatched away by the dry wind.

Concerned, she straightened in her chair. "Mike—?" she began.

But before she could say more, a high beam raked the campsite, and a vehicle bearing the unmistakable insignia of the Department of Wildlife and National Parks rolled to a halt, its engine growling in the stillness.

Two rangers in khaki stepped out, the taller of the two introducing himself and apologising for the disturbance. "Won't take a minute. Just need you to answer a few questions." His tone was casual enough, but there was an undercurrent of suspicion that made Susan's skin prickle.

She turned to Starky, her heart beginning to pound as guilt needled her. She'd told him to fetch his rifle for that stupid photograph, and if the rangers found the dead ostrich and linked the bullet to Starky's Krieghoff, it would all be her fault.

Starky, however, looked perfectly unruffled, as if he had nothing at all to hide, though she noticed the slight tightening around his eyes.

Just a routine check on campers in the area, the rangers explained. An elephant had been poached not far away and, though the kill was a few days old, they were still taking down the names and gun registrations of everyone nearby.

Susan tightened her grip on the metal arms of her camp chair. She recognised the gleam of fear in Mike's and Phil's eyes, but Starky looked entirely unconcerned as he offered the rangers a beer, his charm on easy display.

"Why not?" said the stocky one with a shrug. "We're on our way home, and it's been a long day. First, we need to record your names and rifles, though."

He picked one up from the line against the side of the vehicle and turned to Susan, saying with a wink, "I don't suppose this belongs to the young lady?" He stroked the weapon admiringly. "A Krieghoff double rifle. .470 Nitro Express. Very nice. Not your run-of-the-mill Mauser 98 like the rest of them there."

Susan swallowed and tried to hide her fear.

"So, poachers are in the area?" said Phil, wrinkling his nose. "I hope they get what's coming to them."

"You and me both," said the ranger, still admiring the unusual rifle. "Only big fines are going to work, though. The government's got the right idea."

Picking up a *Fair Lady* magazine, Susan tried to focus on the pictures, though her frightened gaze kept straying back to Starky, who merely grinned at her, then put a forefinger to his lips.

She heard Phil droning on to the rangers, sounding important as he said, "Botswana was one of the countries that agreed to the Convention on International Trade in Endangered Species of Wild Fauna and Flora last year. I agree that we need international cooperation to protect endangered species. Too many vested interests in poaching our natural resources."

Starky's eyes seemed to glow as he fixed them on her. Oh Lord, when had she ever felt so excited?

Or so terrified.

Well, she wasn't going to say anything. But the rangers had better not look at her too closely. Why couldn't she hide her feelings better? If Starky was charged, it would be because she'd asked him to fetch his rifle.

"The Krieghoff's mine. A beauty, isn't she?"

Susan turned towards Jeremy, who—quite unaware of what Starky had done—smilingly claimed ownership of the gun, stroking it just as Susan had once wished he'd stroked her during their two months together. Maybe if he'd been half as interested in Susan as he was in that rifle of his, they'd still be together, she thought, studying his softly curling light brown hair and open, easy smile as relief surged through her.

Though of course she should have realised it was Jeremy's. His Krieghoff was polished enough to see one's reflection in it. Starky's was older, scratched, and clearly hard-used.

"No more guns?" asked the other ranger as they noted the registrations of the three German Mausers before taking a seat and accepting beers.

"No," said Starky, shaking his head. "Though I'd kill to own a Krieghoff."

His words hung in the air, laden with irony.

Liar.

Susan stared at him, amazed by how nonchalant he looked. Even Mike seemed jittery.

Starky was the only one who had committed a crime with a hidden Krieghoff, and yet he looked the least guilty of them all.

And a liar was exactly what she called him to his face when the rangers had finally gone, and Mike, Phil and Jeremy had disappeared into the bush to relieve themselves, the darkness swallowing them whole.

But she said it teasingly, admiringly, and was rewarded when Starky put his hands on her shoulders and lowered his face to hers, pressing her gently against the trunk of the old baobab whose massive girth could have hidden an advancing army from the direction the other three had gone.

"Would you call me a liar if I said you were the cutest chick I've ever met?" His breath tickled her cheek, and she arched into him, the hard grey trunk of the baobab pressed against her back.

"Where did you hide your Krieghoff?" she asked coyly, wriggling against him in invitation because he hadn't quite kissed her yet, and she was determined that he would. She slipped her hands inside his shirt and began gently rubbing his shoulders. They were broad and strong.

So unlike Jeremy's.

So unlike Phil's.

Starky was a real man.

"I hid it in the bush after the photographs were taken. Couldn't be too sure, could I?" His hands came up to cup her face, thumbs grazing her cheekbones as he lowered his mouth to hers. "You're not going to dob me in, are you?"

Susan shook her head as the world seemed to fall away, leaving only the two of them beneath the vast, star-hung Kalahari sky.

She groaned softly as she kissed him back, letting him part her lips while his hands began their own exploration of her body. For now, he'd slipped one hand inside her shirt.

The sound of Mike and the others returning made them jerk apart. Susan felt she might cry, she was so not ready for it to end. Somewhere in the distance a hyena laughed, its eerie call seeming to mock their secrecy.

So when Starky stepped back, carefully buttoning her shirt as he murmured, "Maybe I could slip into your tent when the others are asleep," she gave him a very definite green light with an emphatic nod.

IT SEEMED LIKE AN HOUR PASSED, during which Susan lay on her camp bed, tense and waiting. After the rangers had gone, they'd sat around the fire a little longer, dipping buttermilk rusks into steaming enamel mugs of sweet tea while she exchanged sly smiles with Starky as Philemon washed the dishes some distance away. When Mike had yawned, she'd yawned too, stretching and turning slightly towards Starky as she announced she was going to bed.

But then the men had gone on talking for ages after she'd left.

She'd heard them droning on and on while she tossed and turned, straining for some sign that they were finally turning in. The night sounds of the Kalahari—the rustle of small nocturnal creatures, the far-off roar of a lion, the strange creaks and sighs of the dark—only sharpened her anticipation.

She heard Mike having another go at Starky over the ostrich. Why was Mike so overwrought this weekend? His voice carried an edge she'd never heard before.

Starky, by contrast, remained his usual laconic self. His easy, unruffled replies made her shiver with admiration.

And want.

And need.

The words *diamond* and *liar* floated through the canvas once or twice—those were the ones spoken loudest. Susan wondered vaguely what that was all about before drowsiness overtook her, unease settling over her like an extra blanket.

Then she was woken by the soft sound of the tent zip inching open.

For one breathless second she lay still, trying to steady her breathing, and then Starky was climbing into her sleeping bag. It was a tight fit, but he gave a low laugh as his hands ran the length of her, demanding to know what *these* were.

These were her pyjamas, of course. And it came as a shock to discover that Starky was... stark naked.

"Pyjamas?" he repeated in disgust. "Haven't you ever done this before?"

Susan shook her head, then wriggled obligingly as he removed them for her, murmuring, "Well, my celestial being, I'll have to make sure your first time is the best fun you've ever had. You're quite sure about this, hey?"

Susan clung to him, her whole body feverish as she assured him she'd never been more sure of anything in her life.

And then they were off.

And Starky really was as good as his word, stroking and caressing her until her body did things she hadn't known it could, awakening cravings she hadn't even known existed until he was satisfying them.

At last, when she felt that the fever inside her must consume her completely, the great pressure building within her suddenly broke apart, just as a different kind of pressure breached her.

So this was what it was all about.

She'd heard whispers. She'd glimpsed, very briefly, an indecent picture of what men and women did. But this was the real thing.

And she was doing it with Starky.

For one brief moment, with his weight on top of her,

she thought she might suffocate. Then he rolled aside and drew her against him, cradling her to his chest and stroking her cheek.

"Was that good?" he whispered.

Susan nodded, smiling drowsily, even though she felt tender.

"It was so good."

"Now don't you go telling the world that, will you?" Starky laid one finger lightly against her lips, and she shuddered with soft, happy laughter.

"It'll be our secret to the grave," she whispered. "No one will ever know."

CHAPTER

FOUR

FIFTEEN YEARS LATER
Melbourne, Australia, 1989

Verity stood on a dining chair in the middle of the crowded living room, a champagne flute raised high above her head. Coloured party lights and paper Chinese lanterns cast pockets of red and gold over the faces of the friends and family gathered around her. Someone had cranked up *Love Shack* on the tape deck in the corner, and the smell of curry drifted from the slow cooker in the kitchen, wrapping the winter night in spice and warmth.

She tapped her glass with a spoon until the music was turned down, and the chatter faded.

"When I wrote this speech a week ago," Verity began, "I listed four reasons for tonight's celebration."

In her tight knee-length black skirt and the gold bolero she'd bought especially for the party, she felt both over-dressed and absurdly happy. This was supposed to be James's moment as much as hers, and yet somehow she'd ended up centre stage, wobbling on a chair and speaking for them both.

"You all know the obvious ones," she went on. "This is our housewarming. It's our fifteenth wedding anniversary. And it's proof that some people"—she shot a mock glare towards one of the pilots near the stereo—"were wrong when they said we'd never last."

Laughter rippled through the room. James, leaning against the doorframe with a glass in his hand, grinned and shook his head, his dark hair falling over his brow in the way she'd always loved.

"Yes, Tim," Verity added, "if we've made it to fifteen years, I think we've earned the right to call this a proper marriage."

She reached down to smooth his hair, her fingers brushing his cheek as their friends clapped and whooped.

"The fourth reason," she said, "is that we wanted an excuse for a party. And because when life is good, you should celebrate it."

She was about to go on—about James, about the years of scraping and saving and never quite having enough—when the chair beneath her gave a little wobble.

"Careful," someone called.

Before she could steady herself, James dragged another chair beside hers and jumped up so they stood side by side above their guests.

"You all get the gist of what Verity's saying," he announced, taking the spoon from her. "So I'll keep this short. There's something most of you don't know, because it was only confirmed yesterday—"

"Oh my God, Saskia's getting a brother or sister!" Helen shouted from the back.

The room erupted again.

"Nice try," James said. "But no. The big news is that Verity here"—he slipped an arm around her waist—"is

Flair's new lifestyle editor extraordinaire. She starts on Monday."

The rest of his words were drowned out by clapping, stamping, and the shrill whistles of half a dozen pilots. Verity laughed, a little breathless, as James hopped down, lifted her effortlessly from the chair and spun her into a kiss that tasted of champagne and jubilation.

In that instant, it felt as though every sacrifice, every long-haul contract James had flown, every late-night story she'd filed while Saskia slept down the hall, had finally coalesced into something solid and worthwhile. Fifteen years of trailing around the world, and at last they were settled. A gorgeous home. Secure work. Family.

It had all paid off in the end.

"The news couldn't have been better timed," Verity's best friend Sarah murmured a little later, as the party spilled down the hallway and through the living room. The champagne bottle in Sarah's hand chimed softly against Verity's glass as she poured. "You got your dream house. Then your dream job. Next, world domination."

Verity laughed. "I need to pinch myself every morning I wake up," she admitted.

And she did. A brick house in Melbourne. A teenage daughter she adored. A husband whose smile still made her stomach dip. And now, at last, a job that made her feel important. Silly, perhaps, but after so many years of fill-in work and interrupted ambitions, she felt valued in the workplace for the first time.

"Come on, let's talk in the study," she said, leading the way from the overheated living room where more and more guests had drifted in out of the cold. "That's better," she said, flopping down onto the sofa bed. The warmth from the nearby radiator was a welcome relief from the winter chill outside. "Don't you still do the same? Pinch yourself. I mean—even though Tim's been flying for Ansett for a year now? I remember how gloomy the guys were when they turned thirty and thought they were too old ever to crack the airlines."

Verity and Sarah had become firm friends when their husbands were still at the fledgling stage of their careers, based in the remote Western Australian town of Kununurra, flying sightseers over the Bungle Bungles and other scenic wonders of the outback. Those early years of uncertainty had forged the sort of bond that survived distance, children, and time.

"I do," Sarah replied, straightening her green velvet headband. "Airline pay means better care for Ben. Nothing would make me move again." She grinned. "But Tim knows that. He wouldn't dare."

Verity nodded, acknowledging the strain Sarah and Tim had been under caring for their ten-year-old son, who had cerebral palsy. Sarah took a breath. "Not that the Flying Doctors weren't wonderful to us when Tim was working for them," she went on. "And being so long in one place really helped us get a foothold. But I'm so happy to be in Melbourne and close to good hospitals." She squeezed Verity's arm. "You're the perfect pilot's wife, you know. Six jobs and six towns in fifteen years, and you're still by James's side. Not every pilot's wife is so patient. I don't know that I could have been."

Verity drained her glass and squeezed her friend's shoulder. "You're the most patient person I know," she said. With her own success arriving so close on the heels of James's, she felt almost giddy with happiness, ready to spread it around. There'd been times when she'd despaired of ever getting her on-ice journalism career moving again, forever playing second fiddle to James's flying. But the universe had finally smiled on them both. James's delight in her new job, after all their years of muddling through, was the icing on the cake.

"Ben is so lucky to have parents like you. I don't know that I could have managed the way you and Tim have." Almost overwhelmed by her feelings, Verity didn't bother to hide them. "Isn't it wonderful how much better everything feels when you've struggled for it?" She blinked back another rush of tears. "All those years in general aviation, with companies folding and contracts ending. Packing up another rental, finding another school for Saskia. But now our fellers are airline pilots. Now we're getting some stability in our lives. And finally—maybe—with James having just been checked to line and becoming a first officer with decent pay, it's in time to make a difference for Saskia. Goodness knows, stability is what she needs."

From the adjoining living room, where the guests had drifted back together, a deep, aggrieved male voice cut through the strains of Madonna, and conversation faltered.

"Did you hear what the PM said on the six o'clock news?"

Verity grinned, and Sarah rolled her eyes as they exchanged glances. Sean, one of their more outspoken friends was a regular visitor lately, ever since his marriage had started wobbling was dominating once again. The likeable larrikin had first met easy-going James and Tim at ground school fifteen years earlier, when the three of them were studying for their Commercial Pilot's Licences.

Verity leaned closer and whispered in Sarah's ear, "I suppose I should listen to what Sean's carrying on about now that we're all in this together."

Someone turned down the music, and Sean's strident tones carried through to the study.

"Hawke called us glorified bus drivers!" He almost spluttered with disgust.

Verity peered through the half-open door to see a knot of pilots gathered around him. Sean was declaring that Prime Minister Bob Hawke needed to be reminded that negotiating through a union was a basic right. "Being besties with the Ansett boss has sure made him forget his trade union roots!" he shouted.

Tim gestured for Sean to lower his voice, but although his own answer was more measured, Verity was startled by the anger in his face. Usually Tim was even more easygoing than James, but as he began to speak, something inside her gave a small, inexplicable lurch.

"I got a call at nine on Tuesday night from the company saying they were willing to negotiate my terms and conditions—but not through the Pilot's Federation—"

He got no further. His words were swallowed by a rumble of outrage before Sean's sharper voice cut through again.

"We've had wage suppression for years. If they think we're asking for too much, they should negotiate through the union! And if the government wants to treat us like other employees, then our working conditions should be the same. Normal office hours. Nine to five. Let's see how they like that."

Verity rolled her eyes at Sarah in a private sign that she'd heard enough and was about to suggest they escape to another room and leave the men to their indignation. But Sarah touched her arm. Her expression had changed.

"Verity, I know Tim's the first to say Sean doesn't know what hardship is," she said quietly, "but on this, he agrees with everything Sean's saying." She shrugged. "Me? I don't know what to think."

Sean had always had it easier than most. His father, an Ansett captain on the Boeing 737, had funded his eldest son's training. By contrast, James and Tim had scraped together every cent for their commercial licences. While Sean had walked straight into a cadetship with Ansett, James and Tim had spent years building hours through instructing, joy flights and airborne geophysical survey work all over Australia.

"Are you sure you don't want to get out of here, Sarah?" Verity asked. The hubbub of general resentment was beginning to unsettle her. The evening had started with such warmth and promise, but the grievance running beneath so many of James's pilot friends was stronger than she had realised.

She pushed away the little dart of worry and tried to cling to the joy of the moment. So she was relieved when Sarah stood and followed her out onto the now-empty deck, which offered a quiet, if chilly, refuge from the noise inside.

"And now," Sarah said, settling onto the sofa, "I want to hear about your new job, Verity, which is every bit as exciting as James's. I'm so envious." "No, I'm not," she corrected herself. "I'm proud. And relieved. You've wanted something like this since I first met you. You've worked so hard, and so patiently, always putting James and Saskia first while you've hunkered down and taken whatever work you could find. But now it's your turn. Now you're not just a journalist—you're an editor."

Verity shivered, but not from the cold. It really was a dream come true.

"Sarah, I have a whole ninety-six-page glossy magazine

to look after. Yet for years I've only written the occasional freelance piece for papers and magazines. Now I can commission articles and fashion shoots and pretty much make all of *Flair's* editorial decisions. I know it's a lesser title in Lightning Express's stable of magazines, and you'd be surprised how little the pay is, but my real dream suddenly feels possible."

"And what is that?"

"To become editor of *Stitch and Style Down Under*. That's the flagship title with the big readership, and Carrie Dunbar—the Managing Editor who oversees all six magazines, of which *Flair* is only one of the smaller titles—has hinted there might be a role there for me if I do well."

Curled up on the outdoor sofas with a light throw rug over their legs and a couple of candles flickering on the wooden coffee table between them, the women sipped their drinks. Verity was glad to leave the men to their own concerns in the next room and enjoy again the easy companionship she'd missed so much after Sarah and Tim had moved to Melbourne two years ahead of them.

"Then here's to *Stitch and Style Down Under*." Sarah raised her glass. "James has got where he has because of your sacrifices. Now it's your turn."

"Yeah, they offered me a wage rise, too." Pete paused meaningfully. "Conditional on my leaving the union."

Verity tensed at the conversation going on over her left shoulder while trying to enjoy the artificial bonhomie of the barbecue with a cluster of James's pilot friends.

It was being held at Sean's place in Gisborne, where the view from Skyline Drive took in the Macedon Ranges to the north and the skyscrapers of Melbourne far to the south. With the pilots now engaged in rolling strike action and refusing to fly outside business hours of nine to five, the barbecue had been organised for the Melbourne-based pilots and their families to lift morale.

It was having the opposite effect on Verity.

She had felt a little flutter of excitement when they'd turned into the long gravel driveway. In deference to her new role, she'd cut her light brown hair to her shoulders, which thankfully meant most of her perm had gone south, and she liked the effect of the softer, more natural curls, which looked more 1940s than 1980s.

But the general air of grievance was draining her spirits. Her throat felt dry, and it was hard to smile at Melissa, Sean's wife, as the two of them worked in the gazebo, trying to keep the flies off the food and rescuing the coleslaw, which was already looking watery and defeated beneath its cling wrap.

"I told Sean that if he walked, then I'd walk." Melissa huffed as she rearranged bowls on the trestle table. "If he goes all solidarity on me and throws his career away, he can kiss goodbye to me, the kids, and fifteen years of marriage." With a snap, she tipped the half-empty contents of one plastic container into another, tossed the dirty one into the bin, then straightened. Running an elegantly manicured hand through her short bleached-blonde perm, she fixed Verity with an intense look. "What about you?"

Verity nearly dropped the pavlova she was plating. Melissa was one of the most intimidating women she'd ever met, and that was saying something. She'd thought her boss, Carrie, was fierce until she'd discovered the woman had a heart of gold when she decided someone was worth backing.

"Fifteen years? We've been married fifteen, too."

"I'm not talking about that." Melissa's look sharpened, and Verity felt suddenly gauche and absurdly young, though Melissa was probably no more than five years older. "I mean, a good job like this doesn't come along every day, does it? I was a hostie with TAA when I met Sean. I wasn't born yesterday, and I know what this whole business is about. Yes, I think the pilots are getting a rotten deal from management, from the government, and from the media. But at the end of the day, we've got three kids to feed and clothe, private school bills to pay, and a mortgage. Do you think we can do that on my wage? On one day a week as a beautician?" Tapping her long painted nails on the table, she pressed her thin pink-frosted lips together. "So where do you stand on all this?"

Verity, resealing a bag of white sandwich loaf with unnecessary care, couldn't quite meet Melissa's eye. "James finished his training only a few weeks ago," she said. "This is all pretty new to me."

"The government's bringing in the Air Force to fly domestic passengers. Is that normal? No, the normal response of a rational government to a reasonable pay claim is to negotiate in good faith. Next they'll be bringing in strikebreakers from the rest of the world to do our boys' jobs—"

Verity nearly groaned with relief when Sarah stepped in from the lawn onto the slate, grateful for a patch of shade. And when Melissa thrust a tea towel into Sarah's hands and announced she needed to go and powder her nose, Verity could have hugged her.

"This is ghastly," she hissed the moment Melissa disappeared. "Aren't we supposed to be having a good time?"

"Some people are," Sarah said dryly, nodding towards the wheelchair Ben was strapped into while two four-year-olds played tag, shrieking as they ran circles around him. "Ben hasn't had this much fun in ages."

Verity smiled at her adorable disabled godson before glancing towards the various knots of guests, all deep in earnest conversation over paper plates of sausage and salad. It was not the sort of easy, sunstruck barbecue atmosphere she associated with the outback gatherings they'd attended over the years.

"I thought Melissa was going to take me by the throat and shake me when she more or less said, 'If you're not with us, you're against us.'"

"That pretty much sums it up, I'm afraid." Sarah patted her arm. "Don't let it get to you. It'll get sorted out eventually, even if nobody gets exactly what they want. That's what negotiation is supposed to mean, isn't it? Finding a level maybe not everyone likes, but that everyone can live with." She gave Verity a gentler smile. "Now tell me more about the new job. I haven't seen you since you started. No, don't give me that look. I'm not bored with hearing more."

Verity let out a slow breath, then smiled. "Well, I can honestly say it's even better than I hoped."

Just saying the words loosened something in her chest.

"Carrie's a good trainer, and she gives me a lot of leeway. I have my own office—well, a cubicle really, but I don't share it. I sit at my desk and ring people to ask whether they'd like to be interviewed about their passion, and liaise with our stylists and photographers. Sometimes I do the interviews separately; sometimes I'm there on the shoot, watching Jennie work absolute magic with a camera and three props. Then I work with the graphic designers, leaning over their shoulders, making suggestions while they race towards the deadline, and finally I sign it all off before the magazine goes to print in Singapore at the end of the month." She laughed. "I've only done the first issue, of course, but I think it's going to look fabulous, and Carrie was really pleased."

She knew she was grinning like a schoolgirl, but she couldn't help it. It had been years since she'd had that kind of validation, and for work she genuinely cared about—telling stories, matching words and images, shaping something beautiful for exactly the right reader.

"And what do you like most about it?"

"The fact that I spend my day talking to people about things that make them happy. And then I get paid for it."

Verity tipped her face towards the pale winter sky. "I've done my time as a cadet journalist, chasing ambulances and doing the usual rounds—the police rounds, the courts. I do not miss coming in every morning half-afraid some sub-editor would have photocopied my article and sticky-taped it to my monitor with paragraphs ringed in red and rude comments scribbled all over it. I never missed that side of journalism. But I did miss writing about things people actually cared about in a happy way. This *Flair* job was made for me. I'm finally in my happy place."

BY THE TIME they arrived home at nine, mellow with good humour and good wine, they were delighted to find Saskia curled in front of the television with an open exercise book on her knees and a scattering of old photo albums across the coffee table while *Little House on the Prairie* flickered in the background.

Their daughter looked up with a smile and, for the first time in what felt like weeks, looked animated.

"Hey, Dad, is that you in Africa?" Saskia asked, stabbing a finger at a photograph of a young boy holding a dead bird proudly by its wings, his rifle slung over one shoulder like a trophy in itself.

James and Verity sat down beside her and pulled the album closer.

"It's my cousin Mike holding a spur-winged goose. See? In that other picture, he doesn't look anything like me."

"There's a family resemblance," said Verity, leaning in. "You both had those blonde curls as children, and both of you went darker. And that must be your cousin, Susan. She's gorgeous. Look at those dark curls. Where was this taken? Some hunting trip, by the look of it. But a few years after the one with Mike and the goose."

James lifted the album for a better look. "I think these are the photographs Aunt Bessie sent Mum after Mike was killed." He frowned. "This might even be the trip you and I were supposed to go on, Verity. The timing would fit."

Verity bent closer to the grainy colour photograph. Two young men in their early twenties and a teenage girl were standing with rifles in front of a campfire, faces turned towards the camera, the dark pressing in behind them. There was something about the image—its youth, its innocence, the bush all around—that gave her a curious little chill.

"How awful to think of it. Was this in Zimbabwe?" she asked, reaching back for details she hadn't thought about in years. She'd never made it to Africa, and had only brushed up on the history when they'd once been on the brink of travelling there.

"No, Botswana. In the Kalahari. Dad used to talk about the hunting trips he went on when he was a kid. He missed the country so much he left Australia for a few years when I was in my early teens and went back to Botswana to work at the Orapa diamond mine, which had only just opened. Then he and Mum reconciled, and he came back to Oz."

"Mike was your first cousin, Dad, wasn't he?" Saskia asked. "How was he killed?"

James set the album on his lap. "It was a horrible accident. Susan had a disgruntled ex-boyfriend who followed them to camp, and when he and Mike got into a fight, a gun went off and Mike was killed." He hesitated, then added more quietly, "A lion got to his body before the others came back and brought him in."

Verity remembered the broad outline now. It had

shocked her at the time, though these African cousins had always felt remote and half-mythic, scattered across southern Africa and spoken of more than known.

"Horrible. So which one was the man who did it? Which one was Auntie Susan's ex-boyfriend?" Saskia asked, her finger trailing over the two unrelated young men in the picture beside Mike, both tall and handsome, then over pretty, dark-curled Susan with her elfin features. She bent closer to the caption written beneath in small ballpoint. " 'Mike, Starky, Susan and Phil on their last hunting expedition together. Northern Kalahari. Best friends forever.' " She looked up, wide-eyed. "So, which one killed his best friend? Was it Starky or Phil?"

"Neither. Susan's ex-boyfriend wasn't in this photograph." James worried his lip. "I think his name was something ordinary, like Peter or Mark. No—Jeremy Lawrence."

"What happened to him?"

"He went to gaol and... I think he killed himself in his prison cell before the case went to trial. Anyway, he died not long afterwards. It was all rather horrible."

Verity tucked herself against James on the sofa while Saskia knelt on the floor, still absorbed by the old album and the lives trapped in its pages.

"Poor Susan," said Verity softly. "Losing her brother out there in the bush. She doesn't look much older than Saskia."

She glanced again from the photograph to James, noticing the faint family likeness between him and Mike— the square jaw, the colouring, the look of easy confidence. And suddenly the photo felt less like some distant family relic and more like a warning preserved between plastic sleeves: youth caught in one bright moment before everything went wrong.

"We all got on well as kids," James said. "All us cousins lived in the same small town of Serowe. But Mum and Dad took us to Australia when I was ten, and we didn't really stay in touch. Last I heard, Susan was working in Cape Town." Then, with deliberate briskness, he clapped his hands. "Right. It's great that you've made a start, Saskia, but it's bedtime."

When Saskia had gone upstairs and the living-room door clicked shut behind her, James turned back to Verity with a smile that was part mischief, part invitation.

"And it's our bedtime too."

Heat unfurled low in Verity's belly as she shifted onto his lap and slipped her arms around his neck.

It was exhilarating, this new sense of standing level beside him. James had worked so hard to give her and Saskia a good life, and whenever Verity had floundered through one of her periodic crises of confidence, his first instinct had been to blame himself for uprooting her again, dragging her away from friends, momentum, work. But that had never quite been the point. Usually, the work available to her had been low-paid, stopgap, a way to keep going rather than a path of her own.

For the first time in fifteen years, Verity felt proud not only of James's success, but of her own.

"Take me to bed and love me forever," she whispered, nuzzling his ear and pressing herself against him, refusing for tonight to let the rumblings at the airline intrude.

Carrie had hinted that if Verity proved herself over the next six months, she might be marked out as the eventual successor to *Stitch and Style Down Under*.

"Your wish is my command," James murmured, lifting her in his arms, his mouth never quite leaving hers.

Moonlight filtered through the gauzy curtains, laying

silver bars across the bed, and Verity's heart swelled—with love for him, with pride in the life they had made, with gratitude that after all the moving and muddling through, they had reached this place together.

His hands traced familiar paths across her body as she unbuttoned his shirt. After fifteen years they knew one another's rhythms so well, yet tonight felt touched by something new. An equal partnership. Two people who had both earned the right to feel hopeful.

She threaded her fingers through his dark blond curls, still boyish despite the first threads of grey at his temples.

"I love you," she whispered against his neck. "Thank you for believing in me, even when I didn't believe in myself."

James drew back just enough to look at her, his eyes dark with desire and something deeper, warmer. Understanding?

"You're extraordinary," he murmured before lowering his mouth to hers again.

They moved together with the ease of long practice, each kiss carrying the weight of all they had already survived.

Later, tangled in the sheets, Verity traced idle patterns across his chest and let herself feel, for once, wholly content.

Whatever lay ahead, they would face it together.

CHAPTER
SIX

It had been a long day at work with a social do to
follow, and Verity had returned home full of cheer.
Her first issue of the magazine, now printed and in
most Australian newsagents, was selling beyond expec-
tations.

Carrie had called her into her office to congratulate her,
and Verity had been bursting to tell James.

But now, with Saskia asleep and James almost ready to
turn out the light, she stood in the middle of the rug in their
bedroom, biting her lip and trying to stop her hands from
shaking as she looked first at the Cue shopping bag on the
chair and then at her husband.

That afternoon, between work and the cocktail party,
she had bought a second new suit from David Jones, one
she planned to wear the next day. As a magazine editor,
with a decent salary and a position to dress for, she could
justify a new wardrobe, and the novelty of needing polished
work clothes still hadn't worn off.

The navy linen Cue suit, size six, with its little peplum
at the back, teamed with navy high-heeled sandals, was

exactly the sort of thing she needed to give herself that extra jolt of confidence for the important meetings now filling her diary.

For all those editorial meetings where her opinion mattered.

If there were going to be any more editorial meetings, the way James was talking.

She tried not to let her fury show. James, sitting on the edge of the bed, was explaining for the third time how unions worked. The necessity of solidarity. The fact that being a scab was the quickest way to kill a career. And that, at the end of the day, one had to live with oneself.

Yes, she understood the need for loyalty and honour. But she did not understand the rest of it. Did not understand how, only weeks after completing his 737 endorsement with Ansett, James could be contemplating jeopardising everything he had worked for.

Everything they had worked for.

Was it a crisis of confidence? That did not sound like the James she knew.

"Darling, I don't expect you to understand all this straight away—" James began, his voice carrying frustration and something close to desperation.

She cut him off as she reached for her dressing gown. "What are you saying? That you're prepared to throw away the best job you've ever had and drag us off to Alice Springs or—or Timbuktu?"

"Verity, I know I must sound as if I've completely lost it, but please don't react just yet. Think about what I've said, and we'll talk more in the morning. This pilots' dispute... it's bigger than just me. It's about fair pay, years of wage stagnation, and standing up for what's right."

"I won't sleep a wink if I'm not allowed to talk about it

until then." She heard the petulance in her own voice and hated it, but could not stop pacing. "Tell me what this madness is really about. So the pilots didn't get the pay rise they wanted. Is that it? Well, that doesn't mean you all have to walk. I've just started the best job of my life. Are you asking me to throw that away because of some—some fit of principle?"

"I'd never ask you to do that on a whim." He spoke quietly, but his fingers had gone white where they gripped the carved wooden bedpost. "This is about principles, Verity. About fair treatment. If we don't stand together now, things will only get worse."

"If you ask me, it sounds like an overreaction to not getting your way. The company needs you. Just be patient. Of course they'll come to the table, eventually. You don't have to behave like a sheep and follow the herd."

Her voice broke. Fear and fury crowded her head until there was room for nothing else. She took a breath, but it only seemed to make more space for anger.

"You can't give it all up. What about me?" she flung at him. "What have I done to make you want to scupper my hopes and dreams?"

To her horror, she began to cry. Big, hot tears slid down her cheeks and into her mouth. She wiped them away angrily as she leaned against the wall, then fixed him with a wounded, accusing stare.

James looked wretched.

He rose and took a step towards her, instinctively wanting to comfort her, but she moved away and sat down on the far side of the bed, half-turned towards him but staring at the floor as she tried to absorb what he was saying.

"I'm with the other pilots in this, Verity. I have to be. It's not only about me. It's about all of us. About the future of the profession."

He sounded so unlike himself. Not the easy, vibrant, quick-to-laugh James she knew and loved, but someone older suddenly. More rigid. More burdened.

"So the union tells you to throw away your job in order to stick it to the company, and that's what you all obediently plan to do," she said. "Because they told you to."

"You don't understand," he muttered. "This dispute could change the whole industry. If we don't stand up now, we might never get another chance."

She shook her head. "Too right, I don't understand."

"Then you won't understand if I keep saying it in different words." He rubbed a hand over his face. "Verity, I'm sorry, but I'm going to bed. It's been a god-awful day."

They lay back to back, not touching, yet acutely aware of the narrow strip of mattress between them as if it were a gorge. The weight of all they had not resolved pressed into the dark.

Perhaps Verity snatched a little sleep towards dawn. If she did, it was shallow and unsatisfying. When the alarm finally dragged her awake, she crept into the bathroom as quietly as she could and got ready for work without waking James.

But when she emerged, fully made up and wearing her new Cue suit, James was awake and sitting on the edge of the bed in his pyjama bottoms, raking his hands through his tousled hair.

Verity paused in the doorway and looked at him with brittle composure.

"Carrie has invited me to a board meeting this morning with the editorial director. They're thrilled with how my first issue of *Flair* has been received and want to talk about my ideas for the next one and possibly—even—my taking on the editorship of *Stitch and Style Down Under*."

She bent to straighten the bow on the side of her shoe. Very chic, and bought specifically to go with the sort of suit a women's fashion-and-food magazine editor might wear.

It was hard to keep her voice level, but when she straightened, she found some of the fight had drained away, leaving her only raw and exposed. She felt suddenly as vulnerable as she had in all those months of job hunting.

"Should I say anything," she asked, swallowing, "about... what might be happening?"

James met her eye, then looked away almost at once, fixing his gaze on the back of his hand.

"Leave it for now." He sounded tired to the bone. "I should know more later today. The union's meeting with management again."

Verity nodded. "I'll grab some toast, and then I have to fly."

A few minutes later, as she opened the front door and her heels clicked along the wooden passage, he called after her.

"No kiss? Come on, Verity, please. We can't let this get between us."

Reluctantly, she turned back. She hated the final few metres that seemed to separate them almost as much as the argument itself.

When she reappeared, he said, more softly, "I would never ask you to give up your career for me. I know how hard you've worked for it. I know how good you are. And how much you deserve this."

The sincerity in his face only made it worse.

"But...?" Verity prompted.

He gave a helpless little shrug. "But if there was absolutely no other way..." He stopped, then began again. "You'd trust me to make the right decision for us as a family when it comes to my career, wouldn't you? Even if it meant some short-term sacrifices?"

She shrugged, leaned in, and kissed him briefly on the forehead before retreating again towards the door.

"Right now, I don't know what to think." She fought to steady her voice. Conflict was so rare between them, but she had to say what she felt. "I'm frightened you're being swept up with everyone else, and that you think you're doing the right thing when it'll be the people who put self-interest first who end up having the last laugh."

James was the most loyal and honourable man she knew. It was one of the things she had always loved most in him.

"Please, James... don't do something we'll all regret. Don't be a fool and fall on your sword when you don't have to."

She had never spoken to him so coldly. She felt the chill of it the moment the words left her mouth, but there was no pulling them back.

James looked at her for a long moment. Too long. He had never looked at her with such quiet intensity, and in the end she had to lower her gaze.

"Without the benefit of a crystal ball, Verity, I can only do what I think will let me live with my conscience. You'd do the same in my position."

With a sigh, he dropped his head into his hands.

Verity waited, but when he did not look up, she stepped back into the passage and set off for work with sharp, decisive footsteps.

They had weathered rough patches before—usually in the exhausted months when Saskia had refused to sleep as a baby, or after the collapse of yet another small aviation company James had been flying for, when they'd had to pull up stumps and start again in another town, with another school, another rental, another dispiriting round of job hunting for Verity.

But all of that had been beyond their control.

This was what made the present so unbearable.

Now James had, or seemed to have, some say over his future. The chance, at last, to provide for his family properly. To stand beside his wife while her own career finally took flight.

And yet it looked as if he was prepared to place his sense of duty to the other pilots above the immediate well-being of the family who loved him most.

CHAPTER
SEVEN

And, oh, how prescient that fear of hers had been—that their future might be about to go up in flames, Verity reflected as she ran through the afternoon rain a few days later, thunder rumbling overhead as she knocked on Sarah's front door.

"Oh, Verity." The two women fell into each other's arms as Verity took refuge in the hallway. "It's all over," she sobbed. "It's not just James. All the pilots have resigned en masse." She'd heard the newspaper sellers shouting the story when she'd stepped out at lunchtime to buy a sandwich. *The Age*'s bold headline had screamed the shocking news that around sixteen hundred pilots had been forced to resign to avoid litigation from their employers.

"Ansett, Australian Airlines, East-West... yes, that's what I heard," Sarah said, leading her through to the partly renovated kitchen and living area at the back of what had once been an old miner's cottage.

For a moment they stood in silence, staring at the gutted shell of what would one day be a proper family room. The kitchen was almost finished, but beyond it the rest was still studs, dust and promise.

"Cup of tea?"

Verity nodded, her mind reeling. There was no point in voicing the obvious. How were Sarah and Tim supposed to find the money to finish the building work now that Tim had no job?

And neither did James.

"He could go back under their terms," Verity said, taking a seat at the kitchen counter, hating the desperation in her own voice as her thoughts skittered ahead to James and what he would say when she got home. She shouldn't have made the detour to Sarah's. She knew that. But she needed moral support before she could face her husband. "What is Tim going to do?"

"He's not going to buckle to their demands, Verity. And you know James isn't either." Sarah filled the kettle and set it on. "The way the companies and the government have handled this... it's unprecedented. They're trying to break the union."

"I don't understand. Why couldn't they negotiate? How did it come to this so quickly?" Verity watched Sarah reach for the tea canister and drop an English Breakfast tea bag into each mug. "I thought general aviation was all swings and merry-go-rounds, with constant upheaval and change, but that the airlines were different. I thought that once James got into Ansett, we'd finally stepped into something stable. I thought we were... settled. At last."

"To be honest, I don't fully get it either," Sarah said. Usually the one doing the steadying, even her voice held uncertainty. "I know Tim had been saying for ages there were rumblings, because the pilots hadn't had a pay rise in ten years. But I still assumed they'd put in a claim and negotiate from there. No one expected management to refuse to negotiate at all, let alone for it to blow up this way. Or for the government to back them so hard. When the PM's practically best mates with the airline boss, our blokes haven't got much hope."

Verity pushed back her fringe and took a sip of the scalding tea. "I don't know what to say… or what to think. It wouldn't be so bad if it weren't for my new job. I've barely been in the chair a month and I love it. And they like what I'm bringing to the role. Do you know how good that feels? Do you know how long I've wanted this? How many years I've trailed around after James, being the supportive wife—"

"Being," Sarah said quietly. "Not pretending. Being."

Verity gave a short, helpless laugh that was almost a sob.

"If it was only playing," Sarah went on, leaning against the bench, "then you could simply stay here and let James sort himself out. But it's not that simple, is it?"

"So what am I supposed to do?" Verity burst out. "Choose between my job and my marriage?" The tears threatened again, and she hated them, hated how easily they came when she least wanted them to. "Is that what this comes down to?"

She tried to lift the mug again, but her hand was shaking.

"Do you think Tim would have gone along with the whole flying-nine-to-five strike if he'd known it would end like this?" she asked. Even saying it aloud made the fear in her belly tighten. What were they going to do?

Sarah lifted one shoulder. "I don't know. Would James have?" she asked gently. "Who knows? It's a shock for everyone. The speed of it all... one day they're trying to negotiate, the next they're all out of a job."

"They could still get their jobs back if they agreed to management's terms, couldn't they?" Verity worried the edge of her fingernail with her teeth. "It's not really over, is it? The pilots aren't all going to lose everything, surely?"

Sarah hesitated. "Verity, I don't know. All along, the men have kept saying it isn't just about money. It's about principles. About standing up to what they see as unfair treatment."

"Which is all very noble if you still believe the other side is negotiating in good faith," Verity said, more sharply than she meant to.

Sarah sighed. "And to answer your question... yes, I suspect it may already be too late." Her gaze drifted to a strip of flaking paint on the wall, and she touched it absently. "I don't think any of them understood the cost would be this high."

Verity stared miserably into her tea. "James will have to look for another job in a market flooded with... what? Hundreds? Thousands? He won't get anything in Melbourne. Maybe not even in Australia." Her voice thinned. "And what about Saskia? How will she cope with another move?"

She raked a hand through her hair.

"Well, she hates this latest school even more than the last. Maybe she'll be expelled again. Maybe she'll decide she wants to go with James. Oh, God... and how could I not go too?"

"Shhh." Sarah gave her a sympathetic smile, though the worry around her own eyes betrayed how frightened she was as well. "Saskia will cope if another move comes. And so will you." She tried for lightness, though it didn't quite disguise the strain beneath it. "Whether it's Rome or Timbuktu."

CHAPTER

EIGHT

Verity couldn't disguise her horror.

"*Botswana?*" she repeated, scarcely believing what she was hearing.

Her breakfast cereal turned to ash in her mouth as she conjured the dry, hostile landscape of the Kalahari she'd seen in a documentary the previous month. The word itself seemed to hang in the air between them like a wall.

When she'd returned from Sarah's the night before, James had confirmed the news, but they had both been too wrung out to pick over the details. James had gone to bed early. He'd been asleep by the time Verity finally joined him after watching an episode of *Neighbours*, cleaning the kitchen, then doing the crossword while she tried to think of some artful way to make him see their situation from her point of view.

But now it seemed there was nothing left to argue over.

It was done. Sarah had been right. James could no longer cave in to company demands, because the choice had been taken from him.

Instead, he was trying to get her excited about some God-forsaken country on the far side of the world.

"You remember me telling you about that fellow Cameron I instructed in Kununurra a few years back?" James poured them both more coffee, his movements slow and hesitant, as if he were buying time. "Anyway, he got in touch, knowing what's happened, and said he'd heard there was an operation in the Okavango Delta looking for pilots."

Verity was so aghast she could barely speak. "In Botswana? Are you seriously suggesting we up sticks and move to Botswana?" Her voice climbed with every word.

"To the Okavango."

"Like in that documentary we watched?"

"That was the Kalahari, sweetheart. The Kalahari's hot, dry and dusty. I'm talking about the Okavango. It's lush. Beautiful. I remember going there when I was a kid, and you'd love it." His expression softened, hopeful despite everything. "I'd be taking you to paradise."

Panic fluttered in the pit of Verity's stomach as she stared at him. How brief her sense of home had been. How brief the miracle of finding work that felt meaningful, adult, entirely her own.

She drew a breath and tried to sound calm. James was always measured. James understood reason.

Carefully, she said, "I have a good job here. This isn't final, James. You could still ask for your job back. Management made the offer."

He reached across the breakfast table and took her hand.

"I'm sorry, Verity. But I can't do that."

The finality in his tone made her stomach clench.

She had known that would be his answer, yet still she had to blink back tears.

"It's going to be difficult finding another flying job here with so many pilots looking for work. I really think I need to jump at any decent opportunity." His thumb moved over the back of her hand. "The job's based in Maun, not far from where I grew up. I could show you and Saskia that part of the world."

"But my job..." She dragged in a breath. "Maybe I could stay on here for a while. Just in case... in case Botswana doesn't work out."

Even as she said it, she knew how hopeless it sounded.

His sympathy was almost worse than argument. They couldn't afford two households. Not now. Not for long. An editor's salary—even on a glossy national magazine—was nothing like a first officer's. And when James eventually made captain, he would be earning more than three times what Verity was ever likely to make unless she somehow turned into Ita Buttrose overnight.

"James, you've only just been checked to line as a fully endorsed 737 first officer. Couldn't you wait a little longer until you get the magic five hundred hours? Wouldn't that make a difference later? For job security? For both of us?" Her words tumbled out in a rush, desperate for him to see reason.

For once, she was in a uniform of sorts herself, dressed for work and for meetings where her opinion mattered. To a job that bolstered her self-esteem like none of the endless assortment of jobs she'd held over the years ever had.

When James got his first proper flying job taking tourists over the Kimberleys, Verity had just finished her cadetship on the *Ballarat Courier* and been upgraded to a C-grade journalist.

The extra pay had felt thrilling, but she and James had missed one another so badly that when he asked her to join him, she had been lucky enough to secure six months' unpaid leave.

With nothing available on the local paper in Western Australia, she'd found work at the tourist office instead, with the compensations of meeting people, going bush, and writing up itineraries—things she'd genuinely enjoyed.

Then, two months later, she'd discovered she was pregnant.

Unexpectedly, bewilderingly, joyfully.

They had been young and in love then, and soon they'd been overjoyed too.

Over the years, with the help of occasional freelance work for newspapers and magazines, Verity had contributed as best she could, though most of the jobs she took were stopgaps and dead ends. Even so, she'd built a varied portfolio that had impressed *Flair*'s Managing Editor. They loved her ideas.

And Verity loved everything about this new life. The balance of it. The challenge. The way work gave shape and confidence to the rest of her day.

She could not bear to think it might all be snatched away just as it had finally begun.

"Let's leave it for now. Did Saskia get off to school all right?" James was usually the first up, smartly dressed in dark trousers, white shirt and epaulettes. This morning he was bed-tousled and barefoot in khaki shorts. Under ordinary circumstances it was exactly the look that made Verity want to drag him back to bed.

Not today. Today the distance between them felt uncomfortably real.

"She shot past me in the passage in full school uniform, far too much eye makeup, claiming to be in a huge hurry to catch the bus." Verity forced herself to abandon aviation for the moment. Like Saskia, she had a bus to catch too.

"That doesn't mean she'll get where she's meant to be going. What are the chances Mrs Glendenning rings at lunchtime to say she never turned up?"

Verity let out her breath in a rush. "I can't watch her every minute, can I? She's fifteen. Anyway, I have to go."

She stood quickly, took her unfinished cereal bowl to the sink, then came back to kiss James on the cheek. The gesture felt thin and formal. Hollow. Then she left the kitchen.

James sighed.

"Maybe I should ring the school, given her past history," he called after her.

Relief was the strongest thing Verity felt as she stepped out of the house they had rented with such hope only six months before.

And what about tonight, when she came home?

Would James have seen sense?

Would he finally understand that Verity had a right to her own career?

Or was she making it too simple because fear had made everything feel stark and absolute?

As each step carried her closer to work, she had the wretched sense that she was also walking away from James, and from the life they had spent fifteen years building together.

Carrie Dunbar was impressed by the line-up of stories Verity had planned for the following month. For an hour they sat in Carrie's office while Carrie ran through which stylists and photographers she thought best suited particular features and moods. It was meat and drink to Verity, and she scarcely noticed how the morning had slipped away until Jane, the receptionist, put her head round the door to say there was a phone call for her.

Verity's heart sank the moment she picked up the receiver.

"What are the chances? Saskia's skived off school again!" James fumed down the line. "Mrs Glendenning wants a meeting as soon as possible. She suggested this afternoon."

"James, I—" Verity's voice caught. Instantly she was torn between the world she had fought so hard to enter and the family crisis already dragging at her heels.

"Verity, we're talking about our daughter." James sounded strained rather than angry. "Mrs Glendenning made it sound as though expulsion's on the cards. We can't go through that again. Saskia's going off the rails and we don't know how the hell to stop her. Maybe Mrs Glendenning has some ideas. Maybe the school counsellor knows something we don't. Please. I really think we need to show a united front before the day's out."

There was no argument to make, much as she longed to. Verity could only hope the goodwill she had built up with Carrie would survive this interruption—and that it would not become a pattern.

She met James in the headmistress's office, a rarefied little room that made Verity feel twelve years old again in a rush of schoolgirl dread.

Mrs Glendenning got straight down to business.

"Saskia has been with us for six months, and I have made as many allowances as I consider reasonable in that time."

It sounded grim from the outset. Verity glanced at James. His mouth had taken on that hard, flat line that meant he was fighting to stay calm. He had never liked Saskia's headmistress. In his more exasperated moods at home he called her an old warthog. Verity took care never to say any such thing in front of Saskia, though privately she loathed Mrs Glendenning almost as much as James and Saskia did.

Now, speaking to the woman who held their daughter's future in her hands, Verity said, her voice unsteady, "I know Saskia's behaviour hasn't been ideal, but... how is she doing academically?"

Mrs Glendenning adjusted her wire-rimmed spectacles. "She's scraped through most of her tests, and it's obvious she has ability. But it is equally obvious she has no wish to apply herself. I don't say the blame lies entirely with her, since she could hardly have found more undesirable company. Anabelle Logan is not the sort of girl any mother would want influencing her daughter, and Saskia's behaviour has deteriorated markedly since they took up together. If I could separate them, I would, but that is easier said than done. They've been reported several times smoking behind the shed, and after school while still in uniform. That's when they're actually at school, of course." She folded her hands. "Saskia is a troubled teenager."

Troubled teenager.

The words landed with a thud.

Verity's mind leapt helplessly through the years: the moves, the new schools, the cramped rentals, the fresh starts that weren't really fresh at all. James learning new routes and new aircraft; Verity learning new supermarkets, new phone numbers, new ways to begin again. Saskia dragged from one life into the next before she could ever properly settle into any of them.

Was it any wonder the girl kicked against whatever walls were put around her? Fairmont's rules, its blazers and chapel services and clipped vowels and suspicion of girls who didn't fit neatly into place—perhaps to Saskia it all felt like another cage.

And yet the smoking, the lying, the disappearing—those were not nothing.

Verity fought to keep her composure as the walls of the office seemed to inch inward.

"We understand your concerns, but we're doing our best to guide her through a difficult phase." James's voice held a note of desperation. He had put on a clean shirt and smart trousers for the meeting, and the sight of him—trying so hard, carrying so much—gave Verity an unexpected jolt of tenderness.

"With all due respect, Mr White, if you were doing your best, we wouldn't be having this conversation, would we?" Mrs Glendenning's eyes narrowed.

James stiffened.

"With all due respect, Mrs Glendenning, my wife and I have always taught Saskia right from wrong and tried to give her clear boundaries."

"Well, those lessons don't seem to have taken, do they? Perhaps if you spent less time trying to be her friends and more time being parents, she would be less easily led astray. I see it again and again—permissive parenting sending a child down the path of delinquency."

"Delinquency?" James repeated, his voice low and suddenly cold.

He glanced at Verity, and in that dim, over-heated office

on a gloomy winter afternoon, the look they exchanged pulled taut again every loosened thread between them.

James's deepest fear was not for himself.

It was for his family.

For Verity and Saskia. It always had been.

He rose.

"We've taken up more than enough of your time, Mrs Glendenning. Saskia used to be an A-grade student. I'm not suggesting that Fairmont Ladies College is entirely to blame, but clearly your school's rigid environment does not suit her, when past experience suggests she does better in a less constrained setting." He picked up his car keys. "I think it may be time to move her elsewhere. Good day to you."

CHAPTER

NINE

Sitting in silence in the kitchen at four-thirty, Verity and James glanced up from their respective newspapers at the sound of the front door handle turning very quietly, followed by stealthy footsteps along the passage.

"Saskia!"

Her sigh on the other side of the door was clearly audible, but after a few seconds she slouched into the kitchen, her school blazer hanging off one shoulder, long blonde hair sticking untidily from its two braids.

"What?" Her tone was rude and defiant as she glared at Verity.

Verity clenched her hands in her lap and tried not to rise to the bait. Saskia was spoiling for a fight. She would no doubt engineer the confrontation until it ended in tears—her tears—which would give her the perfect excuse to flee to her room and avoid talking to them any longer.

"Don't be disrespectful to your mother," James said quietly, and Saskia drew in a sharp breath. Clearly she had not realised both her parents were in the kitchen.

"I wasn't," she muttered, sticking out her chin, her eyes narrowing as she took in the smart clothes both her parents were still wearing.

"Mrs Glendenning asked us in for a meeting at the school to discuss your behaviour," Verity said carefully.

Saskia shrugged. "What did the old cow have to say? Nothing nice, I'll bet."

"You're spot on there," James said.

Verity blinked. Saskia, too, looked momentarily thrown.

"You've been at Fairmont Ladies for six months," James went on, "and you don't like it any better now than when you arrived, do you?"

Saskia shook her head.

James sighed. "You're a smart girl, Saskia, but you're losing your way. You can't go on like this." He raked a hand through his hair, looked at Verity, then back at his daughter. "You'll be sixteen soon, and you've still got another eighteen months of school before you matriculate. I'd hoped you might somehow hang in there."

His words seemed to hover between them. Saskia kept staring at her parents as if daring them to say whether she was staying or going.

The silence stretched.

Then Verity said, "But it's obvious you can't, so we're taking you out." She cleared her throat. "Basically, before you get expelled again."

"Oh, so you think some other posh girls' school is going to take me? Or can I just leave and get a job?"

She stood there glaring, truculent and combative, but beneath it Verity caught something else too: hope, bright and frightened, as if Saskia was bracing for the worst while longing for something entirely different.

Verity looked at her daughter, then at James.

"We're taking you with us to Botswana," she said at last. "Your father has been offered a job there."

James stared at her, caught off guard, and the silence broke when Saskia gave a whoop.

"Africa? To live with the animals? To see the wildlife? Really?"

"You'd still have to go to school, Saskia," James said. "You wouldn't be some jungle girl running wild."

"Everyone has to go to school," Saskia said, still fizzing with excitement. "If they don't want to end up on the dole forever, I mean. But I could see the animals on weekends, couldn't I? Maybe I could even get a job with them one day. Botswana." Her eyes shone as she looked at James. "Are we going to where you're from, Dad? Like in those old family photos? Though I don't agree with the shooting part. They don't still hunt there, do they?"

Verity watched her daughter's face come alive in a way it rarely did these days and felt a wrench somewhere beneath her ribs. Fairmont, with its hard-edged rules and lacquered girls, had seemed only to shrink Saskia further into herself or drive her into rebellion. But the thought of Africa—of space, of animals, of a life less hemmed in—had cracked something open in her at once.

For a moment, even Verity could almost see it: floodplains instead of corridors, sky instead of brick walls, a life that might suit a girl who had always seemed to kick against confinement.

When Saskia's excitement had finally burned itself out and she had gone to her room, James shook his head.

"You weren't worried you'd jumped the gun, Verity? We haven't properly talked it through, you know."

Verity closed her eyes and took a deep breath.

"That job you've been offered... you have to take it, don't you? For all the reasons you said."

James nodded and shifted his chair a little closer.

"When do they want you to start?"

"We'd have to discuss that. There's you and Saskia to think about. I'm not going to rush into accepting anything without making sure you're on board once you know all the facts." His voice softened. "I know how much you hate the idea, and I've been racking my brains trying to think of alternatives."

"But there aren't any, are there?" Verity said quietly. "Not really. There's no way through this for you and the other AFAP pilots. It's not just the bosses who want to crush the Australian Federation of Airline Pilots. It's the government as well. Which means you need another job, because we can't live on my salary and still pay rent and Saskia's school fees—well, after today, school fees may be one less thing to worry about. But there's everything else. And you won't find flying work in Australia, will you?"

She stood and turned on the tap, pouring them both a glass of water as she waited for him to answer. When he didn't, she went on, leaning back against the sink.

"I get it, James. I hate it, but I get it. I've heard it so often I'm sick of it. The Prime Minister in bed with the airline bosses so they can break the strike without you blokes even getting a proper hearing over pay after years of frozen salaries. The facts have been skewed. Everyone thinks pilots take home fat salaries and won't stop whingeing for more. They don't know the truth. And if Bob Hawke can go on national television and call you glorified bus drivers, then you don't stand a hope of winning over the public."

James nodded. "Yep. He's thick as thieves with Sir Peter

Abeles. He's brought in the Air Force at enormous cost, and he'll throw as many tax dollars as it takes at Hercules and whatever else to break this strike without us getting near a proper negotiating table. There's been no sensible public debate about it, Verity. None that I can see." He paused. "I won't get my job back. Not with Ansett. Not with any Australian airline."

"So that's that." Verity came round behind his chair and craned over his shoulder to read the letter in his hand. "What does this man in Botswana—Tony..." she squinted at the signature. "Harper—have to say?"

James relaxed a little into his chair. "Duncan spoke well of me, so Tony checked around with a few contacts, including some of my old students from when I was instructing—Barry in Kununurra among them. Now he's asking about my availability. We spoke on the phone, and I've pretty much got the job if I want it. I'm current on the Cessna 206, so licence conversion shouldn't be a problem. There's accommodation for all of us at the Okavango Air compound in Maun, and a shared vehicle goes with the job."

Verity noticed the way his hands tightened when he added, "Of course, I don't expect you to come with me. A lot of the blokes taking overseas jobs are leaving their families here so they don't disrupt schooling and work."

With surprising calm, Verity said, "You're talking about men who've had airline salaries for years and can afford that option. Please don't look at me like that. It's not a cheap shot. But the fact is, we can't afford two households. My job doesn't pay anything like what the title suggests. That's publishing for you. Sounds glamorous, pays like rubbish." She tipped her face towards the ceiling for a moment. "Anyway, I'd never let you live in another city—

let alone another country—without me. We made that rule when we got married."

The disappointment in her gut sat there like a stone, but she still managed a smile.

"So yes. Of course I'm coming with you."

It ought to have hurt more, giving the words life. Yet when she saw the flash of relief that crossed his face, something inside her eased too. Not because she wanted Botswana. Not because she didn't mind sacrificing the job she loved. But because this—this choosing each other in the midst of disappointment—was still the core of what they were.

Then James frowned.

"There are no high schools in Maun. Saskia would have to go to boarding school in South Africa. That might dampen her enthusiasm."

"She might surprise you."

And Verity was right.

"Boarding school?" Saskia cried when they told her. "In South Africa? And holidays on safari in the Okavango?" She could barely keep still. "When do we leave?"

CHAPTER

TEN

FOUR WEEKS LATER

Verity watched the South African Airways check-in girl affix labels to the last of their belongings— three suitcases containing what remained after the garage sale and the painful decisions about what truly mattered.

"That's it then." James squeezed Verity's hand as their bags disappeared from view. "No turning back now."

She nodded, not trusting herself to speak.

The Melbourne terminal bustled around them, people hurrying towards destinations they had chosen for themselves.

Unlike her.

Beside them, Saskia bounced on her toes, her excitement a sharp contrast to Verity's leaden spirits. She seemed a different creature from the lacklustre teenager Verity had grown used to. "I can't believe we're really going to Africa! Will we see elephants from the plane, Dad?"

"Not till we get to Botswana, sweetheart." James ruffled her hair. "But there'll be plenty of time for wildlife spotting once we're there."

The flight to Johannesburg seemed endless. While Saskia read her book and watched *When Harry Met Sally* on the big screen, Verity gave up trying to follow it. The family in the row ahead kept standing up and blocking the screen.

Or perhaps that was only an excuse.

The last thing she felt like right now was a romantic comedy.

As James studied his Botswana aviation maps, Verity stared out of the window at the Indian Ocean far below and thought about her last day at the magazine.

"You're always welcome back," Carrie had said, hugging her goodbye. "Six months—that's how long I'll hold your position. Just in case..."

Just in case what?

In case James changed his mind? In case Botswana was a disaster? In case Verity came home humbled and bruised and needing to pick up the pieces of the life she had only just begun to build?

Below them, the ocean gave way to the African continent. The sun rose over Madagascar, lining the clouds in pink and gold, and gradually the land beneath them changed too—the lush coast flattening into something harsher and drier.

"Look!" Saskia pressed her face to the window as they began their descent into Johannesburg. "Everything's so different!"

Different did not begin to cover it, Verity thought, once they disembarked.

She had never been outside Australia, and the first thing that hit her was the smell and the heat. It was as hot as any outback town she had ever lived in, but somehow this felt different—denser, wilder, less familiar. The very air seemed to carry a note she could not yet place.

James's connecting flight to Gaborone was delayed, so he waited with Verity and Saskia in the terminal until their afternoon bus to Pretoria departed. While they were to spend a week with James's grandmother, James would go on to Gaborone to organise the flight and residence permits required for his new job in Maun.

"You okay?" he asked softly, watching her pick at her airport sandwich.

"Just tired."

It was not exactly a lie. She was tired—bone tired. But it was not only the journey. She felt suspended between one life and another, with no firm ground beneath her feet.

And she was frightened that she was no longer equal to being the sort of wife James needed for this next stage: cheerful, adaptable, all-in.

As she had always been.

Until now.

BUT ONCE THEY REACHED PRETORIA, the visit with Edith Franklin proved pleasanter than Verity had expected. Saskia seemed to genuinely take to the old lady, and Edith's home in Anderson Street, lined with magnificent jacarandas, was lovely, with two gardeners and a maid who made sure Verity did not have to lift a finger.

It was a strange contrast to life in Australia.

Then James joined them, and after a few restful days it was time to say goodbye to Saskia's great-grandmother, who had entertained them royally with stories of James and

Africa, most of them accompanied by her favourite sweet sherry.

Now, as the small plane to Gaborone rattled and bounced in the hot air, Verity watched the veld scroll past below—great stretches of yellowed earth broken only by the occasional smudge of green. So different from the wintry Victorian landscape she had left behind.

At last Maun appeared on the horizon: a scatter of huts and low buildings rising out of the dust like a mirage.

The heat hit them like a wall as they came down the steps from the plane, the air shimmering over the runway.

"Welcome to Botswana," James said, his face alight with an enthusiasm Verity still could not quite match.

A donkey cart rattled past the airport fence. Birds wheeled in the distance against a hard blue sky. Everything felt alien, bright, unreal.

Then Saskia slipped her hand into Verity's, warm and familiar.

"Look, Mum—is that Dad's new company plane? The one he's going to fly?"

A small Cessna sat on the apron, its paint gleaming in the African sun. James was already striding towards it, purposeful, alert, entirely in his element. For all he had striven for the security of an airline job, Verity could see now that this—light aircraft, dust, bush flying—spoke to some deeper, older dream in him.

She drew a breath of hot, dusty air.

Yes, this was their life now. She could either keep fighting it inwardly, or find some way to step into it.

"Come on, then," she said, squeezing Saskia's hand. "Let's go and see your father's new office. And then we'll have something cold to drink at that café we passed—the Duck Inn—and talk about the safari."

As a send-off, Verity's parents had contributed towards a five-night land-and-water safari before Verity was to fly with Saskia to Johannesburg and settle her into her new school.

"No, it's not the Cessna I'm going to fly," James told them after inspecting the aircraft. "Come on—let's get something to drink while we wait for our flight into the Delta."

In the courtyard of the Duck Inn, the three of them sat patiently, apparently the only patrons on this blazing afternoon.

"Do you think they know we're here?" Saskia asked ten minutes later, with an impatient sigh.

Up the road, the tinny thump of transistor music from Elvis Buzz Cuts—operating beneath a tarpaulin strung between two poles—competed with the hum of generators and the hum of a Cessna coming in to land.

Verity took out her diary and made a few notes. The whole racket painted such a vivid picture of a frontier town caught between old and new that she could not resist trying to catch it on paper.

Even the things she disliked.

James fanned himself while watching a donkey wander down the dusty street with a couple of feral dogs trailing behind. Heat shimmered off the unsealed road, making the distance dance.

A waiter had glanced at them when they arrived, then disappeared into the dark interior of the bar.

He still had not returned.

"Relax. Africa time." James looked at his watch. "Shall we walk across to the airport and wait there? We're due to fly out in twenty minutes, anyway."

"But I'm thirsty," Saskia said.

James sighed. "I hope you weren't like this with Granny."

Saskia grinned. "Granny and I got on great guns. She said she was the reason you got interested in flying, Dad. Something about a riot in the mountains in some African country—not Botswana—where she took you when you were a kid and you rescued somebody." She gave him a searching look. "Though I think she was making it up to amuse me."

Verity laughed. "So you don't think your father is hero material? Is that what you're saying?"

James grinned back. "The story's true, but *rescuing* is a bit of a stretch—though I did witness it. There was a riot in the mountains of Lesotho that threatened a pilot's wife over some false accusation that made the pair of them look bad." He sobered. "It was actually pretty frightening. I was only a kid, visiting Granny in Pretoria. I was too young to know that years earlier she and Grandpa had fostered a couple of evacuee children from London during the war. One of them had come back and was flying in the mountains. Anyway, Granny only realised it when she saw it in the newspaper—"

"That her foster son was flying in Africa?" Verity frowned. "You've never told me this story."

"Yes—and that he'd supposedly committed some terrible crime. Stuart Price, his name was. Granny adored him. He was only eight when he came to live with them, and apparently his real family was dreadful. She and Grandpa looked after the siblings for five years and then paid for Stuart to learn to fly back in England. But they became estranged, which just about broke Granny's heart, and then one day she sees in the paper that he's mixed up in some illegal diamond business in Lesotho." James shook his head. "She was looking after me that afternoon, but she simply bundled me into the car, walked out just before a tea party, and drove for hours to find him. I was only a kid and mad about planes, but I'd never been in one until things got rather more dramatic than anyone expected and—"

"Eh, Rra, what will you be wanting?"

The waiter had reappeared at last, bringing with him exactly the laconic, unhurried Motswana manner James had described with such nostalgia.

This was one adventure story Verity was determined to hear to the end, but then Saskia was peppering James with questions about the safari ahead as another small plane came in to land.

The heat was enervating, and while James talked, Verity tried to pay attention. She hoped she was not always going to feel this wilted.

Fortunately, the cold drinks arrived quickly, disappeared just as quickly, and soon the three of them were heading back out into the dusty street towards the terminal building, where the heat struck them again the moment they left the shade.

As James peered through the airport fence, picking out the various light aircraft in the haze and explaining which charter companies flew where, Verity found herself wondering what their life here would really look like.

Maun itself was not much to stir the soul, and she was glad they would soon be out in the bush on safari.

Perhaps if she saw the beauty on their doorstep, she might find the enthusiasm she was still having to fake for James's sake.

For now, she had to arrange her mouth into a smile each time she looked at him.

"Is that what we'll be flying in?" Verity squinted at a

Cessna 206 taxiing towards the apron. When the propeller stopped, the pilot—a broad-shouldered, khaki-clad man in his mid-thirties, with shaggy dark-blond hair—jumped down and went round to open the door for his four passengers.

"It says *Zerangu Hunting Safaris* on the door," said Saskia. "Definitely not what you'll be flying then, Dad. He's all right-looking, though."

"Since when did you start noticing men?" Verity asked, though she had to admit the fellow was handsome in a rough-hewn sort of way. Not like clean-cut James, and not remotely the sort of man she usually found attractive.

She watched the tourists thank the pilot before heading towards the exit. In a few days' time that could just as easily be James, she thought.

He was going to love working here. She could feel it.

James laughed. "She has to start sometime. No, the outfit I'm joining has a fleet of those." He pointed to another Cessna 206 parked a little way off, with the Air Okavango logo on the door. "And they fly to hunting camps as well as photographic ones, so you'll have to keep a lid on your outrage, Saskia, if I'm rostered onto a hunting charter, okay?" Then he glanced at Zerangu's Cessna Caravan—a larger, more powerful aircraft—and added thoughtfully, "Zerangu must be doing well to have its own plane. Big hunting outfit, by the look of it. Don't worry, Saskia. We're not flying with this bloke."

Raised voices cut across the heat-hum of the afternoon, and they turned to see a stocky, dark-haired young man in khaki striding towards the pilot. The two men were arguing, their words carrying clearly on the dry breeze.

"No, man, I don't feel like another stop in Chubaora. I

want to get back to Zerangu," said the pilot, hands on hips. "I've had it up to here with tourists."

"I did your flight when you were in a spot last week." The dark-haired pilot changed tack, his voice now pleading. "Come on, Starky, it's no skin off your nose. You'll be passing over, anyway. It'll mean I can take Sharon to dinner tonight."

The pilot—Starky—brushed past him to slam shut the luggage pod. He appeared unmoved by his colleague's romantic hopes.

"Ach, man," he said, straightening and raking a hand through his thick hair. "I'm sick of having to come up with the same old answers to the same old questions from the same ancient bloody tourists. I told you, I'm not flying them."

Both men stopped abruptly when they noticed James and the girls watching through the fence. Starky's glower turned at once into an apologetic grin, his strong white teeth flashing from ten yards away.

Embarrassed, Verity looked away and followed James towards the terminal—only to find herself almost colliding with Starky, who had now walked outside.

"Forgive the introduction, but you're not the ancient bloody tourists Matt wants me to fly?" he asked, his grin broadening as his glance flicked over Verity in a way that made her skin prickle.

"Okavango Air passengers bound for Chubaora," said James. He hesitated, then held out his hand. "I'm James White. I start with Okavango Air next week, and this is my family—my wife, Verity, and our daughter, Saskia."

"Starky Willis," the pilot said. "Well, then—a comrade-in-arms." He smiled at Verity, then called over his shoulder to the other pilot, who was now trailing behind them.

"Looks like I've painted myself into a corner. All right, Matt —you take Sharon to dinner, and I'll fly these people to Chubaora."

"You will?" James looked taken aback.

"I just might need a favour from you one day, mightn't I? Maun's too small for people not to get along." Then, with a sidelong glance at Verity, he added, "Though if you want the truth, I can't stand the bloody place. Maybe that's the wrong thing to say to newcomers." He grinned. "Where's your luggage? In the terminal? Right-o, I'll send Lesego to fetch it."

"I'm sure I'll like Maun," Verity said. "I've lived in places smaller than this ."

"Then you're a shoo-in," said Starky. "Lucky man, James, having a wife determined to thrive in a dust bowl like this." He turned to Saskia. "And you, young lady—got your checklist ready for the Big Five minus one, eh? No rhino here, but you should see the rest if you're lucky."

Verity sent Saskia a warning look while Saskia, fierce conservationist that she was, said predictably as she flicked back her sun-bleached hair, "And how much do the big game hunters pay these days for a lion's head as a trophy?"

"That's between them and the Botswana Government, but I can assure you, it's a lot of pula." He lifted an eyebrow, then his expression softened. "If you want to preserve the animals, you have to make them worth preserving. Otherwise, local people will hunt them for meat or because they're dangerous. Things aren't so black and white when you're..." He looked at her more closely. "How old are you?"

"Fifteen," Saskia said warily.

"So you'll be off to boarding school after this, I take it? Which means you've got five days to get educated in Botswana's delicate, high-cost, low-impact tourism model." He gave a knowing sigh. "Fifteen-year-olds are very judgmental." He glanced at Verity and James as though inviting them into the joke.

Verity was surprised that this supposed hunting pilot was speaking to their daughter like this, and more surprised still that Saskia—normally so prickly—looked bright and alert, as though she were sparring for pleasure.

"You've got one, then? A teenager?" Verity asked. Starky looked too young, though in truth he was probably not much older than James.

"God, no." Starky laughed. "No wife, no kids. Not that I know of, anyway. But there's plenty of fun to be had in a place like this, so I'm not complaining. The Delta's been home for nearly fifteen years and I'm not going anywhere else." He grinned at James. "You'll have to see my camp. If you're flying for Okavango Air, you'll be dropping in often enough. They do charters for all the camps around here."

"Hunting camps too?" Saskia asked.

"Hunting camps, photographic camps, tourists, supplies, government officials—you name it," Starky said. "The only way into many of the camps this time of year is by light aircraft, and Okavango Air is one of our clients." Then, after barking instructions to Lesego, a young Motswana lad who had appeared at his call, he added, "There's a big enough Aussie contingent around here to make you feel at home. You know any of the blokes, James?"

"My cousin Rod Maxwell knows Tony from Okavango Air. Tony interviewed me over the phone and offered me the job."

"Rod's your cousin?"

"James grew up in Botswana but emigrated to Australia when he was ten," said Verity. Then she hesitated. "Actually, I knew who you were before you came round the corner, once the other pilot said your name."

"What?" He looked suddenly wary, and she hurried to reassure him.

"Nothing bad. There can't be too many Starkys in this part of the world, and I remembered the name from an old photograph album James's aunt sent over years ago."

"There's a picture of me?" Starky's brows shot up.

James nodded. "Your name was in a caption with one of my cousins. You were with Mike, Phil, and Susan on a hunting trip in 1974."

"Mike and Susan are James's cousins," Verity explained. "Well, Susan still is, obviously. James was actually supposed to go on that hunting trip too. Goodness—you look as though you've seen a ghost. Are you all right?"

For a moment Starky really did look discomposed. Then he smiled.

"Man, it's just been so long since I saw those blokes. Now it's like... someone's walked over my grave." He cleared his throat. "Great kid, Susan. I don't think I've seen her since that trip."

"Why's that?" Verity asked politely.

He hesitated. "Some bad business happened." He sent James a wary glance. "I suppose you know all about it, being Mike's cousin." Then he shook his head as if still astonished. "To think we knew each other as kids—briefly. And that you were supposed to be on that hunting trip."

"Yes," said James. "And if I remember rightly, the bloke who shot Mike didn't get what he deserved."

"What happened?" cried Saskia.

Starky looked at James, who said, "A very bad man shot your dad's cousin."

"Who was it again, Dad?"

James glanced at Starky, then said to Saskia, "The boyfriend of my cousin Susan. A man called Jeremy, I think it was. Only he died while on remand—"

"We shouldn't be talking about this so lightly," said Verity.

"We're not talking about it lightly," James said, then seemed to regret the sharpness in his tone.

"Right." Starky clapped his hands lightly. "Looks like Lesego's got your bags and sorted everything else. Shall we go?"

"Are we the only ones?" Verity asked, looking around.

Starky nodded. "The only ones bound for Chubaora this afternoon, yes." He grinned. "You've got yourselves a private charter, folks."

CHAPTER

ELEVEN

Forty-five minutes later, the three of them were blinking in the bright sun.

The young Motswana lad who had leapt from the game vehicle parked at the edge of the dirt airstrip was unloading their luggage from the pod while a petite young woman with strawberry-blonde hair, whom Verity judged to be in her mid-twenties, strode towards them.

"Welcome to Chubaora," she said, shaking hands all round. "I'm Lucy, the camp manager—for the time you're here, anyway. The usual managing couple are still in Jo'burg on leave until the end of January. It's the tail end of the busy season, so there are only three other guests in camp, which means you'll all share one game vehicle for the dawn and dusk drives."

Turning away from them, she greeted Starky, who had just re-emerged from the cockpit. "How was the flight, Starky? Do you want to come back to camp for a cold drink?"

Verity sent Lucy a sidelong glance. The girl fancied their pilot. It was there in the blush, and in the flicker of disappointment she failed to hide when he declined, saying he wanted to get back to Zerangu to prepare for the hunting party arriving the next day.

Starky, Verity thought, probably had that effect on women.

Definitely a ladies' man.

Starky clapped Lucy on the back and said with a smile, "Make sure you look after our guests properly, Luce. James is flying for Okavango Air from next week. And Verity...?" He raised his brows enquiringly. "What are you going to be doing?"

Verity tried to look nonchalant as she shrugged, but James said quickly, "Apart from being a fantastic amateur photographer, Verity is a writer."

"Magazines? Newspapers?" asked Starky. "Maybe Verity would be interested in a job at the *Okavango Observer*. They're looking for someone—"

"She's writing a book," James interrupted.

Verity frowned. Yes, that was what she had told James she meant to do, but she did not appreciate his shutting off other possibilities before she had even had time to consider them.

"Very nice. What about?" Lucy asked.

"A romance," James said.

"Yes, a romance," said Verity. It was what she had always wanted to write, but now she wished James had not said it. She had scarcely thought beyond the vague idea of it and did not want to be quizzed.

"Oh, wow!"

They all turned at Saskia's involuntary gasp. She was gazing across the landing strip at the floodplain melting into the horizon. A herd of zebra stood grazing quietly, their ears flicking now and then while little birds perched upon them, all of them perfectly at ease in a world that still felt impossible to Verity.

"I didn't think I'd see them this close," Saskia whispered.

Verity nudged James in the ribs, but he was already smiling at the wonder on their daughter's face.

Maybe this new adventure was not going to be entirely dreadful.

The three other guests in camp were a flirtatious pair of American newlyweds—Dougie and Brenda Kilmore—and a retired British filmmaker called Rupert Graves, whom Saskia recognised from his television documentaries. With a star-struck look in his direction, she elbowed Verity's ribs.

The Kilmores had just returned from their game drive, flushed with enthusiasm but pleading exhaustion, so they retreated to their tent. Rupert, meanwhile, perched himself on a bar stool and entertained Verity and James with stories of his latest thrilling animal encounters while they waited for dinner, which they all ate at one long table beneath the stars.

Lucy proved an effervescent hostess, drawing Saskia out about her interest in wildlife and assuring her she was almost certain to see lions, as a pride known fondly as *The Boys* frequently wandered through the Chubaora concession.

"And what if a lion strays *out* of the concession?" Saskia's eyes darkened. "Like into a hunting concession next door. Doesn't Starky have a hunting camp with hunters arriving tomorrow? He's not far from here, is he?"

Verity's heart clenched.

For so long Saskia had shown such disregard for everyone else's feelings that it had become hard to reconcile this difficult, prickly girl with the sweet, compassionate child she had once been. It seemed that now, with the toxic influence of her Melbourne friends fading, that softer self was beginning to re-emerge.

"No need to worry about that," Lucy assured her. "The average wildlife concession is about eight hundred square kilometres, though some are as large as two thousand. And it's not as if there's open slather in a hunting concession. They're leased from the government with an emphasis on sustainable practice, and only a few permits are issued each year. I happen to know that there are no lion permits left for Zerangu. Starky can take his wealthy clients out for a few impala and eland, perhaps one of the big four, but not lion."

Brenda leaned forward. "So they don't hunt lion?"

"I didn't say that," Lucy said with a smile. "Each client gets a general game licence—say four impala, four warthog, a couple of kudu, that sort of thing. Then anything else, like lion or elephant, requires a supplementary licence. And as I said, the lion quota for Zerangu has already been filled."

"Someone's already shot a lion?" Saskia screwed up her face.

"About six weeks ago."

"Who would do such a thing?" Saskia looked so accusingly at Rupert that he gave a low chuckle.

"I shoot them with a camera, darling. That's why I've been coming to Chubaora for the past fifteen years. Chubaora is a photographic camp, while Zerangu attracts a rather different kind of visitor." He turned to James. "You'll get to know them all soon enough if you're flying in these parts."

"But who shot the lion?" Saskia persisted.

Lucy shrugged. "I honestly don't remember. Ah—here comes dessert." She broke off as the staff appeared with

Black Bottom Pie. "And don't worry, Saskia, I can promise you that if you see a lion tomorrow, he'll be one hundred percent safe. As for the kudu, I wouldn't be so sure," she added with a wry smile.

Waking for the game drive before dawn was no hardship for Verity, who had been lying awake for what felt like hours by the time the alarm went off.

Too many thoughts had circled through the dark as she lay beside James, and she had not known how to quiet any of them.

Peering at the travel clock, she could just make out the time: 4.45.

Well, she and James had to be at the boma in a little over half an hour, so she might as well get up, she thought, though there was no point waking James yet. He had tossed and turned for hours, and she let him sleep.

The night before, she had set out the clothes she meant to wear—khaki shorts, shirt and boots—on top of her suitcase, so she took them into the little letaka-reed bathroom and dressed by the dim light of a kerosene lamp.

The ensuite had no roof, and as she tied up her hair, she gazed at the brilliant scatter of stars overhead.

The sounds of the night felt sharper here. She could hear a hippo chomping somewhere out in the dark, and farther off came the deep, unmistakable roar of a lion.

It was exciting. She had not really believed she would hear a lion, though Saskia's questions the night before had made everything feel suddenly possible. Perhaps she could write articles about the wildlife here and try to sell them. Not that one could make much of a living from that.

As she tugged her hair into a ponytail, distant voices carried on the stillness, and she paused, not exactly meaning to listen.

They were neither the mid-Atlantic drawl of the American newlyweds nor Rupert's plum-inflected English tones, but a South African male voice, low and soft, answered by Lucy's unmistakable lilting accent and then her giggle.

Verity moved to the reed wall and peered through a gap. In the distance she could make out the faint glow of a hurricane lamp near the manager's tent on the far side of the boma.

Lucy was obviously up early, and soon she and one of the guides would be serving coffee and rusks.

Yet the male voice sounded oddly familiar, and when she angled for a better view, Verity was almost sure that the man striding away in the opposite direction while Lucy headed towards the bar area was Starky.

"You're up early."

Verity jumped as James put a hand on her shoulder.

"You'll get a much better view from the front step," he said. "Or did you hear something behind the tent? I went to sleep listening to hippos chewing, and I woke up to hippos chewing."

"And I'm starving, so the sooner I start chewing on a rusk the better." Verity was keen to test her hunch. Not that it mattered if Starky had come from Lucy's tent. She was simply curious.

Lucy looked sleepy as she stood beside the steaming urn, but she brightened when she greeted Verity and Rupert, who arrived at the bar together.

"I'm hoping for leopard this morning, my girl," said the elderly filmmaker, putting a hand on Lucy's shoulder. "But you've not seen leopard yourself yet, have you, Lucy?" He bit into a buttermilk rusk and crunched loudly. In the still dawn it sounded remarkably like the hippos grazing outside camp.

"Jacob is taking me out in a couple of days and he promises he'll find one," said Lucy. She turned to Verity. "Jacob is one of our local rangers, and famous for his lion story. Saskia will love that one, since she seems to have quite a soft spot for lions."

"And what's Jacob's lion story?"

"He was mauled by a lion when he was a young man, long before he became a ranger. He still has the scars, and it's his favourite fireside tale. Lots of drama. I'm sure you'll hear it tonight."

Verity smiled. "I look forward to it. And when do you go on holiday?"

"In two months. But I'm going to make the most of every minute till then."

"And then, Lucy, you'll have to bring that boyfriend of yours back from Cape Town with you next time and show him what he's missing," Rupert said. He frowned. "Or is that all over and done with?"

Verity noticed that Lucy did not answer. Instead, she looked relieved to move away and greet James and the Kilmores with tea and coffee before escorting them out to the game vehicle, where Jacob, their Motswana guide and hero of the lion story, was already waiting at the wheel.

The weather, which had been so oppressive the previous afternoon, was cool and delicious now as dawn stole across the horizon, washing the bushland and savannah in pink.

For the first few minutes they bumped away from camp in silence. James and Verity sat high in the back, Verity's mind running over the thousand possibilities her new life might hold. James, at least, would be all right. He had his flying. The salary was not spectacular, but they had a roof over their heads and some breathing room, even if they had not yet talked about timelines or next steps.

In the few short hours since arriving in Botswana, James seemed already to have come alive. More than once he had said it felt like coming home.

But this was not home to Verity.

The safari itself gave her a jolt of adrenaline, certainly, but beneath it sat the same old worry: what on earth was she going to do in dusty Maun?

The more she turned it over, the more the possibility Starky had mentioned—the *Okavango Observer*—began to glimmer. It would be a comedown from the hard-won heights of *Flair*, yes, but it would keep her hand in, and if it was the small outfit she imagined, perhaps she might have scope to choose her own stories, perhaps even one day to shape them editorially.

It would also, she realised, give her a reason to get out of Maun and into the Delta. If the paper supported the conservation ethos that governed the region, she could write about things that mattered to her—and to Saskia. Things like wildlife and preservation.

More important than any job, though, was the fact that Saskia had begun to bloom. The girl had hugged her spontaneously the night before for what felt like the first time in years.

Now James's hand slowly folded over hers, and Verity felt her heart soften as she lifted her face to his.

"It's beautiful, isn't it?" she whispered, trying to show in her smile that things might perhaps still be something like the old days, when they had been young and reckless and bound together by shared adventure.

And in love.

"Cheetah!"

Jacob pointed ahead as the vehicle jolted to a stop.

Not merely a cheetah, but a kill.

The hunt took twenty minutes, during which the female cheetah asphyxiated its prey—a young impala—after separating it from the herd and springing onto its back to bring it down.

It was not pleasant to watch.

But there was also something electrifying in witnessing real life stripped of sentiment.

Verity had expected Saskia to be horrified, to insist they rescue the impala or at least drive away.

Instead, her daughter sat very still, watching.

Then, over brunch, Saskia said solemnly, "Life is real."

"Life is real," Rupert agreed with a sage nod. "I'm proud of you, my girl. I did wonder whether you'd keep your head. I always hold, when filming documentaries, that one mustn't interfere with the natural order of things. Predators have to eat too, you know."

LATER THAT AFTERNOON, when Verity found Starky unexpectedly at the wheel of their vehicle, she felt a small frisson of alarm.

What would Saskia say to the hunter if something similarly brutal unfolded on this drive?

As it happened, sightings were sparse compared with the morning, and by the time Starky stopped by a lagoon and hauled out the cooler box with beers and gin and tonic, everyone seemed to have wilted in the heat.

Even the newlyweds were no longer holding hands.

"To new adventures."

Verity turned as James raised his Castle beer in salute. With a smile, she clinked her gin and tonic against the can and reclined in the director's chair Starky had set up well back from the lagoon's edge, which he had deemed too risky.

"Have you ever seen a fish eagle?" Starky asked Saskia, handing her a Sprite. "Better still, have you seen one catch a fish? Because that's what we're about to see." He pointed to the still water and papyrus beyond it while reaching into his pocket for a piece of biltong. "Now watch carefully—but remember what I said about staying away from the edge."

The late-afternoon sun turned the lagoon to beaten gold. Verity watched the fish eagle swoop, its great wings catching the light against the endless sky, and felt a strange calm wash through her.

Saskia, who had been standing midway between the vehicle and the water, edged closer, enthralled. The dried mud crackled beneath her Doc Martens.

"Did you see that?" she cried. "It just snatched that fish straight out of the water!"

Verity's throat tightened.

"Saskia, come back from there."

"It's fine, Mum. I'm not even that close." But she took another step, shading her eyes.

The lagoon looked like glass, disturbed only by the faint ripples where fish broke the surface.

But something darker moved beneath.

A shadow.

A shift.

A wrongness.

"Saskia—"

The water exploded.

Later, Verity would remember it only in fragments: the massive head breaking the surface; the jaws flung wide; the hideous prehistoric flash of scales; the sound—not quite a splash, not quite a roar.

In the instant itself, time seemed to stop.

She saw Saskia's eyes widen as she understood.

Saw her try to leap back.

Too late.

The crocodile struck her daughter's leg like a battering ram, knocking her off balance before its jaws clamped around her ankle.

"No!"

Verity's scream seemed to come from somewhere outside herself. She lunged forward, but someone seized her arms.

"Stay still!"

Starky's voice cracked through the panic. He was already lifting his rifle to his shoulder, all banter gone, his movements swift and terrifyingly precise.

Saskia thrashed in the mud, clawing for purchase as the crocodile dragged her towards deeper water. One Doc Marten scrabbled desperately while the other vanished between those monstrous jaws.

Then the reptile rolled.

Saskia's scream tore across the lagoon.

"Hold still, Saskia!"

Starky's voice carried the sheer command of a man used to being obeyed in dangerous places. Somehow—God knew how—Saskia heard him through her terror. She stopped struggling.

The crocodile stilled too, secure in its grip now.

That was what Starky had been waiting for.

The first shot split the air like thunder.

The crocodile's head jerked, but the jaws did not open.

A second shot followed almost at once.

The grip spasmed.

Then, slowly, the jaws loosened.

Verity wrenched free of whoever had been holding her and ran to her daughter. Saskia lay face-down in the mud, blood already seeping through the torn leather of her boot.

But she was alive.

Alive.

"The boot saved her." Starky's voice sounded oddly far away. "If she hadn't been wearing those heavy boots..."

Verity gathered her daughter into her arms, feeling her shudder with pain, shock and terror. The lowering sun had turned the lagoon red, and somewhere in the distance a fish eagle screamed.

They had been lucky.

A few inches higher. A few seconds longer.

She could not finish the thought.

When she looked up, Starky was still scanning the water with his rifle ready.

"Get her back to the vehicle," he said quietly. "The blood will draw others."

Verity helped Saskia to her feet, supporting her as she hopped on one leg. As they moved away from the water, she heard the soft plop of something heavy slipping beneath the surface.

She did not look back.

"Can you move it?" Starky crouched to inspect the wound while Saskia sat on the edge of the game vehicle, white-faced and wide-eyed, whimpering as she tried to flex her ankle.

"I don't think the damage is too bad, but we need to get her to a hospital. It has to be properly cleaned. Croc bites carry a real risk of infection." He glanced from Saskia to the darkening sky, and Verity's heart clenched.

"Tonight? In Maun?" she asked hopefully.

Starky shook his head. "We'll bypass the clinic and take her straight to Jo'burg first thing in the morning. By the time we get back to camp it'll be dark." He patted Saskia gently on the shoulder. "How much pain are you in? We're going to hit a few bumps, but the bone looks intact. You were lucky. I've dealt with medevacs where the foot was hanging on by tendons. You, my girl, look to have got off with a flesh wound."

Verity was shaking so badly she could barely force out her next question.

"How many guests have been attacked by crocs?"

Starky gave the faintest of smiles. "Saskia's the first. I'm talking about locals. Kids who swim in lagoons, that sort of thing." Then he looked back at Saskia. "Hey, kiddo—what do you call those boots? I think I need a pair."

"Doc Martens," Saskia whispered, managing a weak smile.

Verity squeezed her hand, fighting tears.

"Well, they've done a sterling job protecting you. But the people at Baragwanath in Jo'burg will know better than I do."

"Baragwanath?" James repeated.

"It's one of the best hospitals in the Southern Hemi-sphere," said Rupert. "Had a new ticker put in there myself after the old one gave up during a rather lively filming expedition a few years ago." He squeezed Saskia's shoulder. "Your odds are far better than mine were, and look at me now."

"But we're in the middle of safari," Saskia whispered,

squeezing her eyes shut against the pain. "We only just got here. We can't leave yet. I'll be better in the morning."

James shook his head. "Sorry, sweetheart. Be grateful it wasn't worse. We have to make sure the wound is properly cleaned, as Starky says."

"But—"

"No buts," Starky cut in. "You do as the grown-ups tell you, and I promise I'll take you on a special private game drive next time you're in this neck of the woods. In fact, when you're back in Maun from your fancy boarding school, I'll personally fly you out to Zerangu."

Verity was astonished by the way her daughter's face lit up through the pain.

A hunting camp?

But she bit back the thought. Starky was plainly a charmer.

And after what he had just done, gratitude made every-thing else feel a great deal more complicated.

CHAPTER

TWELVE

WITHIN HOURS of being admitted to hospital, Saskia was in bed in a ward with a pleasant view. Despite receiving intravenous antibiotics, she was remarkably cheerful about her ordeal.

"Wow! Imagine going on safari in Africa and nearly getting taken by a crocodile? Anabelle's not going to believe it?" She grinned as she bit into a biscuit.

"And I can't believe you got off so lightly after you disobeyed Starky's warnings and then nearly gave us all heart attacks." Verity had barely slept while she'd waited for dawn, terrified that Saskia's condition might take a turn for the worse before she was flown to hospital.

"Lucky Rupert just got a new ticker, then," Saskia joked. "Isn't he a lovely man? He told me stories about animal encounters he'd survived in the plane all the way back to Maun." She pulled aside the blanket and wiggled her foot. "It was the Doc Martens that saved me, Mum. And you said I couldn't take them on safari."

"I said there was more appropriate footwear for going on safari," Verity corrected her. But she smiled, overwhelmed by relief. Saskia could have said anything, and she'd still want to hug her. "Now, the hospital wants to keep you in for one more night to make sure infection doesn't set in. So, how about I take a trip into town and buy you some books to read?"

James, who was sitting on the edge of her chair by the bed, put his arm about Verity and gave her a squeeze. He'd suffered just as greatly through Saskia's ordeal, but he said, "How about you spend a couple of hours seeing the city while I keep Saskia company? What about the Carlton Centre? It's the tallest building in Africa with a great view from the observation deck."

"I can't leave you to go sightseeing when it's only by the grace of God you're alive!" Verity protested.

"You mean, by the grace of my Doc Martens," said Saskia, adding with a grin, "Really, Mum, I'm fine. You go into town and buy me some books, and feel free to be as generous as you like, considering you're so happy I'm alive. Dad and I can just chill."

Finally, Verity relented, aware of her pent-up stress only when she was on her own in the city. The observation tower was impressive, but it was a relief to take a seat in the Johannesburg Art Gallery and to try to destress as she stared at its collection of 17th-century Dutch paintings.

How could Saskia nearly have died while under their watch, in front of their very noses? Suddenly she felt very vulnerable. For all of them.

Would Saskia really be alright to go to boarding school in a new country after such a shocking ordeal?

Would James be safe doing his bush flying?

When she returned to the hospital and sat down with James and Saskia in the cafeteria, she shook her head at their enquiries as to whether she'd had a good time. "I've been catastrophising," she said, exhaling with exhaustion. "I couldn't get out of my head how close we were to losing you, Saskia. And then I started worrying about your father flying single-piston engine planes."

"Well, Saskia's hale and hearty, with an adventure to tell, and I think flying a single piston-engine plane around Africa is a lot more exciting than flying a jet between Melbourne and Sydney," said James. He took her hand and gave it a squeeze. "Now we just have to find you something you love doing that'll take your mind off the near misses and *what ifs?* Writing that book will do it. My poor love! It sounds as if your day wasn't as much fun as I'd hoped."

Verity shook her head. "I was still gloom and dooming when a black train conductor told me to get out of the carriage I was in! He said I was sitting in Third Class, which was reserved for Blacks, and that I must go to the more comfortable carriages in the train."

"That's horrible!" gasped Saskia. "What did you say?"

Verity shook her head, embarrassed. "By this stage, I felt so overwhelmed by everything that I started to cry as I stood up, and then I felt even worse because the conductor looked so scared I wondered if he was worried people would think he'd been rude to me. Oh, James, I'm so glad we're in Botswana where there's not this Apartheid. Things feel so different there."

"Oh, Mum! You cried? The poor train conductor." Saskia's eyes widened. In Australia, they'd all seen the television coverage of the riots and unrest in Soweto and other townships. Sporting and other sanctions against South Africa on account of its apartheid regime were regular news.

James put a comforting hand on her knee. "In today's *Argus*, I read that President de Klerk looks like he's open to releasing some political prisoners and relaxing some of the worst apartheid restrictions. South Africa is such a beautiful country, but the politics—"

"And there were so many signs saying Whites Only. At toilet blocks and even on park benches!" Verity interrupted, still thinking about her traumatic day of contrasts. "Oh, James, I can't wait to go home."

"Home?" James repeated, and Verity was stabbed by remorse at the look on his face, adding quickly, "To Maun. Home is where you are, James. That's what I meant." She felt dangerously close to spiralling into an unhelpful morass of emotion and worry so forced herself to add, more robustly, "Anyway, since I've had my day of seeing the city, why don't you contact your cousin, Susan, now that you've learned she's moved up here? Maybe the two of you could catch up tomorrow before Saskia's discharged?" She turned to her daughter. "How about I teach you how to play Canasta while your dad's gone? Would you like that, sweetheart? You mentioned it a while back, but then I got so busy with my job."

"And now you have all the time in the world," Saskia said with a smile, unaware that her words were a double-edged sword and oblivious to the look exchanged by her parents.

"All right, I will," replied James. "Mum gave me her phone number when I called her last night. But if Saskia's all right on her own for an hour or two, maybe you and I could arrange lunch with Susan tomorrow after I visit the Travel Agency to book our flights back to Maun."

Verity shook her head. "Saskia has an appointment with Dr De Villiers before she's discharged, and I'm not sure yet when that's going to be. No, you go. It's a good opportunity for you to reconnect with the Africa side of your family. I'll stay with Saskia until you get back."

IT WAS STRANGE, thought Verity the following morning, but despite the trauma Saskia had experienced, their daughter's spirits were effervescent now that she'd been given the all-clear to be discharged. This was so different from the adolescent who cried if a cut to the finger drew blood and who moped around the house, offering monosyllabic replies to her parents' questions, if she wasn't holed up in her bedroom.

"The doctor says there won't be much of a scar, but there will be some, which is great. I mean, how many people get to say they were attacked by a crocodile and lived to tell the tale?" Saskia swung her legs as she sat on the hospital bed, waiting for the nurse to change the bandage and to arrange crutches for her while James was out at lunch. "Do you think that'll give me street cred at St Anne's?" she asked mischievously, and Verity felt another of those pangs of love and hope that were becoming increasingly frequent. Saskia was blossoming before her eyes.

"Mrs White?" A young nurse put her head around the door. "There's a gentleman asking to see you. Starky Willis."

Verity noticed how Saskia's eyes flashed with excitement. Her own feelings, she had to admit, were mixed. But she nodded and was about to respond when Starky himself appeared, holding a carving of a crocodile that he'd likely bought from one of the many carvers and other artists who sold their work from the city's pavements.

"A good luck talisman," he said. "To remind you of your bravery. And, of course, your *very* good luck. And for you, Mrs White..." He thrust his hand into his pocket and pulled out a letter. "It dropped into Okavango Air's Private Bag just as I was heading off to Jo'burg to get some maintenance done on the Cessna at Lanseria, so I thought I'd drop in to the Bara since it wasn't much of a detour. How's the patient? Hey, but it's getting a bit crowded in here," he said, when the nurse entered to re-do Saskia's bandage, "and I'm sure you don't want your injuries on display—"

But when Saskia protested saying that if he could handle a bit of blood and gore she'd be happy to show him, Starky looked at Verity with raised eyebrows, and said, "Do you want to read your letter in the cafeteria and I'll bring Saskia through when she's finished?"

Verity hesitated. She'd signed the hospital discharge paperwork. The nurse would only be a couple of minutes, so Starky wouldn't spend long with Saskia. "Sure," she said, forcing a smile. "See you in a few minutes."

With a sigh of exhaustion, Verity sat down in the cafeteria and pulled out Sarah's letter as a waitress deposited a cup of unappetising instant coffee made with chicory in front of her.

Smoothing it out, she began to read:

"Dear Verity, I hope this letter finds you well and that you're settling into life in the Okavango Delta. Has the beauty of Botswana's wilderness started to work its magic on you yet? I can only imagine how different it must be from the bustle of your editor's office in Melbourne. How are you coping with the heat and the wildlife? I bet James is in his element, flying that little Cessna over such spectacular scenery.

Things here in Australia have gone from bad to worse since you left. As you know, after the mass resignations, the airlines responded by formally accepting all resignations and terminating any remaining contractual obligations, effectively cutting ties with all the pilots who participated in the action.

But things have gone from bad to worse!

Can you believe it? They're now advertising internationally for replacements! It's an outrage how the government is backing the airlines instead of supporting the workers. And this is a Labour government!

Some pilots who didn't resign are crossing the picket lines to work—we're calling them scabs, of course. It's tearing the community apart.

I saw the "For Sale" sign in front of Sean's Gisborne house the other day, even though it shouldn't have been a shock because he told us he and Melissa are getting divorced, which is hardly a surprise, though that's not as awful as the news about Barry Connelly who took his own life two days ago. Helen found him in the garage. But Barry is not the only suicide. It's horrible.

Everyone is anxious and miserable, and Sean is over here way too much, but I can't say anything except to suggest that, like Tim, he tries harder to find work overseas.

James was lucky to have the job offer in Botswana and leap on it like he did. Tim and all the others who went on strike don't have a chance of getting work for an Australian airline or even one of the smaller aviation companies that have been inundated with pilots job-hunting after the mass resignations. 1650 of them, or thereabouts! Anyway, Tim has applied for a few positions in China, and we're really hopeful he'll get an interview with Cathay Pacific, like Ted, who just got a job offer and is moving to Hong Kong with his family. I'd have to stay here in Melbourne, of course, because of Ben's cerebral palsy treatments, but at least he remains our ray of sunshine through all this.

I know you were upset about having to leave your job, Verity, and I'm so sorry this whole mess has upended your life. But maybe there's a silver lining? Perhaps you could write about your experiences in Botswana—I'm sure your old magazine would love to publish some exotic travel pieces, or there's a local newspaper where you'd be happy. And who knows? Maybe this adventure will open up new opportunities for both you and James. Stay strong. We're all doing our best to weather this storm.

Love, Sarah

She finished reading at the same time as Saskia arrived at the table, laughing at something Starky had said.

"Got to go! Short visit only," he said. "Sorry I can't fly you back to Maun, but I'll be here for a couple of nights and Saskia says you're leaving tomorrow."

And then he was gone, and Verity had to smile and whip up at least a modicum of enthusiasm as Saskia gushed over her visit from Starky.

But she was spared having to agree that he really had to be the most humane hunter in the Okavango by James arriving back from his lunch with Susan, and taking a seat at the table, just as a waitress arrived to take his order for coffee.

"I wouldn't recommend it," said Verity, pulling a face. "It doesn't resemble any of the coffee I've ever had in Melbourne. Anyway, how was your cousin?"

James leaned across the table, his eyes wide as he looked at Saskia and said, "You'll never guess, and what are the chances? But Susan told me that she has a fifteen-year-old daughter boarding at St Anne's too!"

"It's been ten days since we returned to Maun after our dramatic rush to Johannesburg for Saskia's ankle..."

Verity bit the end of her pen and stared at her diary.

What else was there to say?

That it was hot?

That James had delayed his induction in order to spend time with Saskia before she flew back to Johannesburg? He had been wonderful and thoughtful. He had also been brimming with enthusiasm for this new country he had already begun calling home.

And he seemed quite oblivious to Verity's own feelings of isolation and to her growing anxiety about how she was going to carve out a place for herself.

For once the drama of Saskia's crocodile attack had faded, and James had started work—even if he was not yet flying—Verity had been left with her own company for most of the day.

And the cottage, though comfortable enough, was very basic.

Thank goodness she had brought four books.

"Of course, ten days is far too short a time in which to make pronouncements about the future, but..."

Verity looked at the words she had just written, as though silently offering herself advice.

She ought to be more like Sarah.

She ought to accept that Maun would be her home for a very long time.

There would be no job for James as a pilot in Australia —not on a turboprop for one of the smaller companies, and certainly not on a jet. Not for years.

From the bathroom, she could hear him shaving, getting ready for his first proper day on the job. She had woken with the alarm and risen to make his coffee, buying him a few extra minutes in bed.

As she listened now to the sounds of him brushing his teeth, Verity sat up against the pillows and reread Sarah's letter while trying to compose a reply in her head, her diary open on her lap.

Would she be honest with Sarah about how she was feeling, as she had been in the diary? Though perhaps a little more circumspect. Not that she imagined James would snoop, but it would hardly be edifying for him to discover in black and white how unhappy she still was, when the time had surely come to accept reality and do something to improve her mood.

And her life.

That part, at least, was up to her.

Of course, James would tell anyone who asked that his wife was writing a book. But most people on Earth thought they had a book in them, and how many ever stirred themselves to write it, let alone publish it? Not Verity. Long-form narrative was not her strength. She was good at articles. It was on that basis that she had landed the editorship of *Flair*.

Her eyes slid to Carrie Dunbar's farewell card, which ended with a promise to hold a management position open for Verity for six months.

Stitch and Style Down Under.

At the sight of those words, her heart clenched with frustration and longing.

And to think she had truly believed the pilots' dispute might be resolved within that time. After reading Sarah's letter for the third time, she suspected the wounds and loyalties of the pilots' brotherhood would run far too deep for anything to be neatly fixed. Not soon. Perhaps not for years.

No, it was time to think seriously about what she could do in Maun to restore her self-confidence. The growing pressure to contribute financially to their household weighed on her too.

She was not adapting to this new life with Saskia's sudden enthusiasm or James's extraordinary ability to roll with the punches. For Verity, it came down to self-worth. To feeling she was more than James's wife and Saskia's mother, which was what she had been, for the most part— and little more in the eyes of others, she sometimes thought —for fifteen years, as she packed up and followed James wherever necessity took them.

The more she thought about it, the more the job at the *Okavango Observer* seemed the ideal answer.

Not only for her career, but for the family's new life in this place.

The current journalist was not leaving for a few weeks,

apparently, so Verity intended to spend the next few days doing proper research. She had already read several recent issues she'd found on the coffee table at the Okavango Air office.

There was the usual small-town gossip from the two reporters and the editor, but the departing journalist, Tumelo Kgathi, had also written some thoughtful, probing articles about Botswana's heavy reliance on diamond mining—its environmental impact, labour conditions, and the uneven distribution of wealth that followed.

Verity laid one of those articles across her lap and smiled at the byline.

Tumelo.

Faith.

A fitting name for a journalist, she thought—faith being what readers placed in a writer to tell the truth. Perhaps Tumelo had been destined for the profession.

Like Verity.

And perhaps, here, Verity could write about the things she genuinely cared about: environmental questions, conservation, the tensions between hunting and preservation—issues that had hovered beneath the surface of that awkward dinner at Safari South a few nights earlier.

With six years having passed since the ban on elephant hunting, perhaps she could examine what effect that had actually had on elephant populations. Or look at anti-poaching efforts. Or tourism. Or the pressures of development.

Or...

Was she getting ahead of herself?

"I've got to go, darling. Kiss me good luck. Saskia wants a photo of an elephant."

James emerged from the bathroom smelling of Old

Spice. Still buttoning his white shirt, he bent over the bed to kiss her, and she slipped her arms around his neck and pulled him down to deepen it.

"What a pity duty calls," he murmured with a smile.

"We have a fifteen-year-old in the next room," Verity reminded him.

For one moment she considered telling him about her growing determination to apply for the *Okavango Observer* job.

Then she thought better of it.

She wanted to win it on her own merit. If, as she had heard, the editor was still interviewing, James might well put in a good word.

No, she would get that *Observer* job herself and carve out an entirely new professional life here. While James was flying today, she would be researching and drafting her application. The idea that there might be real competition —perhaps from local applicants who understood Botswana far better than she did—only sharpened her resolve.

"I hope the weather's kind to you, and that you have fun and see lots of amazing things," Verity called as he headed for the door, while she pulled a copy of the *Okavango Observer* towards her.

All at once she felt invigorated by the possibility of this job.

She could write the stories closest to her own heart, but also those that mattered to the local community, once she knew it better.

That, after all, was what she had been trained to do.

"I will," James said, turning back to give her one last kiss. "And I'll tell you all about it."

When the door closed behind him, Verity felt her excitement lift another notch, though not without a thread of anxiety.

She could adapt. She had adapted before. She could survive and even thrive in this place, just as she had in all the others.

But so much now seemed to depend on finding work that would give her not merely occupation, but meaning.

Like the job at the *Okavango Observer*.

FOURTEEN

James stepped out of the front door with Verity's kiss still lingering on his lips.

The first rays of sunlight were only just beginning to warm the air, and the world felt alive with possibility.

How much better was this than city life?

Of course, he hadn't actually started flying yet, but that was the easy part. He'd loved showing Saskia and Verity around during the extra few days he'd asked for before starting work.

And Verity really did seem to be acclimatising. She had been resistant—understandably so—but he was sure he could see signs that she was beginning, if not exactly to love this new life, then at least to lean towards it.

October in Maun was not yet brutally hot, but the promise of another scorching day already hung in the air. He inhaled deeply, savouring the earthy smell of the Botswana morning.

"Dumela, Rra."

A familiar voice called out. James turned to see Mothusi, the groundskeeper, methodically raking the sand around the acacia bushes. The old man's weathered face crinkled into a smile.

"A very important day, Captain? I am thinking this is the first time you are flying for Okavango Air." Mothusi rested both hands on the top of his rake, eyes twinkling. "Maybe I must read the bones, eh? For a safe journey?"

James knew Mothusi was not merely the compound's caretaker; he was also a respected *ngaka*, a traditional healer. For a moment he was tempted, wondering whether the old man's insights might offer some useful guidance in this unfamiliar new chapter.

"Thank you, but another time, Mothusi. I'm trusting my flying skills to keep us all safe today."

He nodded in response to the old man's toothless grin and stepped into the road, slowing to let a donkey pass. It was pulling a reconstituted trailer with two chattering children and sacks of mealie meal bouncing in the back.

As he waited, something in the shadows by a letaka reed wall further up the road caught his eye. He looked more closely and saw two figures stepping apart and then walking off in opposite directions.

Lucy and Starky.

Verity had told him of her suspicion that the pair might be carrying on some sort of clandestine relationship. Not that it was any business of theirs.

He was just glad Saskia was still only a schoolgirl. Otherwise, he might have found himself in an awkward position, given the degree of hero worship his daughter now reserved for the man who had—there was no denying it—saved her life.

And now Starky was coming towards him, greeting him with a cheerful, "First day on the job. Nice to get some fresh blood into the business. One gets jaded after a dozen years or so."

James tried to remember what he knew of the man. "You're not originally from Maun, are you? Serowe, wasn't it? But after I left, I think. Is that how you knew Mike and Susan?"

The mention of his cousins stirred a complicated tug of feeling.

Starky nodded. "I moved there with my family when I was ten."

"And you came to Maun... when?"

"I was twenty-three when I settled here and got my business up and running. Big learning curve." He grinned. "The clients drive me mad sometimes, but I wouldn't be anywhere else." Then he added, "What are you and Verity doing tonight? There's some singer Lucy was telling me about at the Duck Inn. Friday night, so there should be a decent crowd. If you're not flying early tomorrow, you should bring her along."

James nodded, already wondering whether he could persuade Verity. She had been reluctant to go out over the last couple of days, saying she needed to stay home with Saskia before she left for school.

But Saskia was fine. She would manage if her parents slipped up the road for an hour or two, and Verity needed to get out and meet people.

"I'll tell Verity. She'd love to come, I'm sure," he said as they parted.

When he reached the airport, Rob was already doing his pre-flight checks. The young Canadian greeted him with much the same thing.

"Will you be at the Duck tonight? Lucy says there's a singer coming up from Jo'burg. Good night to bring Verity."

Jess, one of the Delta's few female pilots, was chatting to Rob beside the plane. She turned and grinned when James arrived.

"I wonder who's sweet on Lucy, then?" she asked, digging Rob in the ribs.

But Rob only flushed and shook his head. "I'm not even sure Lucy's completely finished with that boyfriend of hers in Cape Town, so I'm not making any moves." He glanced anxiously between them. "Better not mention it to anyone else, Jess. Promise? James too, okay?"

James smiled at his earnestness, though with a slight sinking feeling that Rob was probably headed for a bruised heart. But Maun seemed that kind of place—full of expats, jaded old hands, and green young adventurers, all chasing something: money, escape, reinvention, excitement.

He supposed hearts got broken here all the time.

And he was quietly grateful that he and Verity were beyond all that—past the skittish uncertainty of youth and the chaos of searching for love.

Verity did seem a little more settled these last couple of days. He had seen her taking photographs of the town and scribbling page after page in the old notebook she always carried with her.

Ideas for her novel?

If she could find something here that genuinely fulfilled her, he would not feel nearly so bad about derailing her career. Again.

But his was the job that made the money, and however prestigious her title as magazine editor had sounded, her salary was never going to support the three of them. They simply could not make ends meet with James out of work.

After checking the fuel requirements, he turned back

towards the terminal to fetch his passengers—two English-women travelling together and an American couple.

Yes, he thought, if Verity could truly immerse herself in writing a novel, she might begin to feel like herself again.

And that, more than anything, was what James wanted for her.

FIFTEEN

"What do you think, James? Hair up or down?" Verity twisted her shoulder-length brown waves into an updo and batted her eyelashes while James circled her like a predator.

He had that smouldering look that always meant business once they got home, and her heart kicked up several notches. Earlier that day she had gone into the *Okavango Observer* and, although the editor was away on business, she had left her résumé and been told interviews would be held the following week. Verity had not felt so buoyant in a long time.

"Definitely down, Mum. Otherwise, you look like Mrs Glendenning."

"Mrs Glendenning?" Verity and James exclaimed in outraged unison, turning to their daughter, who had just emerged from her room.

"You apologise to your mother this instant," James said with mock severity, while Verity asked, her confidence imploding, "Do I really look like Mrs Glendenning?" and pictured the skeletal spinster with the pointed nose and severely scraped-back hair.

"No. I only thought of her because she always wore her hair in a bun." Saskia bit into an apple as she lounged against the bookshelf, then grinned suddenly. "And because I knew it would upset you. It's my job, you know."

Verity laughed, feeling instantly better. "You don't mind us going out without you, sweetie?" she asked, with a flicker of motherly guilt.

"Course not," said Saskia. "Not while I'm still clunking around on crutches. Have a good time."

"Glad that's settled." James waited while Verity let her hair fall back to her shoulders, then murmured in her ear as they said goodbye to Saskia and stepped outside, "I think you look fabulous, as always. And I'm so glad you're coming. You're going to have a great time and you do *not* look remotely like Mrs Glendenning."

Verity laughed, though her excitement was tinged with nervous anticipation about the Tribune job. "All right. If you say so." She had almost forgotten how reassuring James's certainty could be—that steady belief that things would somehow work out. It buoyed her own hopes for whatever lay ahead.

And what lay ahead, she told herself, was a fulfilling job at the *Okavango Observer*.

Or so she fervently hoped.

It was crowded and noisy when they pushed through the doors of the Duck Inn. The singer from Jo'burg was already performing in the corner, brightly lit by a lamp perched on the bar counter. To the right of her was a scene so bizarre that for a moment Verity could not properly make sense of it.

She craned to see what had attracted the crowd gathered around the counter, for all she could make out at first was a thick *veldschoen* boot jutting out at an odd angle.

As though someone were lying lengthwise along the bar.

Which, she realised a moment later, he was.

As someone stepped aside, she saw more clearly and heard the shirtless man shout drunkenly, "Drink up!"

To Verity's horror, a woman was bent over his bare midriff.

Only when she looked more closely did she realise, with an absurd stab of relief, that the woman was merely drinking shots from his belly button.

"Who's next?" the inebriated exhibit bellowed.

The young woman straightened, wiping the back of her hand across her mouth. Then she turned, saw James, and her eyes widened. Her red-lipsticked mouth curved into a dazzling smile.

"James!" she cried, raking her fingers through her dark shoulder-length curls while her large silver hoops swung wildly. She reminded Verity of the dark-haired singer from The Bangles. "James, Good to see you again! Who'd have thought I'd set foot in dusty old Botswana, but thanks to you, I'm in my spirit place. I don't think I thanked you properly before." Her gaze landed on Verity. "And you must be Verity."

The singer's rendition of *I Wanna Dance with Somebody* was just ending, so it became easier to hear as James steered them into a quieter corner and said, "Verity, this is my cousin Susan." He grinned. "I meant to tell you that she popped up unexpectedly in Maun only the other day. Not a word that she was coming, either." He turned back to

Verity. "As you know, I met Susan for lunch in Jo'burg when she could only spare twenty minutes from—"

"That horrible copywriting job I was doing," Susan cut in, picking up a half-finished drink from a high table near them and knocking it back. James, predictably, asked, "Ladies, what can I get you?"

"A double vodka and lime, please," Susan said, though she looked as if she'd already had quite enough. Still, she smiled warmly at Verity as she added, "Lovely to meet you properly. James talked so much about you." She toyed with the silver cross resting in the hollow of her cleavage.

Verity's eyes flicked involuntarily from the low neckline of Susan's white blouse to her own far more conservative blue-and-white striped shirt and jeans. She felt instantly dowdy beside Susan's skimpy shorts, dramatic eye makeup, and effortless confidence.

"James tells me you're a journalist too," Susan went on. "Like me. Except I got shunted sideways into copywriting at the company where I've been working, which I absolutely loathe and where I might have stayed forever if James hadn't stepped into my life at exactly the right moment."

Verity felt a sudden chill.

"What's this?" James asked, returning from the bar with Susan's double vodka and lime and Verity's gin and tonic.

"You're my saviour. My salvation, James," Susan slurred, throwing an arm around his waist.

James's eyebrows shot up as he exchanged a quick, uncertain glance with Verity.

Susan was very drunk.

"Well, I'm glad you feel that way."

"How long are you staying?" Verity asked.

"I'm here for good. Time to put down roots."

"For good? I suppose you'd know people from the old days. Though you were in Serowe, weren't you?" Verity asked, striving for steadiness.

"There are people I'm sure I recognise from years ago, but it's too dark and I'm too drunk to place anyone properly," Susan said, taking another large swallow of her drink.

Searching for something to say, Verity said, "I guess you know Starky Willis, wouldn't you? He grew up in Serowe and is here now."

Verity was not prepared for the violence of Susan's reaction.

"Starky Willis? Now there's someone whose path I never want to cross again—and yet he's part of the reason I'm here, I suppose you could say."

"Oh really?" said James mildly. "You came back here because of Starky?"

"God, no! I wouldn't care if I never saw him again in my life." Susan drained the rest of her drink. "But I didn't fit in after I left Botswana for Cape Town, and I sure as hell didn't fit in in Jo'burg. Then you told me there was a job going on the *Okavango Observer*, James. So I rang the editor, and he was desperate for someone, and when I said I'd grown up in Bots, that was that."

Verity choked on her drink.

She set down her glass at once, and James patted her on the back as he said to Susan, "Congratulations! You do move fast. Cousins together again, on Botswana soil. Who'd have thought?" He turned to Verity with genuine delight. "Isn't that wonderful, Verity?"

Verity hoped what she managed resembled a smile, but her stomach had dropped as if the floor had fallen away beneath her.

"So you've taken Tumelo Kgathi's position at the

Okavango Observer," she said, keeping her eyes on the table as she fiddled with her straw so neither of them would catch the shine of tears. "When do you start?"

"As soon as possible, Derek says." Susan grinned as she sucked noisily on an ice cube. "Which means as soon as I've recovered from this weekend's hangover."

CHAPTER

SIXTEEN

"Verity, what's the matter? Surely you don't want to leave yet? It's early, and I don't have to fly tomorrow."

Verity hesitated in the doorway, looking over James's shoulder at the crush of bodies inside the Duck. The pulse of the music seemed to throb through the floorboards and up through her feet, and the air was thick with beer, sweat, and cigarette smoke. Susan was on the dance floor, hair a cloud of glossy, damp curls, the buttons of her blouse undone much too far.

"You stay. I'm tired, and I need to check on Saskia," Verity said, raising her voice above the din.

"Saskia doesn't need checking on. Something's upset you. Tell me."

Verity wished he would simply let her go. She was too close to tears and wanted desperately to be by herself.

"It's all right. It's nothing," she said, almost pushing him away. "You stay and have fun. I'm fine to get home on my own."

"Even if you were, I'm not letting you go unless you tell me what happened in there."

He took her hand, but instead of turning back towards the bar, she drew him outside.

The cool night air was a relief after the fug inside.

"Start talking," he said as they began to walk down the dusty street. "One minute you were smiling and looked as though you might finally let your hair down, and the next..."

Verity took a breath. Better to say it here, out in the open, than wait until they were home and risk Saskia overhearing.

"I wanted that job," she said, stopping beneath a flowering bougainvillea and pulling her hand from his. Her breath caught on the words.

For a second, he looked genuinely blank.

"What job?" Then his face changed. "The job Susan got? You wanted the *Okavango Observer* job?"

Verity nodded, fumbling for a tissue and dabbing at her eyes.

"But you never said. I thought you wanted to write a book."

"I don't think I'm ready to write a book," Verity said miserably. "And now I don't know what else I can do. I feel..." Her voice thinned. "Useless."

"Oh, Verity."

James drew her into his arms, the familiar scent of his aftershave comforting despite everything.

"You've never been more needed or more useful. You've been my rock through everything. You've been the best mother Saskia could have had, not just through the recent drama, but through all the rotten times before that."

"You carried it too, on top of a full-time job. But that's

all I am, isn't it? Useful when needed." She buried her face in his chest while he stroked her hair. "I want something more. I wanted to take pictures and write about the animals and the environment. I thought I could do something interesting. Something worthwhile. Something that might make people see the importance of—"

She broke off.

"Oh, I don't know. The moment I try to say it out loud, it sounds ridiculous. Like I'm reaching for something I've no right to want. What could I really contribute that anyone else couldn't?"

"Don't talk like that." James tipped up her face. "You're a beautiful writer, and it excites me to hear you say you want to write about this country. There was a time I thought you'd be on the first plane home if you got half a chance." He kissed her forehead. "I'm so proud of you, Verity. You can do anything you set your mind to—"

"Hey, is that you, James?"

They both turned to see Lucy and Jess waving as they headed towards the Duck.

"Are you coming to hear the singer from Jo'burg everyone's talking about?"

"We were actually on our way home," said James.

"Is she no good?"

"No, she's great," said Verity, summoning a smile. "James was taking me home because I've got a headache, but I don't want to ruin his night when all I really want is to lie down and close my eyes. James, you go back with Lucy."

"No, Verity."

"Please," she urged, squeezing his arm. "There's no need for you to walk me home when we're this close. I'll be fine."

Reluctantly, James let her go only when a couple of

pilots from their compound came by and said they were heading home and would see her safely to the front door.

So she truly did want to be alone.

He turned back towards the Duck, flanked by Jess and Lucy, answering their questions politely while wishing he had ignored Verity's objections and insisted on going with her.

"How's your daughter?" Lucy asked.

"The ankle's going to be fine. She'll be on crutches for a while, but she starts school next week."

It was hard to focus. Verity's face kept rising before him. Had she blamed him for mentioning the paper to Susan? Was that what had happened? Had he somehow, stupidly, helped knock away the one thing she had begun to want for herself?

"That's good to hear," said Lucy. "Rumours were flying all over town."

James nodded. The bass thudded in his chest as they neared the bar. "It was horrific, but she certainly enjoyed the drama. Starky's won himself a fan for life."

Lucy raised an eyebrow. "He's good at that."

"And you?" James asked. "When do you leave the Delta? You said you were only filling in while Chubaora's managing couple were away."

"She's going to hostess on Starky's overland," said Jess, digging Lucy in the ribs.

Lucy blushed but ignored her. "Yes, a German couple and their twenty-one-year-old son arrive in just under a month. I'll stay on and do some work for Wilderness Safaris in the meantime."

"I take it they're hunters?" James asked.

"Lucy's changed her spots," said Jess, grinning. "She's not the same Lucy I first met when she arrived at Chubaora with some very strong ideas about a certain notorious hunter I shall not name."

"How much have you had to drink, Jess?" Lucy swung round. "It's true that when I first came here, I had a very black-and-white view of hunting. But it brings a lot into the economy—"

"What are they hunting?" James cut in, hoping to head off an argument.

Lucy hesitated. "I'm not sure. Anyway, here we are."

The rest was swallowed by the noise as they reached the Duck just as Susan seemed to be propelled through the doors and into the courtyard, where she blinked at James, then collapsed against him and flung her arms around his neck. The smell of alcohol came off her in waves, sharp and sour beneath her perfume.

"This is Susan," he explained, with a faintly pained look for the other girls. "My cousin. She's just arrived in Maun. I think I'd better see her home."

Lucy and Jess exchanged amused glances, then disappeared inside.

"Right," James said, half-supporting Susan. "Time to get you to bed. Did you come here with anyone?"

"Just me," she said, eyes closed. "Always just me."

The words were tossed off carelessly, but something in the flatness beneath them stopped him.

"Where are you staying? Have you got somewhere sorted?"

"I'm at Riley's for tonight. Tomorrow I move to..." She mumbled the rest, but by then James was already steering her towards his vehicle.

The night air was blessedly cool as he drove through the quiet streets of Maun. A night bird called somewhere in the darkness. It was only a few minutes to Riley's, and he did his best to avoid the curious looks from the drinkers outside the hotel bar as he helped her to her room, mercifully without needing to pass through reception.

Once she had flung herself onto the bed, he filled the kettle and made her strong tea. She drank it greedily, then looked up at him with sudden softness.

"It's nice," she said, "having family who'll look after one. And you're not judgmental, like my mother." She sat cross-legged on the bed, blowing across the tea. "That's a novelty."

James gave a faint smile, unsure whether she expected an answer.

"So," he said, "you've made the move on your own? And left your daughter—what's her name?—at boarding school?"

"Angel. Correct. A fresh start for me." She lifted her cup in a mock toast. "Cheers."

"To a fresh start," James echoed, though the phrase sat oddly with him. He was not about to point out that, so far, her new beginning appeared to involve too much vodka and public collapse. "And here's to success at the paper. What do you want to write about?"

Susan tilted her head as if considering how much to give him.

"Corruption," she said at last.

Then, reaching across the bed for the minibar, she misjudged the edge and tumbled inelegantly to the floor. A second later she was on her knees, clutching a tiny bottle of whisky with triumphant delight.

"Want to share?"

James shook his head. "Maybe you shouldn't either. I think you've had quite enough."

"Oh, I've drunk virtually nothing," she said, and took a swig.

"And what sort of corruption do you expect to uncover in Maun?"

Susan lowered the bottle and looked at him through narrowed eyes. "Oh, I think I might start with a few of the hunters," she said. "Zerangu Hunting Safaris, perhaps. See whether they're breaking rules."

"You mean... Starky?"

This time she did not answer straight away. She set the bottle down very carefully and looked at him in a way that made him oddly uncomfortable.

"Maybe," she said at last. "Have you ever wondered how he managed to get granted a hunting concession and lease a plane when he was only twenty-two?"

It had crossed James's mind, certainly, but he shrugged. "His family might have helped. That's how Jango Lodge got started."

"Starky's family was dirt poor."

"An inheritance, then." James stood up. He had no desire to be drawn into drunken speculation, especially if what fuelled it was some old grievance she had not yet named.

"Ah, yes," she said softly. "An inheritance." Then she looked up. "But what kind of inheritance, James?"

There was something in her face then—something feverish and bitter and intent—that made the question feel less like gossip than an accusation. Less like a theory than some memory.

He said nothing.

She gave a short laugh that had no amusement in it.

"That's the trouble with men like Starky. Everyone

wants to believe they're merely lucky." Suddenly she clapped a hand to her mouth and lurched to the bathroom.

James heard her retching violently.

When she emerged again, she looked smaller somehow. The bravado had drained away for the moment, leaving only exhaustion, self-disgust, and the rawness beneath the spite.

"I'm not a drunk," she said heavily, sitting on the bed. "I don't usually get this bad. Not really." She lowered her head. "I thought I might see him tonight, but I didn't. I wanted to talk to him."

James looked at her carefully.

"And tell him you'd got this job at the *Observer* so you could investigate him?" he asked, aiming for humour and missing the mark even as he said it.

"Or give him the chance to stop me."

The words landed harder than he expected.

"I see," James said after a pause, though in truth he did not. Not really. He could hear the threat in what she was saying, and the hurt beneath it, but the shape of it eluded him.

He pulled back the bedcovers. "I think it's time you got some sleep. I need to get back to Verity. But are you going to be all right if I leave you?"

"That's what they all do anyway," Susan said, and now the bitterness was tired rather than theatrical. "Leave."

She fell back onto the pillow and closed her eyes.

Within moments, she was asleep.

James stood there for a second, looking down at her, trying to make sense of the evening. Verity had been devastated, Susan was clearly in pieces beneath all the vodka and venom, and somewhere in the middle of it all he had failed to understand either of them properly.

Then he let himself out quietly and headed back into
the night.

CHAPTER

SEVENTEEN

Saskia was still on crutches when she and Verity took the three-hour flight to Johannesburg to start school.

Her daughter was excited, certainly, but more nervous than Verity could remember seeing her.

"The girls will think I'm a freak, starting school on crutches," Saskia moaned, her breath fogging the glass as she leaned against the cool window, the steady hum of the ATR 42's engines filling the cabin as they droned over the vast, sun-baked country below.

"But I thought you said it might, I don't know, give you street cred," said Verity, gently squeezing her daughter's hand. "I thought you didn't mind."

"That was before," Saskia whispered, closing her eyes.

Verity saw at once that her lashes were damp. This was so unlike her bold, fierce Saskia.

"You'll make friends in no time, I'm sure. You're fun and pretty, and your Aussie accent will be a novelty. And... your cousin is there."

Saskia opened her eyes, the rich brown of her irises

catching the sunlight pouring through the window. "I don't even know her name. And you never invited her mum over before I left. Are you ashamed of me?"

"Oh, Saskia, how can you even ask that?" Verity exclaimed, feeling both guilty that she had not, in fact, asked Susan to the cottage before now, and stung that Saskia's question had landed so close to the truth of her unease.

Since that night at the Duck, Verity had not been able to stop dwelling on the fact that Susan—more like a rock star's groupie than a serious journalist—had got the newspaper job Verity had wanted so desperately.

And now Saskia was going to strike up some cosy cousinly connection as well.

Well, just because they were cousins did not mean they would get on, she told herself, while knowing it was shabby of her even to hope they might not.

AND NOW, the day after Verity had returned to Maun, Susan was standing on the threshold of the cottage saying, "I hope you don't mind me dropping in like this. I bumped into James in the street and he said you'd only got back from Jo'burg yesterday and were at home, and as I'm between stories, I thought I'd come and say hello."

Verity smiled. "Of course not," she said, determined to override her feelings and use this as an opportunity to get to know Susan properly. To try, at least, to like her. "Come in and I'll boil the kettle."

"My word, but you've made this place cosy," Susan said as she stepped through the front door.

Verity looked at the room with fresh eyes and accepted

the compliment. The living room was welcoming after a morning in the blinding sun. Fan blades spun lazily overhead, stirring the warm air. The frayed sofa she had inherited had been brightened with a couple of cheerful cushions. On the built-in shelves, African souvenirs and framed family photographs sat alongside James's flying manuals and their mixed collection of romances and adventure novels.

"Please sit down," she said, indicating one of the two wicker chairs. "Tea or coffee? Or something cold?"

"Cold, definitely," said Susan, pausing by the shelves to look over their books and photographs. "Is that your daughter?" she asked, picking up Verity's favourite picture. "How old is she? She's the same age as mine, I think James said."

"Yes, nearly sixteen."

Verity was just putting a jug of cold water back into the fridge when Susan exclaimed, "Photo albums. Do you mind if I look?"

"Of course not," said Verity, coming through with a jug of lemonade and some biscuits. "You're family."

Susan was more soberly dressed today, in a knee-length khaki skirt and black T-shirt, though her hair was as unruly as ever, her silver hoop earrings swung when she moved, and her eyes were still heavily made up.

Verity knew Susan was about her own age, yet she looked—and somehow seemed—older. Still very attractive, yes, but with the air of someone who had been living too hard and sleeping too little for years.

"I should have made sure Ange knew to look out for her cousin, but I got so caught up with the new job I forgot," Susan said, glancing up from the album she had pulled from the shelf. "Anyway, I'm sure they'll find each other.

You certainly don't look old enough to have a fifteen-year-old."

"Nor you," Verity returned, sitting down and quietly sliding the terrifying Baragwanath hospital bill beneath a magazine on the side table. "I'm sorry, but I've forgotten your daughter's name."

"Ange." Susan took a sip and shrugged. "Short for Angel, not Angela, in case you were wondering." She sent Verity a sly look. "My mother hates the name, so she's Ange or Angie to most people. Anyway, Ange was the reason I left Bots. Back in '74 it was too shameful to be an unmarried mother. I had her in Jo'burg, ran away to Cape Town for a few years, then back to Jo'burg. And now, here I am."

Verity bit back the obvious questions. Had Susan put Ange into boarding school so that she could come to Maun and work? The fees alone would be more than a single mother on a small newspaper salary could easily manage.

Instead, she asked, "Do you like it here?"

"Maun?" Susan gave a little laugh. "I love it and I hate it. But it's the gateway to the Okavango, isn't it? I want to get out into the bush again, like in the old days. I'll get to visit the lodges with the newspaper work. It's what I need. Jo'burg was killing me. Now *that's* a place you don't want to live."

Verity nodded, though she had no idea what Susan really meant. Susan was nothing if not emphatic. And restless. Even seated, there was a tension in her, as if she were only ever partly still.

"Oh my God."

At Susan's sudden exclamation, Verity craned to see what had caused it and found her pointing at the photograph James's aunt had sent them.

"It's me."

"Of course. But I'd completely forgotten we had that. And that you were in it."

Verity moved her chair closer, squinting at the young faces in the faded photograph from those long-ago days. Though perhaps fifteen years was not so very long, when she thought how swiftly Saskia had gone from babyhood to rebellious girlhood.

And, in truth, Saskia had not felt rebellious when Verity had left her in Jo'burg. She had clung to her as though she might never let her go.

"And there's my darling brother."

Susan's voice caught, and Verity felt a rush of sympathy. She had not stopped to think how unsettling this might be for her, seeing herself fixed in time beside the brother she had lost.

"He looks like you," said Verity, studying the picture of the siblings standing side by side. Big brother Mike and little sister Susan, Mike's hair long and curly in the fashion of the day, Susan's spilling past her shoulders.

The girl in the picture had been a beauty.

Verity glanced at the woman beside her. She still was, though the difference between then and now was impossible to ignore. Back then there had been a dewy freshness to her. Now there was something harder about her glamour, as though life had sharpened every edge. She was still striking, but she had what Verity's mother would have called the look of someone who had lived in the fast lane.

"And who are the others?" Verity asked.

"That's Phil. And—"

Susan stopped, her finger hovering just above the photograph.

"Starky."

The name dropped into the room like something cold.

Her voice had changed. Bitter, flat, and so charged that Verity felt the skin tighten on her arms.

"I haven't seen either of them since that day. Talked to them, I mean."

"Not even at the funeral?" Verity asked before she could stop herself.

"I didn't go to the funeral. I was too..." Susan gave a small shrug. "Let's just say I was in no fit state to pay my last respects. I've regretted it ever since. Poor Mike." Her mouth tightened. "He protected me so well when we were growing up, and I took it for granted. In fact, I threw it back at him that day."

Verity tried to read her expression. There was regret there, certainly. But there was something else too—something dark and concentrated, as though the memory was not merely painful but alive. Not dead history at all, but a thing still moving beneath the surface.

Not knowing how to ask, Verity said instead, "Did you know Starky saved Saskia's life?"

"What?"

The force of Susan's reaction made Verity jolt. The colour seemed to leave her face.

"Didn't James tell you?"

Susan shook her head. She looked, for a second, as if she were struggling to steady herself. "He said you were in Jo'burg because Saskia had nearly been dragged into the lagoon by a croc. He never said Starky had anything to do with it."

"Starky shot the croc. If he hadn't, Saskia would be dead."

"My God," Susan said softly. Then, after a beat: "So Starky saved your daughter's life." She gave a strange little laugh with no humour in it at all. "That's rich."

Verity did not know how to answer that.

"It was lucky he had a rifle with him. I'm told it's not usual on photographic safaris. Saskia didn't approve of him at first because she's very conservation-minded. But she's changed her tune." She hesitated as Susan abruptly rose. "Oh—you're going?"

Verity stood too, surprised by the suddenness of it. Susan was rubbing one eye as if something had blown into it.

"Do you want some water?"

"No, no, I'm fine. I completely forgot—I've got my interview now, not at eleven." Susan pushed back her hair with a hand that was not quite steady. "Stupid of me. But I suddenly remembered. Thanks so much for the company. Great photos. I'd love to see more one day. Sorry to rush off."

Bemused, Verity stood in the doorway watching her go, then came back to the albums and looked again at the photograph, trying to work out whether something beyond the sight of her brother had caused such a visceral response.

Nothing leapt out at her.

And yet something about Susan's expression lingered in her mind: not mere grief, not simple nostalgia, but the look of someone who had suddenly recognised something. Something shocking.

She closed the album and put it back on the shelf, and was halfway through the washing-up when James came home.

"Thought I'd grab some lunch between flights. You know you've got a maid to do all that," he said, giving her shoulders a squeeze. "At least there are some compensations for my having dragged you out of the life you wanted."

"Don't say it like that. I wouldn't have come with you if I hadn't wanted to." Verity set down the bowl she had just rinsed and looped her arms around his neck. "Sit down, and I'll make you a sandwich."

"Did Susan come here? I passed her on the road, but she looked in a hurry."

"It was the strangest thing." Verity frowned. "She was looking at that old album on the table, the one with the photograph of her and the boys on that hunting trip. The one your aunt sent. And suddenly she became terribly emotional. Well, I understand that, of course—losing her brother. But it was fifteen years ago, and she looked as if she might lose control altogether. Then she just got up and left."

James shrugged. "Being dropped into new situations can bring things to the surface. Look at Saskia. All bristles and sarcasm, but it doesn't take much to pierce the armour. I hope she'll be all right at St Anne's. At least she'll have her cousin."

"We've no idea what sort of girl Ange is," said Verity mildly.

He smiled. "You don't like Susan, do you?"

"I never said that. I was very friendly when she dropped by. I just think she's wild and... a bit odd."

James laughed. "I don't disagree. Still, blood is thicker than water. Anyway, what are you going to do this afternoon? You should take up Mrs Watkins's offer to teach you Mahjong."

Verity screwed up her eyes as she handed him a ham and cheese sandwich and sat opposite him.

"I need to get a job, James." She reached for the hospital invoice and slid it across the table. "It's enormous."

"Well, there's no need to rush into something you hate. It's a lot, yes, but the insurance should cover most of it." James bit into the sandwich, then paused as a distant rumble of thunder moved across the afternoon sky.

Sighing, Verity fingered the edge of the bill.

"I won't rush," she said softly. "But I'm going to have to do *something* soon, James. Or I'll go mad."

CHAPTER

EIGHTEEN

James had enjoyed his first three weeks of flying.

Verity did her best to sound enthusiastic when he came home full of tales about the wildlife he'd seen from the air—or shooed off the runway before take-off.

Saskia, meanwhile, had written a letter positively fizzing with excitement about meeting her cousin and the friendship that had sprung up almost at once. Angie, she said, was even wilder than Saskia had ever been at her worst, but tremendous fun and super beautiful. She suggested that when the girls had their next holidays, they should all go on safari together. *Starky said he'd take me personally, so I'm sure he wouldn't mind taking Ange too*, she had written.

Verity was glad for both girls.

And yet she chafed at the bit, stuck in a utilitarian cottage in the middle of a town that was growing too quickly to be the quaint little frontier village it might once have been.

In a place this small, everyone knew everyone else—or

worked with them, flew for them, drank with them, slept with them, or all four.

Verity was on the outside. She had no job and no foothold in the little networks and routines that might have given her some sense of belonging if Saskia had been able to go to school in Maun.

One Monday morning she laid Saskia's cheerful letter beside the hospital bill, ran a brush through her hair, changed into navy shorts and a white T-shirt, and set off on foot into town to do the shopping.

Finding fresh produce was hit or miss. It all depended on what had survived the weekly truck journey up from Johannesburg.

After buying condensed milk, she bumped into an acquaintance who kindly invited her to the next regular mahjong afternoon. Then she moved on to the vegetable section, where she found Lucy inspecting a limp lettuce and a clutch of overripe bananas.

"How's Saskia's leg coming along?" Lucy asked with a smile, pushing back her strawberry-blonde hair. "Is she still on crutches?"

"Not anymore, and apparently not even limping," said Verity. "Saskia's quite proud of the scar. She loves the drama of life. And Starky has a fan for life. He was so quick on the uptake. And the fact he shot the croc and not my daughter—" Verity shuddered. Even now she tried not to let herself dwell too long on the horrors that might so easily have happened that evening.

"Yes, he's good with a gun. A crack shot," Lucy agreed. "A very popular guide, too. Some of his clients have been coming back to Zerangu every year since he set up business."

"I used to be thoroughly anti-hunting, and I still mostly

am. But after this experience, I've softened a little, I suppose. I bet you're looking forward to hostessing on Starky's overland trip."

The moment she saw Lucy's face, Verity added quickly, "I'm sorry... did I say something wrong?"

Lucy looked so troubled that Verity did not know what to do. At last, shifting her shoulder bag to the other shoulder and running her fingers through her hair again, Lucy said, "I've had second thoughts. I just pulled out of the trip."

"But isn't the overland next week? Has something happened back home?" Verity knew she ought not to pry, but anyone pulling out of Starky's safari at such short notice suggested something had gone badly wrong.

"I always wondered if it was a good idea for me to go with Starky. He's... charismatic and..."

"Oh yes, he certainly is," Verity agreed with a colluding smile, though she still was not quite following, for she had been almost certain that Lucy and Starky had been involved since before she and James arrived in Maun.

Lucy toyed with the limp lettuce as though she wanted to say more but could not find a safe way into it.

"I had a boyfriend in Jo'burg. I'm not proud of it, but... Starky has a way of making a girl feel..." She gave a helpless shrug. "I don't know. As though she's the only one in the world. I knew I had to be strong and..." She shook her head. "Let's just say I couldn't go."

Verity frowned. "But you're not going back to your ex-boyfriend, are you?"

"Well, it's my mum too." Lucy looked suddenly close to tears. "She hasn't been well."

"Well, I suppose there's always another time," Verity managed, hoping it was the right thing to say.

"Hey, Verity!"

It was Susan, calling from the doorway and breezing towards them just as Lucy made her excuses and slipped away.

"I haven't seen you for ages. Sorry I couldn't come for dinner last night. I told James I had something else on. Life's pretty social here, isn't it?"

Verity smiled. "I suppose if you're single and beautiful, it is."

"Oh, come on. You're married and beautiful. I never see you at the Duck. You should come out tonight. I'm there practically every night and always looking out for you, but James always tells me you're at home."

"You see James there often?" Verity knew James sometimes dropped in for a drink after flying, but Susan made it sound rather more regular than that.

"Course. There's nowhere much else to go unless you sit in somebody's house. And me? I'm not really a cook."

"So you're glad you made the move from Jo'burg, then?" Verity asked. "It's rather a change of pace."

"Sure is. I don't know what I was thinking, moving to the city when I was only eighteen and leaving the bush when that's what I am at heart—a bush girl." Susan flashed a smile. "Come on, let's grab an iced coffee and have a chat. I've got a bit of time to kill."

As they sat in the coffee shop, the ceiling fan whirred uselessly above them, barely troubling the thick afternoon heat. Outside, a couple of donkeys wandered past, stirring up the powdery street. Verity could taste grit on her lips each time she lifted her iced coffee.

"You don't have to be at work?" she asked, glancing at her watch.

"I've just finished an interview for a story in next week's *Observer*. I'm done for the day."

Trying to sound genuinely interested, Verity asked, "What are you working on?"

"A piece on conservation and the contentious role hunting plays in the economy."

Verity blinked. "Is that the sort of thing you wrote for the papers in Jo'burg?"

Susan laughed. "I wish. No, I did advertorials. Hack work. It paid the bills, but I hated it."

"Then... how did you—?"

"Get the job? Get to write this piece?" Susan touched the side of her nose. "Contacts." She threw her head back and laughed. "No, I didn't sleep with the editor, if that's where your mind was going, but I lived in Bots half my life and my family's known around the place. I wasn't hired to write great investigative exposés—never done one in my life. But I pitched Derek a piece on hunting and conservation and all that jazz, and he said if it was good enough, he'd run it. So that means doing my research, doesn't it?" She shrugged. "I figure if I'm interested enough in the subject, and can charm the right people into talking, I'll be able to write about it in a balanced, objective way without passing judgement."

Verity was not at all sure how that was meant to work.

"You should offer to go on Starky's overland trip now that Lucy's dropped out," she said.

Susan pressed her lips together. Only a moment before she had been laughing; now she was definitely not laughing.

"Sorry," Verity said quickly. "I didn't mean to say something offensive. I just meant, since you knew Starky years ago, and since he's a hunter, you'd get a terrific story if you were embedded, so to speak."

"Embedded? With Starky?" Susan's lip curled. "Didn't mean to go all strange on you, but it's a weird thought—hostessing for Starky."

She tipped back her head, ran her fingers through her curls, and closed her eyes. When she opened them again, something had shifted.

"Right. I wasn't going to say this. I wasn't going to say anything. But the truth is that when I was eighteen, I had a huge crush on Starky. He was Mike's best friend, and he'd stayed with my family over two holidays, first when I was fifteen. Of course he didn't notice me then. He was four years older, and I was just a little girl. But when I was eighteen..." She smiled, though the smile did not reach her eyes. "He looked at me as if I wasn't a little girl anymore."

"So is that's why you're here?" Verity's eyes widened. "You and Starky had a thing years ago that you hope to rekindle?"

"Rekindle?" Susan suddenly looked almost amused. "I'm not sure what I want to do. Or plan to do."

There was a flicker in her eyes then—something unreadable, and not at all romantic.

"Does he know you're in town?"

"Of course he does. Well, he must. Though he's done his best to avoid me." Susan's fingers drummed a restless rhythm on the table.

"And what would you do if he walked through that door?"

Susan shrugged, her silver earrings flashing in the fanlight. "He's at Zerangu, but..." She exhaled. "I suppose I've been tense about it for the past two weeks, ever since I got here."

The bell above the coffeeshop door jingled, and both women turned instinctively, as if expecting to see Starky's broad-shouldered silhouette in the doorway.

It was just another customer.

Verity leaned closer. "Susan, Starky's in town, not Zerangu. I saw him in his vehicle this morning. But... I'm curious. That day you were looking at the old photographs... your reaction to seeing Starky... it wasn't just about an old crush, was it? It was something else."

Susan's face gave nothing away, but her knuckles whitened around her glass.

"Verity, there are things about that time, about Starky, that you don't—"

"Susan! Hey, that was a great piece you wrote about the primary school fete."

A large, smiling woman had stopped at their table and launched into chatter with such enthusiasm that she barely seemed likely to pause for breath, much less stop.

Verity's gaze drifted to the window. Vehicles and animals passed in a steady procession. The sky was hard blue with puffs of white cloud, and beyond it all the Okavango Delta stretched away into a pristine, shimmering wilderness.

A landscape James flew over every day and returned from, full of wonder.

A frontier world in which Saskia already seemed to have found a place, marked as she was by her survival of a near-fatal drama in the swamps.

And meanwhile Verity remained stuck in the dirty, dusty gateway to all that beauty, frustrated beyond words.

"Sorry, Verity, I really should be going." Susan had risen, ending the conversation with the other woman, who was now at the counter. "I feel bad. What are you doing this afternoon?"

Verity waved a hand vaguely. What else could she do? She could hardly beg Susan to finish what she had almost said.

As for what she herself was going to do that afternoon...

A sudden thought struck her. If Lucy had pulled out of hostessing Starky's overland trip at such short notice, then surely Starky would be desperate for someone to fill her place.

"I might... go for a walk," she said, rising too.

"In this heat?" Susan swung her bag over her shoulder and raised one eyebrow as she turned towards the door.

"True."

Still, that was exactly what Verity was going to do—though perhaps she ought to think it through a little more carefully.

Yes, Starky would probably have preferred someone single, carefree and unencumbered to hostess his safari.

But he might also be desperate enough to take whoever he could get.

So Starky was in town.

Susan had barely been able to sit still after Verity told her. When had he flown back to Maun? Why had he not come looking for her? Surely he'd seen her? Was he avoiding her?

As she crossed the dusty street towards the compound Zerangu shared with a couple of other safari outfits, the only answer to that question kept needling at her.

Because she was most certainly sure he was avoiding her.

She paused beneath an acacia tree and shaded her eyes. A couple of workers were loading supplies into the back of a Land Cruiser. In their ubiquitous khaki, she could not tell who they were.

Would she even recognise him straight away?

Swallowing, she realised how dry her throat was and thought briefly of turning back for water. What if she could not get the words out? She gave a bitter little laugh. That would be a first—not being able to say what she had to say when those words mattered more than anything else she had ever spoken.

Would she have the nerve to confront him?

Just thinking of him made her body pulse with all those wretched, familiar feelings she had known as a teenager before he kissed her.

And after.

Yes, after had been worse. He had lit a fire in her that she had never quite managed to put out, however creative the means she had employed.

Taking a deep breath, she stepped into the sandy road and made her way along the fence towards the gate.

"Starky!"

Even at this distance, it was easy to pick him out. The way he moved. The easy grace as he strolled from the store-room, exchanging a joke with one of the staff before lifting a heavy box as if it weighed nothing and passing it to one of the men.

He had always carried himself as though the world belonged to him.

And his strength.

And that lazy, infuriating masculinity.

Susan swallowed and closed her eyes for a second as she waited for him to turn. Even after all these years, she could still remember the smell of him. The feel of those hard muscles, sinewy and alive beneath her hands as they had explored one another's bodies in her single sleeping bag.

"Ach, man, I don't believe it. Susan?"

He was smiling as he strode towards her.

As though they had parted only weeks earlier.

"You still recognise me? After fifteen years?"

"You haven't changed a bit," he said, putting his hands on her shoulders and kissing her on the lips before setting her back from him. "You look great. What are you doing in town?"

Susan had to fight to reorient herself.

This was not how it was supposed to go.

This was not how she was supposed to feel.

"I've got a job on the paper," she said, trying with all her might to resist the urge to put her head on his chest. "Didn't you know?" There. The combative tone was a start.

"I heard, and I'm really sorry I haven't had a chance to look in on you. I'm not in town much—"

"You never wrote to me, Starky."

Susan took a shaky breath. If she did not get the accusations out now, he would work the same old magic on her, and she would be as susceptible as she had ever been.

And no closer to the truth.

"Yes, and I'm sorry about that." With a sheepish look, he raked a hand through his tousled hair. "I'm not much good at writing letters."

Susan's vision flashed red.

"Not much good at writing letters? After everything that happened? After Mike died and I was all alone and—"

"Hey, I'm really sorry." He squeezed her shoulder, looking troubled. Troubled, yes—but nowhere near as shaken as she needed him to be. "You know, Mike was my best mate. I went through hell replaying how it might have turned out differently. I know you did too. And I should have followed up."

Followed up?

Susan stared at him. His lazy remorse only deepened the outrage boiling in her. This was supposed to be the moment she found some sort of release. Some kind of truth. Perhaps even forgiveness.

Instead, he sounded as though he were apologising for forgetting to return a library book.

"My brother died! And you were his best friend, and you didn't even come to the funeral!"

"Hey, hey, I know, and I'm sorry. I really am." He shook his head. "Your parents weren't exactly brilliant communicators either. And they never thought I was the greatest influence on Mike. I didn't even know about the funeral till it was too late."

Susan choked back a sob.

"I didn't make it either. I couldn't get out of bed. But if I'd only seen you..." Her voice shook. "I had so many questions, Starky."

"Of course you did. And I did try to get hold of you, but you'd gone away. Then I got the chance to get Zerangu up and running, and it all happened so fast..." He glanced away at the sound of voices. "I realise now I owed you more at the time, Susan."

"So you got my letters, then?" she asked, her hands curling into fists.

"You sent quite a few. I was going to answer. A few

times I started and then didn't know what to say. But I did send you—"

"Hey, Starky! Just checking the Heinrichs' ETA into Maun. They're still coming in on the Friday Jo'burg flight, aren't they?"

One of the office girls had stepped out of the back door and was crossing towards them. Susan did not recognise her, but she was young and pretty and spoke with a plummy accent. She sent Susan a brief smile before turning to Starky.

"I've got a couple of other questions that need answering when you've got a moment."

"Sure, Liv. Now's fine." He gave Susan's arm a quick squeeze, his smile apologetic. "Sorry, Susan. We'll get together sometime. Promise."

And then he turned back towards the office with Liv, leaving Susan standing in the dust with all those unanswered questions settling upon her more heavily than before.

The heaviest of all being this:

How could he live with his conscience?

And underneath that, darker still, another thought took shape.

If he would not tell her the truth, then she would have to prise it out of the past herself—and use whatever she found.

CHAPTER

NINETEEN

At the last moment, Verity had lost her nerve. She couldn't simply walk over to the compound and offer herself as Starky's new hostess without first talking it over with James.

So the next morning she sat listlessly on the cane settee, sipping tea, with the *Okavango Observer* and a paperback lying beside her on the cushion.

James was overnighting at Xakanaxa Camp, and Verity had whiled away the evening reading a Wilbur Smith novel set in Africa that one of the other expat wives had lent her.

She had also skimmed a couple of Susan's pieces. Light stories. Colour pieces. Perfectly fine and readable, but Verity couldn't help wondering whether Susan possessed the instinct—or the discipline—for anything deeper.

She thought of her own years of training on a country daily. At sixteen she had started a four-year cadetship, doing all the usual rounds: police, courts, ambulance-chasing. Everything she wrote had been heavily subbed, and while the experience was often bruising and there were parts of the work she hated, she had learned how to sniff out a story and how to write it cleanly.

Did Susan have that expertise?

Verity sighed. Why on earth was she still obsessing over it? It was time to let it go and focus not on what she had missed, but on what she might still seize.

"Eh, Mma, would you like another cup of tea?"

Kagiso, her maid, stood by the sink, holding up the kettle. Verity liked her friendly, motherly warmth in contrast to Naledi, the other maid in the compound, who was sharper and more abrupt. Kagiso loved giving her opinion and sang while she worked. Verity found both things oddly comforting.

"A cup of tea would be lovely," she said, not realising she had sighed again until Kagiso added, "And what is bothering you, Mma? This is the fourth very big sigh I have heard while I am doing my work."

"Oh." Verity looked up. "Well, I'm trying to decide whether to go on safari or not."

That really was the crux of it.

"And the captain? He has not decided this for you?"

"I think I have to decide first and then ask the captain whether he agrees."

Kagiso was silent while she poured boiling water over the teabag, added long-life milk, and handed the mug to Verity.

"Then we must ask Mothusi."

"Mothusi?"

"Yes, he is raking the sand, but we must talk to him."

"How will Mothusi help me decide whether to go on safari?" Verity asked.

"He will roll the bones, Mma. He will tell you if this plan to go on safari will bring you happiness or danger." Kagiso returned to the sink and gave the steel basin a final scour. "Or both."

"He reads the bones?" Verity found this unexpectedly disconcerting. "He's a witch doctor?"

"A *ngaka*, Mma." There was clear disapproval in Kagiso's tone. "A traditional healer. His pouch of bones can help with answers we ourselves cannot know. I see him through the window. Shall I call him in?"

Kagiso seemed so determined that this might help, and Verity, sceptical though she was, knew that Mothusi's bag of old bones was hardly going to dictate the decision she made. She shrugged.

"Certainly, Kagiso. If you think it will help."

So, a few minutes later, Verity perched on the edge of the settee watching the old groundsman, who now sat cross-legged on the floor, his wrinkled hands carefully untying the cord on a worn leather pouch.

"We begin."

He tipped out the contents onto the colourful woven mat before him. Small bones, shells, and smooth pebbles clattered softly as they fell. Then he closed his eyes, murmured in Setswana, scooped them up and cast them again.

Verity watched Kagiso's face, then Mothusi's. Could they truly believe this? Could people really make life-altering decisions based on what these bits of bone and shell appeared to say?

"Danger."

Mothusi's weathered face tightened in concentration as he bent over the scattered pieces. His finger hovered above a small grey bone near the edge of the mat, then moved to a white shell beside a dark pebble.

"A journey... and a man." His eyes lifted to Verity's, full

of warning. "The bones speak of evil, Mma. A dangerous man. He brings darkness with him."

Verity's heart sank, despite herself. Of course she did not believe in Mothusi's bones, but she would have preferred a more encouraging prophecy.

After nodding gravely, listening to his advice over several more castings, and thanking him and Kagiso for their trouble, she was relieved to see them go.

Then she went to the bedroom, tidied her hair, changed her shoes, and prepared to walk into town.

Whatever the bones had said, she was going to see Starky.

SHE FOUND him at the Wilderness Safaris compound just as Alistair, one of the other safari managers, was leaving after a brief conversation with him.

Nervously, she approached.

He looked up, surprised, before he smiled. "Verity. How's Saskia? All good?"

"She's doing well, thanks. Enjoying school, and her ankle's getting better all the time. But it was something else I wanted to talk to you about."

He raised his eyebrows and jerked his head towards the shade of a nearby acacia. "Come out of the sun, then."

There was something almost lazily masculine about the way he moved—unhurried, assured, as if his body was entirely at home in itself. Even crossing a yard full of dust and fuel drums, he looked like a man built for the bush: broad across the shoulders, lean through the hips, sleeves rolled, forearms browned by sun.

"I hear Lucy's not going on your overland," Verity said,

forcing herself to the point. "And I wondered if you were looking for a hostess."

"Wow. News travels fast." He regarded her thoughtfully. "And who do you suggest?"

Verity gave a small shrug. "Me?"

Might as well bite the bullet.

"You?" He looked faintly amused. "What does James say?"

The question caught her off guard, and she heard the edge in her own voice as she replied, "There'd be nothing to tell him if there wasn't a possibility of my getting the job. I only wanted to know whether there really was one going, and whether you'd consider hiring me."

Starky laughed softly. "Your husband might not be mad about the idea of his wife heading into the bush for ten days with three men." He paused. "One of them being me."

Verity felt the heat rise to her face. "Lucy was going as of yesterday."

"True." He tipped his face briefly to the sky, thinking. Then he looked back at her with a faint frown. "Can you cook? Not that you need to be brilliant. Molemo, my cook, is pretty good, and he's coming. There'll be a couple of camp hands too, plus Florence, one of the waitresses from Zerangu. Mostly you'd need to coordinate things and keep the wife of my client company while he and their son go hunting." He shrugged. "Nothing too strenuous. Do you think you could cope with that? They're arriving from Germany next week and, just so you know, it is very definitely a hunting trip. I wouldn't take you on if there wasn't the wife to entertain, and frankly, you'd probably do that better than some of the younger girls around Maun who've been hinting they want to come."

"Oh."

For some reason, Verity felt absurdly deflated.

"I just want the chance to get out into the bush, and I know I could do what was required." She tried not to let her nervousness show. Mothusi's bone-casting had unsettled her more than she wanted to admit, but it had also stiffened her resolve. She needed to get out of Maun, and this felt like her best chance. "I'm good at coordination and delegation, and I can cook. And I don't have a problem with the men going off hunting. I can do whatever's needed."

"Can you, though?"

His warm brown eyes travelled from her face downward in a way that made her suddenly aware of her bare legs, her pulse, the heat at the base of her throat.

Perhaps he was merely assessing her.

Or perhaps she simply was not used to being looked at that way.

"And you think James will be happy for you to be away for ten days, looking after three blokes?"

"And the wife," Verity said quickly. Then she hesitated. "James knows I'll be happier if I can get out of town for a bit. He feels bad that I had to give up my job as an editor on a magazine in Melbourne. I'd worked hard for it, and... there's not much in that line here."

Starky's expression altered, softened, then sharpened again into practicality.

"Sure. You've got the job." He gave a quick shrug. "It'll save me asking around and trying to find someone else. If you've got time now, I'll give you a quick rundown, then we'll meet, say, two days before we leave Maun. I need to get back to Zerangu this afternoon, but I can give you a list of things I'll need you to buy. That'll be your first job." He looked at her again, more directly this time. "You won't let me down and decide at the last minute you suddenly can't do it, will you?"

Verity shook her head. "I want to do it. I won't let you down."

What she did not say was that she needed to do it. Missing out on the *Okavango Observer* had left such a raw, humiliating hollow in her that this unexpected opening felt almost like a rescue.

~

SHE HAD NOT BEEN PREPARED for James's concern at her impetuosity.

"You already got the job? Without talking it over with me?" He leaned against the chest of drawers in their bedroom, watching as she changed her blouse before they went out to Safari South, where they were meeting a couple of his friends.

Verity looked up, surprised. "I thought you'd be pleased I'd be going into the bush for a bit instead of hanging around town being miserable."

"Are you miserable?" He crossed the room and drew her into his arms. "We don't spend enough time enjoying ourselves the way we used to. I'm sorry this hasn't been as much fun for you as it has for me."

She twisted within his embrace to look up at him. "So you don't mind me going?"

James frowned. "I don't mind you going and doing something you want to do..."

"But what? Is it Starky?"

He nodded. "I've heard things about him."

"From whom?"

"Susan—"

"Susan and Starky had a thing years ago, and she's never got over it. Look, I know Starky's a womaniser, but do you honestly think I'm at risk of succumbing to his charms?" Verity said it lightly, but even as she spoke she was remembering the way he had looked at her beneath the acacia. "I'm going to be there to keep the German hunter's wife company. That's all. And anything Susan says is bound to be coloured by the fact that things didn't work out between them."

James held her close. "Susan's difficult, and if I'm honest, I don't entirely trust her. Or at least, I don't trust the way she tells a story." Then he took her by the shoulders and held her away just far enough to smile at her before kissing the tip of her nose. "But I trust you. And he did save Saskia's life, so there is that."

Verity sagged with relief. She had not realised how much she had wanted this to be his answer.

"So go out into the bush and have your adventure, darling." He kissed her again, this time on the lips. "But come back safe."

Verity kissed him back briefly, then pushed out of his arms. Somehow his words had sounded just the faintest bit condescending. "I hope it'll be more than some self-serving little adventure, James," she said, as she did up the remaining buttons of her blouse, watching him from the other side of the bed. She gave a half-smile, not wanting to spoil the mood, but not wanting to let him off the hook, either.

"I am *trying* to make something more of this new life I'm suddenly having to adjust to."

CHAPTER

TWENTY

ST ANNE'S COLLEGE

Saskia bent her head closer to Angie's as they pretended to do their homework in the study room and whispered, "You mean your mum never said anything? So who do you think he is?"

They were talking about fathers—about their own, after a long and winding path that had started with Saskia telling her new friend about how her dad's job as a pilot had taken them all over Australia. Now Angie had just made the startling revelation that, according to the law at least, she had no father, because no one had been named on her birth certificate.

"That's because he's a murderer." Angie pushed back her dark curls and gave Saskia a defiant look.

Except that they were more than friends. They were second cousins and, for Saskia—who had grown up an only child with no cousins and hardly any extended family close at hand—that was thrilling.

So was this new information.

More thrilling still was the fact that Angie did not seem embarrassed or horrified by her bloodline.

"My cousin Emma says Mum was trying to protect me, and that's why she refused to reveal his name," Angie went on. "Because he killed Mum's brother."

"What?"

"Girls, do I have to separate you?"

Mrs Steadman took a menacing step forward and slapped her ruler against the palm of her hand. "This is quiet study time, not a place for idle chatter."

But this was anything but idle chatter.

Saskia's eyes widened, and she waited until Mrs Steadman had stalked to the far end of the room before she asked in a thrilled whisper, "How did he kill your uncle? When?"

Angie hunched her shoulders and answered softly. "'Em says my father was Mum's old boyfriend, and that he followed her to the hunting camp where she was with Uncle Mike and his friends, and that they got into a fight." She rolled her eyes, but there was strain beneath the performance. "It must have been after…" She lowered her voice. "'You know what' happened. Because then Mum found out she was pregnant, and Granny and Grandpa sent her away to have me. They wanted her to adopt me out, but she ran away instead. It was months before they found her."

"They sound like terrible grandparents," Saskia said, thinking of her own warm, kind grandmothers.

"Not at all. They're wonderful. They saved my life. They're paying my school fees, and I think I've grown on them." Angie grinned, then, almost as if she had said more than she meant to, changed tack abruptly. "Has your ankle healed properly yet? When will you be able to play hockey?"

Angie was captain of the Under-16 girls' hockey team,

and it had been her delighted discovery that Saskia loved the game too, which had properly sealed their bond.

"The doctor says it's healing really well, so I hope it won't be long." Saskia closed her eyes briefly as the memory rushed over her of water, terror, and enormous teeth. "It's still such a blur. I think I must have blacked out, because the next thing I really remember—"

"Girls!" Mrs Steadman had wheeled round and was now bearing down on them again. "If you've finished your homework, then take your conversation outside. I've had enough."

Saskia and Angie rose, scooped up their books, and left with barely a glance at Mrs Steadman. The moment they were out in the corridor and heading towards the gardens on the way back to their dormitory, they picked up the thread as if it had never been broken.

"I must ask Starky to tell me again exactly how it happened and how he knew where to aim, considering the croc had me on the ground. He just whipped up the rifle and fired. How he got the croc and not me, I honestly don't know. Mum said he was a quick-thinking hero. Well, of course he was." Saskia smiled, aware she probably looked as star-struck as she felt.

"Who's this bloke? What did you say his name was?"

"Starky Willis. He's a hunter with a concession in the Okavango, and he was helping out at Chubaora when we were there." She noticed Angie frowning. "What's the matter?"

"I just reckon I know that name. Or ought to." Angie slowed a little as they reached the path between the flowerbeds. "I'm almost sure he was one of the guys with Uncle Mike on the hunting trip where he got killed. It's not the sort of name you forget." She gave a quick grin. "That would be a coincidence, wouldn't it?"

Then her expression changed.

"It would also mean he knows something about my father."

The words seemed to settle between them, heavier than anything they had yet said.

"I know nothing, not even my father's name, though I heard Granny and Grandpa whispering it once. Jeremy." Angie went on. "I haven't even seen a photograph. Mum destroyed everything—every old picture my father was in. I don't even know whether I look like him. I hate not knowing if I have other cousins or family out there somewhere, but Mum changes the subject every time I ask. I mean…" She faltered. "He wasn't a serial killer or anything. It must have been an accident."

She finished in a tone that turned the sentence almost into a question, and when she looked at Saskia, it was with such naked uncertainty that Saskia felt a rush of protective loyalty.

She squeezed Angie's arm.

"It would have to have been an accident," she said firmly. "He'd have had to have been a decent sort if your grandparents accepted him as your mum's boyfriend, wouldn't he?" Then she grew thoughtful. "But you're right. Starky would know. And he'd tell you, even if your mum doesn't want you to know anything, because she can never forgive the man who killed her brother."

She gave Angie's arm another squeeze.

"When it's holiday time, we'll go back to Maun together and you can ask Starky straight out. He'll tell you."

She smiled that absurdly hopeful smile she could never quite suppress when Starky was mentioned. He was her hero, after all, and she would have defended him to the ends of the earth for saving her in such magnificent fashion.

"I'm so happy you're my cousin," she said. "I honestly thought I was completely alone in the world until I came here."

Angie smiled back.

"So did I."

CHAPTER
TWENTY-ONE

"Story's finished!" Susan shoved the typewriter away from her and leaned back, the old vinyl chair creaking beneath her. "Job well done, I'd say. The new ice-cream shop in town has just made front-page news."

She grinned at her colleagues in the cramped, airless office of the *Okavango Observer*, then dragged a pile of old, yellowing newspapers towards her. "There's got to be something more exciting to write about," she said, flicking through them until something caught her eye. No one answered. Only the dry rustle of old newsprint disturbed the stale heat. "I see Starky Willis's hunting lodge was worth a centre-page spread this time last year. Whose palm did he grease to get that position?"

Philomena, the work-experience girl, looked instantly uncomfortable and dropped her gaze when Susan caught her eye. But Mitchell, the other journalist, merely raised an eyebrow and said, in a tone edged with warning, "I'd be careful about rocking the boat, my girl. This might be where you were born, but the whole hunting-and-conservation balance has changed a lot since you've been off in the big smoke."

Susan did not care for the condescension. She had disliked Mitchell from the moment she was told he was the senior reporter and that she was, essentially, to take instructions from him.

"So how did he get such glowing coverage if he wasn't paying for it?"

Mitchell kept typing.

A full ten seconds passed before he stopped, let out a long sigh, and turned his head just enough to say, "A renovated lodge is newsworthy. Hunting lodge or photographic lodge, a makeover is a makeover. Starky hired a decorator from Jo'burg and she did a *lekker* job transforming the place from a rundown operation into something worth a centre spread."

Susan gave a sharp little snort. "Oh yes, his decorator. His girlfriend at the time, wasn't she? And she spent money he didn't have. I'll grant you he was doing all right, but I reckon he's in a hurry now to pull in as many rich trophy hunters as he can before the bank forecloses because he overreached himself. What do you reckon, Mitchell? Can you tell me it's not true?"

She knew her bluntness put certain men's backs up. Men like Mitchell. Plenty of other men too.

Mitchell swore softly under his breath, then swivelled away from the typewriter and looked at her properly. "You're the supposedly investigative journalist, Susan. Maybe you should be the one finding proof before you start making claims that could get you run out of town if you aired them publicly."

He held her gaze.

"People are likely to forgive you a lot of the rubbish

you come out with because you're local. Or were once. I'm not, and I wouldn't dream of saying half the things you do. But you need to be careful. I'm thinking you haven't worked in newspapers long enough to know when speculation is dangerous and when it's smarter to keep your mouth shut until you've got facts. It's obvious you've got something against this man, but don't go shooting your mouth off about Starky Willis until you've got something concrete. Go back and polish your ice-cream parlour story and then get serious if you really want a front-page byline."

Seething, Susan turned away and hunched over the stack of old newspapers, the musty smell of dust and ink rising as she turned the pages more roughly than necessary because she had no ready retort.

Mitchell thought he could put her back in her place.

And perhaps, professionally speaking, he was right. She wanted a big exposé on hunting—something that would shine a merciless light on everything she felt was rotten in Starky's business dealings—but the truth was, she did not yet know where to begin.

She simply knew.

Knew it in her bones.

How else could he have paid for flying lessons, secured himself a hunting concession, and built up that lodge at such a young age when she knew his family had been dirt poor?

And as for the evidence that had convicted Mike's so-called murderer, it rested on one brutal fact: the bullet in her brother's heart had come from a Krieghoff double rifle, .470 Nitro Express. The only Krieghoff the rangers had recorded during their checks on the night before Mike died was the one Jeremy had cheerfully claimed as his own.

But Starky had hidden his Krieghoff in the bushes after shooting the ostrich.

He had never admitted to owning one. Not to the rangers.

And while, technically, the fatal bullet could have come from either Starky's rifle or Jeremy's, Jeremy was no killer.

Jeremy could not have killed a fly.

"Will you stop doing that?"

Mitchell's irritated voice floated across the room, and Susan snapped back, "What?" before realising she had been tapping her fingernails against the desk, the sharp little clicks carrying through the office.

She stopped. Turned another page.

Then gasped.

Out of the corner of her eye, she saw Mitchell roll his eyes, but he said nothing this time as Susan bent closer over the paper, her heart beginning to pound.

The article was eight months old.

It was not even the crime itself that made her reread it with such intensity—a report about Botswana Wildlife and National Parks officers swooping on a poaching ring in the Caprivi Strip and arresting five locals for slaughtering a rhino.

No.

It was the name of the chief investigative officer.

A name so familiar it seemed, for one sickening second, to rise off the page.

Phil Lehmann.

Mike's ring-in friend. The one who had joined that doomed hunting trip after their cousin James pulled out.

Susan remembered, even now, Starky's easy contempt for Phil—how he'd acted the mate to his face while treating him like an inconvenience, a soft-handed nuisance, someone to be tolerated.

And now, it seemed, Phil and Starky stood on opposite sides of the hunting divide.

Susan stared at the newsprint until the black letters blurred, then sharpened again.

A slow, dangerous satisfaction moved through her.

At last.

Now she knew exactly what her next move was going to be.

TWENTY-TWO

It was just after dawn when James dropped Verity at the gate to the Okavango Wilderness Safaris compound in town. The air still held a faint morning coolness, though already there was that brittle brightness which promised another punishing day.

"OK?" he asked. He looked concerned.

Verity nodded, swallowing her apprehension. There was no going back now, which meant there was no point in saying what she really felt.

"The time will fly by," she said with a smile, reaching across the gear stick to kiss his cheek, breathing in the familiar scent of his aftershave.

"Is that all I get when it's going to be two weeks?"

Verity leaned over again, but her thoughts were on the ten days ahead rather than on James. He caught her mouth before she could pull away, kissing her properly, and when she drew back she said, lightly, "I'll see you in a few days when you come into camp with whatever our demanding hunters have run out of. There's Starky already in the compound. I'd better go."

She grabbed her duffel bag from the back seat and hurried through the dust, the thorns of a camel thorn snagging at her khaki shirt as she passed. By the time she reached the storeroom, she found Starky and a group of about ten local Motswana loading the Forward Control, which was already groaning under tents, equipment, crates and sacks of supplies.

"Am I late?" she asked, glancing from the strange, hunched-looking vehicle with its cab perched over the engine to Starky, who was lean and rangy and taut with energy as he jumped down from the back and grinned at her.

"Not if you want to make you and me some coffee."

He hoisted a box of supplies from the ground and shoved it into the rear of the cab, then slammed the door and leaned against it, studying her from the ground up with an ease that made her suddenly aware of her own body—her dusty legs, her shirt sticking faintly to her skin, the hammering of her pulse.

Or perhaps he was only taking stock.

He did not seem to notice her discomfort. Turning to pull a list from the glove box, he said over his shoulder, "I need you to check the inventory and make sure we haven't missed anything." He handed her the paper. "There's also a case of Krug, two of Moët, and some speciality whiskies that need picking up. The clients come off the Jo'burg flight in a couple of hours. You can collect them at the airport and do the small talk at the Duck while I get the plane ready. Then we'll head out to Kwai River Lodge for the night."

Verity was about to leave when a thought occurred to her. "Mrs Heinrich speaks English, doesn't she?"

"Sure. Anyway, Heinrich would have said if she didn't. Now—where's that coffee?"

Verity returned with two chipped mugs of steaming coffee just in time to wave off the forward party: waiting staff, tent ladies and the camp boy. The truck would collect a couple of trackers and skinners from one of the villages on the way to Deception Pan.

Starky watched the vehicle leave in a cloud of ochre dust, then let out a breath and relaxed against his bakkie.

"Glad to see you looking the part. Not bad."

His tone was approving until, in response to her raised eyebrow, he added, "Doesn't a bloke get to compliment a lady in Australia? No need to look so nervous. You're married. This is business. I don't bite. You won't have to be more than a pretty face and keep Mrs Heinrich entertained, and you'll have done your job."

Throughout the morning Verity checked the inventory list, picked up champagne, whisky and flowers, helped with odd jobs, and just before midday set off in the Land Cruiser to the airport.

The daily Air Botswana flight from Johannesburg had just landed and disgorged its passengers, who were now streaming across the tarmac in the hard white glare. It was a surprisingly full flight. Verity held up a card printed with the Heinrich name and scanned the arrivals for a German family.

"Zerangu Hunting Lodge?"

She looked up to find a man in his mid-fifties and a boy of about twenty stopping to squint at the card in her hand.

What surprised her first was how Aryan they looked: white-blond hair, Roman noses, pale blue eyes.

What surprised her more was the woman at the older man's side.

"That's right," said Verity. "I'm Verity White. And you must be Kurt Heinrich and—?"

She tried not to gape at the long-legged blonde in the scandalously short white dress. If the woman had not been clinging to the older man's arm, Verity would have assumed she was the son's girlfriend.

"Charlize de Groot." The girl batted absurdly fake eyelashes as she squeezed her companion's arm.

"Pleased to meet you, Verity."

Kurt Heinrich had a Teutonic intensity that was almost unnervingly severe as he took her measure. Very different from Starky's insolent warmth.

His son, however, had the dreamy, bruised eyes of a poet.

"You must be Thomas," she said.

The boy nodded. He looked younger than the twenty-one years she'd seen listed on the passport details.

"First time in Africa?" she asked, trying to draw him in.

"First time for Thomas," his father answered for him. "I have hunted in Botswana before. Thomas is here to put away his books and learn the skills of the hunter."

His English was excellent, if heavily accented. Starky had told her he had spent years as an investment banker in New York.

"Are you looking forward to the next few days, Thomas?" Verity asked as she led them to the vehicle, the heat already thickening around them.

"I guess." He shrugged, and Verity could not help wondering at the amount of money his father was spending so his son could endure an experience he so plainly did not relish.

"Well, you'll enjoy it a lot more than you would have last month when it was not just steaming hot but rainy as well. Now it's much nicer." She smiled, pushing herself into the role of bright, capable hostess despite the nerves knotting inside her. Poor Thomas looked as though he were here entirely under duress. "And I'm sure it'll be good to spend time with your father."

She stopped, unsure how to refer to the young woman who was laughing at something Kurt had just said as he placed a proprietary hand on her shoulder and drew her slightly away. Surely Charlize de Groot was not his wife.

"Do you think so?" Thomas said, his tone heavy with sarcasm. "For a hot five seconds, I did too—until we stopped at Sun City."

Verity frowned, waiting.

"Then suddenly this woman appeared. Charline... Christine—"

"Charlize," Verity corrected gently.

"Whatever her name is, it doesn't matter. I swear I won't speak one word to her."

"I'm sorry," Verity said softly. "I didn't realise you didn't know her." It was dreadful enough when a parent introduced a new partner. Worse still to be ambushed by one.

"My father never laid eyes on her until yesterday, when we flew into Sun City for a 'business meeting'." He made air quotes with such disgust that Verity would have laughed, if he had not looked so wretched. "Now this woman is going to be his companion for the next two weeks, and I'm expected to keep my mouth shut when we get home to my mother."

His hands were clenched. Behind him, Charlize giggled again and rested her head on Kurt's shoulder.

Verity swallowed. She was suddenly very aware of how far out of her depth she was. Kurt Heinrich's wife was at home, none the wiser, waiting for her husband and son to return from their so-called father-and-son hunting trip.

"Please, come, and I'll take you to our local watering

hole, the Duck Inn, for something to drink before you meet Starky Willis, your safari guide and host," Verity said, making her voice as bright and untroubled as possible. "He'll fly us to Kwai River Lodge, where we'll spend the evening with dinner and drinks round the campfire before heading on to Deception Pan tomorrow, where your camp will already be set up and waiting. I'll be your hostess, so if there's anything you need, please let me know and I'll do whatever I can to help."

Given that these clients were paying upwards of eighty thousand American dollars for a two-week safari, Verity was quite prepared to facilitate almost anything.

Clearly Charlize was on hand to facilitate the rest.

Verity felt desperately sorry for Thomas as he trailed after them.

The Duck was quiet at that time of day. Inside, the dim coolness was a relief after the hammering sun outside. Thomas was just finishing his Coke, Kurt a Castle beer, and Charlize a gin and tonic when Starky strode into the courtyard, his presence somehow making the whole place feel smaller and more charged.

"Mr Heinrich. Good to meet you."

He shook hands with Kurt, who immediately insisted he call him Kurt before introducing his son Thomas and then his "friend and companion for the next two weeks," Charlize de Groot.

Verity did not miss the brief flare of surprise in Starky's eyes as he took in the pairing. Clearly he understood the arrangement at once, but he was as courteous as if the Sun City prostitute were Frau Heinrich herself.

Courteous—but perhaps very slightly more flirtatious.

And when Verity caught that look, a curious sensation fluttered low in her stomach.

Jealousy?

No, not jealousy exactly. Not of Charlize de Groot and the sort of male attention she drew. More an uneasy awareness of something she herself had been missing of late. A sharpened energy. A kind of charged appraisal. The sense of being seen, not as a mother or wife or displaced editor, but as a woman.

James was a warm and wonderful husband who had suffered a terrible professional blow and bounced back with the resilience Verity had always admired.

Had she begun to take that steadiness for granted?

Glancing between cheating Kurt Heinrich and Starky, perennial ladies' man, the contrast between both these men and her own husband could not have been starker.

She felt a little stab of regret at the coolness of her parting kiss that morning, but it was too late now.

Starky put a hand on Verity's shoulder and said, with a glance between the two women, "Even if you don't pick up a rifle on this trip, you're guaranteed a good time, Ms de Groot."

James would be waiting for Verity when she got back from her own small adventure.

And she ought, she told herself, to take comfort in knowing he always would be.

CHAPTER

TWENTY-THREE

James flopped onto the sofa in the living room and stretched out his legs to read the letter that had arrived in the company's private bag that afternoon. A cup of coffee steamed beside him.

He'd been itching to open it from the moment he'd recognised Tim's handwriting and, as today was a day off, he was taking things easy. Later, if he felt like company, he might drop in at Croc Camp.

When James had left Australia, Tim had been hoping for a crack at Cathay Pacific. Unlike James, he had the minimum five hundred hours' jet time, having flown longer for Ansett, whereas James had only just been checked to line.

With the state of the world economy, of which aviation was the canary in the coal mine, James wondered if he'd ever get a jet job with no real time on type.

With a sigh, he tore open the envelope and unfolded the letter. No point in brooding over what he couldn't change.

Dear James—

How's things in beautiful Bots? Are Verity and Saskia adjusting to life in Africa?

Well, I did it. Got the gig with Cathay and I'm already in Hong Kong. I know it's not that far from Melbourne and that I'm lucky I can commute to a degree, but it feels like a world away from home. I'm sharing an apartment with two other blokes in Discovery Bay on Lantau Island, same island as the airport. The views over the South China Sea are spectacular, but it's definitely not home.

Sarah's been a trooper. She loves adventure and would have been here in a heartbeat, but there's no way she can come to Honkers with Ben's treatment regimen. Can't complain, though. You heard about Sean and Melissa, didn't you? Divorced, though that had been coming since the day they got married. And poor Murray... I still can't believe it. Makes us all feel guilty as hell, I tell you.

You made the right decision. I hope Verity knows it. You couldn't have stayed. It's like an invisible line has been drawn, dividing pilots into opposing camps. The camaraderie we once enjoyed in the cockpit feels like a distant memory now. I find myself wondering if anything will ever really get back to normal...

Anyway, no news other than—

James let the letter drop into his lap and stared out of the window. Mothusi was in the yard. Or rather, bent almost double, he was raking the sand at his usual glacial pace.

Verity had told him about the reading of the bones. That Mothusi had foretold danger.

Restlessly, James stuffed Tim's letter back into the envelope and stood up. It was only four o'clock, but it was Saturday, so Croc Camp would already be filling up.

He'd have no trouble finding someone to share a beer with.

"James!"

Sitting at the bar counter, he turned at the sound of his name and forced a smile as he saw Susan rising from a nearby table.

She threaded her way through the drinkers and dropped onto the empty stool beside him. "Missing Verity yet?" There was purpose in her eye and a tightness to her smile. "Has she sent you a message yet to say how it's going? Have the hunters shot anything? Has the boy been blooded?"

James took a swig of his beer. "Your sources are good, Susan," he said. "Who's your intel? Starky?"

"Starky?" she repeated, with open contempt. "All my own sleuthing, James." She touched the side of her nose and smiled, though there was something brittle about it. "I realised early on I had to stay one step ahead of the game if I wanted to survive. I was too trusting back when my innocence was taken. I'm a hard woman these days, James."

"But one who still likes a bit of fun," said James, trying to steer her tone into something lighter.

"Oh, I like fun when I can get it. But most men are bastards. I learned that the hard way."

"Oh." James raised his eyebrows, and Susan, with unsteady hands, pulled a Camel from the packet in her bag and lit it. "Verity's hung around for fifteen years, and good on her. You're one of the decent ones, James, I can tell. I just don't seem to attract the good ones. But I'm damned if I'm going to be a walkover like Verity or anyone else."

"Excuse me?"

"No offence, James." Susan gave a throaty laugh and patted his wrist. "Verity's sweet and all that. But she's taken everything thrown at her lying down. I mean, why didn't she arc up when she had the best job of her life and say her career should take precedence over yours? Why are you here flying a 206 when you could be flying a goddamned jet?"

"Wow." James shook his head. Susan had no grasp of the complexities she was reducing so blithely to a few sharp lines, but there was no point trying to untangle them for her when she was in this mood. "What has Verity said to you?"

Susan gave him a level look through a thread of cigarette smoke. Then she shook her head. "Nothing much. But she was cut up about losing her status. I mean, she finally had status, and you took it away from her." She broke off to flag down a waiter and order more drinks, including a Castle Lager for James, then went on. "And I'm going for status, James. I got knocked down when I was eighteen and dragged myself out of the gutter, only to get knocked down again and again. Every bloke I loved, I thought loved me back. But he was only using me. Well, never again. Now it's time for me to reclaim what I've lost."

She took a long swallow of whisky on the rocks.

"Starky thinks he's above the law. He got away with something very bad when he was young, and it emboldened him. Now he thinks he can get away with anything. But he can't. And it'll be the last person he expects who brings him down."

James studied her. Was she more drunk than she sounded? Her words weren't slurred, but there was something dark and feverish in her tone.

"What are you planning, Susan? And why are you telling me this?" He narrowed his eyes. "I didn't realise you felt quite such... an aversion to Starky."

Susan reached over and gripped his wrist.

"He killed my brother," she said.

Then, still nodding, she stared over his shoulder. "It's taken me fifteen years to admit it, though I've had my suspicions for years. But he killed Mike—your cousin, your best playmate till you left Botswana—in case you don't remember."

James pulled his arm back. "Your ex-boyfriend Jeremy killed Mike," he said. "There's never been any evidence or suggestion otherwise."

"Jeremy didn't do any of the things he was accused of." Susan took an angry drag on her cigarette. "And he died in gaol one day after he was charged. He never had a chance to clear his name."

James shook his head. "Why would Starky have any reason to kill Mike? They were childhood friends. It doesn't make sense." He wrapped his hand around his cold beer. "What evidence do you have? Did he confess to you?"

Susan's look darkened. Her lips thinned. She was silent so long that James thought she had decided not to answer.

Finally, she said, "Jeremy's fancy rifle? His father gave it to him before he died, but Jeremy didn't have the heart to shoot even a guinea fowl with it."

"Well, the evidence was that the bullet came from Jeremy's rifle. I'm not saying it wasn't an accident, but that's what the coroner's report said." He offered her a sympathetic look. "I read it."

Susan's hand shook violently as she lit another cigarette. "Maybe it was an accident, but Starky did it. I know he did," she said stubbornly. "And do you know how else I know Starky is bad to the bone?" She dragged in a shaky breath and let it out through clenched teeth.

"Because I gave him the chance to make things right, and he didn't take it."

James tipped his head to one side, trying to think how to respond, but Susan rushed on.

"You think I don't have a reason to hate Starky? Well, he showed his true colours by the way he responded when I finally managed to ring him a couple of months after Mike's death." She fiddled with her bracelet, then said viciously, "He'd moved to Johannesburg and was doing his flight training at Lanseria when I discovered I was—"

She lifted her head and bored her eyes into his.

"Pregnant."

James was taken aback. Susan was looking at him as if she were daring him not to understand.

He glanced around, but saw no one he knew close enough to overhear, so he lowered his voice. "Starky is the father of your daughter?"

"Yep." Susan nodded. "I slept with him the night before Mike was killed. I'd had such a crush on Starky. For years. Anyway, he charmed me the way he charms all the women around here, as you may have noticed. But for me, it was my first time." She gave a humourless laugh. "Yes, Starky is Angel's father, but my parents were convinced it was Jeremy because of what Mike had written in his diary, which they were given after he died. Not that I knew that at the time. Anyway, when I discovered I was pregnant, all hell broke loose." She tipped her face upwards and mimicked her parents' horror. "'Our daughter is pregnant by a murderer.'"

James frowned. "I'm sorry, Susan. That must have been hard." Briefly, he covered her hand with his. "So Starky is your daughter's father and... I gather he refused to accept paternity."

He remembered Starky's robust denial, weeks ago, when James had asked whether he had children.

When Susan didn't answer, he said, "Why do you think he had anything to do with Mike's death?"

Susan gave a visible shudder, and James wondered if he ought to steer the conversation somewhere safer than this vendetta she was clearly nursing.

But this was exactly where she had wanted things to go, and her expression was almost triumphant now as she said, "Jeremy had already left camp when the three boys went out shooting."

James looked at her blankly, and she went on.

"He left after a fight with my brother. I could hear them while I was in my tent early that morning. Mike was accusing Jeremy of going into my tent in the middle of the night. He'd obviously heard the zip and the whispering and the rustling and assumed it was Jeremy—not Starky— because Jeremy had travelled all that way hoping the two of us might get back together." Susan took a swallow of her drink and looked at James with bleak shame. "Maybe I should have set him straight then and there. But so should Starky. He must have heard what the fight was about. Instead, Jeremy just drove off, and when I came out of the tent, everyone seemed embarrassed, and I certainly wasn't going to say anything. So we all ate breakfast in silence, and then the three boys went out shooting."

James sat with that a moment. So Starky was the father of Susan's daughter. It was quite a revelation. But he dragged his thoughts back to her central accusation.

"So if Jeremy had gone," he said carefully, "what evidence do you have that Starky had anything to do with Mike's death? Jeremy could have come back, like the evidence suggested, with his rifle."

"There was something shifty about Starky after he and Phil came back carrying a dead impala between them, saying they couldn't find Mike, though at the time I thought nothing of it. I mean, I just assumed Mike would saunter back to camp a bit later."

"And when he didn't?"

"The boys didn't seem keen to go looking once it got late, but I made them." Susan's shoulders sagged. "About half an hour later Phil came back…" She swallowed hard. "He was nearly hysterical when he told me they'd found him. Or rather, found his body… half eaten by lions. He said he was coming back for a tarpaulin or something, while Starky stayed there."

James pressed his lips together. "I'm sorry, Susan. I had no idea."

"Yes." She closed her eyes briefly. "Everything after that was a blur. They brought Mike back, and by then I'd done what I could to pack up camp, but they said we had to stay the night because it was too late to get hold of the authorities."

Susan had begun to tremble, so James tried to move her away from the ghastliness of that night and back to the substance of what she was claiming.

The man in whose care James had left Verity.

"But the police obviously had evidence that pointed to Jeremy," he said. "Mike was shot, wasn't he? With a bullet from Jeremy's rifle?"

Susan rubbed at her eyes, smudging her mascara. "Starky and Jeremy had the same type of rifle. A Krieghoff double rifle. Except Starky had never admitted to owning one. He'd already asked me to lie once for him the previous evening when the rangers came to camp asking about a dead ostrich."

"What?"

"Starky had shot an ostrich in the national park. Idiotic, because he should have known they were protected there. He never expected rangers to turn up, and when two Botswana National Parks men came asking questions and wanting names and rifle registrations, Starky made sure I kept quiet after he hid his gun. And because I was madly in love with him at that tender age, I did exactly as he knew I would."

"But killing an ostrich with a Krieghoff—the same kind of rifle Jeremy had—doesn't prove Starky killed Mike."

"Jeremy wouldn't kill a fly."

James narrowed his eyes. "But this was all investigated, wasn't it? Surely the bullet that killed your brother was matched to the weapon? Jeremy's weapon?"

Susan shook her head. "Poor Jeremy probably had no idea what had happened when they brought him in for questioning after the coroner's murder ruling. I had no idea he'd been taken into custody and charged. I was protected from all talk of Mike's death. At first Mum and Dad were silent, and then when they found out I was pregnant they sent me to stay with my grandparents because they didn't know what to do with me. I was a mess. I didn't even make it to Mike's funeral. They had me so full of tranquilisers I could barely think. And later, to find out my ex-boyfriend had been charged with my brother's murder and was now dead too—beaten up in gaol before he ever had a chance to clear his name..." She rubbed her eyes again. "When I finally started thinking straight, I realised nobody would believe me if I said Jeremy wasn't Angel's father. By then it was too late." She gave a bitter laugh. "And now, after everything, I'm glad Starky's name isn't on her birth certificate. The best thing

I can do for Angel now is prove that Starky murdered Mike."

"Because that would prove Jeremy didn't?" James said. "And your daughter wouldn't have a murderer for a father?" He hesitated. "Come on, Susan, even if Starky wouldn't step up when you phoned him, you can't keep lying to Angel about who her father is." He paused. "Are you sure you really gave Starky the chance to do the right thing?"

Susan gave him a steady look. "I left three messages for him with his roommate, each one asking him to ring me back." She paused. "Do you know what he finally did?"

James shook his head.

"He sent me a cheque for two hundred rand and a note saying he was sorry about what had happened and if he could turn back the clock, he would." She made a sound of disgust. "Such a puerile response. Still, the money came in handy when Mum and Dad and everyone else tried to make me give away my baby."

James raised his eyebrows, and Susan gave a humourless grin. "I was able to run away. It took them two months to find me. By then I'd run out of money, but it was too late to make me give up Angel."

She took another deep drag on her cigarette and stubbed it out viciously.

James could see how she might intimidate men. Had she always been so aggressive? Or had injustice and mistreatment scraped away whatever softness she once had?

He hunched forward, clasping his hands around his drink. "You can't keep lying, Susan," he said. More gently he added, "If Jeremy isn't your daughter's father, she needs to know that."

"Oh, believe me, I'm done with living a lie, and I'm done with Starky swanning through life as if he hasn't a care in the world while women throw themselves at his feet and he accepts it like he's some Greek god." She gave him a hard look. "But I am not telling Angel, or anyone else, that Starky is her real father. And if you say it—though why would you?—I'll deny it."

Now James really did begin to wonder whether jealousy —or a deep, unhealed confusion—lay beneath all this. He straightened. Susan's vendetta against Starky clearly sprang from his refusal to acknowledge Angel, but he couldn't yet see how she intended to turn all this into a murder charge after fifteen years.

He was just about to make his excuses and leave when she said, "I didn't see Starky again from the day we left camp—the day Mike died—until I confronted him after I tracked him down at the compound. He denied everything. Can you believe it? What he doesn't know, though, is that I have the means to expose him."

Her smile turned conspiratorial.

"You think you can force him to confess?"

Susan barked out a laugh. "Starky wouldn't confess under torture. He's a hard nut to crack at the best of times. No, I'm organising the evidence as we speak."

James frowned. "You do realise Verity and I are on friendly terms with Starky. Aren't you worried we might... warn him? And you can't suddenly produce evidence after fifteen years, Susan."

He thought of Verity out in the bush with Starky at that very moment, and a spear of alarm went through him. Susan had offered nothing that would stand up as proof. But was she capable of manufacturing something?

"What are you planning to do, Susan?" he asked, more

sharply now. "Verity is out on safari with Starky. You're not planning anything that might put her in harm's way."

"Oh Lord, wouldn't it be nice if a bloke in my life ever gave a thought to *my* safety and well-being?" Susan said, scrabbling in her bag for another packet of cigarettes. "No, Verity's quite safe. I'm going to the source, James. To the only other person who knows the truth about what happened. The bloke who heard Starky and Mike arguing over diamonds." She leaned in. "That's what else I heard from my tent. Mike found a diamond. That's why Starky shot him. So he could steal it. And now, at last, I've discovered where to find the one person who can tell the truth about what happened to Mike that day."

James sat very still.

Susan seemed to savour the fact that she had shocked him into silence.

Finally he said, "So you think Starky's unexplained financial success came from killing your brother for a diamond?"

Susan nodded as she struck a match. "Sure do. But I'm not naming names for you because you don't believe me." She shrugged. "That's all right. I'll have the last laugh when it all comes out."

"Why now, Susan? Surely if you had this so-called evidence, you had it before."

"Well, I did think of tracking him down a few years ago, but I was in a bad place and didn't look very hard. Mum was threatening to take Ange away from me and I was... well, maybe I was a bit too fond of *dagga* and the grog, but I wasn't a bad mother. Hell, I ran away and hid for two months so I could keep my baby, so nobody gets to call me that." She thrust out her chin. "Anyway, I was reading old newspaper files the other day. There was a story about a rhino-poaching sting, and it mentioned the name of the Botswana National Parks chief inspector. So you can probably guess what I'm going to do next, can't you?"

James frowned. "Susan, there's no evidence Starky is planning anything illegal. He'd never risk everything he's built for the sake of letting some clients poach a lion." He was deeply uneasy now. "Verity is on that overland. She helped him prepare. She'd know if he was planning something."

"Would she?" Susan rolled her eyes. "You've got one sweet, trusting wife, but she's no detective. She'd have no idea. Ask Lucy, who was hostess with Starky out at Chubaora. Even had a fling with him, though you'd never know it now, seeing how cutesy she is with that Canadian pilot, Rob. Anyway, ask her why she pulled out of this overland with Starky."

James thought about this, then asked reluctantly, "And what does Lucy say?"

"She says Starky's already fulfilled his lion quota, but that's exactly what this German safari group wants. A Kalahari lion."

"He might simply have fobbed them off with something else. A Kalahari lion's a pretty scrawny beast, most of the time."

Susan shrugged. "Well, that will be for the head of anti-poaching at Botswana National Parks to find out."

CHAPTER

TWENTY-FOUR

"Breakfast!"

The smell of frying bacon and eggs had not yet coaxed Kurt and Charlize from their tent. Nervously, Verity tiptoed past the canvas flap and announced that food was ready in what she hoped was a voice loud enough to be heard but not so loud as to sound intrusive.

Thomas, his hair still wet from his bucket shower, was staring at his father's tent with something close to loathing. He was clearly on the verge of turning away and heading for the breakfast table—with its plates, silverware and all the over-the-top luxury that passed here for a simple morning meal—when his father's paramour suddenly emerged from the tent.

Half-clad in a see-through peignoir, Charlize stood with her eyes still closed, tipped her face to the sun, and ran one hand through her rippling blonde curls.

Verity was mesmerised.

Thomas, she could see at once, was horrified. His

Adam's apple bobbed twice before he turned sharply away and stalked off to breakfast.

Charlize might be a woman of easy virtue, but she was unquestionably beautiful. And when she opened her heavy-lidded eyes and saw Verity watching her, her generous mouth curved into a self-satisfied smile.

"Smells delicious," she said in that husky voice of hers. "I could eat a kudu. That's what Kurt says he'll hunt for me today."

At the sound of his name, Kurt pushed through the tent flap, and Verity caught the brief, startling sight of his rounded belly lolling over the waistband of his boxer shorts before he shrugged into a dressing gown. He was still, in his way, a handsome man, but the years—and an obvious appreciation for food, drink, and indulgence—were beginning to show.

Thomas, by contrast, was lean to the point of weediness, all coltish limbs and the trusting, almost puppyish innocence of someone not yet hardened. But when his father said pointedly, "Today Thomas will hunt you a kudu, *Engelchen*," Thomas swung round from the table and thumped down his mug of coffee hard enough to slop it over the rim.

"I will not."

Verity was standing close enough to the older pair to hear Kurt murmur, "Perhaps you need to have a little conversation with my foolish son, *Liebling*. Use all the wiles at your disposal; I don't mind. My son and I are here to have a good time, and I want Thomas made into a man. So today he will hunt a kudu, and perhaps that will be, in part, because of some very special persuasion from you."

His hand slid from Charlize's shoulder, down over her breast and on to her thigh.

"Or perhaps," he added silkily, "you will give him a very special reward if he hunts you a kudu."

Verity scuttled away, nearly colliding with Starky as he emerged from the kitchen tent with a mug of coffee in one hand.

"What's got you so all-a-flutter?" he asked. "Our great white hunter hasn't propositioned you, I hope?"

"With Miss South Africa at his disposal? I think not—"

"Oh, you're not so hard on the eye, my dear. And if Mr Heinrich likes chestnut—"

"He likes blondes, which is why he chose Charlize." Lowering her voice, Verity added, "But it appears he's encouraging Charlize to introduce Thomas to... the ways of the world."

She felt herself blush violently, more so still when Starky threw back his head and laughed.

"What an unfortunate thing for your poor, innocent ears to overhear." He was still grinning. "Verity, this sort of thing happens, I'm afraid, and you must just do your job and not judge."

"I'm not judging," she protested, even while knowing perfectly well that she was.

Starky squeezed her shoulder, and the warmth in his glance as he moved off towards the breakfast table, where he began at once to draw Thomas into conversation, left her more unsettled than she cared to admit.

Once breakfast was over and the men had departed on the hunt, Verity was left behind to organise the staff and then attend to Charlize's comfort. Starky had made it plain that this was one of the main reasons for hiring her, but Verity had imagined herself keeping respectable Frau Heinrich company, not an escort picked up in a casino.

He had also made it clear that he was entirely satisfied with the substitution.

Verity was not.

Since Charlize had discovered that her every whim would be catered to, she had made full use of it.

Now she lounged in a director's chair by the campfire and beckoned to Verity with one languid finger.

"I'm bored," she said.

That was it. *I'm bored.* As though Verity were meant to snap her fingers and banish it.

"I'll fetch you some *Fair Lady* magazines," Verity suggested, but Charlize flicked her hand as though shooing away a fly.

"No. I need someone to talk to. And there's no one else to talk to, is there?"

Verity considered the question. Was it really her job to indulge this woman—a prostitute picked up only days earlier by their client?

Her whole sensibility recoiled from the situation. Charlize was stunning. She might have made anything of her life, and yet here she was, living off rich men by selling her body.

Verity hesitated.

She had things to do.

Or did she? There were plenty of staff to prepare the next meal, clean and straighten the tents, feed the donkey boilers so there would be hot water on demand, and keep the fire going—the fire in front of which Charlize was now sprawling, its smoke drifting up in a faint blue ribbon into the bleaching afternoon sky.

Verity looked around at their curious little idyll in the African bush. The cluster of East African canvas tents, the neatly laid tables and camp chairs, all stood in improbable elegance against the harshness of the savannah. Inside the tents, luxury reigned. Outside, service was instant, every need anticipated. These clients had travelled from the other side of the world and paid a fortune so that a man and a boy could shoot a few animals over ten days, and with that payment came the right, apparently, to have their every whim indulged.

If Charlize wanted conversation, then conversation was what Verity was paid to provide.

She sat down, casting Charlize a sidelong glance. The younger woman was gazing over the horizon with an oddly distant look. For a moment Verity thought she might actually be struck by the grandeur of the view, until Charlize said, with a curl of her lip, "My God, but it reminds me of the dorp where I grew up."

"Where was that?" Verity asked politely.

"Bethulie. Orange Free State." Charlize turned her head. "You don't know this country very well, do you? How long have you been here?"

"A couple of months. It's my first time out of Australia."

Charlize gave a soft, disdainful laugh. "Then you wouldn't know that Bethulie is not Monte Carlo or Monaco. Now *that's* where I want to go one day. Get out of this dump and never come back."

Verity followed her gaze and saw a very different landscape from the one Charlize described. The bush had already begun to work its spell on her. She no longer saw only scrubby vegetation and dry sand, but a world opening out beyond the umbrella thorn and the termite mounds—a whole new life, strange and beautiful, waiting to be discovered.

Charlize leaned back and wound a strand of pale hair round her finger.

"I'm sure the novelty of Monaco would wear thin too, if you had to stay there long enough," Verity said, not remotely expecting the look of pure loathing Charlize turned on her.

Quickly she added, "But of course it would be glamorous and—"

"And full of sophisticated people who'd appreciate what I have to offer."

"Yes, I'm sure," Verity agreed. "You might even marry a prince. Like Grace Kelly. You're every bit as beautiful."

Charlize tossed her head back. "I'm not marrying anyone while my husband's still alive," she said. "He'll never divorce me. He says he'll kill any man I take up with." She gave a throaty laugh. "That's quite a lot of dead men by now. But he'll have to find me first."

At Verity's look of shock, Charlize's smile shifted, becoming less bitter and almost amused.

"I've no doubt my father would help him. Or do the job himself. He's the fire-and-brimstone sort. Pastor Johannes de Groot of *Gemeente van die Goeie Herder*." She translated with mocking precision. "Congregation of the Good Shepherd."

Verity groped for a response. "You come from a religious family?"

"I suppose that's what it might look like from the outside. Pappa fashioned himself on an Old Testament despot."

Verity flushed. "I'm not very familiar with the Old Testament."

"Lucky you. Genesis 19:8 was Pappa's favourite. Though he had a whole arsenal of verses to justify the things he did to me." Charlize's voice altered, becoming almost sing-song as she quoted: "'Behold, I have two daughters who have not known man. Let me bring them out unto you, and do to them as ye please...'"

At Verity's expression, Charlize gave a small laugh and reached for her coffee.

"Pappa made me marry Corbus when I was eighteen. Oh, I was such a good girl then. Church every Sunday and twice during the week. Ma and I waited on Pappa and all his God-fearing friends, and Pappa offered me up to whichever of them got the handsiest. So many visitors to Pastor Johannes de Groot's *Gemeente van die Goeie Herder*, all of them apparently very taken with Genesis 19:8."

She rubbed finger against thumb in the universal sign for money.

Verity stared. "Why are you telling me all this?"

Charlize shrugged. "Because you're paid to listen when I feel like talking. And because after this safari I'll never see you again."

"I'm sorry this happened to you," Verity said, wishing all the while that she could simply get up and leave.

"I'd be a rich woman if sympathy could be traded for gold coins." Charlize's smile sharpened. "But one day I *will* be a rich woman. You'll see my picture splashed across the papers. No—across the respectable papers. And I won't be some beautiful Afrikaans prostitute you once looked down your nose at."

"I don't!" Verity protested. "Everything you've told me explains why you—"

"Ah, you might understand. But you don't respect me."

Verity swallowed. "I do, Charlize."

"Well, that's nice." Charlize rolled her eyes. "Corbus didn't respect me either, but do you think Pappa cared when I told him this was the man he wanted to force me to marry—a man who touched me where he ought not? No.

The marriage contract was arranged. What could I say? And Ma was no help either. Too frightened of Pappa. Though I'll give her this—she did try, in her way. Not enough to help me escape. Pappa would have beaten her if he'd guessed she was on my side."

"Oh, Charlize. I'm so sorry."

"I don't want your pity!" Charlize snapped. "Just be grateful not to have a husband who did to you what mine did to me."

An image of James rose at once in Verity's mind: his smile, his warmth, and his dependability.

Charlize touched her upper lip. "Beautiful new teeth, you see. After Corbus laid into me. Why? Because I burnt the dinner and lacked enthusiasm in the marriage bed. Three times he hit me, and after that I wasn't standing for any more." She gave a brittle little laugh. "So I packed a bag while he was asleep and jumped on the first train out. Didn't care where it was going. Long story short, I found someone who looked after me a lot better than Corbus and paid for my new teeth. But that didn't last. He had a friend who suggested this line of work. I've been an escort for four years."

"You're estranged from your family?"

"It's either that or be dead. My father would beat me senseless, first for shaming him and the man he sold me to, and then for doing what I do now to survive."

"And Corbus? Aren't you afraid he'll find you?" Verity asked. "You're so beautiful... you're hardly easy to miss."

"That's why I'd like Monaco. Or Monte Carlo. I don't want to spend the rest of my life looking over my shoulder."

"Do you have a plan? Are you saving?"

"A plan? Oh yes, I have a plan." Charlize winked. "I get paid well enough for this lark, and I don't have expenses. I can save. I was always good at that. So as soon as I've sent some boys to Bethulie to give Corbus what he deserves, I'm on the next plane out."

Then, with startling abruptness, she changed tack.

"And what do you think of our handsome hunter, Starky Willis?"

Her look was speculative, and to Verity's horror she felt herself blush. "He's a good hunter, I hear."

Charlize laughed. "I don't care whether he can hunt. I'm talking about what he's like in bed."

Verity gasped, and Charlize chuckled. "I was dying to see your face. So you don't know?"

"Of course not! I'm married!"

Charlize burst out laughing. "What's that got to do with anything? You're out here in the bush with the best-looking man in the Delta, and you're his hostess. What sort of husband lets his wife loose with a man like Starky?"

"My husband trusts me," Verity said, hearing the defensiveness in her own voice.

"Does he? And what about him? While the cat's away..."

"James is not like that. And neither am I."

Charlize shrugged. "Not everyone is what they seem. How do you know your husband doesn't cheat on you?"

Verity was momentarily speechless. "He just wouldn't. He's not that kind of man."

"How long have you two been together?"

"Fifteen years."

Charlize gave a low whistle. "Children?"

"One. She's fifteen."

"I see." Charlize rolled her eyes, and Verity said, more sharply than she intended, "That had nothing to do with it. We were going to marry anyway. We just had children a bit earlier than we'd planned."

"Looks like you managed to stay sweet. That's nice." Charlize's dazzling smile dimmed. "I'd like children. I won't have them though. What man sticks around and stays faithful through the hard bits?" She gave Verity a long look. "And I think you're fooling yourself. If Starky crooks his little finger, you should jump at it. I'll wager your husband hasn't turned down every offer that's come his way. What does he do?"

"He's a pilot," said Verity, just as she was about to hotly rebut everything Charlize had implied.

"A profession full of opportunities," Charlize said lazily. "Yes, I rather like the idea of hunting a pilot. Might get me to Monaco, if nothing else."

"You could always be an air hostess," Verity said, getting to her feet.

"I looked into it. They pay peanuts." Charlize shrugged. "Sorry—you've got to go. But you know where to find me if you ever want to ask what I know about men." Her lips twitched. "I could write an encyclopaedia on the subject. And I'm sorry if I offended you. I shouldn't have said that about your husband without meeting him first." She touched the side of her nose. "But I do have an instinct about men. I knew Corbus was rotten to the core, and I told my father so. But then, he was rotten to the core, too."

She seemed about to say more, but then turned at the sound of a vehicle roaring into camp. Almost at once a door slammed, and Kurt strode over, Starky just behind him. Thomas followed like a forlorn young lamb.

"Come, *Mäuschen*." Kurt put an arm around Charlize's shoulders. "Put on some clothes and get into the vehicle. You too, Verity. We are all going to watch Thomas make his first kill."

CHAPTER

TWENTY-FIVE

An uncomfortable churning in Verity's stomach made it hard to concentrate as they bumped across the veld, weaving between umbrella thorn trees and termite mounds.

She sat in the back on the raised bench seat, with Thomas's profile in front of her and Kurt and Charlize in the middle seat. Heat shimmered off the Land Cruiser's bonnet, blurring the horizon into a wavering mirage.

Thomas's shoulders were hunched. Kurt and Charlize chatted companionably, ignoring him except when Starky pointed out something of interest. A herd of springbok bounded across their path, kicking up dust in their wake.

Verity longed to shout, '*He doesn't want to kill a kudu. You do it*' at Kurt, or perhaps at Starky. But it seemed Thomas, despite being twenty-one, had no autonomy at all in the matter.

At last Starky braked, and they all climbed out into the scant shade of an acacia. Its hooked thorns cast delicate, spiteful shadows over the baked ground.

Before them stretched a wide expanse of yellow grass

and grey earth, the distant line of animals standing out against the shimmering plain. Impala grazed with their noses to the ground while others lifted their heads to scent the air. A few zebras stood not far off, their stripes wavering in the heat haze, and in the distance two giraffes raised their long necks against the washed-blue sky.

And a little closer stood the kudu—the reason they had come.

Verity stared at it and felt the same coldness spread through her veins that she imagined Thomas must feel too. Why this one? Why had they been summoned to witness Thomas shoot this kudu when there must surely have been any number of opportunities for the men to hunt before now?

Thomas stood slightly apart from his father, his arms rigid at his sides. But when Kurt handed him the rifle, to Verity's surprise, he took it.

"We're downwind, but stay quiet all the same," Kurt instructed. Clearly, this was familiar territory to him. He placed his hand over Thomas's and physically guided the barrel upwards. "See it? In the crosshairs?" he asked, winking at Charlize, who lounged against the vehicle with her blonde hair lit like pale fire in the sun.

Verity exchanged a look with Starky, who merely raised his eyebrows. He was keeping out of it. Kurt was the instructor here.

"Down a little. You want the heart. A clean kill. You can do it, son."

But what if he only wounded it?

Verity's nausea worsened. The thought of an amateur killing such a magnificent creature neatly with one shot seemed optimistic at best.

Another wave of sympathy for Thomas washed over her

as she watched him struggle to keep the gun steady, the sights trained on the kudu grazing quietly on the floodplain. A light breeze stirred the grass.

The resemblance between Kurt and Charlize did not escape her. Both possessed something predatory. A hunger that went beyond the hunt itself. Kurt wanted to force Thomas into his own image. Charlize, watching with that hooded, knowing gaze, seemed equally intent on reading where power lay and how best to attach herself to it. The hard African light sharpened every angle of their faces, highlighting their appetite for destruction.

Verity looked at Charlize and thought how she seemed not merely entertained by the prospect of the kill, but invested in it—because if Thomas pleased his father, or became more useful to him, then perhaps Charlize's own position with Kurt was strengthened too. The air itself seemed to crackle with tension.

The kudu stood there, magnificent and unknowing, its coat glowing softly in the late-afternoon light. Verity knew, in theory, that hunting concessions funded the preservation of this fragile ecosystem.

But that knowledge did nothing to ease her revulsion.

"Boom!"

She had turned her head away, unable to watch any longer, and the report made her start violently. Starky, standing beside her, thrust out an arm to steady her, but his quick grin turned almost at once into a grimace.

"Bloody hell."

The oath came from Charlize. The animal she had evidently assumed would drop neatly at one shot was now staggering to its feet, lurching drunkenly in circles while every other animal on the plain scattered in a storm of dust and alarm.

"Try again!"

Kurt snatched up the rifle Thomas had pushed away and thrust it back into his hands. "Finish the job this time!"

His voice was hard and ugly, and Verity quailed for Thomas.

For a second the boy stood absolutely still, staring at his father with naked hatred. Then, as if driven by something darker than obedience, he jerked up the rifle, dropped his eye to the sight, and fired again.

And again.

And again.

Each shot cracked across the savannah, obscene against the peace that had existed only seconds earlier.

"We're going to eat the bloody thing! No need to pepper it with shot!"

Kurt barked something else in German, and Thomas, who had been stiff with fury, suddenly seemed to collapse in on himself. He let the gun drop at his feet and stalked away. The sharp stench of gunpowder hung in the hot air.

"That didn't go very well," Verity whispered to Starky when he came within earshot. Kurt was still shouting at his son in German, so there was little danger of being over-heard. Charlize remained beside the vehicle, arms folded, her expression one of faint amusement, while Thomas had climbed into the Land Cruiser and was staring fixedly at the horizon, refusing to look at his father.

"It happens," Starky said with a shrug. "Kurt has quite a temper, hasn't he? You should have heard him laying into the boy when we came upon the first kudu he wanted him to shoot. Thomas swore he'd only kill one that was already injured, so when Kurt saw this old buck with a torn ear, Thomas had no comeback. Off we came to fetch the women so there'd be an audience while the tracker kept an eye on the animal." He grinned at Verity, then let that grin slide sideways to include Charlize, complete with a wink. "Oh well. Back to camp for something more exciting?"

"More exciting than this?" Charlize's husky voice drifted over on the warm air.

Verity blinked, caught off guard by the current that passed between them as they looked at each other, as if for those few seconds she were not there at all.

Kurt was still venting his anger in German, his whole attention fixed on his son, and Verity had the sudden, unpleasant sensation of being entirely outside the real business of the party. The words crashed through the stillness of the plain like blows.

The drive back to camp was quiet. Either Kurt had exhausted himself, or Thomas had made it plain he had stopped listening.

Verity tried to smile as they climbed out, pretending not to notice the tension thickening the air.

"I'll go and see how dinner is coming along," she said brightly, though her own voice sounded brittle to her ears.

But Kurt was calling to her, and Charlize was already walking away towards the tent. Verity could not immediately see Thomas—until Kurt barked his name again in that same sharp, guttural German and she realised Starky had handed over the vehicle keys, because father and son were now getting back into the Land Cruiser.

A wave of unease washed over her.

In the kitchen tent she busied herself with Florence, who was baking bread and making pepper sauce to go with steaks from a previous impala kill. The comforting aroma of fresh bread, which ordinarily would have had Verity breathing deeply in pleasure, did nothing for her now.

The skinners would still be out there somewhere, skinning and butchering the kudu for the next few meals.

After half an hour, Verity stepped out of the kitchen tent and scanned the horizon for the returning vehicle, but there was still no sign of it. The enormous plain stretched away, gilded now by the lowering sun.

Florence had laid the table. The waitresses were folding napkins and setting silverware while Philomen and Kutlo tended the fire. Verity felt almost absurdly unnecessary, yet busied herself straightening knives and forks.

Her thoughts drifted, as they so often did, to home. The distance between this life and the one she had led in Melbourne seemed immense and impossible to bridge.

Then, from far away, came the distant growl of a lion.

Verity lifted her head sharply, shading her eyes. A shiver ran down her spine. She remembered Kurt mentioning a lion the previous day before Starky had cut him off. Had she imagined the complicit look that had passed between them? The memory unsettled her all over again.

Lucy had been adamant that Starky had used up his lion trophy licences. So Starky could not possibly be planning to let Kurt shoot one.

Could he?

And yet she had heard Kurt mention a Kalahari lion more than once.

As she turned back towards the table, movement at the edge of her vision made her spin around.

Starky had just emerged from Kurt's tent.

The canvas rustled as he bent to secure the fly, and in that same instant Verity glimpsed Charlize's blonde head at about waist height inside the fading shadow of the tent.

For a second, the image refused to make sense.

Then Starky said something low, Charlize laughed, and

the sound carried on the still air. A moment later Charlize reached out and zipped up Starky's fly with a gesture so casual, so intimate, that shock rooted Verity where she stood.

The noises of the camp seemed to recede, swallowed by the violent pounding of her own heart.

She might have stayed there had Starky not looked up, caught her eye, and raised one eyebrow with a slow, provoking smile before turning towards his own tent a little way off.

Drawing in a sharp breath, Verity hurried after him. Her footsteps were muffled by the sandy ground. She caught him just before he disappeared inside, and the words came out before she had properly formed them.

"You and Charlize—"

He straightened from where he had bent to unzip his tent, and a lazy, predatory smile touched his mouth as he waited for her to continue.

But Verity had not prepared what to say. Outrage had propelled her this far, and now his supreme composure left her floundering. Her heart hammered.

Still, she had to say something.

"You were... with Charlize," she accused, her voice barely above a whisper.

"By mutual consent."

"But... that's not right."

"You feel left out?" There was a trace of mockery in his tone.

"Of course not!" Verity burst out, colour rushing to her face. "But Kurt is your client. He's paying for all this—" She flung out both arms, taking in the entire absurd luxury of camp against the savage beauty beyond. "And he's paying for Charlize. Aren't you worried what he'll do if he finds out?"

"Are you going to tell him?"

"Of course not."

"So, what's the trouble?" Starky shrugged, maddeningly unconcerned. "Kurt offered Thomas the opportunity. Charlize offered too, but Thomas wasn't interested. Charlize and I are free to do what we like provided no one gets hurt."

"But... it *does* hurt people." Verity heard her own voice crack.

"You're upset?"

"Not for the reasons you think," she shot back, though in truth his behaviour had disturbed her far more than she liked to admit. "It's just... wrong."

Starky planted his hands on his hips. "You're not the moral police, Verity. You're actually my employee, in case you've forgotten. I'm sure your own behaviour has not been entirely exemplary in every circumstance. Everyone's got a skeleton somewhere."

"Not men, if that's what you're implying. It's only ever been James." She was finding her footing now, propelled by anger. "But that isn't what I'm talking about. I mean morality. Common decency. Charlize is..."

Again those eyebrows lifted, then drew together just slightly.

"Charlize is...?" he prompted. "Go on. Put it into words. Tell me precisely what it is you think is so immoral."

Verity felt her mouth tremble. She wanted to say that sleeping with every woman in town while acting as though it were all nothing was immoral. But the words would not come.

He looked as though he might simply turn his back and go into the tent, so she blurted, "Do you care about right and wrong, Starky? About what's moral and immoral? I think it was wrong that Kurt forced Thomas to shoot that kudu when he didn't want to."

"Kurt is my client, and Thomas is his son. I've got no say in the matter."

"Nor do I. But I can still have an opinion." Her breath came fast now. "I'm paid not to voice it, but I'd like to know what *you* think. We're working together."

"And yet you seem perfectly happy to voice your opinion on what you consider my immoral behaviour," he said, neatly sidestepping her question.

"Is there nothing you'd consider beyond the pale?" she asked, moving slightly to block him as he seemed about to step away.

"I wouldn't kill my best friend, if that's what you want to know. And I've always been good to my mother. There." His face had hardened. "Does that satisfy you?"

TWENTY-SIX

Susan tapped the sandy ground impatiently with her bare-toed slip-ons as she stirred her coffee in the sun-dappled courtyard of the Duck Inn.

Every few minutes she glanced towards the road from Francistown, watching for a newcomer. Traffic was sparse, though she'd been told that soon the road from Maun would be fully tarred and life in the little frontier town would change for everyone.

Some people were fearful. Most were excited.

Susan was excited too, though for reasons very much her own.

At last, a battered Land Rover lurched over the rutted sand, trailing a plume of dust behind it. It pulled up outside the Duck, but its occupant did not immediately emerge. The engine ticked and clicked in the heat as it cooled.

Susan's heart began to hammer.

Could it be him?

Then a tall, rangy man with a shock of silver hair unfolded himself from the driver's seat and stood for a second, shielding his eyes against the white glare of the afternoon.

Susan caught his eye and stared.

Phil had once been dark, so surely—

"Susan?"

He blinked, peering at her uncertainly, and then his face broke into surprised recognition as he strode across the yard, his boots grinding into the grit.

"Wow. You haven't changed a bit."

"You have," Susan said with a laugh, nodding towards his hair.

He grinned. "Life's obviously been rougher on me. Prematurely grey at thirty-six."

"I bet women love it. Or perhaps all that stopped years ago and, unlike me, you've settled down."

"Still single," he said, lowering himself onto the low wall before taking the chair opposite and continuing to study her. "The job's murder on relationships. But wow. Fifteen years." He shook his head. "I never expected to see you again. And when you wrote, I didn't realise it was you. In my head, you're still Suze."

"I can't believe you came."

Susan glanced up as the waiter arrived and took his order, then watched him settle properly at the table. Only one other table was occupied, a family of tourists. She was glad of the empty space around them. She had hoped for this conversation in private.

"I'm not entirely sure why I did," Phil admitted. "You hinted you had something, and even though you were cryptic as hell, it was enough to make me pull up stumps and drive all the way from Gaborone." He swept a hand at the town beyond the courtyard. "This is prime hunting country, and in my opinion some of these concessions are not policed nearly as tightly as they should be. If someone is stepping outside the law, then yes—you came to the right person." He tapped his chest, then leaned in. "To be honest, I might have sent someone else if I'd known it was you." He frowned. "The memories of the last time I saw your brother are not easy to live with."

Susan, who had been about to speak, said nothing. He was going to talk about Mike. She had been starved for details for so long—shielded, silenced, then packed off out of Serowe—that there had never been the closure she needed. Perhaps Phil's memories could fill some of that terrible blank space.

"It was such a dreadful thing." To her surprise, he reached across the table and gripped her hand impulsively. "If I could turn the clock back, I would. We've all suffered for it."

"Not Starky," Susan shot back.

The force of her own bitterness startled even her, though not the jolt she felt at Phil's brief squeeze of her hand. She and her friends had laughed behind his back when he was a lanky, awkward teenager with a peeling nose and too much earnestness. He had been nothing like broad, easy Mike or handsome, cunning Starky.

But now, with that prematurely grey hair and the authority that came from doing difficult, dangerous work, he struck her very differently.

Yes, he was solid. Still earnest. And potentially invaluable.

He was her man.

"What do you mean?" he asked, his eyes narrowing.

"Starky was—"

"Hi, Susan. We're always bumping into each other. Don't you ever work?"

Susan looked up, irritation flashing across her face before she smoothed it into a smile and introduced her cousin, James.

"All the way from Australia?" Phil said, catching James's accent at once. His eyes flicked to the white pilot's shirt and stripes. "What brings you here? You don't look like you're on holiday."

"I fly for Okavango Air. Change of pace." James smiled. "It's good to come back to the country where I was born and be with family." He nodded towards Susan, who smiled too, hoping it looked natural enough.

Inside, she was seething.

She had been right on the edge of something important with Phil before James had wandered into the Duck at precisely the wrong moment.

"Philip's an old friend," Susan said, hearing the tightness in her own voice.

James might be kind and decent, but if he guessed this was the man she hoped would help bring Starky down, he might start trying to mediate. Or worse, get friendly with Phil and turn cautious and reasonable all over the whole thing. Men did that. They circled around one another, protected one another, made excuses for one another. She had seen enough of life to know.

James looked as if he might sit down and join them, but Susan had no intention of letting that happen.

Phil was here for her.

She glanced at her watch. "Hey, Phil, I've got to go and write a story about the local bookshop. Do you want to come along?"

He looked up, surprised, then gave a small shrug.

"Sorry, James," Susan said with a bright, brittle grin. "Some of us have got work to do."

James was lovely and kind, but he would not see this the way she did.

This was her cause.

And she did not want James's qualms muddying what had to be done.

She and Phil needed to talk through exactly what she was after when they were alone.

Perhaps over a quiet dinner at Safari South, where, if luck was finally with her, no one would interrupt.

TWENTY-SEVEN

Despite their well-known tendency to chatter, Saskia and Angie had been teamed up to do a project on famous explorers. It was due by the end of the week, but with only three days to go, precious little progress had been made on Burke and Wills or Sir Ernest Shackleton, and a great deal of progress had been made on a far more pressing personal project that had consumed them ever since Angie produced the latest letter from her mother.

How best to approach Starky with questions about Angie's father.

"Holidays aren't for ages. If we could just get to Maun before then," Angie moaned as they sat with their heads together over one book on the ill-fated Australian explorers Burke and Wills and another on the Antarctic explorer Sir Ernest Shackleton. They had not yet decided who most deserved their attention.

Not when there were so many more important matters to consider.

The library was quiet, and so their voices travelled

farther than they meant them to in the lofty room.

"I'm going to Maun this weekend."

Both girls froze.

Who had spoken?

Cathy Sterling—not a close friend but friendly enough —poked her head around the side of the cubicle beside them, where she had been studying with far more diligence than either of them. Blonde and blue-eyed, and one of those girls who always seemed to belong wherever she went, Cathy was popular enough that Saskia was surprised she had bothered to chime in at all.

"You can come too, if you want," Cathy said. "School's off for three days from Friday, so my folks thought we'd go up to the swamps. I'm not taking anyone with us into the Delta, but you're welcome to come for the ride to Maun and back. My brother Richard's just got a new Bonanza and can't wait to fly up."

Saskia smiled politely. "That's kind, but—"

Angie spoke straight over her.

"We'd love to. Thanks!" she said, with such enthusiasm that she dug Saskia sharply in the ribs under the table.

After a brief exchange about times and arrangements, Cathy withdrew, and the two girls retreated to the hush of their cubicles again.

Saskia leaned towards Angie with a frown. "Have you forgotten my mum's away on that overland with Starky? They're camped at Deception Pan in the desert. And Dad's probably away too. There's no point going to Maun this weekend if nobody's even there. Well—you can, I suppose, and see your mum."

Angie crinkled her nose. "No thanks. I'm not spending the weekend alone with my mum."

"What about before you came here?"

"Why do you think I kept running away until my grand-parents finally shoved me into this place?" Angie swept a hand around the beautiful wood-panelled room, all polished new money and generous alumni donations. "Mum has a thing for unsuitable men. That's what I heard Granny say. And her last unsuitable man got handsy with me, and I told Granny." Angie grinned. "I should have told her years ago."

Saskia gasped. "Oh, Angie. Nothing... nothing actually happened, did it?"

Angie snorted and held up her hands like claws, flexing her fingers. "I learned to take care of myself. Mum was useless at that sort of thing. At home, if we wanted anything half decent, Granny or I made it. Granny taught me to cook. Granny's wonderful. Mum...?" She gave a shrug. "I heard Granny say to Grampa she thought it was because my dad's a murderer and—"

To Saskia's surprise, Angie suddenly lost all her spark. It was as though someone had let the air out of her. She fell silent, swallowed hard, and looked away, clasping her hands together so tightly that her knuckles whitened.

"You can tell me, Ange." Saskia reached out and laid a hand over hers. She was not usually a girl given to touch, but the bleakness that had settled over Angie's face moved her in a way she couldn't ignore. Saskia knew what loneli-ness felt like. She had recognised something of herself in Angie from the start.

And maybe if Angie had been merely a friend and not blood—a real cousin, a kind of sister—Saskia might have let it lie. But part of loving someone, she thought, was knowing when they needed help carrying what they could not say aloud.

"What did you hear your granny tell your grandpa?" she asked softly.

Cathy and her study partner had gone. There was no one else in the library.

Then, to Saskia's growing alarm, she saw a fat tear slip down Angie's cheek.

Angie sucked in a breath and whispered brokenly, "She said she wouldn't be surprised if my dad had... had raped Mum. Because why else would she have come back from the hunting trip so changed? So shut down?"

"Oh, Angie."

Saskia had no idea what to say to something so dreadful. So she simply kept hold of Angie's wrist and squeezed it, hoping that would be enough for now.

After a moment, Angie straightened. She lifted her chin, blinked away the wetness in her eyes, and when she spoke again, her voice had sharpened.

"So all the better to find out what I need to know by catching Starky by surprise."

"But Starky's on safari."

"Yes, you said." Angie gave Saskia a smile that suggested the objection was barely worth answering. "He's at Deception Pan, which Richard will be flying over on the way to Maun—except that I'll get him to drop us at the landing strip there."

"How do you know there's a landing strip?"

"Mum used to camp there when she was a kid. It's flat as a table around there, so there has to be somewhere a plane can land, and Richard will want to impress us."

"Have you even met him?"

"No." Angie winked. "But he's eighteen and Mummy and Daddy have bought him a plane. Of course he'll want to show off. He can drop us at Deception Pan for a couple of hours while we catch Starky off guard, and then pick us up again on the way back." Her smile broadened as she leaned back in her chair. "Mum always thought she knew how to get away with things without being caught, but believe me, I'm far better at that than she is." She wrapped a smoky dark curl around one finger and batted her eyelashes. "I'll get Richard to fly us exactly where we need to go, and I'll get Starky to talk."

Saskia swallowed. Suddenly this no longer sounded exciting, so much as alarming.

"But he'll be on safari with rich clients. He might not exactly welcome two schoolgirls arriving without warning." For all her closeness with Angie, Saskia was beginning to realise that they understood the world very differently. Saskia was rebellious, but she ultimately toed the line. Angie, by contrast, seemed to view rules as merely obstacles to be sidestepped.

"Starky loves you," Angie said, spreading her hands dramatically. Then, with a thoughtful frown, she corrected herself. "Well—at the very least, he feels terribly guilty because you nearly died on his watch, and a truly competent guide would never have let that happen."

"That's not true! Starky's a hero!" Saskia shot back hotly.

But Angie only held up her hands again, one of her wicked grins returning.

"It doesn't matter what's true. We'll use whichever version works best, depending on how he reacts to us dropping in." Then she leaned forward, her face alight with excitement. "Because this weekend is my perfect chance to learn everything I need to know from the one person who was there. Flying up with Cathy's brother and catching Starky by surprise so he spills everything about my father and what happened on that hunting trip is going to be brilliant."

"But what about permission?" Saskia asked, at last catching up with the sheer audacity of the plan. Angie's mother, by the sound of things, might not be overly concerned, but Saskia knew very well that her own parents would be horrified.

"Don't you worry." Angie leaned over the desk and patted Saskia's shoulder in a mockingly soothing way that did not soothe her in the least. "I'll make sure I've got everything covered. They won't know a thing."

And the way she said it—with such confidence, such relish—made Saskia realise with a tiny chill that, impossible or not, Angie fully intended to do exactly as she pleased.

CHAPTER

TWENTY-EIGHT

Susan was more in her element by the time the sun was over the yardarm and she and Phil had reconvened at Safari South, where music drifted in the background and the wine was being poured.

"So," she said, offering him a cigarette, "do you want to hear what I know? And what I suspect?"

"Fire away. And I don't smoke," said Phil.

"You don't mind if I do?" Susan asked, remembering that she'd thought Phil a little priggish when they were teenagers. But if his looks had changed so dramatically, perhaps other things had too. He certainly enjoyed a drink now, though he hadn't even had a Castle lager back on that disastrous camping trip fifteen years before.

"You can do whatever you want," Phil said with a shrug. "I'm not your keeper. But you summoned me here because you hinted at something 'big'—an operation you thought was about to stray into illegal territory. That's what you wrote when I didn't even know who you were. Now you tell me the man involved is Starky. So?" He leaned back and laced his hands over his stomach. Susan couldn't help noticing how lean and taut he'd become. No trace now of the stripling boy he'd once been. "What exactly do you want me to do?"

"You mean… you'll do it?" Susan felt her mouth stretch into a smile as she leaned forward. "You'll go after Starky?"

Phil gave her a laconic grin. "Did I say that? Go after Starky? Of course I won't. Starky's my friend, remember?"

"Is he really, though?" Susan shot back. "And surely you wouldn't let him get away with illegally shooting a lion just so he can pocket dirty profits from his rich German clients?"

Phil blinked. "You think that's what he's going to do?"

"I'm sure of it. Well—almost. When I saw your name and what you do, I thought you'd have every reason to back me up."

Phil took his time over that. "Wow, Suze. For someone who wasn't exactly averse to Starky's attentions all those years ago, you've certainly got it in for him now."

Susan glowered. "He's got away with too much. It's time for justice."

"And what do you want justice for, exactly?" Phil lifted his brows. "What did he supposedly get away with?"

"I'll get to that," Susan said. "Right now, I'm concerned about an illegal hunt. A crime, I have it on good authority, he's about to commit."

"Poaching?"

"He's going to let a client shoot a lion when he has no hunting permit for it."

Phil took a sip of beer and carefully set the bottle back down. "And when is this supposed to happen?"

"They're on safari right now."

"Then it might already be too late to do anything."

"Why?" Susan jerked forward. This was not what she had wanted to hear. Or expected. "You say Starky's your friend—but he's not. You didn't even like each other fifteen years ago. I'd bet you haven't laid eyes on him since then. I'm asking you to catch him in the act of poaching a lion. Isn't that your job?"

"Steady on," said Phil mildly. "I was only able to come here because I was passing through on the way to start my holiday. I don't have the resources to pull men off another operation on a hunch."

"But you could do it," Susan cried.

Phil was silent for a moment, studying her. "You hate him that much?" he asked at last. "What did he do to you?"

"He killed Mike. You know he did. You must." The words came out ragged. "But did he ever pay the price? No, everyone blamed Jeremy because Jeremy was convenient. A perfect scapegoat. Especially once he died the day after he was thrown in gaol."

"How do you know Starky did it?" Phil asked, his face unreadable. "Mike's body was found half mauled by a lion—"

"Yes, but you know the coroner ruled it murder because of the gunshot wound, and Starky—" She broke off, lit one cigarette from the dying end of another, and cursed the tremor in her hand. "I might not have learned the findings until much later, but I knew things about what really happened that no one ever bothered asking an eighteen-year-old girl."

"He could have shot himself, and the lion got to him later."

Susan stared at him. "You know he didn't. You all went out hunting together. That's ridiculous. And how can you sound so cold when it's my brother you're talking about?" Her voice thickened. "You have no idea how determined I am to get to the bottom of this. For fifteen years I've had to keep my mouth shut. And all because of Starky. He ruined my life. I was complicit in letting him off the hook by not speaking up when I should have—by not telling the authorities that Starky had the same gun as Jeremy. The same gun, with the same kind of bullet, that killed Mike." Her hand moved unconsciously to her belly. How bitterly ironic that part of the reason she had stayed silent was to protect the unborn child she already half suspected might be Starky's. "At the time, I didn't realise I was protecting my brother's murderer."

She sucked in a shaking breath. "Well, I'm not going to be a dormouse or a liar any longer. I'm going to do whatever it takes to make Starky admit with his own lips that he killed my brother that awful day, and that it wasn't Jeremy, like everyone said."

Phil wrapped his fingers around his beer and raised his brows. "Jeremy was convicted on sound evidence." Then, unexpectedly, he smiled. "You certainly have more fire than I remember, Suze. Or does no one call you that these days?"

A rush of feeling swept through Susan at the nickname. And at his composure. That had been Phil even then: always observing, rarely giving much away. Yet life had done something to him. Toughened him, sharpened him. Perhaps she'd been wrong about him all those years.

"Not anymore. I've grown up a lot since you last saw me," she murmured.

"You have."

She stared at the hand he had laid on her wrist. And left there. What was it—comfort? Interest? Something more? She was so used to reading men quickly that she was almost thrown when he merely gave her a steadying squeeze and said, "Getting upset rarely helps your cause,

Suze. I can see how much emotion is driving you right now. So let me suggest something."

She blinked at him, hope plain on her face.

"I'm on leave for two weeks, and although I was on my way to visit a friend, I can spare a few days to do what you've asked."

"You'd do that?"

"Mike was my friend, too."

"And do you know what happened? Like—did you see Starky pull the trigger? Would you testify?" She was trembling so much now she could barely form the words.

Phil frowned. "Testify? Suze, a minute ago we were talking about catching someone in the act of poaching a lion. That I can do. That is my job. But testify? Where? On what basis? Surely you don't imagine you can reopen a case that was closed fifteen years ago. Concrete evidence convicted your ex-boyfriend, in case you've forgotten."

Susan wiped the back of her hand over her wet lashes, guilt needling at her afresh. She was glad Phil had not pressed too hard on why she wanted the old evidence overturned.

"You're right," she said. "I know I can't reopen it. The only way I can make Starky pay is by having him caught red-handed as a poacher. That will ruin him." Then she drew breath. "But please—tell me what you know about the last day of the hunt. Mike and Starky got into a fight. What was it about? You were there." She leaned in, hoping perhaps to wrong-foot him. "Did you see Starky pull the trigger out there in the bush?"

When he said nothing, she pressed harder. "Or did you only hear the gunshot, and that's why you stayed quiet and let everyone assume Jeremy was the murderer?"

Phil let out a long breath. "Wow, Suze. That's a hell of

an accusation from someone who wasn't there and had nothing to do with the investigation. If you thought Jeremy was innocent, why didn't you say something then?"

Susan covered her face with both hands. The guilt was like acid. She had stayed silent for so many reasons, and every one of them had turned rotten in hindsight. Shame kept her quiet now.

"Suze," Phil said more gently, "I don't know who fired the shot. Maybe Jeremy did come back—"

"But Mike and Starky fought. I know they did because I heard them arguing that morning. And Starky had a cut over his eye when he came back from the hunt." She swallowed. "What were they fighting about? Was it a diamond?"

Phil blinked. "A diamond? No, they were fighting over you."

Susan's eyes widened. "Starky wouldn't have killed Mike for that."

"Mike was defending your honour, Suze." Phil's voice had turned low, almost tender. His hand was still on her wrist. He seemed to weigh something, then added, "And yes. There was the diamond too." After a pause, he asked quietly, "What did you hear about the diamond?"

"Only the word itself. A couple of times. I was in my tent and I heard Mike and Starky arguing before breakfast." She studied him carefully, needing to know he believed her —or was at least listening properly. "Mike had found one somewhere. I don't know where, but I think he'd promised to show Starky the place. Later, when I kept trying to work out how Starky got the money to pay for his flying licence and secure such a large hunting concession so quickly, it seemed obvious. He cashed in on my brother's diamond after Mike died. After he killed him."

Slowly, Phil ran the tip of one finger over the inside of her wrist, making her shiver despite herself. He appeared to be thinking hard.

"Have you ever put any of this to Starky?"

Susan gave a bitter shrug. "I wrote. I phoned. And when I finally saw him a few days ago, I tried to get him to talk, but he…" She gave a short, ugly laugh. "He pretty much brushed me off. That's how I know he's guilty. All the little things add up."

"So now you want him to pay for what he did to your brother. For supposedly killing Mike—though you have no proof—and then denying you what would, in a sense, have been yours if he stole Mike's diamond?"

Susan leaned forward sharply. "So Mike *did* have a diamond?"

Phil paused. "He did. That doesn't prove Starky took it."

"He must have. Otherwise Mum and Dad would have got it back with Mike's things!" Susan cried. "Do you think Starky killed him for it? Do you think he used me as the excuse for a fight, so he could fire his gun and later claim self-defence?"

"Suze, this is wild. Calm down." Phil caught both her hands in his and leaned towards her. "You weren't there, and I didn't see what happened. I've already told you there is no evidence after all this time to reopen your brother's murder. But I also told you that if there is credible evidence Starky is about to poach a lion, then I'll do what can be done to catch him."

"Yes. That would satisfy me." Susan gripped his hands as if they were the only solid thing in the room. "You'll go to Deception Pan as soon as you can? They're only halfway through a ten-day safari. You could catch him in the act.

I've read about you in the paper. You're good at this. You'll get Starky for me, won't you?"

Phil squeezed her hands, then rose, glancing at his watch. He cupped her cheek for a brief second before letting it go.

"If he hasn't already killed the lion, I'll do what I can."

"So you'll go to Deception Pan tomorrow?"

"There's a fair bit to put in place first. Logistics. Transport. I'll need a decent tracker too."

"My cousin James could fly you. I'm sure he would. He'd want justice for Mike, and he works for Okavango Air. He could make a supply stop. Maybe someone's due to take things into camp, anyway."

Phil raked a hand through his hair. "How long did you say they were staying at Deception Pan?"

"Another week or so." Susan clasped her hands together to stop them shaking. She felt almost giddy with relief. "I can't believe you'd really do this for me, Phil. Get Starky the comeuppance he's dodged for fifteen years."

"I head a unit of integrity and I do not use my position for vengeance, Suze," said Phil. "But I *will* investigate this suspected lion poaching, not as a favour to you, but because it's my job." He gave a dry laugh. "Even if I'd much rather be enjoying my holiday in Hermanus."

Susan could not sleep that night. She lay in her cottage with the ceiling fan pushing the hot Maun air around without cooling it, and sleep would not come.

Not with memories of that night fifteen years ago pressing in, as vivid as the day they happened.

Even with her eyes shut, she could recall every breath, every sound, every beat of her heart.

The canvas of her tent had glowed silver in the moonlight. That she remembered clearly.

She had been trembling—from nerves, from desire, from the forbidden thrill of doing something she knew would infuriate Mike if he discovered it.

"Hey."

Starky's whisper had been warm against her ear as he slipped into her sleeping bag.

"You're sure about this?"

She had never been more sure of anything. She had loved him for three years, watching him over the tops of her schoolbooks whenever he came to see Mike. Watching the way he moved, the way he smiled, the way girls brighter and prettier than she was tilted towards him like flowers towards the sun.

But he had never once looked at her that way.

Not until that evening, when she caught him watching her across the campfire.

"I've been waiting," she whispered back, her heart pounding so loudly she was certain the whole camp must hear it. "For you to notice me."

His laugh had been soft, almost gentle. So unlike his usual easy swagger.

"I noticed. Believe me, I noticed. But Mike would have killed me for looking at his baby sister that way."

"I'm not a baby." She had pressed closer in the darkness, suddenly reckless. "I'm eighteen."

"No." His hands had moved over her skin, leaving sparks behind them. "You're definitely not a baby."

The memory of that touch still burned.

She had been so naïve. So certain it meant something. That she meant something.

"When we get back to Serowe..." He had traced idle patterns over her bare shoulder. "Maybe we could see each other properly. Not just sneaking around."

"Really?" She had lifted herself on one elbow to look at him, moonlight silvering his face. "You'd want that?"

"Why wouldn't I?" He had kissed her then, slow and deep. "You're beautiful, Suze. And smart. And brave." Another kiss. "I've been fighting this for months."

She had melted into him, believing every word. Believing in the future he seemed to be offering—cinema dates, hands held in public, a life in which she was more than Mike's little sister.

"I think I'm in love with you," she had whispered against his mouth.

He had not said it back.

She saw that now. He had simply kissed her harder instead of answering.

Later, when he held her against him and his heartbeat slowed under her cheek, he had murmured, "No regrets?"

"Never," she had promised.

Then everything had changed.

Mike was dead. Jeremy was in gaol. And Starky—

Starky had not even returned her calls.

Susan rolled onto her side and pressed her face into the pillow. Fifteen years later, and it still hurt. The betrayal. The silence. The ease with which he had let another man shoulder the blame while her whole life collapsed around her.

She had been so young. So foolish. So certain that love meant something.

Now she knew better.

Love was only another weapon. And it cut both ways.

Let Starky think she had forgotten.

Let him think the past was buried.

She had Phil now. Phil, who understood duty, consequences, and how to hunt down men who thought they were untouchable.

Outside, a nightjar called—the same sound she remembered from that long-ago safari. She closed her eyes, but still sleep would not come.

Some memories did not fade.

Some waited in the dark, patient as predators, until at last they had the chance to strike.

CHAPTER
TWENTY-NINE

"Got everything?" Rob rolled down the window and called to James from the Land Cruiser idling by the gate. "Booze? Books?"

"Books! I nearly forgot!"

James dumped his backpack on the front step and ran back inside the cottage. Leaning across the bed, he snatched up Verity's Wilbur Smith novel from her bedside table, spun round, and strode back through the living room—only to catch his foot on the doormat and send the book skidding across the polished concrete floor.

Outside, Rob beeped the horn.

Cursing under his breath, James bent to retrieve it, a sheet of paper fluttering loose behind him.

Verity's bookmark, he thought at first.

But no.

A letter.

He stooped to pick it up, and the opening line caught his eye before he could help himself.

I am so unhappy...

James stopped dead.

His eyes dropped helplessly to the next lines.

I feel like a fish out of water and I can't expect James to under-stand. Carrie Dunbar contacted me again to ask if there was any chance I'd be back within six months, as she's holding my job open, and you know... I want that more than anything. But how do I tell James?

He stared at the words.

For one strange, suspended second, the cottage seemed to hold its breath with him.

Outside, Rob called, "James? Are you coming? I've got passengers to pick up!"

"Coming."

Swallowing hard against the tightness in his throat, James slipped the letter back between the pages of the book, then strode out to the vehicle with a smile so forced it hurt his face.

TWENTY MINUTES later the plane lifted off, leaving the dusty village behind and heading out over the Boro River, which shone below them like a glinting snake threading its way through the flat green country.

Some people called the Okavango a swamp or a marsh, but it was a world unlike any other, forever changing. At this time of year the waters were at their lowest. The flood, born of rain in the Angolan highlands, took months to work its way south, reaching the northern Delta around May, bringing nutrients and life and turning dry country into a glittering web of wetlands full of game.

James stared out of the window and tried to lose himself in the immense beauty of it—the flood inching and spreading through the waterways like a slow pulse from the air.

"I bet you can't wait to see Verity again," Rob shouted over the engine noise. "Unexpected trip and all."

James nodded and tried to smile.

Ordinarily, that would have been true. But now the thought of seeing Verity again made him feel hollow.

He would have to tackle her about the letter.

She would know he had seen it. Obviously he'd put the bookmark in the wrong page.

How was that conversation supposed to go?

In fifteen years together, they had been almost inseparable. They had got on as they always had—first as best friends, then as lovers, then as husband and wife. But lately he had become increasingly aware of something wearing thin between them, something once effortless and alive.

Her last goodbye had been lukewarm.

So this was why? She truly hated this new life into which he had thrust her?

For weeks she'd been floundering, and he hadn't seen it, so enthused had he been by the daily awe that flooded him as he flew above the spectacular Okavango Delta.

But Verity was confined to dusty, utilitarian Maun. He'd robbed her of her career. He'd kiboshed her chance at a job on the *Okavango Observer*, effectively handing it to Susan, though he'd done so unconsciously.

Briefly, he closed his eyes. Uprooting the girls so thoroughly from home—friends and family—had been done in the name of honour and principle.

That's how he'd explained it to himself. To them. It sounded noble, couched in those terms.

But if extinguishing Verity's optimism and enthusiasm meant a breakdown in their marriage—would it have been worth it?

He stared grimly at the vastness through the windshield. *No, it certainly would not.*

"Oh, and I saw your cousin this morning," Rob added. "Susan. Nice girl."

"Yes," said James, with another tight smile.

Earlier that day, Susan had waylaid him in town and been fizzing with excitement over something she refused to name. Of course, almost immediately she had hinted that she had found the perfect plan to nail Starky.

Looking back, James wondered if she had been drinking. There had been a dangerous brightness in her eyes and the faintest pause after each carefully chosen sentence, as though she was working very hard to sound steadier than she felt.

He would not have put it past Susan to manufacture mystery where none existed. That, he was coming to see, was part of her style.

"I hear you and Lucy are getting married. Congratulations," he said, more to change the subject than anything else.

Through the crackle of the headset, Rob's grin came through in his voice. Lucy and Rob's courtship had been a whirlwind, and Rob's mad romantic gesture—arriving in his microlight to spirit Lucy away from camp before she flew home under the watchful eye of the boyfriend, or ex-boyfriend, who had been trying to reclaim her—was already becoming Delta legend.

James felt a sudden, irrational pang of envy.

Was that what Verity wanted? A hero? Not the dependable husband she had married fifteen years ago, but someone dramatic, noble, and charismatic?

After some more talk of the wedding, Rob landed at the strip outside Xakanaxa camp, where Jane and Derek were waiting, and then James took the controls, nosing the little plane towards the sun, his heart beginning to pound as they neared their destination.

He would have to come in low to find the rough airstrip at Deception Pan.

But it was easier than expected, because the game vehicle was already parked there, acting as a beacon after having driven the game away from the area.

When James greeted his wife a few minutes later, he was glad to find her alone.

She did not leap out to hug him.

Instead, she smiled and offered him her cheek when he climbed into the passenger seat, while the young local lad she had brought along jumped down to unload the boxes from the luggage pod and carry them to the back of the vehicle.

"So good that you got to do this drop-off, James." Her smile was warm enough, but when he reached for her hand, she pretended to brush hair from her face before settling both hands on the steering wheel.

"What have you enjoyed most?" he asked.

"The sunrises and sunsets."

James studied her covertly, trying to work out what had shifted.

She looked just the same. More than that—she looked lovely. Her dark-blonde hair was tied back in a ponytail; her skin and eyes were bright; she looked years younger than thirty-five. Yet she was speaking to him as if he were someone merely familiar in her life.

Not the man she loved.

"What's Starky like to work for?" he asked. "And how are the clients? I heard some speculation that the woman isn't the boy's mother but some sort of trophy second wife. Though I suppose at least, it's nice to have another woman there."

Verity gave a short laugh. "Wife? He picked her up at Sun City just before they got here. A Bophuthatswana prostitute. She's beautiful, but as calculating as they come. No, we don't have much in common."

James grinned, though unease was tightening in his chest. "And Starky?"

He was almost sure she stiffened. There was the smallest pause before she answered, too smoothly. "As you'd expect. Now—shall we drive back to camp? I'm sure you'd like something cold before you head off again."

James frowned. "That sounds awfully businesslike, Verity."

This time he set his hand on her thigh, and she turned towards him.

"I thought you might be a little more pleased to see me. I didn't get more than the quickest peck on the lips."

"I *am* pleased to see you," she said, and tried to brush it off with a laugh that didn't reach her eyes. "But I'm working and you're working. You didn't expect grand passion in the bush, did you?"

"There hasn't been much grand passion for a while, so no, I didn't."

He knew there was a stiffness in his voice, and the look she sent him was more defensive than sorry.

"I'm sorry you feel that way, James," she said, shifting the Land Cruiser into gear. "There's been so much change, and I suppose there were other priorities. Have you heard from Saskia?"

James sighed. "No. She'll be on holidays in a few weeks, and then she and Angie are travelling up together."

"So nice that they found each other. I wonder if Angie is anything like her mother."

"I wonder," James murmured, staring ahead.

After a few moments' silence, as they bumped over the sandy hummocks, he tried again.

"Any hint of trouble in paradise? Rob mentioned the reason Lucy pulled out of hostessing for this overland. She was worried by rumours that Starky intended to sanction an illegal lion kill." He frowned. "I don't want you mixed up in something like that."

"It's fine, James." There was real irritation in her voice now. "I haven't seen or heard anything to suggest that this isn't above board. The men have shot a kudu and a few other things for the pot."

"I doubt they've come all this way just to hunt for the pot. They'll want something impressive to take back to Germany and hang on a wall. A kudu isn't going to cut it."

"They're looking for a leopard. That's what Starky says. You know they speak German. Starky knows a bit, and sometimes they talk in front of me so I can't follow everything."

James's unease deepened. "On purpose? So their real intentions aren't obvious to you?"

"Oh, James." She let out a breath of exasperation. "Why did you even agree to let me come if you were going to start down the conspiracy path?"

"Because you were bored and fed up in Maun, and I wasn't about to stop you when you, quite understandably, wanted some adventure. I only heard the lion rumours after you'd already agreed to come. Don't blame me for worrying about you."

"I'm not blaming you for anything," Verity said, her voice tightening. "You had your reasons for leaving Ansett. Reasons important enough to uproot all of us... and I'm trying to make the best of it. Look how lucky I am." She waved one hand at the scrub and open sky around them. "I'm on safari in Africa. Everyone back home would envy me. Don't get cross with me again, James. I'm doing my best."

He wanted to keep going. There was so much still unsaid. He needed to ask about the letter. About Carrie. About what Verity truly wanted.

But by then they were back in camp, and Starky was already striding towards them, smiling, handsome, entirely at home in this place.

With a sharp little jolt, James wondered whether the man's easy charisma really *could* be having an effect on Verity. They had both laughed at the idea before she left Maun. Yet out here, in this isolation, with a husband who suddenly felt dull and overfamiliar even to himself, James could not help wondering.

"Where's the Krug?"

James looked over Starky's shoulder towards the statuesque blonde who had asked the question. So this was the call girl the Germans had picked up.

"Hi James. Good flight?" said Starky, with that easy manner that was beginning to grate. "This is Charlize, Kurt Heinrich's companion. Apparently the only champagne worth drinking is Krug, which I discovered after making the mistake of ordering mostly Moët." He grinned as James and Verity climbed out and followed him towards the circle of chairs by the fire. "You do realise the only real reason you were asked to come was for this. Didn't desperately need anything else. But we do what we can to please the ladies, eh?"

James blinked. Charlize and Starky looked very... companionable.

Then a much older man with greying hair, a reddened face and a military way of carrying himself strode towards them, followed by a thin, unhappy-looking boy, and James stopped wondering why Verity had not seemed exactly transported by the company.

The tension in the air was almost palpable.

"You're this young lady's husband, I hear. Pleased to meet you," Kurt said, thrusting out a hand without smiling. "Verity has done an excellent job catering to all our needs and keeping my dear Charlize company."

He laid a heavy hand on Charlize's shoulder.

She gave a little laugh and nuzzled his fingers. "Verity is very... entertaining," she said in her thick Afrikaans accent. "She has told me all about you, James."

She sent Verity a look so knowing it was almost a taunt, as though she had spent the past days being confided in intimately.

Then Starky was calling for Kutlo to bring champagne glasses and biltong. "Better than beef jerky, eh?" he said, easing himself back against the canvas chair with an air of complete contentment as he chewed a strip of dried meat.

"Good biltong," James said shortly.

Thomas looked up. "Is it from the impala my dad shot a couple of days ago?"

Starky laughed. "No, not from any of the game taken on this trip. It takes weeks to dry properly while staying moist. Fine art, that. My mother did it better than anyone."

"And what trophies are you here to hunt?" James asked, unable to keep the edge from his voice.

"My father wants to hunt a lion," Thomas said slowly, shooting an uncertain glance at Kurt.

But Starky cut in at once.

"We're looking for a leopard. Saw one today, in fact, which was lucky in itself. Damned difficult to spot, let alone shoot. But we'll find one." Then, with maddening smoothness, he shifted the subject. "And what are you going to do with yourself in Maun without your lovely wife?"

James flicked a glance at Verity, then back to Starky. He hated leaving her here.

"My cousin Susan's recently arrived in Maun. She's having birthday drinks at Croc Camp." He hesitated, holding Starky's gaze. "You remember Susan Jensen, don't you?"

Starky nodded. "It's been a long time, but of course I do. She was with us on that awful expedition where her brother was killed. Girl was barely out of school." He smiled. "Had the most tremendous crush on me, if I remember rightly. So how is she? I barely had time to say two words when I bumped into her the other day."

"She's fine. And she hasn't forgotten you," James said.

He meant the words to carry more than they could safely say in company. What else *could* he say here? He wondered suddenly whether he ought to say something to Verity on the drive back. Or would that only further burden her when, really, it should be Susan who confronted Starky over both the paternity and the old accusations?

"Well, I *am* rather unforgettable," Starky said with that glib smile, beckoning Florence over to top up the ladies' glasses. "Another Coke, James? You'll want to slake your thirst before you head back up. Can't stay long, I suppose."

"No. You're right." James checked his watch and stood. He glanced at Verity, who rose and reached for the keys to the Land Cruiser where they lay on an upturned log.

"Sorry to see me go so soon?" he asked as they drove back to the strip, the silence between them tight as wire.

"A bit of moral support might have been nice." Verity's smile was wry. "You do know Charlize was lying when she hinted that I'd bared my heart and soul to her."

"Of course I do." He was quiet for a while, then said, "Though it would be nice if you'd do that with me, once in a while."

"What do you mean?"

"You can be a closed book sometimes."

"I just don't have as many wins to record as you."

"So competitive," he said, letting out a breath. "And I don't feel I've got all that many wins to record these days. Still, it's an adventure. And you're having an adventure too."

"If you can call pandering to a group of vain, rich, arrogant men—and a vain, social-climbing prostitute—an adventure." She gave a sudden grin. "I suppose I am learning how the other half live. The rich ones like Kurt, and the women they can afford to buy. I'm right there in the middle, observing. It's a bit voyeuristic."

"You? Miss Goody Two-Shoes?" James pinched her cheek lightly. "Just come back safe and sound... and, ideally, wanting to turn your adventurous, voyeuristic eye towards me."

"I suppose we all have different ideas about what adventure really is." She smiled as she brought the vehicle to a stop, then let him kiss her.

No arms around his neck. No lingering softness. The distance between them felt vast.

"Verity... we *are* all right, aren't we?" He had to ask.

"Of course we are," she said at once.

As if he were a dear friend.

Not as if he were a lover. Or a husband whose heart was in his mouth.

With a sigh, he picked up the Wilbur Smith novel from the glove box and handed it to her. "I nearly forgot. I brought you this. It was on your bedside table."

As she reached for it, he saw the flicker of uncertainty she could not quite hide.

And when he held her gaze, her eyelids fluttered, and her lips pressed together. For a second the book hung between them, one edge in each of their hands.

Then James let go.

He opened the door and stepped down onto the dust.

"Be safe, Verity," he said. "Be happy."

He took a couple of steps back, one hand lifted to shade his eyes as he looked at her.

"When all's said and done, you know I wouldn't hold you back from doing what's best for you." He gave her a smile that cost him. "From having the kind of adventure you really want."

THIRTY

Susan was feeling drunk with success by the time her party really began to gather momentum. It was standing room only at the bar at Croc Camp, balloons and streamers looped from the beams while tinny music blasted from a boom box perched beside the Sambuca.

She had been in Maun barely a month, and already she had friends. Loads of them. Friends who had made sure her birthday would be one to remember, and who were now knocking back beers and bourbons and whisky and wine while the whole place throbbed with heat, noise and laughter.

"You were passing through town at exactly the right time, weren't you?" she shouted over the music to Phil as she gyrated on the dance floor.

He sat on a bar stool, watching her—or rather, watching everything, as was more his style—with a beer in hand and a half-smile playing about his lips.

"Wow, Suze, you've turned out even wilder than I

thought you would," he shouted back. "Quite the firebrand."

"And you're less boring than I thought you'd be, getting to know you," Susan grinned, draping herself over him.

They had spent the afternoon together after meeting at the Duck and doing a little shopping before coffee at Riley's, where Phil was staying. He had told her about his work, about the breakup with his girlfriend of five years, and about his love of animals.

"And you *love* lions, don't you?" Susan had pressed. "You're not going to let Starky get away with shooting a magnificent lion, are you?"

Phil had merely laid his hand on her arm and said that he had already promised to do what time and resources permitted. Then he had changed the subject.

But he had left his hand where it was for a good while longer, and Susan had not failed to notice the intimacy of that.

Now, squinting at him through the dimness of the bar while she swayed to Boney M, she thought that really, Phil was far cuter than she had ever given him credit for. She liked that he had called her a firebrand. Too many men in her life had treated that as a flaw. The moment she showed feeling, or hunger, or ambition, they either took fright or took advantage.

But Phil had said it as though it were something admirable.

"Another drink?" he asked a few minutes later while *Sugar Man* was playing. He had to shout above the crush of voices. A truckload of backpackers had come into town and discovered Croc Camp, and suddenly the place was heaving, the atmosphere humming.

Susan wiped the sweat from her forehead, pushed her

damp dark curls behind her ears, and fanned the front of her white blouse. "What a sight I must look," she gasped.

But Phil only raised his eyebrows and gave her an appreciative look.

"I think you look great."

"Do you?" She bit her lip and shot him a teasing glance. "Then maybe you should take me home."

"Maybe I should."

His hand skimmed from her shoulder to her waist, then briefly shaped itself to the curve of her backside.

A dart of desire went straight through her. She sucked in a breath, then slid her hand into the crook of his arm.

"Lead the way."

They were both a little drunk, but Susan didn't care. Drink made it easier not to think about life's injustices, or how men always seemed to come into her life, kindle hope, and then disappear the instant she let herself feel attached. She was not going to think long-term with Phil. She wanted him. And if sleeping with him also helped shore up his willingness to bring Starky to account, then all the better.

They stumbled into the main room of her thatched cottage, laughing and fumbling at one another, hands everywhere. Or perhaps it was only Susan laughing. She felt intoxicated less by vodka than by momentum. By opportunity.

What a coup.

Phil could answer her questions—but not, she suspected, without the right encouragement. He had always been a cool customer. Still was. But he had thawed tonight, and although he had already said he would do what he could, Susan felt she needed to seal the advantage.

"Come here," she slurred, unbuttoning her blouse as

she fell back onto the bed and dragged him down with her. "Show me what you couldn't fifteen years ago."

"You were not old enough fifteen years ago," he said, his breath hot against her ear.

"Well, you might have been alone in thinking that." Susan hiccuped, then reached for the waistband of his shorts. "Now let's get this gear off you, hey?"

She fumbled with his fly while he nuzzled her neck, heavy on top of her. She wriggled herself more securely onto the mattress, and he followed, his weight solid and not at all unpleasant.

Susan liked sex. She had lost count of the men by now, but she had never had a truly unpleasant encounter at the beginning of an affair.

And who knew, she thought suddenly, where things might go with Phil? He had done well for himself. He had status now. Authority. Perhaps she needn't keep looking.

After that, she stopped thinking in any proper sense. Not about the future, anyway. She simply met his urgency with her own, moaning softly as he entered her and then moving with him as they found a rhythm together.

It was over quickly, but she'd had fun. He wasn't a bad lover, and he had made a clear enough effort to see that she enjoyed herself too.

Afterwards, Susan curled herself against his side and nuzzled his neck, hooking one leg over his in a post-coital cuddle.

"I never thought the day would come," she said with a soft laugh. "Not really my type, back in the day, Phil Lehmann. You are full of surprises."

The ceiling fan rattled above them, stirring the air over their heated, naked skin. Susan laid her head on Phil's chest and cupped his flank.

"Who'd have thought, fifteen years ago, that we'd end up here?"

Phil said nothing.

"Who'd have thought, fifteen years ago, that all those awful things would happen? That Mike would be killed. That Jeremy would go to prison and die." She trailed her fingers over his torso. "You must know he didn't do it. Not poor Jeremy, whom I let down so badly when I always knew Starky was guilty." She sighed. "Now Starky has to pay. For what he did. For what he let Jeremy take the blame for."

For a moment, Susan thought Phil might have drifted off. Then he said softly, "Jeremy shouldn't have done what he did to you."

Susan lifted her head. "What do you mean?"

"You were just a kid. I wouldn't have taken advantage of you fifteen years ago. Not like…" He hesitated.

Susan went rigid.

"Not like who? Jeremy?" she demanded, half sitting up. "Is that what you really believed all these years? That it was Jeremy in my tent?" She hardly noticed how shrill and defensive she sounded. When emotion took hold, subtlety deserted her.

"I read Mike's diary," said Phil quietly. "I had to, before I handed it over to the police."

Susan scrambled onto her knees beside him.

"You did? Well, Mike got it wrong! It was Starky who came into my tent!" She was breathing hard now. "Only he wasn't man enough to admit it."

"Hush, Susan," Phil said, trying to draw her back down beside him. "It doesn't matter now. You were a teenager, and so what if your parents blamed the wrong man?"

"It matters because for fifteen years they have believed my daughter's father is a murderer!"

"What?"

Now Phil really did sound shocked. He half-sat up too.

"You have a child?"

"Yes. Angel. She's fifteen." Susan heard the bitterness flooding back into her voice. "Conceived the night before Mike died. Starky and I—well, you know what I mean. I was a virgin. I didn't even think about pregnancy. Then, when my parents found out, all hell broke loose. They sent me to a home for unmarried mothers and wanted me to sign adoption papers, but I ran away. When I tried to tell them Jeremy wasn't the father, they didn't believe me. No one ever believed me over Mike. Mike was the model child, the scholar, the golden one. I was always the difficult daughter." She stared at him. "But I can't believe *you* read Mike's diary too. That's why Mum and Dad got the wrong idea. I didn't know you knew all that. What else did Mike write?"

Phil ran a hand through his hair. "I wish I hadn't said anything."

Then, after a pause, he went on. "All right. Mike wrote that he heard Jeremy go to your tent after everyone had gone to bed, and that in the morning he confronted him. When Jeremy denied it, Mike punched him. That's why Jeremy left."

"Oh, God."

Susan covered her face with her hands.

"As if I didn't hate Starky enough already. Why should Jeremy have taken the fall for that as well, when there was just as much evidence pointing to Starky? Which he must have done, since Jeremy wouldn't kill a fly."

Phil cleared his throat. After a short silence, he asked, "What do you know about this evidence that would have convicted Starky? Didn't you ask me before whether I saw him pull the trigger?"

"Starky had a Krieghoff too. Just like Jeremy. A double rifle, .470 Nitro Express, firing the same type of bullet the autopsy found." Susan lowered her hands and glared at him. "Oh, for goodness' sake, Phil. You know Starky hid his. You were there."

She sat upright. "Starky asked me to keep quiet about his Krieghoff when the rangers came into camp, so that kind of rifle was never officially associated with him. And I never said a word during the investigation. I didn't know Jeremy had been charged... and by the time I did, he was already dead. But I should have said something."

"Whoa. All right. But the investigation concluded Jeremy killed your brother. There must have been other factors feeding into that verdict." Phil put a hand on her shoulder and tried to guide her back down. "I'm sorry you've carried all this guilt. And about everyone thinking Jeremy is your daughter's father. I had no idea you even had a child. God..." He scrubbed at his hair again. "I never saw you after that trip. Then everything was in the papers. I assumed you'd told them whatever you knew and that the investigation was sound. But you're saying it wasn't?"

"Not when Starky profited from Mike's death," Susan snapped, resisting the pressure of his hand. She folded her arms across her chest. "I once heard Mike tell Starky he'd found a diamond in the Makgadikgadi Pans. I'm sure he showed him one." She hesitated, then plunged on. "Sometimes I read Mike's diary. Yes, I know it was sneaky. One time he wrote that he was excited about our cousin James coming because his father worked at Orapa." She sat straighter. "Why would Mike write that if he hadn't found a diamond? And how else do you explain Starky suddenly having money after Mike died? After I heard them arguing over a diamond? His family was dirt poor. He didn't even finish varsity. One minute he's dropping out, the next he's swimming in cash, with a camp, a concession and a plane. That's why I asked you to come."

Phil lay back and stared at the ceiling.

"OK," he said at last. "I thought you'd already told me why you wanted me here."

"It's true that I want you to catch him in whatever illegal thing he's planning now. But only because *you've* persuaded me that I can't get justice for Mike after fifteen years." She took a deep breath. "My parents have spent my daughter's entire life believing Jeremy murdered Mike. They believed my daughter's father was a murderer, and they told her so. My daughter believes her father is a murderer." Her voice softened. "There's no need for them to know Starky is really Angel's father. Or for Starky to know. Or Angel. God knows I don't want Angel knowing that. But if the truth can somehow come out about Starky being responsible for Mike's death—because he had the same rifle, and a motive, and probably stole Mike's diamond— then Angel can go on believing Jeremy is her father, only a father who was exonerated after death."

Susan turned towards Phil, her hands moving over his flanks as she whispered, "Because I would do anything— *anything*—not to have my Angel grow up with the blight of having a monster for a father."

THIRTY-ONE

Verity gazed up at the cirrus clouds drifting across the bright blue sky, hoping to be inspired by the majesty of the world around her. Hoping to feel *something* infuse her soul with light.

But all she could think of was the pain she'd caused James.

So unjustly.

That half-written letter for Sarah had not been intended for his eyes. It probably wouldn't ever have made its way into Sarah's hands, either. It was the jottings of a woman painfully torn between the conflicting desires in her life: duty and career.

Verity's feelings for James were in a whole different basket. He was loyal and good, and she wouldn't hurt him for the world.

With a sigh, she returned to the task of scraping the vegetable peelings off the board and into the bushes. It had been a relief to step away from camp for a short while before returning to help Florence and Kutlo prepare lunch and get the table laid for lunch a little later in the day.

Starky and the clients had been up at dawn and had returned an hour ago. But camp was quiet as they'd all retired to their tents, although Verity had heard the muted sounds of lovemaking when she'd passed Kurt and Charlize's tent. She presumed it was Charlize and Kurt.

Scraping the last of the carrot and potato peelings into the dirt, she wondered why it should matter. She'd taken Starky to task, but he didn't pretend to be what he wasn't. And Charlize was a prostitute, for God's sake. James and Starky were right. She really was Miss Goody Two-Shoes, holier than thou. Not much fun for anyone, much less for James right now.

Love was another matter. She loved James, but it was a relief to be out in the bush so she didn't have to sleep next to him, feeling guilty about her lack of desire for sex.

For fifteen years, she'd been perfectly happy about their bedroom activities, even when she was exhausted with child-rearing, or fed up with being moved to another town because either the charter company for whom James had been flying had folded, or he'd got a better job elsewhere.

Verity accepted all that as par for the course. It was the lot of a pilot's wife.

But later was when the real test had come.

Love? Or her career?

She'd choose love every time, of course. She just wished she could recapture the feeling.

"I thought you were a wild creature. You were so still, looking into the bushes there." It was Starky, his voice jerking her into awareness. "What are you thinking about that's made you look like the world is about to end? Whoa, and you've got a knife. I'd better be careful since you objected so greatly to what I had to say last time you took issue with me."

Verity gave him a wry smile as she glanced at the knife she'd carried with her to scrape the peelings from the board.

"You're lucky I don't have a volatile temperament, then."

"Passive and judgmental. Not volatile."

Verity gasped. "That's a horrible thing to say."

Starky shrugged. "Is it? I have a bad habit of saying what I think."

"Given your track record with women, your opinion about what you think of me doesn't improve my mood."

Starky grinned. "I think you're an enigma. A beautiful, fragile, damaged enigma."

Verity's mouth dropped open. "Rather deep, coming from you. An enigma? Damaged and fragile? I've worked hard doing whatever job I can pick up in countless towns throughout Australia. There's nothing fragile about me."

Starky thought a moment. "Oh, you're fragile. Let's say vulnerable, then, shall we? You'll always be vulnerable when you think you haven't got what you deserve. I'm right, aren't I? The reason you're so unhappy is that you feel let down. So, who's the culprit? James?"

"I'm very happily married, thank you."

"That's not what it looked like to me when James dropped by. Poor man was raking you with puppy dog eyes and you could barely give him the time of day."

Verity's gasp of outrage made him smile. "Too close to the bone? I'm good at seeing what you think I can't." He took a step closer, and Verity felt her breath hitch as she watched him warily.

"What do you want, Starky? To hear me confess? To say you hit the nail on the head, you clever man, and praise you as you always expect to be praised? And then be grateful that you took the time to listen to my woes and grievances?"

"All that would be very nice. Touching and vindicating. I like to know I'm right. But that's no secret." Starky put out a hand, which he rested on her shoulder. Verity looked at it suspiciously. Her first instinct was to jerk away, but perhaps he really was trying to extend an olive branch.

"I also like to make beautiful women feel better about themselves, and James certainly isn't doing a good job in that department."

She watched—as if it were happening to someone else, not to her—as his fingertips trailed from the sleeve of her khaki shirt down the flesh of her forearm. This is where she should feel something. Desire?

Verity shivered. No, it was anger growing inside her. She'd slap his face if he didn't break contact in just a second, but, oh, how good it was to feel something that wasn't self-pity.

"Poor Verity. You think you're so alone right now, but you aren't. Truly, you aren't."

His palms were cupping the back of her head, his lips poised just above hers. She could feel his warm breath as he whispered, "Beautiful, fragile, lonely Verity. Let me make you feel better."

Then his lips were upon hers, soft, practiced, sending a charge of something powerful through her.

But it wasn't desire.

Outrage!

Starky, the master of manipulating women into panting with want for him, had failed.

"How dare you!" she gasped, leaping back as if stung. "Do you think I'm such an easy conquest?"

"No." Starky was grinning that infuriating grin of his,

his hands thrust into his pockets. "But it did confirm that you are much more unhappy than I had thought you. Bravo, Verity. James is lucky for your loyalty, though for a moment there, I thought it was going my way. Never mind, perhaps next time. And if not, your secret's safe with me."

And then he was sauntering back through the bush towards camp while Verity stood shaking in the shade of a jackalberry tree, her fingertips to her lips, trying not to cry.

THIRTY-TWO

Verity waited a few minutes before returning to camp. The guests expected to be waited on. It was her job. There was no time to stand gazing at the sky or glowering into the bushes or railing at fate or obsessing over the fact that she had let Starky kiss her.

She had known what he was about to do. He had been setting the scene, coaxing the moment into being, and she had simply stood there, waiting for him to make his move.

And she had let him. Oh dear God, she had let Starky kiss her. *Why?*

Why? Because she'd been desperate to feel *anything*—to shock her own numb system back to life

So, no, she did not regret it. The anger had been cathartic.

"Did something spook you out there in the bushes, Verity?" Charlize, curled in a recliner, lifted her head from the book she was reading and looked up. "You look as if you've seen a ghost."

"A ghost? I don't know why you'd think that." Verity barely glanced at her as she crossed to the fire a little way off. Charlize did not deserve a proper answer when she was so plainly motivated by prurient curiosity. Perhaps she had seen them. Perhaps she was now amusing herself by needling Verity with it.

"You know the men are going to shoot a lion tomorrow?"

Verity's head came up sharply. She bit back the instinctive protest.

No, they can't.

"Or maybe it's a leopard." Charlize lowered her eyes to the page again, as though the distinction were trivial. As though one great predator or another made no difference.

Verity knew Zerangu had no lion licences left.

"Do you know which?" she asked, striving for carelessness as she stirred the fire.

Charlize shrugged. "Does it matter? They're just boys with big guns pretending to be men. They think killing predators makes them special. They're not special. They simply have the money to do what they like. And as long as a little of it comes my way, I don't much care what they do."

Verity sent her a cool look. Charlize, with that magnificent mane of golden hair, those long legs and lithe body, might have been a film star. A supermodel. Yes, she had had a terrible life, but how could she sell herself so cheaply? The hard shell she had cultivated made sympathy difficult.

"Do you enjoy this line of work?" Verity asked. "At least you get to see the world." She had to talk of something, she supposed.

"Mostly it's the inside of hotel rooms. This is a change. Not sure I enjoy a camp bed as much as a queen at the Hilton." Charlize turned a page. "But it pays the bills, and I'm careful with money. I intend to retire at thirty-five. Unless marriage proves the better proposition." She gave a short laugh. "Not sure marriage suits anyone though. You and that husband of yours aren't exactly the strongest advertisement for the long-term variety. Though yours at least seems to let you out a little more than my father did my mother, or Corbus let me."

"I hardly think they're the same," said Verity, trying to keep the acid from her tone. "Do you really think you can make assumptions on the basis of five minutes?" She snapped a branch against her knee and fed it to the flames. "My husband is kind, and he does what he can to make me and my daughter happy. He's a man of integrity. That's why we're in Botswana. If we'd stayed in Australia for a better-paying job, it would have meant compromising his ideals. He is a good and moral man who couldn't live with himself if he did what he believed was wrong."

She realised too late that her voice had risen in defence of James, and saw Charlize's lush mouth curve into one of her rare smiles.

"Touched a nerve, did I?" she murmured. "I take it you weren't quite as keen as James was to see him walk away from a well-paying job."

Verity felt shame flare first, then anger. She bent for another thicker branch from the pile by the fire.

And then another voice cut in.

"But did he do it for the right reasons?"

It was Starky, emerging from the trees. Verity had stopped listening for the sounds of him working on the vehicle and had not realised he was so close.

She could barely bring herself to look at him. But he came straight over, took the branch from her hand—the one she had been struggling to break—and snapped it neatly in two with one quick movement.

It hissed and spat when he tossed it onto the flames.

"Were you eavesdropping, Starky?"

"I have the ears of a hunter, Verity. I was only walking back through the bush when I heard you extolling your husband's virtues." He tilted his head. "Or were you defending them?"

"I was simply telling Charlize why we came here."

Starky planted one boot on a log. "I should take James hunting one day. Strange to think we knew each other as kids. He's become the proper Aussie now."

"I don't think James would like to go hunting."

"Is that because you don't think James should go hunting?" He smiled as if it were a joke. "I think perhaps you like telling him what to do, and usually he lets you. Just not this time."

Verity stepped back from the fire, stung. Charlize had lowered her book and was watching from over the top of it, eyes bright with interest.

"I think you make a great many assumptions on very little fact," said Verity. "You may have the eyes and ears of a hunter, but you haven't got fifteen years of marriage behind you."

"No, thank God," said Starky.

Charlize laughed.

"I think Verity believes you are a wicked man, Starky," she drawled. "You and me both."

Verity turned away from their shared amusement with the excuse of going to the kitchen tent just as Kurt and his son appeared at the edge of the clearing.

She heard Kurt ask for a whisky and Coke. He said something curt to Thomas too, but then the sound of a plane, unusually low and close, made everyone lift their heads.

They all looked up, shading their eyes, searching the sky until the small dot in the distance grew steadily larger.

"Visitors?" Charlize asked.

But Starky shook his head. "Tracking overhead. No one comes into a place this remote without us knowing first." He smiled at her. "Want a drink? Verity's fixing your man something, but I don't think your order has been seen to."

Verity caught the secret smile that passed between them. Did Kurt know? And if he didn't, what would he do if he found out that the woman he was paying for had been—

She would not let herself finish the thought.

Starky was so wrapped up in his own charm and appetite that he seemed unable to imagine consequences. Any woman was merely a game to him.

Including Verity.

"It is landing here!" Charlize cried a few minutes later, surprise sharpening her voice. The low drone of the engine had deepened, and the little plane was now clearly lining up the rough strip about ten minutes' walk away.

"I don't recognise it." Starky frowned, then turned to Kurt. "Don't worry. We have squatter's rights. I'll tell them to move on."

"Maybe they're in trouble," said Verity. "Or perhaps they'll go as soon as they realise the strip's occupied. Shall I drive out and see?" She didn't want to, but she did want to be seen to be useful.

Starky had already sunk back into his seat. "Relax. It's their problem, not ours. If they show up, we'll give them a drink and send them on their way."

Verity nodded and poured Coke into Kurt's whisky before handing him the crystal tumbler. He had drawn his chair close to Charlize and was stroking her hand. Charlize looked perfectly content. She played her role beautifully—

stroking his hand back just enough to keep him satisfied, while holding back just enough to keep him trying.

And it really was a performance.

Just as Starky's attempted seduction of Verity had been a performance.

And James? That was all too real. Yet lately, even that had begun to feel strained and stage-managed.

Suddenly she longed for the old days. She wanted to ache with anticipation at seeing him return each evening. Wanted to want him in the uncomplicated way she once had.

She hated this deadening of feeling—the absence of that old desire, that sense of oneness they had once shared so naturally.

"I think our visitors are about to show themselves," Starky murmured.

That surprised Verity, because though they had all heard the plane land some minutes earlier, what Starky seemed to be referring to now was the faint crackle of branches and the soft tread of feet through scrub.

But then even he looked briefly baffled when the plane engine coughed back into life and, within seconds, the little Beechcraft Bonanza was roaring down the strip and lifting off again.

"Hello!" came a young female voice.

And then another, with a giggle: "Dr Livingstone, I presume?"

THIRTY-THREE

Verity blinked.

Were her eyes deceiving her?

For a moment there was complete silence as the two girls emerged from the cluster of acacias.

Verity was the first to find her voice.

"Saskia? Good Lord! What are you doing here?"

Horror flooded her. Her own daughter had turned up in the wilds of Africa in the middle of Starky's overland. This was not good. Not good at all.

Surely Saskia understood that her mother was here working for rich clients?

"Mum! And Starky! Surprise. Meet my friend and second cousin, Angie." Saskia smiled at the group. She did not look remotely overawed by their collective shock. If anything, she looked amused by it.

Verity, it seemed, was the first to recover her wits.

"Saskia, you can't do this. Just... arrive unannounced. What about lions? This is a private safari, and there's no tent for you—"

"Whoa, Mum. Relax." Saskia's smile remained firmly in

place. "Richard is picking us up in a couple of hours. And he checked for lions. He did a low pass to frighten them away—"

"Who is Richard?"

"The brother of one of our school friends. It's my birthday present. My sixteenth birthday, in case you'd forgotten. Thank you for the present you sent last week. But anyway, Richard was flying to Maun this weekend and agreed to take us. When I asked if he could drop us at Deception Pan for a couple of hours, he said it was no problem, because he was going virtually overhead—"

"What about... immigration?" Verity asked, her mind scrambling to grasp the sheer recklessness of it.

"Oh, Richard made sure that wasn't a problem. We hopped aboard after he'd cleared customs in Lanseria. And he's picking us up again later, anyway, at the end of some game flying."

"This Richard did not check that you girls were safely with the right people?" Starky's face darkened. "How old is he? Nineteen?"

"Eighteen. He only got his licence last week, and he was very keen to take us, in case you think we were imposing on his good nature."

A slight defensiveness crept into Saskia's tone. But then she turned to Starky and, to Verity's astonishment, used precisely the kind of charm Starky himself wielded so effortlessly.

She smiled the most seductive smile Verity had ever seen on her daughter's face.

It was so unsettling that Verity could barely bear to watch. Her little girl had grown up without her noticing. She was sixteen.

And very suddenly, very disturbingly, a young woman.

Saskia twirled a strand of blonde hair around her finger and said, with her eyes widened just enough, "You don't mind visitors for a couple of hours, do you, Starky? Ange and I can help Mum. We can pour the drinks and do all that sort of thing." Her mouth trembled ever so slightly. "And when you comforted me after you rescued me from the crocodile on that game drive, you *did* say I was welcome to visit you any time I was in Maun."

"You did?" Verity heard the odd note in her own voice—suspicion, alarm, something uglier—and even Starky blinked.

"I was calming a fifteen-year-old girl who'd been badly frightened and mauled." Now he was the one sounding defensive. "Of course I said that. And I meant it." Then he turned with quick ease to the others. "You and your friend are very welcome for a couple of hours, aren't they, Kurt? Thomas?" He included Charlize too, with a particularly warm smile, Verity thought.

And Thomas, who was only a few years older than Saskia, made it abundantly clear that he found the sudden appearance of two attractive teenage girls in camp an excellent idea. Hardly surprising, perhaps, given how thoroughly bored he had seemed by the company of adults.

Well, Verity supposed, girls nearer his own age were bound to appeal more than hunting.

"Of course, you are very welcome," Kurt said at last.

Verity had been on tenterhooks waiting for his response. He was the client paying a fortune for these few days at Deception Pan, and it was highly irregular for the teenage daughter of the camp hostess to suddenly fly herself in with a friend.

But as Verity watched his gaze move between Thomas

and the girls, she realised he had immediately seen the advantages.

The realisation both relieved and dismayed her.

So long as Saskia was safe.

"And Angie." Forcing herself to smile after thanking Kurt for being so gracious, Verity turned to Susan's daughter. "How pleased I am to meet you. Your mother has told me all about you."

The words were out before she could stop them, and as she darted a glance at Starky, her stomach clenched.

Oh Lord.

Did he know Angie was Susan's daughter?

Verity was not even sure whether he had properly seen Susan since her arrival in Maun.

But Starky gave no sign of anything, and Verity decided to keep very quiet while desperately hoping the girls would be gone again before any deeper connection was made.

It was strange to think that the two girls were cousins. There was no resemblance at all. Angie had her mother's dark curly hair, tied back in a ponytail, and those large eyes and lush lips in a heart-shaped face that gave her an almost elfin beauty. Saskia's straight blonde hair, which seemed longer than when Verity had last seen her six weeks ago, fell in a glossy sheet down her back.

"Come and have a drink. We can offer Coke or lemonade. There's Fanta too, which is Thomas's favourite tipple," Starky said with a wink.

A wink at the girls as much as at Charlize, Verity realised with a fresh start of unease.

Yet perhaps she was not the only one who felt some of the strain in camp ease with the arrival of two pretty, clearly delighted girls. Angie had seated herself between Thomas and Charlize and was already asking eager questions about the animals they had seen—and hunted—while Saskia was standing at Starky's elbow, bringing him up to date on school and how astonished she was to find she liked it, talking to him as if they were old friends.

And Starky?

Verity realised she was watching like some absurdly vigilant mother hen. Only minutes earlier he had been trying to kiss her. Now her younger, prettier daughter was laughing up at him.

Except...

Verity hesitated.

Saskia and Starky were laughing about something Saskia had said, but there did seem to be an innocence to it. An ease. Maybe Saskia, traumatised and young, had simply drawn out whatever protective instinct Starky possessed. Maybe he was not quite as ethically bankrupt as Verity preferred to think.

It was Kurt who suggested they all go on a game drive. He was expansive after another whisky. Saskia and Angie were thrilled, and as Starky pointed out, they would easily hear the return of the Cessna when it came back for them.

So the seven of them piled into the vehicle: Thomas squeezed in at the back with the girls, visibly happier already; Kurt beside Starky in front; and Verity and Charlize shoulder to shoulder in the middle seat.

"I'm not sure what to think about Saskia and Angie arriving like this," Verity muttered to Charlize as the vehicle jolted forward. "James would have a fit if he knew."

"The joys of being young, I suppose. Not that I'd know." Charlize's mouth twisted. "Your daughter is very charming. She's nothing like you."

Verity could not decide whether it was meant as an insult. English was, after all, Charlize's second language.

"People say she takes after James. I'm the serious one. Too serious." She stared out into the bush. Too quiet. Too inward. Too lost in her own thoughts. She had heard all of that before. "James was the party animal back in the day," she added with a smile. "Not that you'd guess it now. I first met him when he was dancing on a table in the uni bar. I walked in just as he announced he was going to dance with the next girl to come through the door. That turned out to be me."

"You liked the idea?"

"Hated it. Hated being the centre of attention. But my friend dragged me over and then suddenly I was hauled onto the table with James, who promptly spilled his drink all over me." Verity was surprised by how much she was saying. As the vehicle bounced over the track and impala scattered ahead, the old memory rose with painful clarity. "You couldn't imagine two people less suited."

And despite herself, she smiled, remembering those bright, heady days. Like Verity, James had always worked hard. But once, he had played hard too.

"Yet here you are, fifteen years later? Fifteen, you said? Like your daughter?"

"She's just turned sixteen, but yes, she's the reason we got married." Verity sighed. "I've never regretted it, and James says he hasn't either. But a child is never the best reason to marry, I suppose. Still, it's been an interesting life."

"But this isn't home, and you want Melbourne back? Do you not love this open land?" Charlize gave a sudden laugh. "I hate it too. Monte Carlo—that's where I'm going. I told you."

"Oh, I don't hate it here," Verity said, startled. "I hate that I'm nobody and nothing here, when I had just started a job that made me feel I really was somebody." She broke off. "Not that I'd expect you to understand."

"You think a job makes you somebody?" Charlize's tone turned contemptuous. "I want money. And a husband I respect, who does not cheat on me. Is that really too much to ask?"

"But... is there nothing you actually want to *do*?" Verity regretted the words as soon as Charlize turned and glared.

"This *is* my job," Charlize snapped. "Just as you fold the serviettes and make sure there is food and drink enough to keep this safari running and earn your wage, I make sure the men who hire me feel important and that I give them pleasure. Why is it different? You use your hands and your brain. I use my body."

"Oh, look! A lion!" Saskia cried suddenly. "Is that a Kalahari lion?"

Starky stopped the vehicle at once, and they all stared at the great tawny beast moving through the tall grass. He seemed entirely untroubled by their presence, ambling on without hurry or apparent care.

Verity stole a glance at Kurt and Starky in the front seat.

Was that what they intended to slaughter the moment the rest of them were out of the way?

"It is," said Thomas, and Verity turned. His mouth was set in a grim line. "He is not a very fine specimen, is he, Father?"

Kurt gave no sign that he had registered the challenge. "If I were to bag a lion, it would need to be a finer specimen."

"And this is where I saw the lioness yesterday," said Starky. Then he glanced at the sky and turned to the girls. "Your friend is taking his time. He'll need to get back to Maun before dark. Is he reliable?"

Saskia and Angie exchanged a look.

"We only met him this morning."

"What about his father?"

"He's in Johannesburg."

"And where is this friend staying in Maun?"

"I don't know," the girls chorused.

Starky twisted in his seat. "I'll get one of the lads to put up a tent for the girls, just in case."

"I'm so sorry they're imposing like this," Verity said, flushed with embarrassment.

"Not at all," said Kurt. "The girls can keep Thomas company while Starky and I go hunting tomorrow if their friend does not return. Hopefully, nothing serious has delayed him."

And as he said it, with that bland assumption that the girls might simply be absorbed into camp for the night and beyond, Verity felt the first real stab of alarm.

This was no longer a surprise visit. It was becoming something else altogether.

CHAPTER
THIRTY-FOUR

James stared miserably into his coffee.

He was sitting alone in the coffee shop, but even had he been in company, he would still have felt alone.

Not alone in the way he had during that first week in Botswana, making arrangements for his new job while Verity and Saskia stayed with his grandmother. At least then he had been too fired up by shock, anger and adrenaline to feel the real emptiness that came with solitude.

Back then, in Gaborone, before he joined the girls, he had worked through the disbelief that the job he had spent fifteen years striving for—his first proper jet job—had been lost to him unless he sacrificed his principles.

"Hey, Adam?"

Though the greeting was not meant for him, James glanced up and saw a tall, rangy, grey-haired man standing in the doorway. He recognised him dimly from when Susan had briefly introduced them a few days before.

Adam, one of the Ngami Air pilots, waved him over to his table.

"So, Phil, I hear you're headed for Deception Pan."

James had no intention of eavesdropping, but neither was he about to shut his ears to a conversation taking place only a few tables away.

Not when Deception Pan was where Verity was.

It turned out Phil had been commissioned by a Johannesburg magazine to take photographs of Kalahari lions to accompany an article by a regular visitor to the region.

James's attention sharpened at the name that followed.

Rupert Graves.

Lucky Phil, he thought with a sudden twist of feeling. Verity would have loved to be part of something like that—writing for a glossy magazine and going out on location.

If they had stayed longer at Chubaora before Saskia's accident, perhaps Rupert and Verity might have discovered how much they had in common. Perhaps he might have appreciated her background and experience. Perhaps one day she could have written for that Johannesburg magazine —or others like it.

James glanced over, but Phil gave no sign of recognising him.

What a pity Phil had not chartered Okavango Air. James would have liked to learn more about the magazine and the opportunities there might be for Verity.

He's have liked to have seen Verity again, too.

The thought sent a shiver through him.

Could a man feel longing and apprehension at the same time?

He took another sip of coffee, then stilled as Phil's tone sharpened his attention once more.

"I don't want to be dropped at the airstrip at Deception Pan. There's a group of tourists there, and I don't want to intrude."

"Ach, man, it's an airstrip," Adam said. "You go your way and they'll go theirs."

"No. I've got coordinates for another place to land a little distance away," Phil insisted. "I want you to put me down there."

James turned his head slightly, a prickling sense of unease taking root. It was an odd request.

The two men were bent over the coffees that had just arrived and seemed quite unaware of him. For several more minutes they discussed arrangements before parting. James was about to leave as well when Jack Vickers, one of the game rangers from Meno a Kweno, slid into the chair opposite and said, "Who was that I just passed on my way out?"

James shook his head. "Not sure. Friend of yours?"

Jack grunted. "Definitely not. Anyway, the man I thought it was wouldn't show his face in a place like this, and this *oke's* a lot greyer, so I go it wrong."

"Well, this bloke's called Phil, and he's off to Deception Pan to do some photography for a wildlife magazine." James hesitated. "I wish I could go too."

"And see your girl?" Jack grinned. "Anyway, how's the overland going? Maybe Verity will take more to that kind of work."

James did his best to sound upbeat as he said he shouldn't complain since he had seen her only yesterday and the safari seemed to be going very well. He agreed that Botswana had a way of growing on a person and that Verity was settling into it more every day.

Even as the words came out, he felt like a fraud.

He felt slightly sick in fact.

He still had to speak to her about the letter he had found, and dread sat in his gut at the thought. What if he had opened Pandora's box? What if drawing out her real feelings unleashed a flood of painful truths about how little contentment she had found in the life he had given her?

At least he could honestly tell Jack that Saskia was loving her new boarding school and already looking forward to another trip into the bush when she next came to Maun.

"Gotta run," said Jack, glancing at his watch. "Told them I'd organise what to do with the Bonanza abandoned out at the airfield."

James raised his eyebrows. He had noticed the little plane earlier and wondered whose it was.

"Some young bloke too rich and too young to have a machine like that wrapped a *bakkie* round a tree after a big night at Safari South."

"Ach, was it bad?"

"Not sure. Rob medevac'd him to Jo'burg in the Caravan around midnight."

"Poor kid. So the red Bonanza up by the fence belongs to him?"

"Birthday present," Jack said with a grin, pushing back his chair. "You on this afternoon?"

James wished he were. It was a quiet day for him, and tomorrow morning too. If Verity had been home, he might have suggested they head into the bush together. He would have taken her to Third Bridge, where someone had told him a crimson-breasted shrike had been seen regularly. The dainty black bird with that impossible, brilliant red breast was his favourite, and perhaps finding it together might bridge something that lately seemed to have opened up between them.

Verity had never shown much interest in wildlife back when they had lived in remote Australian towns. Kangaroos and koalas were nothing special to her, she used to say. Two a penny.

Yet she had been unexpectedly moved on their short safari to Chubaora before Saskia's accident. The fact that the trip had been cut short only made James more determined to take her back into the bush as soon as he could. If he could help her fall in love with this landscape—its vastness, its birds, its beauty—and perhaps, eventually, find opportunities like the one Phil was chasing, perhaps she might be happier here.

The thought hit him like a blow.

But would something like that ever really compensate for the career she had left behind? For the high-pressure glossy magazine world, she had been on the brink of entering properly?

Saskia, he knew, would leap at any adventure into the bush.

Shortly after Jack left, James stood up. He would ring his daughter right now and see how she was getting on. It was Saturday, so he had a better chance of catching her.

But when he rang the school, he was told Saskia had gone away with a friend.

Apparently she and Angie had made a last-minute dash with a mutual school friend called Cathy Stirling, whose brother had flown them somewhere.

The school administrator, apologetic to the point of fluster, explained that they had on file a letter apparently signed by James giving permission.

James put down the phone very carefully.

Then picked it up again and asked to hear it all once more.

By the time he finally replaced the receiver, he was shaking with anger and disbelief.

This was like the old Saskia—the Saskia who lied about smoking behind the sheds, who played truant, who kept one step ahead of consequences until they came crashing down on everyone else.

He had truly believed those days were over.

It was one thing to spend a weekend at a school friend's home.

It was quite another to climb into a plane and fly off to God knew where with a young man her parents had never even met—after forging her father's signature to do it.

Surely she must have known how worried they would be.

He rang the Stirling household next, using the number the school receptionist had given him. There was no answer. He left a message, though he had no idea whether anyone would hear it in time to matter.

Then he left the office and made his way home, confused and sick with worry over Saskia's whereabouts, and feeling vaguely uneasy as to why this photographer would want a covert drop-off near his wife's camp.

Whatever foolish, reckless place Saskia thought she had flown off to, James knew one thing with terrible certainty.

When he finally got hold of her, there would be strong words.

And if anything had happened to her in the meantime, strong words would be the least of it.

THIRTY-FIVE

"Isn't Starky great?" Saskia whispered as the two girls wandered across the salt pan to look at a pair of elegant kori bustards strutting through the sparse grass. The big grey birds, with their white-striped necks and solemn, superior air, seemed utterly unfazed by the girls' approach.

"God, Saskia, you've told me a thousand times. Yes, I know—he's a hero, and he saved your life." Angie rolled her eyes. "And yes, he's great, though if you ask me he's a bit too handsome for his own good, and I reckon he knows it."

A small herd of springbok grazed in the distance, their tan-and-white coats melting into the pale landscape. One of them suddenly pronked high into the air, all four legs stiff, like a creature showing off for its own amusement.

Saskia was far too affronted by Angie's remark to find any of it funny.

"Ange!" she cried. "It's not as if he's coming on to either of us. Do you always have to think like that?"

"Well, all I'm *really* thinking about is what he might tell me about my father, and trying to pick the right moment to ask him, if you really want to know."

Angie bit her lower lip, and Saskia gave her a brisk clap on the shoulder.

"Then ask him," she said, bending to scratch at her still-sensitive ankle before sucking in a sharp breath through her teeth.

"What's wrong? Does it hurt?" Angie snapped off a twig and waited for her to straighten. "You've been fiddling with it a lot lately."

"It's fine," Saskia said, brushing off the concern because the more pressing matter still loomed before them. "But we came all this way to ask him. You can't chicken out now. There might not be another chance."

Angie swung around, her eyes suddenly bright. "How was I supposed to ask him with all those people around? And Richard will be coming back soon to fetch us, so that's that."

Saskia gave her a wicked smile.

"Richard might not necessarily be coming back for us."

Angie stared.

"I mean, obviously we had to tell him he should," Saskia went on. "And tell everyone else he would. But just after we landed, I happened to mention that if he got caught up and couldn't make it back before dark, then not to worry because Mum had an extra tent."

"How did you know that?"

"Well, of course I didn't. But it stood to reason she would. And then, what do you know—Starky came to the rescue and had one set up. So we're fine." She winked. "I rather fancy the idea of staying overnight. And I think Thomas does, too."

A solitary bat-eared fox trotted past a termite mound

some distance away, its vast ears flicking like radar dishes as it hunted for insects in the cracked earth. The girls paused to watch it, then Saskia went on, lowering her voice with satisfaction.

"I also gave Richard a massive wink when I said it didn't matter if he couldn't make it back tonight, so I doubt he'll bother now it's getting late. I knew they'd have to have spare tents in case one got shredded during a lion attack or something."

Angie made a growling sort of noise. "You really don't know anything about this country. A lion won't shred a tent. Honestly, you nearly got taken by a croc on your first trip out and still haven't learned a thing. Wow. And Mum's always carrying on about *me* being spontaneous and disorganised—"

"Excuse me, but I have been extremely strategic, actually." Saskia huffed. "Very insulting, after all I've done for you. You'd better start being nicer if you want me to do what you want."

"Do I sniff blackmail in the air?"

To both girls' shock, Starky himself stepped out from a little stand of acacias, catching them completely off guard. There had been no sound to warn of his approach in that stark, open stretch of sand.

"So," he said mildly, "what does your friend want you to do, Saskia, that you don't want to do?"

Saskia smiled at once to disguise the leap of panic inside her.

But this was Starky. Easy to talk to. Warm and nice and, on the whole, impossible not to like.

And because opportunism came naturally to her, and because Angie's look had flashed to hers for only a second, she blurted out, "Angie wants to find out more about her father."

"Your father?" Starky looked taken aback. "I take it you didn't fly all the way out to this God-forsaken place just for that? Who's your father, by the way? Anyone I know?"

Saskia shot a nervous glance at Angie. She did not know how Angie had intended to begin, or whether she had wanted privacy for the momentous question. But perhaps this was as good a chance as any.

And Saskia was suddenly glad to be part of it.

What, after all, would Starky say about a man all but branded a murderer?

"Jeremy," Angie said in a rush. "That's his name. I don't even know his surname because my mum won't tell me. She won't tell me anything. He's not even on my birth certificate. But when I met Saskia, and she told me about you, I realised you might be the only person who could tell me what I need to know, because his parents are dead and he was an only child. Yes, I know he was a murderer, but shouldn't I know *something* more about my own father?"

The outburst was long and breathless and clearly stunned Starky. The easy smile disappeared. First came a frown. Then something like horror.

And as Angie's voice broke, and she began to cry, Starky took an involuntary step forward as if to put a hand on her shoulder—then stopped himself and stepped back again, throwing one quick, almost helpless glance at Saskia as though she might somehow know how to fix this.

"Hey," he said slowly. "Look, I'm really sorry if you came all this way hoping I could help. But if you're so upset because you think your father was a murderer, then—"

He swallowed hard. Saskia saw his Adam's apple jump in his throat.

"Jesus. Don't tell me your mother is Susan Jensen."

"I thought you knew." Angie scrubbed at her eyes. "Mum said she knew you. And Saskia told everyone we were cousins. I thought she'd said when we arrived."

"Well, yes, but I didn't make the connection and, to be fair, you didn't exactly make it obvious." Starky cleared his throat. He tried to smile, though it looked strained. Saskia hadn't realised until then that she'd been holding her breath. "Sorry," Angie whispered.

"No, don't be." He looked oddly at a loss, flexing his hands as though unsure what to do with them. Then at last he said, "To answer your question, I don't think I really can tell you more about your father, because I think your mother has not... well, I won't say not told the truth exactly, but I think you're under a misapprehension. I do not believe this man Jeremy could have been your father."

"Why not?" Hope leapt into Angie's voice so nakedly that Saskia felt it too.

"Because the only Jeremy I know—assuming we're talking about the one who was on that hunting trip with your mother and me—died two days after he was charged with the terrible crime of..." Starky stopped short. His face shuttered. "He killed your uncle and went straight to prison."

"But he was Mum's boyfriend at the time."

"Her *ex*-boyfriend, and your mother had never—" Starky broke off abruptly and looked away, up at the sky. "I think your mother must have had another boyfriend called Jeremy. Not long after that trip. It's not exactly an uncommon name. I've known lots of blokes called Jeremy." He cleared his throat again. "But whatever the case, your father—even if you don't know who he is—is not, I'm sure, a murderer. There. I hope that sets your mind at rest."

But Angie's frown did not ease. Saskia could see Starky was trying—really trying—to reassure her, and yet the more he said, the more troubled Angie looked.

"I overheard my grandfather saying it was true," she whispered. "Mum said she got pregnant during the hunting trip, but her parents didn't realise until she was showing. And when they tried to put her in a home for unmarried mothers, she ran away. And when they wanted to put *me* up for adoption, she ran away again. I heard my grandfather telling my grandmother they could hardly call to account the parents of a murderer now that the murderer was dead." Angie swallowed. "I heard him say it. And then I walked into the room and asked what he meant. That's when they said I was old enough to know the truth, and told me. They said Mum got pregnant during that hunting trip, and my father was a man called Jeremy who died in prison. But they said I was nothing like him, and could still grow up to be a good girl. They said even good people sometimes made mistakes and did bad things, and that must have been what happened to my father, who was only eighteen, and that something must have gone terribly wrong, only no one knew what because he died before he could tell his side of the story."

Saskia had been watching Angie with anxious sympathy. Now she looked at Starky.

She had expected sorrow, perhaps, or simple pity. Maybe some measure of shock, because it *was* shocking.

But she had not expected the expression that now seemed to wrench his face out of shape.

It was not sympathy.

It was horror.

"Starky! Kurt's asking for you."

Saskia did not know whether she was relieved or not

that her mother chose that moment to break into the conversation. She wanted Starky to explain that look, yet at the same time dreaded what might come next. There was Angie, heart laid bare, and Starky insisting she had the whole story wrong.

"And, Starky, it's getting very late," Verity added. "I'm so sorry, but I don't think this young man, Richard, is going to be collecting the girls today."

"Right. Well then, Kutlo will have set up the tent already."

Starky sounded brisk now, retreating into practicality as Verity gave a brief nod and headed back towards camp.

Then Starky placed a hand on Angie's shoulder.

"I'm sorry I couldn't help you more," he said. He hesitated. "And... perhaps don't bring this up with your mother. I mean, you don't want to upset her any more than she's already been upset. Obviously, it was wrong if your grandparents told you all this."

"Can you at least tell me his surname?" Angie pleaded, following him as he began to walk after Verity. "The Jeremy who was on the hunting trip? Or... any other Jeremy you knew in Bots back then," she added desperately.

Starky shook his head. "Sorry, Angie. I can't help you. The guy was in camp for only a few hours. I didn't know him. I only knew he'd followed your mum there to try to get her back. And I really don't think we're talking about the same Jeremy." He gave a frustrated shrug. "I'm really sorry I can't tell you any more."

And then he was gone. They both were. And Angie looked so stricken that Saskia wrapped her arms around her.

For the first time, it occurred to her that Starky had not handled this nearly as well as she would have expected.

Because she was suddenly quite certain of one thing.
He knew more than he had said.

THIRTY-SIX

The afternoon was cooling when James cut the engine after taxiing onto the apron at Maun airport.

He had finally managed to get through to the Stirling household the previous night and speak to the maid, who told him the whole family had gone to the Okavango Delta for the weekend and that she would pass on James's message for his daughter to phone him.

James suspected Saskia's intention had been to surprise him. She might even be waiting at the cottage now, ready to fling her arms around him the moment she got back from the bush. He was still cross, though he knew perfectly well he would forgive her as soon as he saw her. That did not mean she would escape some sort of dressing-down.

He had just dropped off a party of English tourists at Xakanaxa and returned empty, so when he saw Rob heading towards his Cessna in the company of Rupert Graves, and he had a little time to spare, he wandered over.

"How's your gorgeous girl?" Rupert asked warmly, waiting

while Rob prepared for the flight. Rupert came to the Delta often enough these days that he seemed more one of them than a tourist, and James was glad of the chance to pick his brains.

"Which one?" James smiled. "I suppose you mean Saskia, given the dramatic circumstances under which we all left Chubaora. The good news is she's making a full recovery. And she's loving St Anne's."

"So good to hear. And of course, it would be remiss of me not to ask after that other gorgeous girl, Verity. What's she doing with herself?"

"Actually, she's hostessing for Starky on his overland at Deception Pan." James thought quickly, trying to find the right shape for the question he really wanted to ask. "She's fallen in love with this country."

A little artistic licence, he thought, might be forgiven if it helped him achieve the desired outcome.

Rupert opened his mouth, but James was afraid he might take the conversation elsewhere, so he hurried on.

"She used to be a journalist and was editor of a glossy magazine when I had to drag her away from her dream job. So I was wondering—"

Rupert raised his eyebrows.

James changed tack. He could hardly ask the man for a favour outright.

"This new fellow in Maun, Phil—I'm afraid I don't know his surname. But I mean the photographer who's flying into Deception Pan to take the shots for the Kalahari lion piece you're writing for a wildlife magazine. Anyway, I wondered if—"

Rupert held up a hand.

"Sorry, but I don't know of any photographer taking pictures for any article I'm writing. And I'm certainly not writing about Kalahari lions. I did that only three months ago."

"Oh."

James felt a flush of embarrassment. Immediately it was replaced by another prickle of unease. He really didn't think he'd got the end of the stick when he overheard the conversation between Phil, who wanted the out-of-town pilot to drop him at Deception Pan.

But Rupert was speaking again, offering exactly what James had hoped he would.

"If Verity wanted to join me sometime when I'm going bush, I'd be very happy for the company."

James nodded, smiling. Suddenly he couldn't wait to see Verity again. Wouldn't she be ecstatic when he told her of Rupert's offer?

"I read some of her articles," Rupert went on. "She mentioned in passing at camp that she was a journalist, and I was curious enough to look up a couple of pieces. They were very good."

Rob appeared at James's elbow then, one eye on the plane. "Ready to go? It's getting on a bit, and I need to do a pickup at Zerangu Hunting Lodge and be back before dusk."

"I thought the place would be empty with Starky at Deception," said James.

"Someone's still got to run the show," said Rob. "But, actually, Starky asked me to collect a couple of crates to hand over to Jack, who's flying into their camp at Deception tomorrow. I got the impression tomorrow's the client's big day. Lesego told me the tracker has found the trophy that ticks all the boxes. Seems this German fellow likes an audience and wants everyone around when he goes in for the kill."

James frowned, wondering if he could ask to swap. But

Jack was flying for a different charter company. It wouldn't be ethical. Troubled, he asked, "What's the trophy? It's not a lion, is it?"

"Starky wouldn't be stupid enough to risk his concession and the fines by shooting a lion without a licence," Rob said, sounding unconcerned.

"I'm sure he wouldn't," Rupert chimed in. "He may be a devil with the ladies, but he's not a fool. He built that thriving business while still in his twenties."

James chewed his lip, debating whether to say more. But Verity was out there, and he needed to know she was not going to get caught up in anything illegal. Or dangerous.

"And besides, Verity wouldn't stand for it," James added, forcing a grin. "She can be rather outspoken when it comes to crossing red lines." With an unexpected surge of panic, he suddenly wondered if Verity imagined that James, himself, had crossed any red lines. Could there be something she'd been incorrectly told about his behaviour? Maun was a hotbed of gossip. He'd learned that in a short time.

Rupert clapped him on the shoulder.

"My dear boy, you can set your mind at rest about Verity. I've known Starky for decades. He'd never lead a colleague's wife into anything dubious."

Still unsettled, James went looking for his cousin. Rupert had not eased his mind much about the intended trophy, and the fact he knew nothing of this so-called photographer Phil, who wasn't really a photographer, and who was planning to fly into Deception Pan, was troubling him more and more. Susan, he hoped, might be able to shed some more light on him.

And hopefully, she might know where the girls had gone.

It was not yet 4 o'clock, and Susan was still at work, but the moment James stepped into the newspaper office, she rose from her desk.

"Knock-off time. You'll be right without me, Mitchell?" she called, turning to a balding middle-aged man with a cigarette stuck between his lips. "I'm working on a thrilling exposé for next week's front page. Gotta go!"

James noticed the sour look Mitchell sent her, and the half-grunt that followed. Susan, it seemed, was not exactly endearing herself to her colleagues. Perhaps Verity might still have a chance at a reporter's job on the *Okavango Observer* after all.

"So, what's up?" Susan asked once they were out in the street. "Want to get a drink at the Duck?"

"Not tonight." James shook his head. "I wondered whether you'd heard anything about Saskia and Angie."

"They're at school, aren't they?"

"No. They took off with a school friend yesterday. After Saskia forged my signature to get permission, apparently. They climbed aboard a plane flown by a friend's older brother. I've no idea what they were thinking. The maid said they'd gone off to the swamps with their friends' parents and with this lad at the controls. Perhaps they're waiting to surprise us at your cottage."

Susan grinned. "I was a tearaway at her age too. Ange obviously takes after me."

That was not the response James had been hoping for.

"So, you've heard nothing. Anyway, I'm extremely unhappy about it, and I'd like to know where they are. Verity would too, I'm sure. All I know is that the family name is Stirling."

Susan shrugged as they walked. "Sorry, it's news to me." Then she put a hand on his shoulder and sent him a look of exaggerated sympathy. "Don't worry, James. If anyone knows how to look after themselves, it's Angel. I'm sure the family is perfectly respectable, otherwise the school would never have let them go."

He stared at her. It struck him how little concern she seemed to feel.

Just as she was about to turn into the Duck courtyard, he asked, "One other thing, Suze. That fellow you introduced me to the other day. Phil, wasn't it? What can you tell me about him? Is he a photographer? I thought I overheard he was going to Deception Pan tomorrow to do a lion photo shoot."

Susan blinked. Then smiled.

"That's right. But I'm afraid you can't go with him to see Verity," she added too quickly. "He's not going anywhere near their camp. Anyway, I've got to go."

"So you're not having that drink after all?"

Susan had already retraced her steps and now seemed to be heading back towards the airport road.

"Nope. Just remembered something," she called over her shoulder.

James watched her go.

Clearly, she was not about to tell him what she knew about Phil. And it was odd that she'd endorsed the fact he was off to Deception to do some photography, though it was possible it might be for another job.

Jess and a group of pilots called to him from the Duck courtyard, but James shook his head.

He needed to go home and think. Later, perhaps, he might come back for a drink. But it was not yet four o'clock.

Back at the Okavango Air compound, Mothusi was

raking the dusty yard into neat stripes, his back bent permanently at the waist, it seemed.

"*Dumela, Rra,*" James greeted him as he passed, then let himself into the cottage, nearly skidding on the envelope that had been pushed under the door.

It was brown and unmarked, except for his name written on the front in neat, looping handwriting.

He set it on the kitchen table, lit the gas beneath the kettle, and sank onto the cane settee, tearing it open as he put his feet on the coffee table.

There was no signature.

The handwriting inside was rushed and difficult to decipher, and he had to read it twice before the meaning fully sank in.

Captain White, I am contacting you because you have a plane. A plane is necessary to prevent a terrible crime. I am hoping to meet you by the bougainvillea outside Safari South at 8 p.m. tonight. I am not dangerous.

James stared at the note.

The kettle began to whistle on the stove.

But for a moment, he did not move.

A plane. A terrible crime. No signature.

And Verity out at Deception, Saskia vanished into the Delta, and Susan behaving like she had something to hide.

Under other circumstances, James might not have been concerned.

But right now, he had the grim, immediate certainty that this message was not some prank.

THIRTY-SEVEN

Susan had considered dashing back to her cottage to freshen her lipstick and dab on perfume, but time was of the essence.

And when Phil opened the door of his hotel room and said he had to leave within the hour because his flight to Deception Pan had been brought forward, she was glad she had come straight from seeing James.

"Then there's still time for a farewell drink if you're only taking off at five," she said, leaning against the doorframe. "Aren't you going to ask me in? It looks as though you're all packed and ready to go, with time to kill."

Phil's previously harried expression shifted into an uncharacteristic grin as he stood back and held the door open.

Susan swept in.

She had seen the hungry look he tried to hide, and the sight of it made her feel suddenly powerful. She lowered herself onto the bed, leaned back on one hand, and regarded him.

"So, you really do mean business," she said. "I'm impressed. I'd also like a whisky if you have one."

"The minibar was restocked this morning. I'm sure I can oblige."

He poured her a drink, then came and sat beside her.

"Not joining me?" she asked, taking a swallow before setting the glass aside and stretching herself back across the mattress, one arm above her head.

"Oh, I'm joining you," he said. "I'm simply not having a drink."

Then he leaned over her, his face inches from hers, and his hand slid up her thigh beneath her short khaki skirt.

He tugged gently at the elastic of her knickers, and Susan wriggled to help him as she purred, "Nice to know we're on the same page."

Kicking off the black lace, she grinned and sat up to straddle him, working at the buckle of his belt.

"So, you believe me, then? And you're doing this for me?" Her smile widened as she unzipped his fly and slipped her hand inside to cup him. "You're off to get justice for me?"

Phil closed his eyes and shuddered.

"I'm off to get justice for all of us," he said with a low groan, removing her hand only long enough to free himself and grip her waist. "Oh God, that's good," he muttered as he slid into her and she began to move.

"And you're going to catch Starky in the act of doing something illegal, and make him admit he killed Mike, and confirm Jeremy isn't my daughter's father?"

Phil's rhythm quickened.

"Can we talk about this later?" he ground out.

Susan didn't answer. She was already too caught up in the fierce, heady pleasure of sleeping with the man who had taken up her cause and seemed poised to deliver what she had wanted for fifteen years.

It was over quickly.

With a shudder Phil came, and Susan rolled off him, glancing sideways and feeling a thrill at the expression on his face. His eyes were closed. His lean, sharp-featured face looked almost heroic in repose.

Gently, she ran her fingers through his hair.

"Who's flying you to Deception Pan?" she whispered.

"I found an out-of-towner. Not a Maun pilot," he said, still with his eyes shut.

Susan thought about that. She had not climaxed and was left with a slight ache of frustration, but she supposed that had never really been the point of this seduction. Her own satisfaction could wait.

Phil rolled over, opened his eyes, and smiled into her face as he traced the line of her nose with one finger.

"You can understand that, with the delicacy of this operation, I'd want to make sure no one local was involved."

Susan nodded, her heart tightening unexpectedly at his gentleness. She could not remember when a man had last treated her with anything like kindness. And Phil was going out on a limb for her.

"That was clever," she murmured, catching his finger playfully between her lips. "You are the most incredible lover."

Her voice came out huskier than she intended. She badly wanted the rest of the whisky she could see on the table, but she also wanted him to know how much she appreciated him. So she deepened the admiration in her tone and said, "I can't imagine how neatly you've managed to put this together in so little time. How will you know when the moment is right to catch him?"

His smile broadened.

"You want me to give away all my secrets?"

"It's *our* secret," she reminded him. "I just can't believe you've managed to build a workable plan so quickly. But obviously you have." Then, all at once, a flicker of doubt ran through her and she blurted, "You're not just making this up to fob me off, are you, Phil?"

He looked genuinely offended.

"One of Starky's trackers is keeping me informed through locals along the line. That's how I got word so quickly that it's happening tomorrow. They've found a lion big and fine enough to satisfy the client, and Starky means to take them there in the early afternoon." As he toyed with one of her nipples, he added, "Generally speaking, the Kala-hari lion is a poor, scrawny beast compared with lions else-where on the continent. But this one is apparently exceptional. A beauty. Which means it'll fetch a better price."

"But hasn't the client already paid a fortune for it?" Susan asked.

"He has," said Phil. "I'm only saying it makes for a more exciting proposition than one of the usual miserable Kala-hari specimens." He pinched her nose lightly. "Don't second-guess my prowess in every arena, Susan. Tomorrow, mid-afternoon, justice will be delivered."

Susan let out a long breath. "I wish I could be there to see it."

Phil rose from the bed and began to dress.

"I think it's better if you're not. It could get messy."

Susan pushed herself up on one elbow. "Messy? What do you mean?"

"I mean, we have a shoot-to-kill policy when it comes to poaching," Phil said, zipping up his fly and buckling his belt.

Susan went cold.

"You're not going to shoot Starky, are you?"

Phil glanced at her without expression.

"I didn't think you cared."

"Not like *that*." She heard the alarm in her own voice. "I don't want to think I was responsible for... for his death."

"Well, you think he was responsible for your brother's."

"Yes... but—"

"Hey, relax." Phil smiled then, but there was something in it that did not reassure her. He picked up his overnight bag and swung it over his shoulder. "No one's going to get hurt except those who had it coming. Don't worry about Starky. I've got it all covered." He nodded towards the door. "Now, could you drive me to the airport? This fellow's coming in with his Bonanza, and he won't wait around. Better to leave the hire car here at Riley's than out by the perimeter fence where everyone can see it."

THIRTY-EIGHT

"Mothusi!" James strode out into the yard, waving the letter he'd just opened. "Did you see anyone deliver this?"

The old man nodded.

"Can you describe him to me?" James inhaled, trying to keep the concern from his voice. "Is he... perhaps dangerous?"

Mothusi's eyes widened. "It was Moses Moatlhodi. He comes from a very honest family. He is wise and respected, and not dangerous."

James fingered the letter, unsure how much more to say. "He wants me to meet him because I have a plane, and he says it is to prevent trouble. Have you any idea what that could mean?"

"Eh, Rra, are you asking me to roll the bones? Your wife asked me this too, and I warned her to beware of danger. Miss Verity, she is well?"

"Quite well, thank you, and no, I don't need you to roll the bones. I just want to know what sort of trouble Moses could be referring to."

Mothusi thought for a moment. "A cattle dispute, perhaps?" He frowned, leaning on his rake. "But I am surprised if Mr Moatlhodi would ask for your plane if that were the reason for his very great concern. Still... he has a son who is not quite so respectful as Mr Moatlhodi himself."

"He's asked me to meet him later this evening at Safari South. I just wondered if it was safe."

"Mr Moatlhodi is a very safe man, Rra."

Despite that reassurance ringing in his ears, James's concern was mounting. If it wasn't for the fact that he needed to be in Maun in order to discover where Saskia had disappeared to, he'd be engineering a way he could take Jack's place and fly to Deception Pan tomorrow. Suddenly, he was overwhelmed by the need to see Verity again.

And to reassure himself that she was safe.

However, right now, he needed to discover Saskia's whereabouts, so he turned his footsteps in the direction of the Okavango Air compound so he could make another call to the Stirling household.

He'd just parked near the airport and was climbing out when Alan and Jess crossed the road.

"Nice little Bonanza," said Jess, shading her eyes. James followed her gaze and saw she meant the red Beechcraft lifting off from the airport. "Is it the one that belonged to the Stirling boy who crashed his vehicle? Who is flying it back to Jo'burg for him?"

"Stirling?" James swung round so sharply he almost lost his footing. Red hot alarm speared him. "You're saying the Bonanza that flew in here two days ago belonged to someone called Stirling?"

Jess looked at Alan, who nodded. "Richard Stirling."

Out of the corner of his eye, James saw Susan heading

out through the airport gate towards her car. She was moving quickly and had not looked their way. When he called her, she seemed oddly reluctant to come over.

"What is it?" she asked.

James tried to stop his voice from shaking. "Alan says the lad who crashed his vehicle was called Richard Stirling. I was told that Richard Stirling is the name of the lad who flew our girls to the swamps. Was that his Bonanza that just took off? Have you heard anything more about where the girls are this weekend?"

Her eyes widened. "No, that wasn't his Bonanza," she said too quickly. "Some chap from Francistown did a touch-and-go to pick up—" Then she clapped a hand over her mouth. "So this lad, Richard Stirling, is the one who crashed his vehicle and was medevacced out of here two nights ago? Oh, my God. Was there anyone with him? Does anyone know? Could Angel and Saskia be out in the bush somewhere, hurt, and we don't even—" She drew another ragged breath. "What if some wild animal... a lion—"

Panic rose, hot and sour in James's throat. He turned to Alan and Jess, explaining in clipped, disbelieving bursts.

"Susan and I found out yesterday that our girls had skipped off somewhere in a plane with a lad who'd only just got his private pilot's licence. We thought they were safe with this family, whose name is Stirling, but the parents left this lad and our girls to it, while they continued into the delta with their daughter. I had no idea until now that it was *his* Bonanza parked out there. And if he's in hospital in Jo'burg—"

"Then where are the girls?" Susan broke in on a shrill cry.

"God, that's awful," said Jess. "Is there anything we can do?"

James looked around wildly, searching for some practical next step. "Let's go to the Duck and ask around. Someone must know something."

"Who was it who medevac'ed the Stirling boy?" Susan asked shakily as the four of them hurried towards the local watering hole.

"Jack flew him down to Jo'burg, but he's now delayed with engine trouble," said Jess. "Brenda in the office got a call from him." She frowned. "Now I come to think of it, Brenda said Jack sounded a bit upset. He was meant to meet Starky tomorrow at Deception Pan but with the engine trouble, he obviously can't make it. But—surely he'd have said something if the girls had been in the vehicle with the bloke he flew out."

The Duck Inn was busy when they arrived. Geraldine, working behind the bar, said she had seen the Stirling lad after he was brought back to town from the crash.

"He was cut up pretty badly, but Alison stitched him up as best she could before they put him on a stretcher and loaded him into the Caravan. Jack flew him down to Jo'burg."

"Was anyone else in the vehicle with him?"

Geraldine shook her head. "Not as far as I know. I'm sure I'd have heard. Why?"

Susan and James exchanged a look.

"We've just learned our daughters climbed aboard a plane in Jo'burg with a fellow called Stirling," Susan said.

"To Maun?"

"Into the Okavango, we heard. But if that's his plane, maybe he dropped the girls and his parents somewhere in the swamps before he came back here."

James looked at Susan, but she said doubtfully, "It's

possible he left them somewhere safe and they're already back at school."

James shook his head. "No. I checked."

"Hey, Preibus!" Geraldine called to the other barman. "Do you know whether there were any girls with the young fellow who hit the tree last night?"

Preibus shook his head. "Don't know. But ask Dean Fletcher. He was in the car with the lad. Richard Stirling— that's his name, isn't it? I know they're friends."

It took them the better part of an hour to work out where Dean Fletcher might be found, and when they finally got to his cottage, the maid told them he was out and she had no idea when he would return.

"Please make sure he gets this," James said, scribbling a note and thrusting it into her hand. "I'll come back later and check. He can also find me—or leave a message for me —at the Okavango Air office or my cottage. Or, even at the Duck Inn. Please tell him it's important."

"Oh God, I don't know what to do!" wailed Susan once they were back at the Duck. She collapsed onto a bar stool and put her head in her hands. "Except have a double whisky. Want to join me?"

James shook his head. "I'm going back to the office to ring the Stirlings again. I'll keep trying until I hear some- thing. If you need me, I'll be by the phone."

This time he got through straight away, but it was Richard's aunt who answered. And she had nothing new to tell him.

"I'm so sorry to be so unhelpful," she said. "I've only just returned from the hospital. Richard was in surgery last night." Her voice caught. "The doctors say he'll make a full recovery and, of course, I'll ask him about your daughter the moment the anaesthetic wears off. My brother and his wife and daughter are still in the swamps, and I haven't managed to get hold of them, so I can't tell you anything more."

James thanked her and put the phone down.

When he looked at his watch, it was nearly eight.

There was no more he could do for the next half an hour, so he set off for Safari South.

He could ask around there too, before meeting the anonymous author of the letter who claimed not to be dangerous, whose name was Moses Moatlhodi, and whose son had perhaps talked his respectable father into asking a man with a plane to help settle some cattle dispute.

But he doubted that was the reason for this meeting.

Suddenly he was sick with worry—and foreboding.

Saskia was missing somewhere in the Delta, Verity might potentially be caught up in something shady at Deception Pan, and Susan was half hysterical and completely useless. She'd soon, no doubt, be completely shickered.

Everything seemed to be gathering towards a perfect storm.

THIRTY-NINE

Trying to think and act rationally, James parked beneath an acacia tree, exchanged greetings with an old man and his wife in a rickety trailer drawn by a donkey, then crossed the road.

Noise from the bar drifted out into the street, but apart from a few people moving in and out of Safari South, the night was quiet. He glanced towards the bougainvillea and, seeing no one, wondered if whoever had written the note had given up. He was twenty minutes late.

Then, as a little group who had briefly blocked his view peeled away and went inside the lodge, he saw a figure step out from the bushes and look around.

Moses Moatlhodi?

The well-dressed Motswana gentleman was stooped now, his hair grey and grizzled. He certainly did not look dangerous.

James moved forward with the customary greeting. "Dumela, Rra."

"Dumela, Captain." The old man bowed his head. "I am

Moses Moatlhodi, and I am very glad you are thinking it is a good idea to come here and speak to me. I am thinking you believe what I have to tell you is important. It makes this old man happy to be trusted with a very great secret."

James glanced over his shoulder as he took this in. The man did seem to have a flair for the dramatic. Saskia and her whereabouts were his chief worry. Concern over Verity came a close second.

He really did not have time for theatrics.

"I'm afraid I have to leave soon," he said, his mind still snagged on Saskia. "But I'm listening."

"This will not take long, Captain. I will tell you my story, and then you will see why it is important to find out what this Mr Phil is doing, so that he does not bring any more calamity than he already has to our village."

The name stopped James cold.

"Which Mr Phil are you talking about?"

"The Mr Phil who has dared to show his face in Maun and is thinking that the terrible thing he did has been forgotten. It has not." Moses drew himself up a little. "So when I see this Mr Phil in Maun village, and then I hear he is going to Deception Pan, I know he is planning a very bad thing. You have a plane, so you can follow him and, I hope, stop him. I could have asked any captain with a plane. Maybe they would believe me, and maybe they would not. But because I also know you have a wife at Deception Pan, whose safety would concern you, I think you are the best man to speak to."

A chill ran through James.

This man was suggesting Verity might be in danger.

And that Phil had something to do with it.

"I heard Mr Phil is a wildlife photographer," James said

carefully. "That's why he's going to Deception Pan. He shoots animals with a camera, not a gun."

"Captain, Mr Phil gets other men to shoot the animals that are forbidden to shoot, and then he takes the animal and sells it for money. This is how it works with Mr Phil."

James stared at him. "When has he done this?"

He had been worrying about Starky, and what Starky might be about to do. But Phil, surely, was unconnected to him.

Or had he been lying all along?

"He did this when one of the young men in our village near Tsau did a very terrible thing. This young man shot a lion that was causing great fear. The lion had killed a boy. The people called the young man a hero. But the authorities do not think like this. They think only of the lion, and of the tourists who must keep coming."

"And how is Mr Phil connected to that?"

"Mr Phil was with Botswana National Parks and Wildlife. He was nearby when this happened, and he came and made sure the young man went to prison."

"And did he?"

"Yes. This young man, who was brave and good, went to prison."

"But that was the law, Moses. I'm sorry it turned out that way. If the young man had had a proper defence, perhaps—"

"This young man went to prison, and Mr Phil took the lion. He put it in the back of his bakkie, and we all thought this was simply the justice of the white man." Moses's voice roughened. "But then Mr Phil sold the lion and made a lot of money. He said the lion was lost when he crossed a flooded river and the water came over the back and carried it away. But that is not true."

"How do you know?"

"Because one of Mr Phil's rangers, who is an honest man, said so. He says he knows Mr Phil took the lion to someone who skinned it. Then Mr Phil had a friend in Customs, and he paid him to look the other way."

James exhaled slowly. "How am I supposed to know whether any of this is true? Why ask me? What can I do? I need to get a message to Gaborone, to BNPW. They can send someone."

"Of course you can do that, Captain," Moses said. "But it will be too late by the time they come."

James narrowed his eyes. "How do you know something illegal is about to happen?"

"A young man I know is a camp hand on Mr Starky's safari. His name is Kutlo Ramotswe, which means obedience, and he is a good man. He heard that the German tourist wants to shoot a lion. He is worried because he knows it is against the law, and he does not want what happened to that brave young man in our village to happen again."

James felt a rush of blood to the head.

And Verity was there. In the middle of it.

To those who didn't know her, Verity could seem quiet, even passive. But when she saw injustice, she did not stay silent. What if she put herself squarely in the path of whatever was about to happen?

He shut his eyes for a second.

Moses went on. "I was refuelling the plane Mr Phil came in on when someone said to me, 'Moses, that is Mr Phil who stole the skin of the lion that sent Thabo Mogae to prison. Where is this bad man going?' And I said he was going to Deception Pan to photograph a lion, because that is what he told me. But the man said, 'No, he is going to get the lion, not the photograph. He is going to get the lion from the man who shoots it by pretending he is the law. Then he will get the money for it. That is how Mr Phil works.'"

Moses studied James a moment before adding, "And then I remembered you. Two days ago you told me you were going to Deception Pan to see your wife. Perhaps you do not remember me as the man who refuelled your plane. So I thought: you are the pilot who will want to make sure the bad thing Mr Phil and Mr Starky plan to do does not become a bad thing for your wife."

James swallowed hard. "Thank you for telling me, Moses. You're right that I need to go to Deception Pan." He looked up at the darkening sky. "But I can't go now. It's too dark. There's no way to get there before tomorrow. I'll have to leave at first light, though even that may be difficult. It's my rostered day off tomorrow, and I can't simply take a plane without authorisation."

"You will find a way, Captain. And I can be there to refuel your plane as early as you need me."

James left him with his head buzzing.

After a couple of fruitless enquiries at the bar in Safari South about the girls, he drove back into Maun, his heart pounding. Deception Pan was impossible to reach before morning, even if he left now. The roads were sandy and impassable at night.

No, he would have to be patient.

But was Verity safe in the meantime?

Was Moses telling the truth about Phil, whose surname the old man could not even give him?

Moses was even suggesting Starky might be involved in a poaching operation with Phil. Yet Starky had lived in

Maun for fifteen years. He had friends here. Allies. James had arrived only weeks ago.

How was he supposed to requisition a plane and go tearing off at dawn on the strength of one old man's story? Of course, he could pass on what Moses had told him to the authorities, but it was Sunday tomorrow, and by then, if the suspected poaching was real, it would already be underway.

On the way back, he stopped again at the Duck Inn in case there was any news of Saskia and Angie. They had not been seen for more than twenty-four hours now, and by this point he was sick with fear.

Susan was at the bar. The instant she saw him, she broke away from the people around her and hurried over. Her mascara had run. She was clearly a little drunk, but the panic on her face was real as she seized his arm.

"Ange and Saskia got dropped at Deception Pan yesterday by that Stirling kid who's now in hospital in Jo'burg!"

"How did you learn this?"

"Someone came into the bar saying there was an urgent phone call for you at the Okavango Air office while you were away, and I said I'd take it." Susan gulped. "It was the aunt. She started talking about Richard and his accident and all the rest of it, and I said I didn't give a shit about Richard; I wanted to know about the girls. She got all snaky and repeated that Richard had taken the girls to Maun, but they weren't in the car with him, so they must still be there. Then I lost it a bit and said there was no sign of them in Maun and they weren't back at school either, so somebody had to know something." She sucked in a breath. "Actually, I yelled at her and put the phone down. I didn't think she'd ring again, but she did. She finally got hold of her brother and his family, who'd come back from the swamps after hearing about Richard, and the niece said he had dropped Ange and Saskia at Deception Pan because they wanted to surprise Verity." Susan shook her head. "It sounds so out of character. Would Saskia really do that? What the hell were they thinking?"

James closed his eyes as relief surged through him.

At least now they knew where the girls were.

Safe?

Were they really safe?

The thought hit him a split second later with such force it was almost physical.

Susan gave a shaky smile. "I'm sure Verity's got them working in camp and they're fine and they're not in any…" Her voice trailed off. Her hands trembled as she lifted her glass, drained it, then said more forcefully, "My God, I am going to have words with Angel. James, you have to go to Deception Pan tomorrow. First thing. And bring them back."

James shut his eyes again against the force of what was now colliding in his mind.

The girls were with Verity. At Deception Pan.

And that was where Phil was headed for his supposedly nefarious purpose.

Tomorrow.

He had to get there tomorrow at first light. There was no other option. Whatever was brewing out there, he had to be there before it broke over the people he loved.

If he could have gone that very minute, he would have.

"I'm going at first light," he said grimly.

"At first light?" Susan sagged with relief and let her head fall onto the bar.

James frowned. He put a hand on her back and gave her a gentle shake.

"Suze. You don't think they're in any danger, do you?"

"Danger?" She looked up too quickly. "What danger could they be in?"

James hesitated.

Then, very carefully, he said, "Suze... what can you tell me about this bloke you've been seeing? Phil?"

CHAPTER

FORTY

The mood in camp was strained.

Verity made breakfast with the girls' help while Charlize lolled on a recliner and watched them. Saskia seemed fascinated by the woman, whispering about her to Angie. When she asked whether Charlize was Kurt's wife, Verity merely shook her head.

"They're friends," she said, unwilling to elaborate.

Having her daughter in camp constrained everything. Starky seemed tense and abrupt, which she might have put down to the girls having gatecrashed the safari, except that Kurt and Thomas were in unusually good spirits. And they were the ones paying the bill. Surely that ought to have smoothed the scowl from Starky's brow.

When Richard failed to turn up for a second day running, Verity's nails were nearly bitten to the quick. In fact, Starky took her severely to task when he found her worrying at the cuticle of her little finger after she'd walked a short distance from camp to stare out over the endless, dusty plains.

"It's my job to worry about this safari," he said.

"I feel terrible that the girls are still here. What do you suppose could have happened to that young man? What if he's had an accident?"

Starky grunted. "Nothing we can do about that, is there? We'll hear soon enough."

"Having two uninvited sixteen-year-olds in camp is hardly what Kurt bargained for," she said grimly. "I'm so sorry. I've put them to work. At least Thomas is smiling for the first time."

"And there's a lot to be said for that. Sullen little twerp," Starky muttered. "If I had a son like that, I'd whip him into shape. Make him a man."

"Poor future son," said Verity, with just enough sarcasm to let him know what she thought. "Let's hope you have only girls, then."

He only grunted again.

When he didn't answer, she thought perhaps she had overstepped. Not that he hadn't trampled over the employee boundary already. But then he turned and said, with sudden seriousness, "And what if I did suddenly discover I had a daughter? Except that nobody knew but the mother, who never said anything? Or maybe she did, only I didn't realise that's what she was trying to tell me. What should I do then?"

Verity blinked.

"Goodness—how could you ever be sure if nobody has said anything?" It was rare for Starky to speak so openly about anything private. Perhaps, now that she had properly rebuffed him, he felt safer asking for advice as a friend. "I suppose it's always a risk," she said. "You are... popular with the ladies."

"Ha." His look was bleak. "Always waiting for the right

one, I suppose. I've not been lucky like you, Verity. You found your man right off the bat."

"Did I?"

He raised one eyebrow. "Don't give me that. Whatever I may have said before, anyone can see you and James are great together. When he came into camp and I sensed trouble in paradise, I decided to give you a bit of a wake-up call." He sent her a half-smile. "And you thought it was all about me, didn't you?"

But the flicker of humour vanished as quickly as it came, and Verity's stomach twisted again at the thought of the pain she had caused James.

Surely he could not really believe she would trade her life with him to go back to Melbourne for that glamorous job. Yet that might well be what he had read into the letter she had never intended to send to Sarah—and which no longer truly represented what she felt.

"I suppose I should thank you for reminding me not to take the good things in life for granted," she said.

Starky smiled, but distractedly. Was he thinking about this vague paternity question, or about the hunt? Verity still could not decide whether he had the recklessness to risk poaching, and her adrenaline peaked once more at the thought. If she witnessed anything she believed was truly illegal, what could she do?

So far, the men had shot a few animals, but nothing larger than the ill-fated kudu that Thomas had peppered. Clearly, Kurt was champing at the bit for something more impressive—like a mighty predator. Xixae, the San tracker, had come into camp several times chattering excitedly about some lion spoor he had found, and from Starky's response it was obvious he believed it would delight his client.

A lion? Surely, when it came to it, Starky wouldn't allow Kurt to shoot a lion?

Verity felt increasingly awkward under the silence that fell as Starky stared out over the plains.

"You must miss your hunting lodge," she said at last, hoping she sounded casual. "I heard you once had a girlfriend who did the decorating. I saw a double-page spread in the *Okavango Observer*. People say it's one of the best hunting lodges in the Delta."

"People say that, do they?" He rolled his eyes. "I bet they say plenty of other things too."

Verity felt abruptly snubbed until he turned with a rueful grin.

"Sorry. Just tense, that's all. Kurt is more demanding than he looks."

"I hope Charlize is all right," Verity said instinctively, and his mouth twisted.

"Charlize knows how to look after herself. I wouldn't worry too much about her. That wet-behind-the-ears Thomas is the one you should feel sorry for. Not that I do. He's a milksop."

"Because he doesn't want to be on a hunt his father dragged him on?" Verity raised an eyebrow. "He has principles. That's heroic, not milksoppish."

"Ah, Verity. It all depends on how you choose to see it, doesn't it? So many shades of grey. Nobody all good, nobody all bad. Though some people seem determined to think I'm entirely bad."

Verity pressed her palms together, summoning the courage to ask what she most wanted to know.

"What is Kurt going to shoot on the big hunt?"

Starky turned, looking for a moment as if he might answer properly. Then his expression shut down.

"Anything that gives him kudos back home. Don't worry—Kurt won't leave unsatisfied. Men like him never do."

The bitterness in his tone took Verity aback, and before she could respond the two girls appeared between the acacias.

"Mum, Charlize wants a cup of tea and some of that camp-oven bread you've got cooking in the fire," Saskia called, with Angie beside her.

"Well, Charlize can wait," said Verity more sharply than she intended. Then she looked more closely at Angie and noticed the shadows beneath her eyes. "Are you all right, Angie?"

"I didn't sleep well," the girl said, looking away.

"Are you worried about that boy, Richard Stirling? And why he hasn't come back for you?" Verity hesitated, wondering whether he might be more than just a pilot friend, and was about to ask something gentler when Saskia repeated, "Mum, Charlize is really hungry."

"It won't be ready for another ten minutes." Verity sighed. Of all the clients, Charlize was the most demanding. "There are more important things to worry about, you know."

Saskia glanced between her mother and Starky. "Do you mean us being here? I'm really sorry!" she said, turning appealingly to Starky. "It's my fault that boy didn't come back. I told Richard that Mum had an extra tent and basically gave him the signal that we could stay here. I didn't think it'd be for more than one night. But Thomas really likes having us here," she added brightly.

That, at least, made Starky laugh for the first time all day.

His whole face changed when he smiled. The severity

lifted; the charm returned; and for a second Verity was struck afresh by how alarmingly handsome he was. The jolt she felt was oddly similar to the jolt she had once felt meeting James at university—not sexual in the same way; but the force of his personality.

James had had that force too, back then: young, driven, determined to make a career in a brutal industry. His passion for flying had eclipsed everything, and she had admired that tenacity in him as she had never admired it in any other boy she'd dated.

She needed to tell James that.

"Yes, you girls have been quite the tonic for young Thomas," said Starky. "Why don't you get him a cup of tea and some of that camp-oven bread and wait on him a bit? Earn your keep by making him feel he's landed in Nirvana—"

He lifted a hand to halt the protest he plainly expected from Verity.

"Since Thomas is not a hunter and hates being here. He's not exactly used to young ladies who speak to him. His English isn't too bad, is it?"

"It's all right," Saskia conceded, then she suddenly bent with a gasp of pain.

Both Verity and Starky turned at once.

"What's wrong?" Starky asked sharply. "The ankle's all right, isn't it? You got the all-clear from Bara before discharge, didn't you?"

Saskia nodded. "It's fine. Just sometimes there's a pain, but it goes away quickly."

"In the bone?" Starky asked.

Saskia nodded again, then widened her eyes. "The croc couldn't have injected poison into me like—"

"A zombie!" Angie burst out with a shaky laugh.

"Maybe Saskia will turn into a zombie. Or a baby crocodile right in front of my eyes."

It was the first spark of humour Angie had shown in hours, but it vanished almost at once as Saskia tugged at her sleeve and led her back towards camp.

Verity watched them go with a frown, then turned back to Starky.

"I'm worried about Angie. You don't suppose Thomas has behaved inappropriately?"

"That little milksop? No. I don't think Thomas is the danger here." He glanced after the girls. "I'd be more concerned about Saskia's leg." Then, seeing the alarm that flashed across Verity's face, he added quickly, "I don't want to frighten you, but even if the bite healed perfectly on the surface, there's a chance of a flare-up. Osteomyelitis can appear later if infection lingers in the bone."

Verity went cold.

At once he patted her on the back. "It's rare. Very rare. I'm only warning you so that if she gets sudden pain or a fever, you know not to muck around. She'd need a hospital."

"I thought she was completely out of the woods. This is the first time she's mentioned pain."

"Then it's probably nothing."

Verity turned, ready to head back to camp, but Starky touched her arm to stop her.

"Hey—since you noticed Angie seems down, I need to ask your advice."

Verity frowned, her anxiety shifting course yet again.

Starky shoved his hands into his pockets and looked at the ground before clearing his throat.

"I found out yesterday that the reason the girls flew all the way here was because Angie wanted information about her... dad. They came all this way to corner me and give me the third degree. I don't know how much of the story you've heard."

"I do!" Verity gasped. "Susan told me. The girl's father was Susan's ex-boyfriend who killed Mike, her brother. Oh, poor Angie. What a dreadful burden to grow up with."

"Who told you that? Susan?"

Verity had just begun to repeat the little she knew about the disastrous hunting trip when she stopped short.

"What's the matter? Has Susan got it wrong? You were both there."

"Susan wasn't on the hunt. She stayed in camp while the rest of us went out shooting. Obviously." Starky's tone sharpened. "She wasn't there when Jeremy got into a fight with Mike, or to hear what was said, or to know when he left or why."

"But the fight between Mike and Jeremy was because Mike discovered Jeremy had behaved... improperly with his sister." Verity blushed. "Couldn't you at least tell Angie something kind about Jeremy? That he was only a boy? That it must have been an accident? Surely he'd have stood a chance in court, even on a manslaughter charge, if he'd lived long enough to give his side? It was appalling bad luck that he died first. Couldn't you just say a few decent things to ease Angie's mind? It must have been awful growing up believing her father was a murderer. That he'd killed her own mother's brother." She shuddered. "Please, Starky. Surely you can say something to lighten that burden."

Starky made a sound of frustration.

"Verity, that's just it. I don't know how much of the truth I ought to tell her."

"What do you mean?"

He looked at her, then up at the fierce blue sky above

them. The silence stretched between them and Verity tensed as she watched the muscles work in his face. *The truth?* What the hell did that mean?

Starky snapped a twig in two as he avoided her look. "All right," he said slowly, as if the words were painful. "You know what? I'm going to tell you. You might help me work this out."

"You want me to be your therapist?"

"I want you to listen." He drew in another slow breath. "The truth is, I barely thought about Susan Jensen at all until I heard she was back in Maun."

"Though she was your best friend's sister, and you grew up together? I have got that right, haven't I?" She hesitated. "Or maybe 'best friend' is going too far."

Starky shook his head energetically. "He *was* my best friend. I arrived in a new town when I was ten. We were inseparable. Susan was four years younger. A baby, we thought at the time. Well, because she was. But when we went on that hunting trip—" He closed his eyes as if the memory pained him, "I couldn't help being aware of how her eyes followed me everywhere. I could see she was absolutely...smitten. And, suddenly, she wasn't a baby anymore. She was—Well, she was quite gorgeous. And...oh, so willing. God, I shouldn't have done it, but—"

"But what... Starky?" The vague unease Verity had been feeling over this revelation was coalescing into something a good deal more concrete.

"But I had a fling with her." He closed his eyes, raising his head to the sky, then swung round, blinking, as he added, roughly, "No, I goddamed couldn't do the decent thing, even then, when it came to women. I went to bed with her. I took her virginity. Oh, she wanted it. She wanted it so much, but—"

The air seemed to have left Verity's lungs. She didn't know what to say.

Starky exhaled, shakily. "I knew it was wrong. God knows why I'd do that to my best friend—"

"To your best friend's *sister*—!" Verity ground out.

"All right, all right, yes! My best friend's sister," Starky muttered. "When we went hunting the next day, I'd never felt so bad. I didn't know what to do because I knew Mike would skin me alive if he found out. I just hoped he never would. But then, when we went camping, Mike confronted Jeremy. He'd heard rustlings in Susan's tent during the night. He knew someone had spent the night with her and he assumed it was Jeremy. Mike was livid. He flew into a rage like I'd never seen before."

"And you didn't say anything to set the record straight?" Verity asked.

Starky hesitated. "After Mike punched Jeremy, Jeremy just staggered off. We watched him go. Mike, Phil, and me. And I just let him leave. I remember being so relieved that my best mate was still my best mate." He shrugged and looked at Verity, as if challenging her comment.

"Why didn't you tell the truth later? If you were so worried about losing Mike's friendship, why not tell the truth after he'd died? When losing his friendship didn't matter anymore?"

Verity was working hard to keep up, putting the puzzle pieces together. Was Starky really saying, between the lines, that he was the one who had got Susan pregnant? Of course he was, and it was shocking. But if that were the case, the bigger question was why he still hadn't done the right thing, later—when it was, if anything, even more important?

"Ah, Verity, there is so much more to the story." His look

was almost pitying. "But now is not the place. Let me just say that…I got a reprieve. Mike had written in his diary that Jeremy had slept with Susan and that he'd laid into him. That they'd had a fight and Jeremy had stormed off. Well, that diary went to Mike's parents, and…suddenly I was off the hook." He shook his head, then ran a calloused hand across his sweaty brow. "I didn't know there was more to it than I knew."

"You didn't?"

Starky scuffed the dirt with the toe of his boot. He couldn't have missed the scepticism in Verity's tone.

"A couple of months after the hunting expedition," he said, "I was in Jo'burg, getting my flying licence at Lanseria, when my flatmate passed on a message from Suze. It was muddled. Maybe he muddled it, maybe she did. But what I took from it was that she'd read Mike's diary and now she needed help. Money."

"She'd read Mike's diary? But then, she must have read that her brother wrongly accused Jeremy? Of course, she'd want to call you and…tell you."

"Tell me? God, I didn't even think she might have anything worse to tell me than that she'd read about the diamond—"

"The diamond? Starky, what are you saying? How could you not have considered that Susan was pregnant?" She wanted to quiz him more about this sudden deviation. A diamond? But Angie's parentage was what she really needed to understand.

He shrugged. "I just didn't. I'd slept with girls before. Quite a few of them, actually. And none of them had got pregnant. Oh, I'm not proud of it, Verity, but if a girl looked at me a certain way, and was happy to go all the way, then I figured that just having a good time for an hour or two was all there was to it. Time to move on, after that." He kicked the dirt. "I'm a bastard, through and through. But—" He straightened and looked her in the eye, "I do know that if I'd realised, I'd got my best mate's sister in the family way, I would have done the right thing. I can say that with confidence because—

"Well?"

"Because Mike was my best mate. Anyway, when I got these messages from Susan, I didn't want to go into the whole diamond thing because I knew she'd got the wrong end of the stick. To be honest, I thought she was trying to blackmail me into giving her something to keep her mouth shut, so—" He paused. "Well, I sent her two hundred rand."

The diamond again. Resisting the urge to circle back, Verity replied, ""You didn't ring her back to...to challenge Susan about why she was asking for money?"

"No." Starky wiped the sweat from his forehead. "I thought Mike must have written something about—" He broke off, regrouped, and began again. "A few months before, Mike and I had made an unexpected discovery on a trip to Makgadikgadi Pan. Something that could have made us rich. We were still arguing about what to do with it when we went on that hunt. At first, he wanted me to show my dad, but I said it was just a rock, and probably not worth much. You see, I knew my dad would just steal it if he knew we had it." Grimly, he added, "I'm just a chip off the old block, aren't I? Anyway, yes, it was a diamond. And, it just so happened that your husband, James's father, was working at the Orapa Diamond Mine at the time. Mike's uncle seemed the perfect—and safest—person to consult, so we were really disappointed when James pulled out of 1974 safari." His lips quirked as he looked at Verity. "Why *did* James pull out?"

This time it was Verity who scuffed the dirt with her toe. "I got pregnant."

She was surprised when Starky burst out laughing. "You and Susan, both, it would appear!" Then he sobered suddenly. "Oh God, I'm a father," he whispered. "What do I do?"

His pain was so abrupt, but so real, she touched his arm in sympathy.

"I swear to God, I would have done the right thing if I'd known," he said, gripping her hand. "I'd have done it long before now, if only to honour Mike's memory."

"And to do the right thing by Susan and Angie," Verity had to remind him as he gripped her arm more tightly, before adding softly, "And Jeremy."

"Mum!"

It was Saskia again, appearing from between the acacias. She stopped short, her eyes flicking between them. Verity and Starky had stepped apart so quickly it looked awkward all the same.

"Charlize is getting antsy," Saskia said, giving them a distinctly suspicious look.

Verity took a careful step to widen the distance between herself and Starky. What had Saskia seen? It didn't appear she'd overheard, but the suspicious way she was eyeing Verity made her wonder.

"She really wants that damper."

"And you can't get it for her? Honestly, Saskia, you might at least do something to earn your keep." Verity was torn, reluctant to break leave Starky.

But Saskia remained where she was, hands planted on her hips, watching the two of them.

Then she sighed. "I don't know if it's ready, Mum. You'll have to come. *Please!*" she added, snatching Verity's hand

and starting to pull her away. As if she suddenly feared something she didn't understand.

"Sorry," Verity whispered to Starky as she allowed her daughter to drag her back towards camp, where Charlize was exactly as she had been left: stretched on her lounger, twisting a strand of hair round her finger as she read.

"Thank God Kurt has finally found something to kill," Charlize said, glancing up with a bright, avid look. "Until he bags his trophy and can channel his virility elsewhere, I shall be working hard for my money when the lights go out."

The suggestive laugh that followed took Verity aback and made her dislike the coarse but beautiful young woman even more.

"And what, exactly, is this trophy he is going to bag?" Verity asked.

"Starky says Xixae found the spoor of a lion this afternoon. A Kalahari lion of greater than usual magnificence."

Verity froze. Then carefully she straightened as she lifted the damper from the fire. "I do not believe Kurt is allowed to shoot a lion," she said as she began unwrapping the foil. "Starky has already used up his big-cat quota this year."

Charlize pushed her hair back, a slow, predatory smile touching her mouth.

"If Kurt wants a lion, he will get one." She sighed. "And we shall all be made to watch. Kurt is dramatic beneath that cold, military exterior. He likes an audience. If Xixae has truly found him a glorious male with a full mane, then it doesn't matter whether Starky has exhausted his quota, or however you phrase it. Kurt will get his lion."

She stretched luxuriously.

"Me? I've got my sights on a rather different kind of

trophy." She gave a short laugh. "Kurt has shown me the spot in his grand Munich home where his lion skin will lie. The home he shares with his fat little hausfrau. But I'm much more interested in where *I* fit into that picture." Her eyes glittered. "I'm very good at stalking prey, you see, and I think I'll be making a trip to Munich before very long."

Verity busied herself scraping the blackened crust from the bread. There seemed little point in arguing over lions and quotas. She wondered whether Kurt's intentions and Charlize's ambitions were as aligned as Charlize believed. Beauty made a useful weapon, but it did not always make a woman safe.

And if this was an illegal kill, then Verity would not keep her mouth shut. Not like Starky had when the truth would have saved so many so much pain. Blood coursed through her body at the thought. Inside, she was in turmoil, but on the outside, she was surprised at the calm she was able to project.

"What about you, Verity?" Charlize asked, feigning concern. "You're fretting over a lion when perhaps you should be fretting more about keeping sweet that nice husband you take for granted. Me? I take nothing for granted, and I'm a far better hunter than Kurt will ever be. Let him have his little boy games in the bush. Boom!" She mimed sighting down a rifle and firing. "He gets his lion. Then what? His pleasure lasts five minutes. Clever women like me play the long game. We hunt in boardrooms and bedrooms. We are strategic. Careful. The real trophies are not found in the bush."

Her pupils in her blue gaze seemed to pierce her. Verity turned away in disgust.

"You worry about what your eyes can see, but your thinking doesn't go any deeper?"

Then, with a little laugh full of condescension, she added, "Even if you do not know Starky as intimately as I do, surely even you can see it makes no sense for an admired professional hunter like him to risk everything he has built over twenty years by letting a client shoot whatever he wants if it is against the law? Why would Starky risk gaol when it would take only you, or me, or one of the local camp hands, to whisper it to the authorities?"

She stretched again, catlike. "Ah, if we only understood the ways of the world and how far men like Starky and Kurt will go to get what they want. Now put some butter on that damper. It may be an athletic night. I'll need all my reserves."

FORTY-ONE

Sleep eluded Verity.

Charlize's words kept circling in her mind: *Your reasoning does not take you deeper.*

She tossed restlessly on her camp bed, listening to the night sounds of the African bush.

Then a whispered conversation outside her tent made her freeze.

"...must move tonight."

Starky's voice, pitched low but urgent.

Another voice answered in Setswana, too quick and quiet for her to catch, but Starky's reply was unmistakable.

"No. Tell him to wait. The German knows what he's paying for."

The voices faded. Only the rasp of cicadas and the distant laugh of a hyena carried in the stillness.

Verity's heart began to pound. She was not meant to hear that.

Or was she imagining a conspiracy where none existed?

She rolled onto her side, thinking of Charlize and that knowing little smile. Perhaps the call girl understood far more than Verity had given her credit for. After all, wasn't that Charlize's trade—observing men, studying their weaknesses, appetites and secrets, then using what she learned?

A branch snapped outside.

Through a gap in the tent flaps, Verity glimpsed Xixae moving through the shadows. He was carrying something wrapped in canvas. The bundle disappeared into Starky's tent.

Sleep was out of the question now.

Verity slipped on her boots and crept to the tent opening. Camp lay still beneath the moon, washed pale and silver. Only the embers of the fire held any colour, glowing a dull orange. As she watched, Starky emerged from his tent and crossed to the vehicle, moving with quiet purpose. He reached into the back and drew out something long, wrapped in cloth.

A rifle?

But why the secrecy?

The crack of another twig made her jump. Starky's head snapped up and for one sickening moment his gaze seemed to fix on her tent. She held her breath and did not dare move.

At last he turned away and disappeared into the shadows beyond the firelight, the long wrapped object in his hands. A few minutes later, the low rumble of the vehicle's engine fractured the silence. It faded quickly. He must have pushed the vehicle some distance before starting it.

Verity zipped her tent shut with trembling fingers.

There could be innocent explanations for what she had seen.

But as she lay in the dark, listening to the rustling of the surrounding bush, one thought kept returning:

What kind of hunt required such secrecy?

VERITY WOKE at dawn after a broken, unsatisfying sleep.

It was not only the strangeness of what she had heard and seen. There was also the moral dilemma of keeping from Angie information the girl surely had a right to know.

And yet it was not Verity's place to tell her.

If Starky had never found the right moment to tell Mike that it was he—and not Jeremy—who had slept with Susan, then he certainly needed to choose his moment with Angie carefully. The poor girl had been quiet and withdrawn all evening, and Verity's heart clenched for her.

Around the campfire after dinner, Verity had also watched Saskia like a hawk for any sign of pain in her ankle, relieved each time her daughter seemed her usual healthy, exuberant self.

Now she breathed in the cool pre-dawn air and wished she did not have to get up at all. Today promised to be trying in far too many ways.

If Kurt really was going to hunt a lion—and wanted an audience for it—Verity wished neither to witness the death of a magnificent wild cat nor an illegal act. She would have to tell the authorities. How could she not? But at what risk to herself? To the girls?

What was Starky thinking?

Charlize's cryptic words niggled at her each time she turned them over.

She was distracted at last by rustling and low sounds of excitement from the nearby tent. At first she thought it must be Kurt and Charlize, but when she peered through the netting into the pale pink dawn, she realised Xixae had come into camp and was relaying news about the impending hunt.

Or rather, about the impending trophy.

When Verity had pulled on her khakis and stepped outside, Thomas was standing by the crackling fire looking anything but delighted, a shadow beside the looming presence of his father. Charlize was up too, looking absurdly beautiful for a woman not yet wearing makeup.

"I told you it would be today," Charlize was saying, and there was triumph in her voice. "I told you I was good luck and you would finally find a Kalahari lion worth something."

A few feet away, Starky was speaking to Xixae in pidgin, full of guttural clicks and quick emphatic sounds. He looked animated. Verity felt the foreboding return in full force.

A Kalahari lion.

She still could not quite believe that was really what they intended.

"What's the plan?" she asked, intercepting him as he strode towards the vehicle.

He opened the back. The guns in the rack gleamed dully, and Verity felt her heart clench. Was last night's overheard conversation nothing more than ordinary preparation for a major hunt? Was she now reading menace into everything?

"Xixae is going to lead us to the trophy," Starky said briskly. "Could take an hour. Could take eight. We leave in twenty minutes. Make sure there's enough food and drink packed for any contingency."

Verity hesitated. The words caught in her throat.

Then they burst out.

"But... shooting a lion is illegal."

Starky turned on her at once.

"Are you accusing me of breaking the law, Verity?"

His tone was so sharp that she physically stepped back,

winded by her own boldness. Confrontation was not her natural mode, and in this case it might be downright dangerous. Why had she blurted it out?

Starky returned to arranging equipment in the back of the vehicle, but his voice remained clipped and hard.

"You accepted this job. You heard the rumours. You knew the risks. Don't start getting precious on me now."

Verity swallowed hard. Then, on impulse, said quietly, "Be careful, Starky."

He stopped. Looked at her. And chose to hear something else in her words.

"Careful?" A hint of softness crossed his face. "I'm always careful, petal."

Then he brushed past her to speak to Kurt before returning for more equipment.

Sleepily, Angie and Saskia emerged from their tent, rubbing their eyes as they took in the scene. The low sun cast long shadows across the camp and made the girls' hair glow. Angie looked wan and miserable, sending dark, resentful looks in Starky's direction.

Starky, Verity noticed, looked oddly reticent and uncertain when Saskia approached, dragging Angie behind her.

"Hey, Starky, good luck!" Saskia chirped, all youthful enthusiasm in painful contrast to the heaviness of the morning. "You'll get your kill just like you got that croc that nearly did me in. Ange, cheer up. There'll be lots to talk about when the fellas get back."

Verity took it as an oblique attempt to lift her cousin's spirits and wondered, not for the first time, when Starky would find the courage to tell Angie the truth. The more she looked at the two of them, the more certain she became that Susan had not lied.

Starky most definitely was Angie's father.

He jumped into the passenger seat and revved the engine, shattering the dawn quiet as Florence packed the cooler boxes with the provisions Verity had organised. Kurt climbed in beside him, while Thomas, Kutlo and Xixae clambered into the back.

"It'll be great, Thomas. Whatever happens!" Saskia called, running forward to squeeze Thomas's hand.

For the first time that morning, a ghost of a smile crossed the boy's face.

When the vehicle finally pulled away, Verity returned to the centre of camp—the fire—with a sinking feeling. With the men gone, the place felt oddly hollow. The excitement had gone with them, leaving behind only two women, two adolescent girls and Philemon, the remaining camp attendant, all waiting for news of what the men would bring back.

She wondered what James would think of any of it. He was against hunting, certainly, though if Verity had not realised she was pregnant all those years ago, he would have gone on that ill-fated 1974 hunt with his cousins.

Might he have prevented what happened to Mike?

Might he have become fast friends with Starky instead, over beers and cigarettes and that careless adolescent freedom?

She would never know.

"Mum! Charlize is speaking to you."

Saskia's voice snapped her out of it.

Charlize was staring at her with a look of bored distaste.

"I asked if you wanted to see the kill," Charlize drawled, taking a sip from the flask on the camp table. "Kurt says we're welcome to. Well, he wants me to witness his prowess and is sending the vehicle back if the tracker runs it to ground close enough. I don't want to, but I suppose I should."

"Why would I want to watch a poor creature killed just to inflate Kurt's ego? Or yours, for that matter?" Verity asked, more sharply than she intended.

Charlize shrugged, unoffended. "I don't. But I will. I thought I'd ask you all the same." She inspected her nails. "Have you got any more *Fair Lady* magazines?"

Verity felt herself colour under the scrutiny of the girls. Why was she so prickly? Because she had been thinking about James? Worrying about him? About them?

And, of course, about the lion.

"Can we go if Starky sends the vehicle back?" Saskia pleaded, her eyes bright with excitement. "Just because *you* don't want to go doesn't mean you should stop us."

That was emotional manipulation, and Saskia was a master of it.

"No, you can't, Saskia. This is for the paying clients. We need to respect that."

"Please, Mum. You can't say no. Thomas really wants us to go."

"Thomas is not paying for this safari. His father is," said Verity tightly. "I will only allow you to go if Kurt explicitly asks for your company, which I think is highly unlikely."

FORTY-TWO

James glanced from his watch to the pink glow spreading along the horizon.

He had tried to put Susan off the idea of coming with him, but she had been tenacious. When he had finally told her there was more at stake than simply retrieving two runaway teenagers, she had stuck out her chin and demanded to know what he meant.

"This guy, Phil? You tell me he's off to Deception Pan to take photographs? My intel is that he's a poacher."

That had taken the wind out of her sails. But only for a moment.

Immediately she had snapped, "You've got it all wrong! He's anti-poaching. He heads up the Botswana National Parks and Wildlife anti-poaching unit, and that's why I got him to come up here. To investigate Starky, who is about to take a client on an illegal lion hunt. Phil is the good guy."

Then, at the sceptical look on James's face, she had added even more vehemently, "Do you think I'd be stupid enough to get involved with some shady character—a man heading towards where my daughter currently is? Ange is with Starky, and Phil's out to *get* Starky—"

James had been baffled. "Because you told him to? Why? Starky was your brother's friend."

At that, Susan had burst into tears, after which James had got nothing coherent out of her.

So he was surprised now to see her hailing him from the edge of the airfield as he climbed into the Cessna. Since Jack had been unable to do the scheduled supply run into Deception, James had managed to swap rosters with the pilot taking his place. He was leaving earlier than planned, determined either to reach Deception or at least be in place to intercept Phil.

"Weren't you going to wait for me?" Susan demanded, puffing from the effort of running over from where she had parked. "My daughter's out there too!"

James, who had jumped back down to the tarmac to open the passenger door for her, gave her a quick look up and down.

"Have you even been to bed?"

Her hair was tangled. Her eye makeup was smeared.

"Oh God, do I look that bad?" she asked, climbing in. Then, as he reached across to fasten the harness, she sent him a baleful look. "Is this really necessary? I've done the waist belt. You know I hate being constrained."

"Yes, I'd gathered that," said James drily. "And the shoulder harness is necessary, otherwise I'm not taking you anywhere."

Despite himself, he smiled. "And you don't look that bad. Not for someone who's plainly had only a few hours' sleep and as much to drink as you have."

"Do you think I drink too much?" she asked once they were airborne. "I do, don't I?"

James shrugged. "How much is too much? I've no idea how much you drink. And I'm not your conscience."

"It's one of the reasons my parents sent Angie to boarding school. I'm a terrible mother. They should have done it years earlier, they said. Neglectful, they called me." She swallowed. "Well, I'm not neglectful now. Angie is out there with Starky and I've got to save her."

James tried to reassure her. "Why are you so worried about Starky? Phil's the one we may need to worry about. Verity is with Angie and Saskia. The girls will be fine. They're hardly going to be anywhere near Starky when his client bags his lion."

"You've got it wrong about Phil. And you don't know Starky will keep the girls away from danger."

"No, I don't," James admitted. "But there's no point spinning out worst-case scenarios while we're still up here. We just need to get there as fast as we can and see what's going on. If Starky really is planning something illegal, maybe our turning up will stop him. And if your friend Phil is unethical, perhaps he'll hold back too. Nobody is going to start shooting up the place if we suddenly appear. There'll be too many witnesses."

He really did wish Susan had not come. She was only going to complicate things.

Earlier that morning he had contacted BNPW in Gaborone and passed on the Deception Pan coordinates with a stripped-back message conveying his suspicions.

He did not hold out much hope of action from that quarter, which was all the more reason he had to do what he could himself.

He glanced at Susan. Her eyes were closed as they flew over the dry yellow Kalahari. The moment he landed at Deception, he would settle her in camp where she could do the least harm. Then he would see whether one of the camp hands could guide him to Starky and the hunting party.

Moses, while refuelling, had relayed the latest intelligence: the hunt was expected to take place sometime between midday and three.

"You should have come on that hunt, James."

Susan's voice was low. He had thought she was asleep, but now in the dim light her eyes glowed strangely.

"You should have been there, James. You were coming over from Australia to see the family. That's why Mike arranged the hunt. He wouldn't have done it if you weren't coming."

James wondered if she was accusing him of being complicit in her brother's death.

She sighed and closed her eyes again. "I suppose it wasn't your fault that Verity got pregnant and you couldn't come, was it? Lucky for Verity that she had you. I had no one."

James was not sure he was up to this kind of conversation when Susan was plainly still carrying last night's alcohol in her system. Keeping his eyes on the horizon, he nodded, remembering the whispers he had once overheard between his parents: their horror that Susan had borne a child out of wedlock, and that the child's father was believed to be the man who had murdered Susan's brother on the very day the child had been conceived.

Susan made a sound like a muffled sob, and James slid a glance her way. Her face was clouded with grief and guilt.

She was an attractive woman. The inky black curls, the dark eyes, the exotic air she carried when she was not being defiant or, as his mother used to put it, acting out.

"I'm sorry about everything that happened, Susan," he said quietly, fixing his gaze on the horizon rather than risk meeting her eyes. "I'm sorry none of us can wind the clock back and do it differently. But life doesn't allow that. It keeps springing surprises on you."

She gave a shrug. "I suppose you should be flying a jet. That's what Verity says."

James smiled faintly. "I like it here more than I expected. Most of the time, anyway."

"Like when Verity's not around making you feel you should be flying a jet?" Susan asked. "I had a boyfriend like that once. Always trying to improve me. Made me feel I wasn't enough whenever I wasn't doing what he thought I should."

James frowned. "Verity's not like that."

"You're too noble, James." Susan gave a hollow laugh, then started coughing. When she reached for a packet of Camels, he said sharply, "No, you can't smoke in here."

With a frustrated sigh, she shoved them away.

"Can't believe we're related," she muttered. "Noble ideals were never my thing. Mike had them, though. That's why Mum and Dad were so cut up when their favourite died. Mike, the golden boy." She sniffed. "What sort of boy writes in a diary every night? That diary ruined my life. If Mike hadn't got it wrong... if I'd only known earlier that Mum and Dad had read it, I wouldn't be here right now."

James turned slightly. "What do you mean?"

"You may not think I can prove it, but I know Starky killed Mike." She lifted her chin. "And now I've got proof."

James looked sharply at her.

"That man you thought was a photographer. The Phil you keep asking me about? Phil Lehmann?" She gave him a triumphant look. "Phil saw Starky take his Krieghoff hunting, when no one knew Starky had the same gun the coroner said had killed Mike. And Phil saw Starky pull the trigger."

James swung around to look at her properly. "I'm not at all sure you should be placing this much faith in Phil."

"Oh yeah? Well, you don't know him."

"How do you know he's telling the truth?"

Susan glared. "Because I asked him here, if you must know. I asked him because he was on that hunt, because he knows what happened, and because he was uniquely qualified both to tell the truth and to investigate—catch Starky red-handed—in the crime that's about to happen."

James shook his head. "You're living in La-La Land, Suze. You say Phil's anti-poaching BNPW, but how can you trust what he says when you haven't seen him for fifteen years? You've no idea what his motives are for... pleasing you."

"Don't twist this around!" Susan flared. "Phil has an important position. Authority. People believe him. And when he says Starky killed my brother, they'll believe him too."

James groaned. "Susan, the case is closed. Even if Phil catches Starky poaching, he's not going to magically wring a confession out of him for a crime with no other proof."

Then, more frustrated still, he added, "And if Starky is Angie's father, then she deserves the truth. Why would you want him publicly branded a murderer? That poor child already believes that of the man she thinks was her father. Why not give her the greatest gift possible? A father who isn't a convicted murderer. Whatever you think of him."

Susan shook her head fiercely. "Starky refused to accept paternity."

"That was a long time ago. He may have changed."

Her mouth twisted grimly. She toyed with the unlit cigarette between her fingers.

"You think so, do you? Well, I think you're wrong. There was a time when I seemed only to attract unsuitable men. But you know what?"

James lifted his eyebrows, inviting her to continue.

"Phil bucks the trend. For once, I know I've got it right."

She rummaged in her handbag, pulled out a lipstick, and began applying it with aggressive care.

"Just you wait and see," she said, pausing to inspect herself in the little mirror. "If you think this is only about collecting the girls from Deception Pan, you've got another thing coming. I've got a whole lot more up my sleeve. And every bit of it is going to prove that Phil is my knight in shining armour."

She hesitated, then snapped the mirror shut and turned on him with sudden menace.

"And if you dare breathe a word to Angie about who her father is, I swear I will never forgive you. Ever."

FORTY-THREE

"Please come back with me?" Thomas pleaded as he climbed out of the vehicle, with Kutlo at the wheel.

Verity tried to hold firm while the girls begged to be allowed to join the lad and drive to where his father was waiting, about twenty minutes away. Charlize sat in the front passenger seat, looking bored.

"You've always deplored hunting, Saskia." Verity planted her hands on her hips and shook her head. "Why would you want to witness this?"

"I don't," said Saskia, sobering suddenly and sending a guilty look at her cousin. "Maybe we shouldn't go."

"But they've paid for it, and it helps balance the ecology," Angie said with the breezy certainty of someone whose love of nature was a little too transactional. In that regard, Angie was definitely her mother's daughter. "Come on, Saskia, you want to go, don't you? Of course, you do. It's a once-in-a-lifetime thing, and if it proves how horrible the whole hunting business is, surely that's useful? I want to go so I can see what the fuss is about. We're on a hunting safari."

Kutlo glanced at his watch and revved the engine impatiently.

"Please, Auntie Verity, can we go?" Angie tried once more, her expression a masterclass in charm, respect, and appeal. "Starky knows what he's doing. He'll keep us safe. That's his job."

Starky.

The name hung in the air, and in that moment Angie channelled so much of her father's charisma that Verity felt a little jolt.

Angie was begging to see her father do the thing for which he was admired. And even if Verity disapproved, could she really be the one to stand in the way?

Starky needed to tell her the truth. He needed to do it before Angie flew back to boarding school. The poor girl was carrying the weight of a lie that had shaped her whole sense of herself.

"All right. We'll all go. Just give me a minute."

The girls needed a chaperone. Not Charlize. But Verity first had to update Philemon and Florence and tell them to prepare some late-afternoon refreshments in case the whole absurd business dragged on.

Soon she was in the back seat behind Saskia and Angie as they bumped over the sandy track towards the men who wanted an audience.

"Over there!" Kutlo pointed into the distance, where a small cluster of figures could be seen under an acacia.

Kurt was seated in a director's chair, fanning himself and looking impatient rather than excited until the vehicle rolled to a halt and the girls jumped out.

Charlize unfolded herself from the front seat with all

the easy poise of an actress hitting her mark. She strolled straight to Kurt, laid a hand on his shoulder, and slowly stroked his cheek.

"So," she said, "you're going to show me what you're made of?" She tipped up her face for his kiss. "You're going to put your manly eye to the sight, pull the trigger, and that magnificent beast lounging out there somewhere is simply going to roll over and die from one shot. How thrilling."

Though the sarcasm in her voice was unmistakable, Verity was shocked by the hunger in Kurt's face as he let his hand slide down Charlize's arm.

She was about to move away from the intimacy of it when she heard him say, in a low growl, "Come back to Munich with me."

The slow satisfaction on Charlize's face did not surprise her. What did surprise her was how genuine Kurt sounded.

Well, time would tell, Verity supposed. Kurt could offer Charlize a far better life than the one she had in South Africa. Monte Carlo was still a fantasy. Munich, perhaps, was not. And maybe Charlize really could retire before she was thirty.

Verity found herself grudgingly admiring her.

Then Starky strode over.

"Thanks for coming," he said to Verity. "Kurt was keen for the womenfolk to witness this."

Only the faint lift of his eyebrow betrayed a touch of contempt for his wealthy client.

Before Verity could answer, Angie broke away from Thomas and came towards them.

"Are you going to hunt the lion on foot?" she asked, bright-eyed and visibly excited. Yesterday's despair had vanished completely. "What rifle are you going to use?"

Verity caught the fractional pause before Starky

answered. "A .375 H&H Magnum," he said. "Ever heard of one?"

Angie shook her head. "I know nothing about guns. But I reckon I wouldn't mind learning. Not in the city, obviously."

"Well, your mother lives out in the bush. Ask her." Then, with a quick grin: "Or better still, tell her you want to learn to shoot properly."

He winked, and Angie laughed.

"No good asking Mum to do anything. She never follows through. Anyway, I don't want to shoot animals like your client does, but I think it'd be cool to be a really good shot. Like, if there were another croc attack, I'd want to do what you did and grab a rifle and make the shot. That'd be cool."

Verity saw Starky's eyes flick briefly to Kurt, as if he knew that at such a moment his attention ought to be on his client, yet found himself more caught up in this conversation than he had expected.

With his daughter.

Then Kurt began striding over, his face bright with what Verity could only think of as killing lust. He nodded towards the rifle in Starky's hands. Charlize clung to his arm as he told her, "We're going to track him on foot from here."

"Where is it?" Charlize asked, shading her eyes, and Kurt pointed.

The reclining lion was only a tawny speck in the distance, its mane catching the late-afternoon sun. It looked indolent, majestic, entirely unaware that death had already entered its orbit.

"It doesn't look very dangerous," Charlize said.

As if to contradict her, the lion gave a distant, guttural

roar that rolled across the flats and made her squeak and step back.

Kurt only grinned and patted her hand. "We're downwind. He's got no idea we're here."

Then, turning briskly authoritative, he went on, "You and the other women stay exactly where Starky tells you. Thomas!"

He beckoned to his son, then added to Charlize, "We men are going hunting. Stay by the vehicle until you get the all-clear, eh, Starky?" He chucked her lightly under the chin. "I've done this before."

So Verity, Saskia and Angie withdrew with Charlize to stand by the vehicle in the scant shade of a couple of acacias.

Kurt shouldered his rifle.

"Be careful," Charlize called, suddenly all concern. She kissed her fingertips and flicked them towards him like a blessing.

"Come, Thomas!" Kurt barked over his shoulder.

Thomas gave Saskia and Angie a bleakly bemused look and muttered, "Do not think I am going to shoot anything."

He took a step, then turned back with a sudden grin. "And if I get killed by the lion, it was fun to have you in camp."

"Thomas!"

With an impish smile, Angie dashed forward and tugged at his arm. "A quick kiss, in case you don't come back."

A fierce blush flooded his pale face. He ducked his head, let her kiss him quickly, then hurried off through the rough grass to catch up with the others.

Verity sank into one of the director's chairs Kutlo had unfolded from the back of the vehicle.

"There's a thermos of tea and some biscuits if anyone wants them," she said. She felt strangely flat. Three men were walking out towards a lion with rifles. So what?

So Kurt could lay its skin on the floor of his entrance hall in Munich?

"What do we do now?" asked Saskia. "Just sit here until they come back? I thought Kurt wanted us here to see the action, but then Starky said we couldn't go any closer. I heard him telling Kurt it was unsafe to have us there. This is nuts."

Verity thought the same, though she kept it to herself. Instead she pointed to the sky.

"Look! There's a plane coming in to land at Deception Pan. It must be your friend, Richard."

"No need to stress about it, Mum," said Saskia, chewing the end of her plait. "He can just wait. Or will this take all day? I thought it was going to be exciting, but it's not."

"I thought you were against killing wildlife," said Verity.

"Yeah, well, Kurt is paying huge money, and that goes back into the economy and conservation, so I suppose sometimes it's all right," Saskia said, though without much conviction.

Except it wasn't all right.

This particular trophy was going to line Starky's pockets, surely. Verity could not see how it could be otherwise, and the fear simmering inside her began to harden into anger.

But what could she actually do?

Report it afterwards? That was one thing. March into the middle of it now, accusing them all? Quite another.

She worried her lower lip as she watched the aircraft overhead.

"I suppose Florence or Philemon will tell him where we are. I only hope they don't give him free rein with the other vehicle. He might arrive just in time to ruin the hunt."

Though perhaps that would be the best thing.

Except, then, Starky would not be caught red-handed.

And was that not, at some level, what she now wanted, if he really was a criminal?

"Richard would never manage to drive that old monster," Saskia said dismissively. "It's a hideous ten-tonne truck that makes no sense. I've never seen anything like it. Angie and I were looking at it yesterday."

"You don't drive, Saskia, so how would you know?" Verity asked.

Her daughter looked at her steadily.

"I can drive." Then, after a beat: "There are lots of things you don't know about me, Mum." She drew a breath and added softly, "Or about what's happening around you."

FORTY-FOUR

James nosed the plane down and lined up the dirt runway. A low pass over camp had confirmed that only one of the vehicles was there, which could only mean the other was out in the bush and Starky and his clients were already tracking—or hunting—the lion.

His throat felt dry as he brought the plane in to land, and the air felt drier still when they jumped out.

The bleakness of the place hit him forcibly after the lushness of the Okavango.

It felt barren. Stripped bare. The emptiness itself seemed ominous as they set off on the ten-minute walk towards camp, stretching their legs and squinting against the glare.

"Where is everybody?" Susan asked, shading her eyes as she stared ahead at the camp, barely visible through the heat shimmer. "No welcoming party? Oh God, what if we're too late? Come on! We've got to find the girls! I don't want them anywhere near the action."

James lengthened his stride after her.

"Starky's a professional hunter, Susan. He wouldn't let the girls anywhere near real danger."

But Susan either didn't hear or chose not to. She forged ahead.

"Phil's out here somewhere," she said when they reached the edge of the empty camp, shading her eyes again as she scanned the yellow landscape dissolving into haze. "He promised he'd apprehend Starky the moment the fatal bullet found its mark. The moment Starky committed his crime. Phil's unit will have joined him by now. They'll have rifles."

She stopped abruptly, chewing the knuckles of her right hand, and then suddenly fixed on the vehicle parked beneath a stand of acacias.

"We've got to go after them!"

"Susan!" James ran to catch up with her. "We'll find the girls. They may not be anywhere near the hunt. Yes, I'm worried too, but slow down. We can't just hurl ourselves into something where somebody could get killed."

"Phil says his unit has a shoot-to-kill policy. I don't want Angel anywhere near that!"

James seized her arm and swung her around. "You don't trust him? Well, neither do I. But we can't be rash."

They both turned at the sound of shouting from near the fire.

"Captain!"

A Tswana lad came hurrying through the smoke, breathless, and introduced himself as Philemon, the camp hand. "Moses said you would come!"

"You got word already?" James asked, startled.

"It was passed by HF from the Maun office and then a runner took it on to me. Everyone is very excited for this Mr Lehmann to go to gaol. Please take that." He pointed towards the vehicle under the acacias. "I think you are not too late if you go now. Please, Captain, this Mr Lehmann is a very bad man and his illegal hunting is very bad for Botswana."

Susan narrowed her eyes. "Starky Willis is the poacher. Phil Lehmann is with Botswana National Parks and Wildlife and has come to apprehend him," she said sharply.

Philemon looked at James with embarrassed uncertainty, as though unwilling to contradict her outright.

There was no point arguing it here.

"Thank you, Philemon," James said, heading for the vehicle, then stopping short. "You'd better stay here, Susan. It may not be safe—"

But she shoved past him and leapt in, scrambling over the centre console as if she didn't trust him to wait while she went round. Dark hair clung damply to her face, and her eyes blazed.

"Of course I'm coming. Not only to make sure Angie and Saskia are all right, but to prove that I knew exactly what I was doing when I got Phil involved. I was onto this long before you. Phil's the BNPW man, head of the anti-poaching unit, and his people are already on site. Now we're going to where the action is happening and we'll see who's right."

"I think you're going to find you placed your faith in a felon, Susan," James said, fighting to keep his temper in check as he crunched the gears and the vehicle lurched across the rough ground. "If you and I are talking about the same man, my intel is that Phil Lehmann has been present at least one poaching incident where the trophy animal then conveniently disappeared. More than one person has said he pockets the proceeds through coercion or blackmail. You've played straight into his hands."

She shook her head violently. "You're wrong. Starky's the felon and I don't want my Angel anywhere near him."

"She'll have to know one day that he's her father."

"No, she won't." Susan rounded on him. "Starky's about to be caught poaching, and then he'll confess to firing the Krieghoff that killed Mike."

James shot her a look. "You really believe that?"

"I do, and I've got proof!" she flung back. "It's in your living room, in case you didn't know."

"Oh, really?" James said with a disbelieving snort. "And what proof is that?"

"That photograph in Verity's album. The one taken the evening before Mike was killed. Afterwards, when the rangers came through camp and registered everyone's names and rifle details, the only Krieghoff they recorded was Jeremy's. But in that photograph there are two Krieghoffs—Jeremy's and Starky's."

She sent him a fierce, triumphant look. "Phil was there. He's in the picture, so he knows exactly what he saw. He says Mike and Starky argued. He says Starky went hunting with his own Krieghoff. He says Starky pulled the trigger and Mike died. The bullet mentioned in the coroner's report came from Starky's rifle, not Jeremy's."

James gripped the wheel harder. "And what does Phil supposedly plan to do with all this?" he asked.

"What he promised. Pressure Starky into confessing. Yes, I know it's too late for my brother's murderer to get justice in a gaol cell, but I can still see him punished for poaching." Her voice rose with every sentence. "Then, once that photograph showing Starky holding his Krieghoff becomes public, Angel can go on believing Jeremy was her father—but Jeremy will be exonerated. He won't be remembered as a murderer." She drew a shuddering breath.

"That's why Phil is here. To expose Starky for what he is. A poacher and a liar."

James sucked in a breath. "No. Phil is about to expose you, Susan. That's what I heard—from another source, and a reliable one." He glanced across at her. "And if we get there and Phil is on site, I do not want you running into his arms like he's some conquering hero, because he's the bad guy. You have to understand that."

FORTY-FIVE

Verity fanned her sweating cheeks, seeking relief from the relentless Kalahari sun, and wondered for the hundredth time why she had ever allowed the girls to come.

The four women had been reduced to Kurt's future cheer squad, left to endure the heat and discomfort while they waited. Shimmering waves rose from the parched earth, harsh and endless.

Even so, the sparse acacias on the horizon had their own melancholy beauty. The wild animals roaming the plains still stirred something in her.

But just now they were all on tenterhooks because of brutal men's business.

She could not fathom how Kurt imagined he would rise in anyone's estimation by slaughtering a wild animal at close range with a high-powered rifle.

The thought of James stirred mixed feelings.

More than anything, she longed for his steady presence. But she had hurt him. Made him feel somehow lacking; given him reason to think he was being weighed against

Starky and found wanting—when nothing could have been further from the truth.

And for that she felt deeply ashamed.

"I miss Dad," Saskia said with a sigh, both hands clasped around her ankle.

Verity sent an anxious glance at the injury and saw at once that the redness had spread.

"Lucky you. I wish I knew my dad. Even if he were a murderer," Angie murmured.

"But you have a wonderful mother who loves you," said Verity, leaning forward to get a better look at Saskia's flushed face.

"Mum! What are you doing?" Saskia cried as Verity pressed a hand to her forehead.

"Checking you haven't got a temperature. I'm worried about your ankle." Verity tried to smile reassuringly as Starky's warnings echoed in her mind.

"It does throb," Saskia admitted.

But Angie, consumed by her own misery, said bitterly, "No she doesn't. Mum was glad Granny and Grandpa paid to send me to boarding school. She wishes I'd never been born. I ruined her life."

"That's not true!" Verity protested. "She would do anything for you. She loves you."

"Like you love Dad?"

The accusation in Saskia's voice made Verity recoil.

"Don't speak to me like that, Saskia."

"But do you?" her daughter demanded, narrowing her eyes. "Because I saw you with Starky. Not once. Twice."

"What are you implying?" Verity gave an outraged half-laugh. "I love your father more than any man. I would go anywhere to be with him. I would do anything for him."

"It'd be nice if you didn't make him feel so bad about

bringing us to Africa, then," Saskia muttered, bending her head to trace the angry redness around her scar.

"Keep your voice down, Saskia," Verity hissed, darting a glance towards Charlize, who was studying her fingernails with every appearance of not listening. Angie, fortunately, had risen and was pacing in front of the vehicle, too restless to sit still.

"Why?" Saskia shot back. "Because you don't want anyone else to hear that you let Starky kiss you?"

"I did not!" Heat surged through Verity. Out of the corner of her eye, she saw Charlize's shoulders move, as if with silent laughter. Of course, she could hear every word.

Saskia had never known shame. Not really. She had always flung things out, raw and public and unforgiving. No—Verity corrected herself bitterly—that wasn't quite fair. From the age of twelve, when hormones had transformed her daughter into something fierce and difficult, Verity had struggled to control her while keeping her own disappointments tightly buttoned in.

Stoically.

Not like the martyr Saskia clearly thought her.

And yet some tiny part of Verity acknowledged the barb in what her daughter was saying. She had not borne the changes forced upon them with James's stoicism.

Not at first.

"I did not let Starky kiss me." Verity threw another glance at Charlize, whose pink mouth was pursed with amusement. "I did not know he was going to."

"Convenient excuse, Mum. So, are you going to tell Dad? Or just keep one more secret from him? You think I don't know anything just because I'm at boarding school?"

"Stop it!" Verity reached for Saskia's arm, but Saskia jerked away.

"You don't love Dad. Not like I love Dad. He's done everything for us. He brought us here for us. Dad has morals and principles, which is more than you do."

Angie had stopped pacing and was staring now, wide-eyed. Charlize watched with detached interest and murmured only, "You'll get heatstroke if you go on like this."

"That's enough, Saskia." Verity's voice trembled. "You have no idea what goes into the decisions adults make when we're trying to protect our children from truths they are not ready for."

"For our own good?" Saskia's voice rose. "Do you really think it's for *my* own good that I'm kept out of decisions about where we live and why? Is it for Angie's own good that no one tells her that her father might not have been all bad, when all she's known her whole life is that he murdered her uncle?"

Saskia's face was blotchy with heat and fury. Verity could hear her own blood pounding in her ears.

"We keep things from you to protect you," she said again, though it sounded weak even to her. "Whoever Angie's father is makes no difference to the wonderful young woman Angie is. That all happened in the past, and when Angie's mother thinks she's ready to know every-thing, she'll tell her. It isn't our place to interfere—"

"What do you mean, it isn't our place?" Saskia demanded. "Are you saying Angie doesn't know the truth?"

"The truth about—yes—of course. Whatever that truth is, her mother will tell her when the time is right."

Verity heard herself floundering. The girls' expressions shifted from confusion to outrage so quickly it made her feel sick.

Angie came at her.

"What do you know that you're not telling me? What has Mum said about my dad? That he was a murderer and then killed himself? That a killer's blood is running through my veins?" Her voice shook violently. "Sometimes when I feel the rage inside me, I think maybe I could be capable of killing too. And then I get scared and think maybe I should kill myself before I ever kill someone else."

"Angie, no!"

Horrified, Verity stepped towards her. But Saskia moved between them as if Verity herself were the threat. Verity reached out again, pleading. "Don't ever think like that. Don't ever let that idea take hold. Your mother would be distraught to hear you say such a thing."

"My mother won't talk about it. Full stop. I've tried, but she brushes me off. She's told me nothing about my murdering father—"

"Your father's not a murderer, and she should have told you that!"

The words burst out of Verity before she could stop them.

Silence crashed down.

She saw confusion blaze on both girls' faces.

Angie's voice tightened to a thread. "How can you say that when he was charged and sent to gaol?"

"That's not the man who fathered you—"

The words were out, and this time Verity did not regret them.

Susan should have told Angie long ago. How could she have let the girl carry such torment for so many years?

"What?" Angie's mouth opened and closed, but it was Saskia who stepped forward.

"What do you know that Angie doesn't? What else have

you kept from her? If you know her father wasn't a murderer, then who is he? You know, don't you, Mum? Who is he?"

Angie's shock changed into something darker, more dangerous. She was trembling from head to toe; her face drained white, her eyes huge and black.

"Who's my father?" she whispered. "Please tell me. Because Mum will never tell me. She'll keep it from me my whole life. She's like that. Please. If you know, tell me."

Verity sucked in a breath and glanced helplessly at Charlize, who said coolly, "I think you've dug too deep a hole, Verity. If you know the truth, you should tell her."

Closing her eyes for the briefest instant, bracing herself for Susan's rage, Verity forced herself to calm.

Then quietly, she said, "Starky is your father."

For a second, nothing moved.

Angie's mouth fell open. Her eyes seemed to widen impossibly.

Saskia's half-formed expletive turned into a wail of horror.

Even Charlize jerked forward.

And then a single rifle shot cracked across the plains.

The sound hit them all like a blow. Instinctively, they turned towards the distant figures of Kurt, Thomas, and Starky. Clearly, they had done what they had gone out to do: brought down one of Africa's great wild beasts.

Even from several hundred metres away, the shot seemed to go on reverberating through the air.

The women stood rooted to the spot, frozen by the life-changing revelation Verity had just loosed into the world.

All except Angie.

She recovered first.

Before Verity could stop her, Angie spun around and began to run across the veld, a lone, vulnerable figure racing towards the men.

Towards Thomas.

Towards Kurt.

Towards Starky.

FORTY-SIX

"Can you see the men over there, Captain?" Philemon asked excitedly as they clambered out of the Bedford, the hard African sun beating down on them. "And the lion? He is in the tall grass."

He pointed as Susan jumped down and came around the vehicle, shading her eyes against the glare, her voice taut with worry.

"What about the girls? They're not here. Where are they?"

James laid a steadying hand on her shoulder, feeling the tension coiled tight in her muscles.

"Starky would have made sure they were safe." He tried to sound certain. In truth, he was weighing the scene with an acute awareness of how little he understood compared with a man like Starky. James had known Botswana as a boy. But not like this. Not as a hunter. Not as a man used to reading danger on open ground.

Starky had planned for this moment over days, perhaps weeks. Beside him were the rich clients who had paid handsomely for whatever was about to unfold.

A sliver of doubt pierced James.

What if he and Susan had got it wrong? What if the permit had been obtained after all? The BNPW had already been tipped off and would make their own enquiries. What did it matter if James arrived a little after the lion was shot?

Except that wasn't why he was here.

His real reason was Verity. Saskia. Their safety.

And they weren't with the men.

None of the girls were.

Yes, Moses had wanted Phil stopped from profiting at the expense of the Batswana people. But James's first concern was Verity, Saskia and Angie.

He swept the horizon again.

No sign of Phil. No sign of any BNPW contingent.

Perhaps Starky had got wind that Phil was coming. Perhaps he would abandon the plan. Perhaps he had only taken his clients out to look at the lion—

Boom!

The gunshot split the stillness of the savannah.

James and Susan jerked instinctively, hands half rising to their ears, their eyes snapping to the three men in the distance. The older German was striding forward now, his rifle slung carelessly over one shoulder.

Starky stood a little behind him.

The younger man—Thomas—had not moved.

And several metres away lay the lion.

Inert.

One shot. Dead cleanly.

A trophy for a rich tourist.

Disgust rolled through James.

Then, at the edge of his vision, something shifted.

Two other figures had emerged from the scrub: a tall, thin white man with grey hair, dressed in khaki, and a muscular local man beside him. They were heading straight for the hunters, moving with purpose, kicking up little puffs of dust at each step.

Reluctantly taking the rifle Philemon thrust into his hands, James moved forward with Susan and the lad, then stopped under the shade of an acacia to assess the scene.

Philemon motioned urgently, and following his lead they crouched low and slipped into the cover of a nearby thicket, still unseen.

Then Starky's voice carried clearly on the hot wind.

"Phil? God, man, what are you doing here?"

So Starky did recognise him.

Of course he did.

Susan clapped a hand over her mouth. The rangy newcomer gave a harsh, sarcastic laugh.

"I thought that'd be obvious. What a pity I'm too late to stop this abomination." He turned to the German, his tone hardening. "You know this hunt is illegal. There's no permit for it. I'm here on the orders of Botswana National Parks and Wildlife to arrest you."

He dug into his pocket and produced what James assumed was identification.

Starky regarded him coolly. The two Germans remained silent, clearly taking their cue from him, though confusion was written across both their faces.

"Or," Phil added, with a little shrug, "I can simply take the animal and let you walk away."

He nodded towards the dead lion, and at a click of his fingers a group of local young men in khaki, AK-47s slung at the ready, materialised from the nearby scrub and moved towards the carcass.

"Why would I do that?" Starky asked.

James could see contempt radiating from him.

Phil smiled, though there was nothing pleasant in it. "Let's say I'm evening the score."

Susan made a sound of outrage and James dug her sharply in the ribs to keep her quiet.

"Even the score?" Starky drew himself up, fists bunching. "Who are you to talk?"

Phil's smugness did not falter. "I'm not here for idle chitchat. You don't have a permit for that lion," he repeated. When Starky said nothing, he gave a short, mirthless laugh. "So why don't you and your clients just get in the vehicle and leave? Let me deal with the rest." He indicated the lion again, then the armed young men behind him. "You're outnumbered."

"You expect me to slink off and let you skin the beast and pocket the proceeds?" Starky said with a contemptuous laugh. "That's your plan, isn't it? Just as you've done before whenever you've turned the integrity of the BNPW anti-poaching unit into your own little profit machine."

Phil's eyes narrowed. "You're hardly one to talk. Weren't you the opportunist who pocketed Mike Jensen's diamond fifteen years ago?" He flicked a glance at the Germans, then back at Starky. "Oh yes, I've watched you build your little empire. You had nothing. A twenty-year-old kid with big dreams and no money. Your family was dirt poor. Yet the moment Mike was dead you were flying your own plane and winning tenders for a concession. People say you made it big. But you did it at the expense of our mate Mike."

Susan's fury practically vibrated off her. James had to seize her arm and haul her back as she started to surge forward.

Starky's voice was low and dangerous. "Mike and I found that diamond together. He wrote about it in his diary after our trip to Makgadikgadi two months earlier. *You* were the opportunist, Phil." He gave a small, hard shake of the head. "I'd like to think it was an accident, but you engineered the whole thing. You made sure Mike took a swing at me, then grabbed my rifle and claimed self-defence. *You* pulled the trigger. *You* fired the shot that killed Mike."

Phil flicked a glance at the Germans. Behind him, his armed followers shifted restlessly, dry grass crackling under their boots. With their machine guns at the ready, they looked menacing.

But there was something about Starky's stillness—his refusal to flinch—that drew the eye and held it.

Phil tried to take back control.

"I intervened when you and Mike started that stoush after he found out you'd been in his sister's tent. You were a fool, Starky. Could never leave the ladies alone, could you? But Mike was your friend, and his sister should have been off-limits. If you hadn't slept with Suze, you'd never have got into the fight that ended his life."

"You engineered that fight," Starky said again, his voice thickening with anger. "Mike thought Jeremy had been in Suze's tent until *you* took it upon yourself to tell him it was me. You did everything you could to rile him. And when he punched me, neither of us was holding a rifle. You picked up my Krieghoff—"

"I saved your life!" Phil shouted suddenly, thrusting back his shoulders. "Mike was going for it and he would have shot you through the head. I saved your life!"

Phil's voice rang out across the flat land, but it was Susan's strangled gasp in James's ear that made him turn.

The horror on her face told him she had heard it too.

Phil had confessed.

Perhaps he had not even realised it yet, pushed as he

was by Starky into saying far more than he intended. But now he plunged on with reckless bravado. "No one will believe you, Starky. And who cares anyway? Neither of us is going to prison over that." He wiped sweat from his brow. "But you *will* go to prison for poaching a lion—unless you hand it over to me. I won't press charges. I'll let you walk."

He jerked a thumb towards the dead lion.

The older German made a sound like a groan. Thomas stared, white-faced and motionless.

"That sounds a little irregular," Starky said. James had to admire his composure. "I'm not sure that's how BNPW operates. But then, you always were a law unto yourself. If you thought you could get away with it, you'd have shot me too, all those years ago. I saw it in your face." He shook his head. "And all over a diamond. A diamond you knew Mike had in his pocket and which none of us—young fools that we were—knew how to sell legally. You wanted it."

Phil's face flushed dark with anger.

"Drop your weapon, Starky. Get your client to drop his too, and I'll let you walk."

Starky shifted his rifle to his other shoulder and shook his head.

"I wouldn't trust you to let me walk free after what you did to Jeremy. I learned only later that it was *you* who reported him to the authorities. He died in that gaol cell the day after he was remanded, because of your lies. So, no—I don't believe you'd let me walk free, even if I *were* guilty of poaching. Which I'm not."

And then, to James's astonishment, Starky smiled.

He glanced at his clients, then back at Phil.

"I happen to have a licence, despite rumours to the contrary. Yes, it was a ruse to flush you out. You've cheated the people of Botswana long enough, and they're tired of it. If there isn't enough evidence yet regarding your earlier crimes, there are dozens of witnesses already prepared to testify to the plans you made to walk off with this magnificent animal." He nodded at the lion. "You pretended to Susan Jensen that you had come here to avenge her brother. Yes, you fed her exactly what she wanted to hear—that I was responsible for Mike's death, when it was you. All the while you were arranging to appear here, with your hired gunmen, at this exact moment so you could claim the lion as poached contraband and sell it on."

"Enough!" Phil barked. He raised his rifle a fraction. "Poaching is a crime with severe penalties. I have shoot-to-kill powers when dealing with poachers." He nodded at the Germans. "I don't know how much you understand, but I'm giving you a chance. Turn around and walk away, and this ends here."

He signalled to the armed young men, and they took another ominous step forward.

Susan dug her nails into James's arm and shot him a look of desperation, but he shook his head. Even with the rifle in his hands, there was nothing he could do against a group of armed men.

Helpless, he felt fear ratchet tighter as they moved into position. Starky may have laid a trap for Phil, but from where James crouched it looked horribly possible that Phil had brought enough firepower to spring it right back on him.

The Germans looked uncertainly towards Starky.

Was James about to witness a massacre?

His finger drifted towards the trigger of the Mauser. He had never fired a rifle before.

No—that was not quite true. Mike had shown him

once, when he was ten, just before the family had gone to Australia.

And then, out of the acacia scrub behind Starky, more armed men appeared.

Relief surged through him.

Of course. Starky had backup. James should never have doubted that a professional hunter, a man who understood ambush and risk and armed confrontations in wild country, would have prepared for every contingency.

Starky would have calculated how to protect his clients.

How to protect his girls too, even when they had complicated everything by turning up unexpectedly.

"Oh, my God."

At Susan's strangled gasp, James turned.

And all his confidence evaporated.

Because how could Starky possibly have prepared for this?

"It's Angie," Susan whispered.

James clapped a hand over her mouth at once. If Susan had seen the girl break away from another group far in the distance behind them, then it was vital that Phil's men were not alerted.

Dressed in khaki, long legs eating up the ground, Angie was racing across the open plain straight towards Starky.

What had possessed her?

But it was not lions James feared in that first second. It was the armed standoff she was running into without knowing it.

"James! Stop her!" Susan hissed, while James shifted the unfamiliar weapon Philemon had insisted he carry for protection against predators. "Philemon?" she begged the Tswana lad, but he shook his head helplessly. He carried no gun; he said he did not know how to use one.

Angie kept running.

In moments her path would take her perhaps twenty metres in front of where James and Susan were hiding. A few more strides beyond that and she would be in full view of Starky, Phil, and the armed men.

James scanned the ground. If he belly-crawled to the patch of acacias behind him, he might get far enough around to intercept her before she reached them.

Beside him, Susan could bear it no longer. She surged upright, waving her arms wildly, before James yanked her back down.

"Don't let the men know we're here," he hissed. "Who knows what they'll make of her—or what they'll do."

He slung the rifle over his shoulder, flattened himself to the ground, and began to crawl. "I'll try to head her off. Get her into the trees."

Quickly he made his way over the rough, tufted earth towards Angie, who had stopped now and was looking uncertainly between her mother, half hidden in the scrub, and Starky in the distance.

Even from here, James could tell she was confused.

But too far away, surely, to see what he now saw.

Twenty metres to Angie's left, half concealed in the long grass, something moved.

The flick of a tail.

The shift of grass.

A second hunter.

"Angie, stop!"

James changed course at once, angling to get between her and the danger, clutching the rifle across his chest.

But Angie ignored him. She clearly had no idea what threatened her.

"Stop!"

He ran as fast as the uneven ground allowed, lungs burning, eyes darting between Angie and the grass.

Then he saw her properly.

A lioness.

No mane. Just tawny power, low in the grass.

Beyond her, in deeper shade, he caught the shape of the rest of the pride: another female, perhaps two cubs.

The lioness rose. Stretched.

She had seen Angie break away from the others. Seen her vulnerability.

He shouted again, hoping the noise alone might turn her.

Behind him, he heard Susan gasping and stumbling in pursuit.

"Angie! Stop!"

But the girl kept running, breath hitching in ragged sobs now, clearly frightened but still not understanding from where the true danger came.

The lioness waited. Assessed. Her ears twitched. Her tail flicked once.

Then she moved.

Not a charge yet. Just that terrible, fluid gathering of power as she came through the grass, closing.

"No, Angie!"

James knew at once he would never reach her in time.

He stopped, planted his feet, threw the rifle to his shoulder and fired a warning shot into the air.

The report cracked across the veld.

Angie stopped dead.

Now, at last, she understood.

James saw confusion vanish from her face, replaced by naked terror as she fixed on the lioness.

The cat had halted too, reassessing.

The warning shot had drawn her attention away from Angie.

And onto him.

"Back away, Angie!" James shouted. "Slowly! I'll draw her off!"

The lioness's eyes seemed to glow. James stared back, rooted to the spot, every instinct screaming at him to move while another told him that movement might be the thing that doomed him.

The beast watched him. Measured him.

Then she opened her jaws, and what might almost have been a yawn turned into a deep, rolling growl that vibrated in his bones.

James adjusted his stance.

Only the slightest shift of footing on the sandy tussock.

But it was enough.

The lioness decided.

With one great bound she came at him, closing the distance in a blur of tawny muscle and force, and sound.

James fired.

Nothing.

An empty click.

The breath went out of him in one sick rush of horror.

And then the lioness hit him, knocking him sprawling.

When James opened his eyes again, the world had gone dark and close and full of animal smell.

He could feel the coarse rasp of her coat.

Smell the musky, overpowering rankness of her.

And then he realised he was staring straight into the black cavern of her open jaws.

~

Verity was halfway across the veld before she understood that what was unfolding in the distance was far more than Starky facilitating Kurt's hunting triumph.

Angie was ahead of her. Verity was gaining slightly, eyes mostly on the ground so she would not break an ankle on the tussocks. It was only when she looked up that she grasped the scale of the danger.

Angie was running straight into an ambush.

Not a simple hunting scene. Not some tense confrontation. An actual armed standoff.

A grey-haired man stood facing Starky, flanked by half a dozen men in khaki with machine guns.

"Angie! Stop!"

Dear God, what was happening?

Sweat stung Verity's eyes. For one awful moment she could not tell who was threatened and who was threatening.

Then, almost immediately, she saw the second danger.

The lion.

Or rather, the lioness, because in that first instant her lack of a mane barely registered. It hardly mattered when the bloodlust in her eyes was visible even from this distance. The animal was crouched low in the grass, still as death except for the twitch of its tail.

"No, Angie!"

But though the girl had hesitated briefly, she kept going, still not seeing what she was running towards.

And then Verity registered someone else.

James.

He was angling across the ground, trying to intercept Angie and head off the danger.

Horror surged through her.

James was putting himself directly in the path of the beast. He did not stand a chance.

"Stop! James! Don't!"

He halted, though not because he had heard her. He had not even seen her.

Instead he crouched, shouldered the rifle, and took aim.

Relief made her almost dizzy.

He could defend himself.

He wasn't simply throwing himself into danger bare-handed. He was doing what he had come to do—protecting his girls.

Why else would he be here? Right in the middle of all this?

And then, in the same breath, she saw how much bigger the danger was. The lioness was only one terror. Beyond her were the armed men.

Her gaze flew to the standoff. What was happening? Was Starky being arrested by the anti-poaching unit? Had James somehow brought them?

And then the lioness growled.

James's shot misfired.

The next instant she saw the cat launch and James go down beneath it.

"James! God, no!"

She ran harder, stumbling, leaping, no longer caring if she fell.

Angie had stopped dead, her face a mask of horror as she watched James in bloody combat with the lioness.

And there was nothing Verity could do but run towards the man she loved while he was being torn apart before her eyes.

CHAPTER
FORTY-SEVEN

Verity was still running when she saw James go down beneath the lioness.

For one frozen second, she could not understand what she was seeing. The world seemed to narrow to tawny fur, a flash of teeth, James's sprawled body, and Angie standing only yards away, rooted in horror.

Then sound came back in a rush.

Susan screaming. Saskia sobbing behind her. The shout of men.

And Starky's voice, sharp as a rifle crack.

"Down! Everybody bloody down!"

He had wheeled at the warning shot. Now, taking in the scene at one glance—the girl in the open, James on the ground, the lioness half over him—he barked something rapid in Setswana to the men who had emerged from the acacias. His own backup moved at once, spreading, weapons trained not on the lioness but on Phil and the youths with him.

Phil shouted something too, furious and incredulous, but Starky was already moving.

"Don't shoot!" he snapped at Kurt, who had half raised his rifle. "Not with James there!"

That was what brought home to Verity the awful precision of it. Anyone could fire at a lion. Only a fool would fire when the beast was on a man.

James had rolled partly onto his side, the rifle trapped between himself and the lioness. One of her paws was planted on his chest. Her head was low, shoulders bunching, as though uncertain whether to finish him or turn on the shouting figures closing from different directions.

"James!" Verity screamed.

His head moved.

He was alive.

The lioness lifted her face from him, lips peeled back, and gave a guttural snarl in Starky's direction.

Starky had not run straight at her. He had cut at an angle, swift and low, putting distance between himself and the others, forcing the lioness to choose which threat to face. He held the .375 to his shoulder, but did not fire. Not yet.

"James!" he shouted. "Don't move!"

Verity was close enough now to hear James's ragged breathing. Close enough to see the dark blood soaking his shirt and the ruin of his trouser leg. But she also saw what Starky had seen: the lioness was not settled into the kill. She was conflicted, attention divided.

Oh God, stay undecided, she thought wildly. Just until Starky has time to act.

"Back, Angie!" Starky roared without taking his eye off the sight. "Get her back!"

At last, Angie moved. Not backwards, as instructed, but sideways, stumbling in shock towards Susan, who had broken from the scrub and was now running awkwardly across the tussocks, arms outstretched.

Phil chose that moment to make his move.

Whether he thought Starky distracted enough to be caught off guard, or whether he simply could not bear the spectacle of losing control, Verity could not know. But she saw him swing his rifle up and heard him shout in fury to his men.

"Now!"

He got no further.

One of Starky's men slammed the butt of his gun into Phil's shoulder from behind, knocking his aim aside. Another shouted something fierce in Setswana at the others. The hired youths, who had looked menacing enough when they believed themselves part of an easy operation, now looked what they were: young, uncertain, and suddenly not at all sure they wanted to die for Phil Lehmann.

Two lowered their rifles at once.

One dropped his outright.

The local man beside Phil took a step back.

And in that split second, the balance tipped.

The lioness gathered herself.

Not towards James this time.

Towards Starky.

"No!" Verity cried, though whether for James or Starky she did not know.

The beast launched.

Starky fired.

The first shot struck her high in the chest and checked her mid-bound, twisting her sideways in the air. She hit the ground heavily, rolled, tried to rise, and came on in a staggering, terrible half-charge.

He fired again.

This time she dropped for good, kicking once in the dust, then lay still.

Silence followed, drawn-out and unnatural.

It lasted perhaps no more than a second.

Then everyone moved at once.

Verity reached James first and fell to her knees beside him. "James. James—oh God—"

His face was grey beneath the blood and dust. One side of his cheek had been laid open, and his trouser leg was shredded from thigh to calf, blood seeping fast into the earth beneath him.

But his eyes opened.

"Hello, darling," he whispered, with the ghost of a smile that was so heartbreakingly brave she nearly collapsed with relief. "I didn't quite get that right, did I?"

"You were amazing," she said through her tears. "Like you always are."

"Oh, Verity..." His voice was barely there. "I'm glad... to see you again."

She stroked his brow, careful to avoid his shredded cheek, and for a second the armed men, the dead lioness, the shouting, the heat, all vanished. There was only James.

Alive.

Alive.

Behind her, Susan had reached Angie and was clutching her hard. Glancing up, Verity saw her half shaking her daughter, half crushing her to her chest.

"What did you think you were doing? What did you think you were doing?" she kept saying, even while kissing the top of her head and then pushing her back to look at her, as if to confirm she was really there and whole.

Angie, ash-white now, stared over Susan's shoulder at James.

"He saved me," she said in a torn whisper. "He saved me."

Saskia arrived limping badly, Charlize hard on her heels, for once without any trace of languor or mockery. Thomas came at a run from the other direction, white-faced and panting.

Phil, however, had not given up.

Even as Starky strode towards James, barking orders to Kutlo and the others, Phil wrenched himself half free and shouted, "Arrest him! Arrest the bastard! He shot a protected lioness!"

"Shut up," said Kurt Heinrich, with surprising venom.

Everyone turned.

The German was standing with his rifle in both hands, no longer the smug trophy hunter but a furious, sun-reddened man whose expensive safari had turned into something so much more. His son stood behind him, clearly shaken and unsure what to do.

"Did you think Starky would lead us on an illegal hunt?" Kurt demanded of Phil, not Starky. "You try to extort us? You threaten us with these bandits?" He spat into the dust. "I will testify to everything."

Phil's face changed then. Not merely rage now, but fear.

"Bind him," Starky said curtly to one of his backup, dropping to one knee beside James. "And take the weapons. All of them. If anyone moves, break his arm."

Though he said most of it in Setswana, Verity knew exactly what he'd commanded, for the men obeyed immediately.

Then Starky turned all his attention to James.

Verity saw at once that whatever Starky might be—

charmer, womaniser, secretive bastard—at this moment he was exactly what he was reputed to be: a man who did not lose his head.

"Verity, listen to me." His tone was brisk. "He's lost a lot of blood, but the wounds to the leg are worse than the face. We need pressure here and here." He took her hands and placed them where he wanted them. "Don't let up unless I tell you."

Verity obeyed instantly.

James made a sound between a groan and a laugh. "Nice of Starky... to bring us together like this."

"Oh, for heaven's sake, my darling, be quiet," she said, sobbing now.

Starky had begun issuing further orders.

"Kutlo! Get the vehicle. Now. Thomas, bring the first-aid kit. Charlize—water, and whatever you can find to staunch the blood." He jerked his head around. "Susan, keep the girls back."

"I'm not moving," said Angie, voice shaking.

"You're going exactly where your mother puts you," said Starky, and the tone sounded so much like that of a father issuing orders that even in the horror of the moment Angie stared at him.

Then, he added more softly, "Please, Angie. Do this for me now and... and we can talk about it later."

That did it.

Angie began to cry.

Susan pulled her close, but her own eyes were on Starky —furious, wounded, confused, and grateful, all at once.

Saskia swayed. "Mum," she whispered.

Verity looked up sharply. Her daughter's face had gone an odd waxy colour.

Starky saw it too. "What's wrong?" he demanded.

"My leg."

The words were scarcely out when Saskia sagged, and Thomas lunged forward just in time to catch her before she hit the ground.

"Damn," Starky muttered, crossing to her in two strides and pressing the back of his hand to her face. "She's burning up."

Verity stared from James to Saskia and back again, her whole world tilting.

No. No, this could not be happening. "Osteomyelitis?" she whispered.

"Looks like it." His face hardened. "We're not waiting on anybody. We medevac both of them now."

It was Charlize, of all people, who got things moving.

"Well?" she snapped at the men standing around Phil and his disarmed followers. "Are we all just going to stare while people die?"

That seemed to jolt everyone.

Within moments, the dead lioness had become irrelevant.

Kurt and Thomas lifted James into the vehicle with Starky directing operations. Susan and Angie got Saskia between them, though Angie kept weeping and wiping her face furiously as if ashamed of it. Charlize climbed into the back and took Saskia's limp head in her lap without being asked, one hand smoothing the hair off the girl's clammy forehead with surprising tenderness.

Phil, wrists bound behind his back with leather thongs, shouted abuse at all of them until one of the local men stuffed a rag in his mouth.

No one protested.

As the vehicle lurched back towards camp, Verity sat wedged between James and Saskia, one hand still pressed to James's blood-slick leg, the other clutching her daughter's fingers.

James drifted in and out.

Saskia moaned whenever the truck hit a rut.

And Verity, looking from husband to daughter, felt as though her heart had been torn in two and left exposed to the sun.

At camp, everything happened at once.

HF messages crackled out to Maun as the plane was readied for its two critical passengers.

Starky leapt into the left hand seat, directing Kurt to take charge of those remaining.

Rob would meet them in Maun with Starky's plane, already refuelled, so they could continue without delay to Johannesburg.

James caught Verity's wrist as they loaded him. "Don't look like that," he whispered through split lips. "I'm not dead yet."

She bent and kissed his forehead, her tears splashing into his eyes. "I've never been more proud of you, though I was proud of you before," she whispered. "When you stood up for your principles back in Melbourne. It was the only thing you could do. And Angie...you saved her life."

His fingers tightened weakly over hers. "An interesting introduction to my niece," he said, with a half-laugh, before squeezing her hand harder. "Look after Saskia. She needs you most."

"You're not going anywhere, James. You'll be there for both of us," Verity said fiercely.

Starky climbed into the cockpit, while Susan stood below the wing with Angie pressed into her side.

Verity, glancing out of the window, saw her raise her hand and smile.

Not at her. But at Starky.

From behind, she saw Starky incline his head in acknowledgement.

And then the engine roared louder as the brakes were released, and the plane tore down the uneven dirt landing strip, carrying James and Saskia and Verity towards whatever came next, the dust rising up behind them like smoke.

CHAPTER

FORTY-EIGHT

FOUR WEEKS LATER

Verity had not realised until they touched down at Maun airport just how tightly strung she still was.

As the jet from Johannesburg made a smooth landing, her body reacted as if bracing for more bad news— for another doctor appearing at the end of a corridor, another phone call in the middle of the night, another crisis requiring impossible decisions.

She ought to have been relieved to be here.

James was alive. Saskia was healing. The worst, everyone kept assuring her, was over.

And yet, as she climbed down into the heat and glare of northern Botswana, her heart hammered as if she were stepping towards another reckoning.

"Mum, I'm nervous."

Saskia stood beside her on the tarmac at the bottom of the steps, and Verity felt an answering flutter in her own belly. But she asked calmly, "What is there to be nervous about? Starky has invited us all to his hunting lodge to celebrate your dad's recovery—and yours—"

"And to make some other important announcement. What do you suppose he's going to announce? He's not exactly into big secrets, is he?"

Verity was not about to say that most of what went on in Starky's life appeared to have been a secret from someone or other, so she simply smiled.

"Do you suppose he's going to announce an engagement between him and Susan?" Saskia asked.

At that, Verity gave the first genuine laugh she'd managed in what felt like weeks.

"Susan and Starky? I really don't think so, darling. But it is good that they're on speaking terms now, and that he's acknowledged Angie. Right—are you ready?"

"Do I look ready? I mean, do I look all right?"

Saskia seemed suddenly very young. She had flown up from boarding school that morning, Verity having been in Johannesburg for, hopefully, what would be one of her daughter's last hospital appointments.

Saskia's leg was still bandaged, though the graft had taken well, and despite all her brave chatter there was a new caution in the way she moved, as though some part of her no longer trusted her own body.

"I wish Dad could have been here," Saskia said with a sigh, looking about her.

Dust swirled in little eddies across the ground, and a group of children stood at the wire staring in at the planes.

"Well, your dad is very much looking forward to seeing you at Zerangu."

"He's been away such a long time, Mum." Saskia looked down, worrying her lip. "Are you sure...?"

"Sure of what?"

Saskia hesitated. "That you and Dad aren't going to tell me something I don't want to hear."

"Oh, Saskia, how can you think such a thing?" Verity asked, genuinely shocked.

Yes, communication had been difficult, with Saskia transferred to a specialist unit in Cape Town while James's treatment continued at Johannesburg's Baragwanath. James had insisted Verity base herself by the coast so she could be closer to their daughter.

It meant she had seen James only at the beginning of his treatment. The long physical distance had made it all but impossible to properly address the emotional distance that had grown between them in the days leading up to the attack.

For weeks Verity had carried layers of fear and doubt about how she would tackle the obvious questions James must surely have.

She also feared that Saskia had seen too much, guessed too much, misunderstood too much.

"Now, come along," she said lightly. "There's Rob and Lucy. They're flying us to Zerangu. No more ominous questions."

She was glad, almost at once, to be spared saying any more, because Lucy and Rob were already waving them over to Rob's 206 parked at the edge of the tarmac.

"How's James doing?" Of course that was Lucy's first question, and Verity wished she could answer in some way that conveyed the depth of what they had all been through, rather than simply with the reassuring shorthand people seemed to want.

"He's made great progress."

Lucy smiled. "Thank goodness for the world-class expertise at the Bara. I heard James had an excellent surgeon. But what a shame Saskia had to go all the way down to Cape Town for treatment." Lucy put a hand on Verity's arm. "My, your family has really been through the wringer these past weeks. Has Saskia even seen her dad since the attack?"

Before Verity could answer in the negative, Rob joined Lucy, shaking his head.

"No one would blame you if you wanted to leave the Okavango after all that's happened, though I hope you won't." He opened the door of the waiting plane and offered a hand to help them both in, then glanced at Saskia's calf. "And now you're all off to Starky's lodge. Any special occasion other than the fact you can all walk on two legs now?" He winced. "I'm really sorry. That was not thoughtfully phrased."

"It's OK," said Saskia as she settled herself in the back. "I've got a story to tell and so has Dad." She managed a smile. "Not every father and daughter get attacked by a crocodile and a lion within the space of two months."

"No, they don't," said Verity, buckling herself in beside her. "And I haven't the faintest idea why Starky invited us all to his lodge, or why James suggested we meet him there rather than back in Maun."

"Yes, that does sound a little secretive," Lucy agreed with a smile. "But James is a romantic, isn't he?"

Verity tried to smile back, despite one of the familiar little stabs of fear that had assailed her ever since the attack.

She had spent hours by James's bedside—but only in those first days after the injuries he had sustained, when too often he had been under anaesthetic or half lost to morphine.

While he was still fighting through emergency surgery

on the lacerations to his face and leg, Saskia had been whisked into surgery to manage the osteomyelitis Starky had feared was the cause of her sudden fever.

It was Starky who had medevac'ed them to Johannesburg, upbeat and reassuring the whole way. As though he knew exactly how to play the role required of him.

Even now, remembering that day, Verity could see the astonishing efficiency with which he had taken command. Despite everything exploding around him—Phil exposed, armed men disarmed, Angie in shock, James bleeding in the dust—Starky had kept his head. His barked orders to his own backup had turned Phil's ragged little militia from dangerous accomplices into frightened young men desperate to save themselves. Phil had not understood Starky's barrage of Setswana, but he had understood the moment his men dropped their weapons and melted away, leaving him alone.

And then James's rifle had gone off, and the whole focus of the danger had shifted.

"Yes," Verity said quietly, almost to herself. "James is a romantic."

But even as she said it, she wondered again why James had asked her to meet him—fresh from the Bara—at Starky's lodge.

Neutral territory.

Or had he chosen it because Saskia had said something? Because he believed, however fleetingly, some ugly misunderstanding about Verity and Starky that he now intended to clear up once and for all?

She sent a worried glance at her daughter. "You've spoken to your dad more recently than I have, maybe? Are you sure you don't know what this surprise is?"

Saskia shook her head, looking as mystified as Verity felt. "Not a clue."

By the time Rob landed them at Zerangu forty-five minutes later, where Kutlo was waiting with the vehicle to drive them the last short distance to the lodge, Verity felt close to breaking point.

Of course, she and James had spoken at the hospital. She had held his hand and told him that she loved him. But he had been weak, bandaged, drifting in and out of sleep. She had gone back to him whenever she could, but after the first tremendous relief of learning he would survive, Saskia had needed her more.

And James had urged her to leave his bedside. It hadn't been her idea that she transfer her time and attention to where their daughter was frightened and ill and far from home, in Cape Town.

"Verity! Good to see you! And you too, Saskia!" Starky was waiting at the top of the steps to his lodge like the consummate host.

Behind him, on the broad wooden verandah, James raised a hand in greeting from his chair, part of an elegant arrangement of leather and timber furniture that melded luxuriously into the safari setting. His right leg was still heavily bandaged, but when he saw her, his face changed.

"I'd get up if I could," he called, with a smile warmer than anything she had imagined on the journey there, "but I'm going to have to ask you to come over here if you want a proper welcome kiss."

Something inside her loosened at once.

Saskia ran ahead to hug her father, while Verity followed more slowly, almost afraid to trust the relief flooding through her. "James?"

She put out her hand, and he took it at once, holding it rather than merely patting the seat beside him.

"Hello, darling," he said, and though he looked tired and thinner and battle-worn, and half his face was still bandaged, she could only see the James she loved. "I feel as if I haven't seen you in years, when it's only been three weeks. Come here."

He tugged gently at her hand until she bent, and he kissed her properly—nothing theatrical, only enough to tell her what she most needed to know.

That he loved her.

That he knew she loved him.

That whatever else had happened, they were still solid.

By the time she sat beside him, her own knees felt unsteady.

"Saskia's bouncing around like a gazelle," he added with a crooked smile. "I'm afraid I've got rather further to go."

He nodded at his bandaged leg. The scar crossing his cheek would not be as dreadful as Verity had first feared. Most of the worst damage had been to his thigh and leg.

Saskia, still leaning against him, suddenly gave a squeal and leapt up, wincing at the sudden movement though her smile broadened.

"Angie! What are you doing here?" She hobbled across the deck to greet her cousin.

Verity turned back to James. "Angie's here? What about Susan?"

"They're both here," James said. Then, giving her hand another squeeze, he added, "I'm glad you came, Verity. There's something important I want to talk to you about."

A flicker of nerves returned at once, though now it was tempered by hope rather than dread.

"Verity! I haven't seen you since—" Susan broke off as she approached, colouring slightly, as if the words *since the lion attack* were too raw to say aloud.

It brought home to Verity how little she and James had properly tackled the attack itself. Their conversations had been by phone or fax and mostly confined to the practical: stitches, antibiotics, dressings, grafts, the long slow business of recovery. Nothing had yet come wholly from the heart.

"Not since the day James became even more of a hero," Verity said, smiling. "It was so good of Starky to invite him to convalesce at Zerangu this last week while I stayed in Cape Town for Saskia's final skin graft. There's still a bit of a way to go, but they're both out of the woods now, and that's the main thing."

"Hey everyone, so glad you could all make it."

Near the bar, where staff were laying out champagne flutes, Starky clapped his hands and drew everyone's attention.

"I know you've only just arrived, and usually we'd let you unwind first. But James isn't yet up to a long sociable session, so let's move to the dining table, let Florence fill our glasses, and get on with it, shall we?"

Verity helped James carefully to his feet and waited while he steadied himself.

"I'm such an invalid," he muttered. "Don't worry. I'll be back on my feet in a few weeks."

This time the reassuring look he gave her was unmistakable.

And for the first time since the horrors of Deception Pan, she allowed herself to believe that perhaps—just perhaps—the worst really was over.

Only when she stood at her place at the long table in

the dining room overlooking the floodplain did she properly take in the guests.

It was an unusual gathering. A couple of people from the Maun office were there, including Rebecca, the new manager at Mombo. Rob and Lucy had taken seats together, and Verity was glad to see, smiling kindly from farther down the table, Rupert Graves, the wildlife documentary-maker who had been so good to Saskia during their stay at Chubaora. Then there were Susan and Angie and, of course, her husband and daughter.

Champagne was poured, and they all raised their glasses to James and Saskia, and to continued healing.

When the entrée arrived—tiger fish pâté with a small fillet of crocodile—Verity could not help smiling at Starky's sense of theatre.

"A reminder," he said, "of what Saskia went through on her first safari with us, and a chance for her to taste victory now that she has come out the winner. Though let me reassure everyone—crocodile attacks on our clients are not common."

"That was only because you came to the rescue just in time," said Saskia, blushing as all eyes turned towards her. "You killed that crocodile seconds before it killed me. And you killed that lion before it killed Dad."

A burst of clapping greeted this, but Starky only inclined his head.

"I had a gun. I'm no hero. Your father is the real hero."

James gave an embarrassed roll of his eyes. "Good God, no. I had a gun and no idea how to use it. When it jammed, I was reduced to using it as a club and trying to stick the barrel into the lioness's eye. I couldn't have held her off any longer. Starky arrived in the nick of time."

"But you saw the danger Angie was running into," said

Starky. "You risked your life and prevented my daughter from being killed by a lion before she'd even had the chance to know me."

Verity put a hand to her mouth as tears pricked unexpectedly. Lucy was dabbing at her own eyes with a handkerchief Rob had passed her, while Susan tipped back her champagne and said, "Oh my God, Starky, you do have a flair for dramatic phrasing."

But she was grinning, and the tension at the table loosened.

"Thank you," said Starky gravely. Then, with a flourish, he indicated the dapper older gentleman seated a little farther down. "Most of you know Rupert Graves and know what he does. But I'll still give him a proper introduction and then let him explain a project the pair of us—with assistance—have put together, and which I hope some of you may be part of."

With that, Rupert pushed back his chair and rose, sweeping a hand through the white hair that fell across his forehead.

Verity smiled across at Saskia, knowing how much her daughter admired him.

Rupert cleared his throat.

"I was in Maun and on the point of returning to Johannesburg when I heard what had happened at Deception Pan," he began. Then, with a nod towards Saskia, he added, "And when I heard that the father of the young lady who had recently featured in the *Okavango Observer*, because of her flirtation with a crocodile, had then been mauled by a lion, I confess I thought it impossible that one family could encounter such extraordinary misfortune in so short a time."

He paused.

"Though on reflection, perhaps it was good fortune too. For everyone survived. And some remarkable truths came to light. Not least the truth that brought together two very special people—Starky and the daughter he never knew he had, Angie."

There was more clapping at that, and Angie, seated beside Starky, leaned her head briefly against his shoulder. The look on Starky's face was pure pride and something quite unexpectedly tender.

Verity felt herself choke up again. She turned to James and found his own eyes suspiciously bright.

"What a lucky man," he murmured, squeezing her hand beneath the table. "Nearly as lucky as I am."

That little squeeze was enough to make her heart soar to the skies.

Rupert, however, was not done.

"But that lion attack," he said, and a hush fell over the table. "What a brilliant, dangerous, and ultimately successful trap Starky laid for a man long suspected of corruption within BNPW, though no one had yet been able to prove it. By allowing the rumour to circulate that Zerangu Safaris had exhausted its lion trophy allocation, and by appearing to take those German hunters on an illegal safari, Starky flushed out Phil Lehmann."

Susan covered her face with both hands.

Rupert continued more gently. "And yes, Susan played a part too."

"In other words, I have the worst judgement and taste in men," Susan wailed.

"No, you don't," said Starky at once, while Angie grinned and several people laughed.

"I thought Phil was the good guy," Susan went on miserably. "I invited him up to Maun. It's all my fault."

Verity exchanged a glance with James. His look mirrored her own thought exactly: Susan did know how to make herself the centre of any catastrophe.

But Starky surprised her by raising his glass to Susan and speaking with real kindness.

"You did invite him. But no, it is not all your fault. It helped convince Phil he could do more than just steal a trophy and pocket the proceeds. It emboldened him. It made him boast about what he'd done fifteen years ago, because he believed he'd got away with it." He paused, then added, "Be proud of what you did. It came from loyalty to your brother. And because of it, Phil now faces charges not only for profiteering from poaching but also"—he swallowed—"for his role in Mike's death."

Verity felt the catharsis of it like a physical thing.

Susan signalled for her glass to be refilled before saying, almost wonderingly, "I still can't quite believe Phil was the one who... did it."

Then she narrowed her eyes at Starky, and the question she did not speak hung in the silence.

Why hadn't you said anything before?

Verity thought she knew part of the answer. Enough, at least, to understand why Starky had carried it so long.

But then he said something that startled even her.

"Phil didn't kill Mike outright. Mike was mauled by a lion after I left him wounded and went back to camp for help."

A ripple of shock went round the table.

Starky's eyes flicked to Susan, as though he knew such details were dangerous to unveil in public if she was hearing them fully for the first time.

But Susan had already leaned forward.

"What are you saying? You left Mike alive?"

"Yes." Starky's voice was steady. "He was badly wounded. Phil and I had done what we could. I told Phil to stay with him while I went for help."

"But he didn't." Susan sat back, rigid with outrage. "So he should face charges for that too. And poor Jeremy still got the blame."

"And that is my greatest regret," said Starky quietly. "That I went to Mozambique not long after and never learned Jeremy had been charged, let alone that he had died in gaol branded a murderer because that is what the newspapers said before the coroner's report was properly understood."

"My parents never said anything about the lion," Susan said. "I was always told Mike was killed by a single bullet from a Krieghoff. And Jeremy was *supposedly* the only one who had one."

She glared at Starky, who looked away.

From the verandah, the floodplain stretched to the horizon. As Starky spoke on, Verity caught sight of a giraffe's head floating above an umbrella thorn, and somewhere in the distance a hyena laughed.

Mocking sound though it was, it made her glad—glad to be alive, glad to be here, glad that justice, however imperfect and delayed, had at last asserted itself.

What did it matter now how Starky had first made his money? That he had probably sold, illegally, the stone he and Mike had found together, and that this had helped set in motion the chain of events which Phil had exploited with such disastrous rashness?

Starky had not killed Mike. He had acknowledged Angie. He and Susan, improbably, had found some kind of truce. Was that not what mattered most now?

Botswana was still wild and beautiful, and dangerous.

All of them had suffered in different ways because of it. Yet as Verity watched the contentment on James's face and the quiet look that passed between Starky and Angie, she felt, for the first time in months, something like peace.

She was so lost in that feeling that she did not at first realise her name had been spoken.

"Mum!"

Saskia's excited voice made her look up just as Starky, who was still standing, said, "—and immediately Verity came to mind."

James took her hand and murmured, "I thought that might please you, darling."

But it was Rupert, rising again beside Starky and clearly noticing that Verity had missed the lead-in entirely, who took pity on her.

"Let me say it plainly," he said, looking directly at her. "Your husband's idea, and the way he put it to me, made a powerful impression. When I visited him in hospital, he showed me more of your writing and your photographs. I was impressed—though I already knew you had ability. But it was your particular journey through this country, and what you have seen of its beauty and its danger, that made me keep turning the notion over on my flight back to Johannesburg."

Verity sat very still.

Rupert smiled.

"I think you would make the perfect wildlife documentary presenter, Verity. I'm too old to front this new series alone, and a younger face—an intelligent one, and yes, a pretty one too, if I may say it—is exactly what my producers and I now believe it needs. So forgive me if this is not the most discreet or elegant way to ask. It simply seemed, after all your family has lived through, a fitting place to say that I hope this may be the beginning of a long partnership."

Verity knew her mouth had fallen open. She had heard him perfectly clearly. She simply could not seem to absorb it.

She turned to James. "Did Rupert just ask me to co-host a documentary series with him?"

"He did," said James, cradling her hand on the tabletop.

"And I'm going to be a consultant!" Susan crowed. "I started writing a big piece on poaching because I was trying to investigate Starky, and when Rupert—"

As Susan's enthusiasm carried her away, James leaned closer and whispered, "That's a bit of a sop. Rupert doesn't mind if she dabbles in the background. It's you he really wants. You on camera. You in the bush. You doing the research and photographing the animals."

Verity put a hand to her mouth.

She was trembling now. James was smiling, and everyone else had fallen silent and was looking at her.

"I did hope you'd agree, Verity," Rupert said, with just enough anxiety to make him suddenly endearing. "I did such a splendid job persuading the producers that I'd hate to have to begin all over again."

"I'd do it!" Susan cried.

"Me too!" said Angie and Saskia in chorus.

"I'm afraid I want Verity," Rupert said over them.

"And so do I," James murmured, squeezing her hand again. "She's perfect."

Rupert smiled and nodded as James kissed her cheek.

"I've always been so proud of the way you've risen to the challenge every time I've uprooted you," he said softly. "You truly deserve this."

Verity lowered her head and wiped away the tear that slipped from the corner of her eye.

"I'd do it all over again," she whispered. "I want you to know that." Her breath hitched. "And I want you to know how incredibly proud I am of you—not just your bravery in taking on a lion, but for refusing to compromise your principles when you made the decision to bring us to this... this wild, beautiful country."

James's fingers tightened around hers.

Then, smiling at him first, and then at the others, she lifted her gaze to Rupert. "I would be honoured to accept."

James squeezed her hand, more tightly this time, his eyes glowing with pride. "I'm so glad, darling," he murmured, kissing her fingers. "Rupert couldn't have found anyone more perfect. I can't wait for the world to get to know the smart, talented woman I fell in love with."

THE END

Ready for more adventure in the Okavango?
1996, Botswana
Angie thought she'd left Maun—and its dangers—behind.

But when a powerful man dies and suspicion falls close to home, she is pulled back into a world of buried secrets, old betrayals, and the bush pilot she has never quite forgotten.

NOTES FROM THE DELTA: MY LIFE AS A SAFARI HOSTESS

In 1992, I travelled to Botswana for a fly-in fly-out safari, just like the two main characters in this book, James and Verity White.

I was accompanying my father, Spencer (Ted) Nettelton, who wanted to show me the country where he was born and brought up.

While there, the wonderfully kind and charismatic Chris Kruger, then managing director of Okavango Wilderness Safaris, offered me a relief-management role at Mombo Camp over Christmas a few months hence, and, after accepting, I took time off from my job as a journalist on a South Australian metropolitan newspaper.

Many of the adventures and day-to-day activities recounted in *Whispers in the Kalahari* are based on my experiences working at Mombo and Jedibe luxury safari lodges in the Okavango Delta.

As fate would have it, the day before I was due to fly home to Australia to marry my boyfriend of seven years, I met the handsome Norwegian bush pilot whom I married instead, after a whirlwind courtship encompassing eight months of letter-writing, and a short two-week stint in each other's company.

Hitching my star to the amazing, adventurous, and exciting Eivind Eikli was the best decision I've made.

It's taken decades to feel ready to translate so much of my life onto the page in the form of this fictional romance about a journalist giving up her career to follow her husband to Africa, though, unlike my heroine, I had no misgivings and have never regretted my choices.

Like all the characters in this book, irresistible hunter, pilot and womaniser, Starky Willis, is not based on anyone living or dead. Rather, he is an amalgamation of the many pilots, rangers, and other charismatic men I worked with in the safari industry, and flew with daily in my subsequent career in airborne geophysical survey. Any similarities to any person, living or dead, are purely coincidental.

The bitter and divisive Australian Pilot's Dispute of 1989 is pivotal to the plot, and I mention this in greater detail over the page.

It provided the ideal vehicle for precipitating my characters to Africa, and while I have tried to present different viewpoints, I am sensitive to the fact that this hugely emotive event, which changed Australian aviation history, continues to resonate.

Finally, the discovery of a diamond in Makgadigadi Pans in *Whispers in the Kalahari* is based on a true story my father recounted, in which a pilot and his passenger were found dead only metres away from a fully serviceable light plane, with working radio. The speculation was that their deaths occurred over the unexpected discovery of a diamond, glittering on the salt pan.

This, really, was my starting point for creating the mystery in this novel.

I hope you enjoyed it.

Warm regards,

Beverley Nettelton (also writing as Beverley Oakley and Beverley Eikli)

A PERSONAL NOTE ABOUT THE AUSTRALIAN PILOT'S DISPUTE AND THE WORLD OF AVIATION.

When I sat down to write *Whispers in the Kalahari*, I was drawing from a well of deep personal experience. Like Verity, I was a young journalist when I first moved to Botswana. And, like her, I found myself in the heart of the Okavango Delta, working as a safari hostess and manager for a lodge. The world you've just read—the scent of the Kalahari dust, the sound of a lion roaring in the dark, and the lifeline of small planes landing on a dirt airstrip—is a world I know intimately.

But this book was also inspired by a very specific moment in history, one that I, too, was caught up in: the 1989 Australian pilots' dispute.

This was not a simple industrial disagreement. It was a bitter, high-stakes confrontation that brought a nation to a standstill. When the Australian Federation of Air Pilots (AFAP) claimed a 29.5% pay rise, it was seen as a direct challenge to the government's entire national economic strategy. The government, in a move that shocked the nation, sided with the airlines. They declared a national emergency, bringing in the Royal Australian Air Force (RAAF) to fly domestic routes and, crucially, began recruiting overseas pilots to permanently replace the striking Australian workforce.

The dispute was divisive, and "strike breaker" became one of the ugliest terms in the industry. More than 1,600 Australian pilots eventually resigned, their careers and lives irrevocably broken.

It was in the immediate aftermath of this historic dispute, with its shockwaves felt by pilots around the world, that I was working in the Okavango Delta. And it was there, just before I was due to fly home, that I met the man who would become my husband: a dashing Norwegian bush pilot named Eivind.

Like many pilots of his generation, his own career had been stalled by a global economic downturn. He had trained in the United States and Canada, but returned to a Scandinavia with no aviation jobs, eventually finding his way to Botswana to fly Cessnas and Islanders for the safari industry. He recalls seeing the full-page ads in international papers advertising for pilots in Australia. It was the promise of an airline job, a dream for any pilot. But, like James in this novel, he knew he was not prepared to be a strike breaker.

That decision, that moral crossroads where personal ambition collides with loyalty, became the heart of this story.

My life has been inextricably linked to the "boom and bust" cycle of general aviation. I have moved countries as my husband's flying companies folded or as he moved up the ladder. This world of pilots, of high stakes and fragile careers, is one I am very familiar with. *Whispers in the Kalahari* is my tribute to that time—to the wild beauty of

Botswana and to the men and women who, in a moment of historic crisis, were forced to choose who they really were and what they were prepared to stand up for.

Thank you for taking this journey with Verity and James.

WINGS OVER AFRICA SERIES

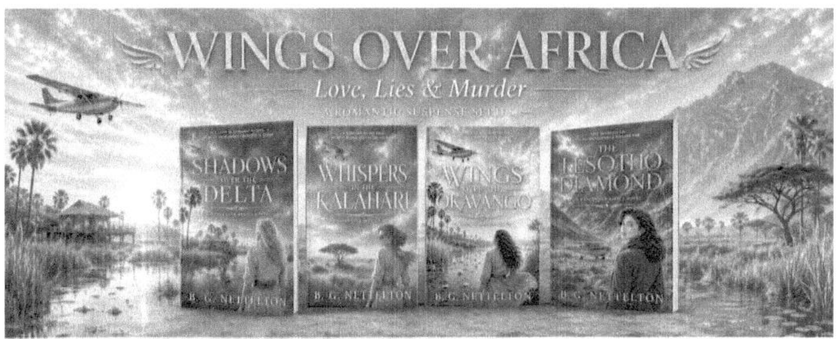

From the snow-dusted peaks of 1960s Lesotho to the lion-haunted floodplains of 1980s Botswana, the *Wings over Africa* series tells sweeping, emotionally charged stories of love, danger, murder, and survival beneath vast African skies.

WHISPERS IN THE KALAHARI (Book 1)

In ***Whispers in the Kalahari*** (1989, Botswana), a bush pilot's wife, adrift after an airline dispute shatters her life, must confront a fractured marriage, a long-buried death on a remote safari camp, and the brutal shadow of a poaching ring before she can reclaim herself.

Perfect for readers who love atmospheric, Africa-set fiction where the wilderness is as powerful and unpredictable as the human heart.

WINGS OVER THE OKAVANGO (Book 2)

1996, Botswana

Six years after discovering who her father really is, Angie returns to Maun with a broken heart and no intention of staying. But when a wealthy hunter dies and suspicion falls on her father, Starky Willis, she is drawn into a dangerous web of secrets, betrayal, and old wounds.

And when the bush pilot she once loved steps back into her life,

Angie must decide whether to trust her heart before the truth
turns deadly.

THE LESOTHO DIAMOND (Book 3)

In **The Lesotho Diamond** (1962, Lesotho), a forced landing, a
reckless lie about a marriage, and a cache of illicit diamonds
entangle a District Commissioner's daughter and a bush pilot in a
deadly web of blackmail and forbidden love in an African
mountain kingdom on the brink of change.

*Perfect for readers of Wilbur Smith's epic African adventures and Kate
Quinn's character-driven historical sagas.*

The mystery of Starky Willis began long before the Kalahari.

At a remote safari lodge in the Okavango Delta, Lucy Brennan falls under the spell of a man haunted by rumours of poaching, scandal, and a fifteen-year-old death.

Read **Shadows over the Delta**, the irresistible prequel to **Whispers in the Kalahari.**

Drawn from the author's own real-life experiences managing a luxury safari lodge in Botswana's Okavango Delta.

THE MEMOIRS THAT INSPIRED THE FICTION

The novels in the 'Wings over Africa' saga are fiction, but they are deeply rooted in incredible true events.

They were directly inspired by the real-life memoirs of my father, S.E. "Ted" Nettelton, who grew up in Botswana in the 1930s and 40s, and served as a District Commissioner in colonial Lesotho in the 1960s. For readers who wish to dive deeper into the true history, here are the original memoirs that inspired it all.

GROWING UP IN BOTSWANA IN THE 1930S AND 40S
(TALES OF ADVENTURE IN COLONIAL AFRICA
BOOK 1)

by Spencer 'Ted' Nettelton

Spencer 'Ted' Nettelton grew up in Botswana during the 1930s and 40s when herds of wildebeest stretched across the horizon and locally shot game was part of the staple diet.

In Volume I of his memoirs, Ted describes the daily life of an adventurous boy living in the bush, and the impact on his family when caught in the spotlight of international events.

From the banishment of Botswana's King Seretse Khama - later elected Botswana's first president - to the birth of a new African nation - Lesotho - Ted and his family played integral roles.

Educated in Cape Town, Ted followed his father into

the British Colonial Service, was posted to the mountains of Lesotho in the 1950s, organised the country's Independence Celebrations a decade later, and then served as Secretary to Lesotho's first democratically elected Prime Minister, Leabua Jonathan, with whom he enjoyed an enduring friendship.

Paperback (Colour) ISBN: 978-0-6486221-9-2

Case Laminate hardcover ISBN: 978-0-6486506-0-7

WORKING IN THE COLONIAL SERVICE IN LESOTHO (1952-69) : TALES OF ADVENTURE IN COLONIAL AFRICA

by Spencer 'Ted' Nettelton

Book 2: Tales of Adventure in Colonial Africa

During the 1960s, Lesotho gained its independence and the Basotho people elected their first Prime Minister

In Volume 2 of his memoirs, Spencer 'Ted' Nettelton reflects on the momentous changes he witnessed during nineteen years working in Lesotho as a District Commissioner in the British Colonial service. In 1966, he organised Lesotho's Independence Celebrations before serving as Secretary to the country's first democratically elected Prime Minister Chief Leabua Jonathan.

Accompanying Leabua to the US where the prime minister delivered his first address to the United Nations General Assembly, Ted and the PM were guests of President Lyndon Johnston at the White House during a hugely successful tour of the country.

Supported by dozens of contemporary newspaper clippings, Ted describes the masterful juggling act of an astute prime minister at the helm of a newly independent African nation landlocked by apartheid South Africa.

From Constitutional crisis on the eve of Independence to the machinations employed by Russia, China and South Africa to gain influence in the strategically positioned country, Ted's memoir provides a snapshot of daily life and a broader picture of a bygone era punctuated by medicine murder and illegal diamond buying overlaid by the irrepressible spirit and strength of the Basotho people amongst whom he had many good friends.

Paperback (Colour) ISBN: 9780648650614

Case Laminate (Hardcover) ISBN: 978064840599

EXCERPT OF 'THE LESOTHO DIAMOND' (BOOK 3)

Welcome to the world of *The Lesotho Diamond*. The story you are about to read is deeply personal as it's set in the 1960s African mountain kingdom where I spent my formative years, and is an amalgamation of the real-life memoirs of my father, who served as the last British District Commissioner, and the partying world my left when she married him.

It's also a fictionalised account of the dangerous world Dad navigated in his daily working life—a volatile frontier grappling with a "Wild West" diamond rush and the chilling, culturally-sanctioned 'medicine murders' he was tasked with investigating.

But it begins in my mother's world of parties and university life, of hopes for a good marriage, and the divide between those who are comfortable—like my heroine, Philippa—and those struggling to rise above the disadvantages life has thrown them, determined to make their mark —like my hero, Stuart, and the firebrand agitator Moses Shakane.

CAPE TOWN, 1961

6pm! Where was Matthew?

Philippa, still dressed only in her cream silk slip, craned her head out of the top-floor dormitory window, leaning into the cool evening air. Far below, the red terracotta roofs of Fuller Hall's lower wings spread out, catching the last rays of sun as she scanned the long, curved driveway that led up to Cape Town University's women's residence.

Taking a deep breath to quell the familiar flutter in her heart that always preceded large social gatherings, she managed a smile for her roommate, Susan, who joined her at the window.

"Be honest now—are you in love with Matthew or just that sports car of his?" Susan's voice carried a hint of mockery as they both shielded their eyes from the late afternoon sun, now glinting off the sleek green MG that had finally appeared at the entrance to the avenue.

Against the grandeur of Table Mountain's backdrop, the sports car appeared diminutive, but Philippa Tremain had grown up amid even more impressive peaks in neighbouring Basutoland. The view from their window, sweeping over the manicured lawns of the university and across the suburbs to the shimmering ocean, was more of a novelty. She hoped that after Angela's party that night, Matthew might propose a visit to the beautiful... romantic... beach.

"The sports car, silly!" Philippa pretended to play along as she turned, reaching for the burnt-orange, full-skirted evening dress draped over her desk chair. "Promise you won't tell Matthew, though. Now, won't you help me into this? I should have been ready ages ago."

"The orange is so daring, but it contrasts beautifully

with your dark hair. Honestly, Matthew doesn't deserve you." Susan sighed as she followed Philippa to the small mirror near the door. "And he's always late," she added as she zipped up Philippa's dress, her tone no longer light-hearted. "You know, it wouldn't hurt to make him wait now and then."

Ignoring her, Philippa pulled on her elbow-length gloves and smoothed her sleek chignon before twirling around. "How do I look?" Her confidence was wavering, wracked with sudden nerves.

"Not bad." Susan grinned as she turned to focus on her own reflection in the little mirror above the basin, helping herself to Philippa's new Revlon mascara. "But you know that."

"Come on, Susan, what do you really think?" Philippa's heart fluttered dangerously, and for a moment, she thought she might be ill. Matthew's approval mattered more than she cared to admit to Susan, who always expressed such disdain for her new boyfriend.

Surely Philippa could call him that after five weeks of exclusive dating?

Susan darkened her sandy lashes before turning back to Philippa with another sigh. "Are you asking me if Matthew will approve? Of course he will. You're stunning—and this year's Rag Queen!" she said, and Philippa wondered if that was jealousy she detected.

Poor Susan was not a beauty, it was generally acknowl-edged, with her sandy hair more frizzy than curly and her freckled face. But the two girls had been friends for as long as Philippa could remember—neighbours and schoolmates —both of them travelling the thousand miles from Mokhotlong in the African mountain kingdom of Basu-toland where they'd grown up, to begin university in the exciting, cosmopolitan city of Cape Town on South Africa's southern tip, where the Atlantic and Indian Oceans met in a swirl of currents beneath the watchful gaze of Table Mountain.

Susan continued applying her makeup before glancing out of the window, saying in that faux-surprise tone that generally irked Philippa, "Well, the young man is ready to escort you to the party at last, you'll be happy to know, though it seems Eliza has captured his attention. He hasn't even got out of his car. Maybe I will be ready in time to go with both of you to the party." She hesitated, adding, "Except—I forgot!—there's only room for two in his MG."

Philippa, who'd been ready to dash out the door to greet her beloved, hesitated as she put her hand on the door handle, remembering Susan's words from last week:

Matthew Myburgh is rich and entitled. He'll play with your heart and then trample on it.

Was Susan really jealous? Did she truly feel Philippa had prioritised her budding relationship with Matthew at the expense of their friendship?

Hesitating, she spun around on her elegant new kitten heels. "Oh, Susan, I completely forgot!" she said, dashing over to the chest of drawers at the foot of her bed. "I meant to give you this to wear with your blue chiffon dress."

Susan frowned at the white silk scarf Philippa held out. "I might spill something on it," she said, her tone more churlish than grateful.

"That wouldn't matter since I'm giving it to you." Philippa tried not to let Susan's tone rankle. Susan hadn't always been the most gracious of playmates since their days of playing with dolls. But it was thanks to Philippa's beautiful, kind late mother that Philippa now saw this as reflective of Susan's own perceived inadequacies rather than ingratitude.

"All right then. If you think my blue chiffon needs something extra," Susan said, reaching for the scarf while Philippa, anxious to be gone, nervously smoothed the lovely burnt-orange creation her talented mother had made for her nineteenth birthday nearly two years before. She turned the doorknob and smiled at Susan. "See you at the party, then."

Susan nodded as she stroked the white silk scarf she'd openly admired when Philippa had received it from her father for her last birthday. "Just make sure Matthew takes you to Angela's and doesn't whisk you off to see the whales instead," she said to Philippa's departing back. "You know how unpredictable Matthew is, and you know how much I hate parties when you're not there to help me talk to people."

"Matthew!" Philippa greeted him with a smile, forcing herself to slow her pace as she descended the last few wide stone steps of the residence entrance; forcing herself to remember the poise drilled into her at finishing school while she curved her lips the way her mother, a celebrated English beauty, had shown her for such situations: welcoming, but not overenthusiastic.

Matthew Myburgh might be rich, but Philippa's mother had been one of the Richmond sisters, featured in magazines throughout the thirties and forties, famed for their ivory skin, lustrous dark hair, and violet eyes.

And their propensity for marrying into the aristocracy.

Except for Eleanor Richmond, Philippa's mother. The

black sheep of the family. Arguably the most beautiful of the three girls, and certainly the most wilful, Eleanor had been disowned when she'd eloped with a Colonial to live in the tiny mountainous kingdom of Basutoland just six months before Philippa had been born.

The scandal had been enormous. The sacrifice, greater still. Eleanor had given up wealth, position, and family for love—a choice Philippa had never fully understood, having grown up craving the glamorous life her mother had abandoned.

Still, Philippa's family could hold their own, she reminded herself as she assessed Matthew's handsome tousled head and muscled torso from the other side of his sports car as he chatted with his rugby mate, Hugh, and Hugh's girlfriend, Eliza.

Square-jawed, blue-eyed and fair-haired, Matthew had the Adonis good looks that made the girls either tongue-tied in his presence, or over-talkative. Philippa fell into the latter category, though she'd worked hard lately to emulate those sultry, dark-haired beauties of the screen who made more impact by being silent and enigmatic.

"Philippa! Sorry I'm late!" Matthew looked up from his conversation as Hugh farewelled him with a salute and a 'good luck' for their rugby match the following day.

His white teeth gleamed as he came round from the driver's side to greet her.

Why did his smile always make her knees feel weak? Literally, weak. And why did it also stir something uneasy in her chest—a quiet voice that whispered this was too easy, too perfect?

Because, really, the last five weeks with Matthew lavishing her with his company had been more than she could have dreamed of.

Except that, right now, this was not acceptable—

Interpreting her frown, Matthew gave a sheepish glance at his filthy rugby jersey and mud-stained shorts. "I got caught up at rugby practice."

"Philippa! Your father's on the phone!" Susan's voice floated down from an open window above the portico.

Philippa ignored her. "But, Matthew... the party starts in ten minutes."

"Philippa! It's long distance!"

"And it'll only take me ten minutes to get changed." Matthew's tone was soothing.

No, it won't. Philippa didn't need to put that into words. She managed a shaky smile, though she felt like stamping her foot or crying as she stepped back from his approach.

"Come on, darling, don't give me that cross look," he said, attempting to kiss her.

"I'll kiss you when you won't get mud on my dress," grumbled Philippa, remembering all the disdainful things Susan had said about him. As usual, Matthew expected Philippa to forgive him.

Yet the things Susan said were true. Many of them, anyway. Matthew was always late. And he did always expect her to forgive him.

Should she stop making so many allowances if he was to respect her?

"Tell Daddy I'm coming now!" she shouted back to Susan. Turning on her heel, she said in clipped tones over her shoulder to Matthew, now lounging against the spotless green paintwork of his car, "I'll see you at the party, later. Daddy's probably waited an hour to get put through. I wouldn't dream of keeping *him* waiting."

No doubt the irony was wasted on Matthew, she thought, as she marched back up the grand steps, past the heavy oak doors, ignoring Susan's enquiring look and settling herself on a chair in the corridor by the communal telephone. The scent of floor polish and old wood filled the hallway.

"Sorry I took so long, Daddy," she said, picking up the receiver Susan had left hanging by its cord, and trying to sound cheerful. "Everyone's in a mad rush here. We're off to Angela Myers's twenty-first birthday. How are things in the mountains?"

Philippa's father's role as District Commissioner in Mokhotlong—known also as the British Empire's remotest outpost at 10,000 feet amidst the rocky peaks—required a broad repertoire of skills. Philippa never knew whether he was currently investigating illegal diamond trading or culturally sanctioned 'medicine' murder, whereby a local chief shored up his power by inducing fear amongst their villagers using the flesh of some unfortunate victim.

Using the crackling down the phone line to give her time to calm her anger and disappointment over Matthew's behaviour, she waited for her father's response. She had done the right thing, hadn't she? Susan would be proud of her for standing up for herself and making it clear to Matthew that she wouldn't be treated with such cavalier disregard. Susan's phrase.

"... another murder last week in the Qthing district. I doubt you'd have read about it yet, but it's in the Cape Times."

Her father's voice was suddenly clear enough to understand, and Philippa drew in a quick breath. "Again? I thought the evidence was sufficient to convict. Do you think—?" She wasn't sure whether she should ask. Now that her focus was on her father's troubles, and how she could help, even by being just a sounding board, she had to tread carefully. Her father's disappointment that there'd been no justice for those responsible for the mutilation and murder of a young boy the previous year tended to make him irritable. "Do you think the same chief is responsible for this one, too?"

"It doesn't matter what I believe. Let's see what evidence turns up this time, eh?"

The line crackled once more before her father's voice returned, crisp and businesslike. "Now... I wondered if you'd thought about coming home for half term."

Philippa hesitated, reluctant to say no. Her father had been so lonely since her mother died.

"There's room on the Saturday flight from Maseru to Mokhotlong."

She cringed. Her father sounded so hopeful.

"Diana from Drakensberg Air said Mrs Vermoed just cancelled as she's staying in Durban another week. Of course, it's a long journey to make from Cape Town, but I thought I'd put it to you, nonetheless."

Philippa breathed out slowly. Mrs Myburgh was hosting a tennis party the following Saturday, and Philippa desperately hoped Matthew would invite her to the family home, a sprawling mansion in Kenilworth. Even though she was angry with him right now. She knew five weeks was early days, but such an invitation would surely be a sign that Matthew intended their relationship to be more... permanent?

"I'm so sorry, but I can't, Daddy," she said in a rush. "There are quite a few things on and... Matthew's introducing me to his parents," she lied, hating herself for the deception but knowing it was the only excuse her father would readily accept.

"Of course, of course." Her father sounded understanding, which was a relief. "And is this boy worthy of you, my darling? Mrs Lehmann asked if she'll be hearing wedding bells soon."

Philippa tried for a light-hearted laugh. "We've only been seeing each other for a few weeks. I can't wait for you to meet him, though. Oh, and, Daddy! He said he'd love to go on trek if you had something interesting that coincides with the end of term." Another half-truth—Matthew had expressed vague interest when she'd mentioned her father's work, but nothing committal.

"I'm sure that could be arranged. As long as he can stay on a Basuto pony for six hours at a time and isn't afraid of heights." With few roads traversing the treacherous terrain this was a requirement. Her father sounded more relaxed now. "Why don't you bring him home with you at Christmas? I'd like to reassure your dear mother that I've done my due diligence when it's my time to meet her at the pearly gates." He paused. "It's been two years, my girl. My, but you've grown up in that time. She'd be so proud."

Philippa shifted, feeling uncomfortable. She hadn't exactly distinguished herself in her academic career to date. And her mother would have considered that more important than the fact that Philippa had been chosen Cape Town University's Rag Queen and was going out with the only son of the famous Myburgh diamond dynasty.

A niggling kernel of doubt made her squirm as she went on, "Mummy would definitely have approved of not just Matthew but of Mrs Myburgh, too. Or at least, her dress sense." She laughed to diffuse the tension. "Mrs Myburgh was in the social columns of Saturday's Argus and this month's Fair Lady Magazine."

There was more crackling before their connection resumed.

Then Philippa heard, "Well, good for her. Now, if you've got a party to go to, I won't keep you talking."

"It's all right. Matthew—" She hesitated. "Matthew was held up after rugby, so I'll see him at the party later. Tell me more about the investigation. What you're allowed to, anyway." Despite her focus on Cape Town society, Philippa couldn't deny the pull of her father's world—the mysteries and challenges of colonial administration that had formed the backdrop of her childhood.

"You have your mother's tact," her father remarked. "Well, for one thing, it means long days for me. And for the police troopers. They're doing an excellent job, as they did last time. Don't envy the poor fellows. The resident commissioner wants the preliminary report on his desk by next week. And then Stuart's flying me up to Letseng-la-Terai tomorrow. The miners were snowed in last week."

"Stuart, the pilot? I thought he went back to England." Philippa felt a quickening of interest despite herself.

"For his mother's funeral. He returned to Maseru on the first of this month." He chuckled. "I wondered if you'd ask. You had quite the schoolgirl crush on him, if I recall. I have no doubt the Lehmanns and Oosthuysen were all involved in making sure he was rostered to fly you out to St Anne's each term."

"Oh, Daddy, that was when I was sixteen!" Philippa felt her cheeks burn at the memory of the taciturn English pilot with his angular jaw, rock star good looks, and piercing eyes who'd treated her with amused indulgence. "Didn't those gossips have anything better to do?" She turned at the sound of heels clicking down the stairs.

Josie, holding the arm of her latest boyfriend Frank, who played left wing with Matthew, stopped in the corridor to silently mouth an offer of a lift to the party as she pointed to Frank's car keys.

Philippa nodded vigorously.

Let Matthew go to the party on his own. She wasn't always going to be at his beck and call.

"Daddy, I have to go now." She stood up to finish the conversation. "My friends are waiting. Have a good weekend!"

"Don't you two look a sight for sore eyes?" remarked Frank gallantly as Philippa replaced the handset. "Susan got a lift with Barney," he added, offering Philippa his free arm to lead the girls down the steps towards his car.

"And Matthew's gone back to his digs to get changed. He'll meet us at Angela's." Philippa hoped she didn't sound disappointed. "That's if he doesn't fall asleep instead."

Frank flicked a wry glance at Josie. "I'd do the same if I could get away with it. I'm hardly going to be rested for tomorrow's match, am I, Josie, my girl?" He pinched her ear playfully. "Wouldn't you rather hang off the arm of a top South African rugger bugger than—?"

"You boys have never let a good party get in the way of anything," Josie interrupted as he opened the car door. "You drink yourselves stupid the night before and think you can play the hero on the rugby field the day after. And mostly you do, though don't think you can get away with it forever," she grumbled, running one hand through her pixie cut and the other down her emerald green slim-line dress.

"It's called sowing our wild oats. We can't change what nature intended. Why hurry into dull domesticity before we have to?"

Philippa decided to ignore Frank's feigned solemnity as she climbed into the car, shivering in the evening breeze.

Her shiver was from anticipation, too.

Domesticity wasn't dull if one was successful in one's career.

Mr and Mrs Myburgh were successful, and they'd got married when they were younger than Matthew and Philippa. Success was a big house with a swimming pool, parties, clothes and frequent mentions in the press.

That had been Philippa's mother's world back in England, and Philippa was sure her mother would be proud if Philippa regained what had been lost.

Not that Philippa was ashamed of how she'd been brought up, but wouldn't it be wonderful to win back the love and acceptance of her mother's estranged family? To restore the Richmond name to its former glory?

Philippa was every bit Matthew's equal, she reminded herself fiercely. And he was ready to settle down.

Even if he didn't yet know it.

Frank turned onto the jacaranda-lined avenue in front of the cottage where Angela and her two university girlfriends had digs. Music spilled out onto the street and, excitedly, the girls tugged at their gloves and bit colour into their lips as they climbed out of the car.

Matthew was unlikely to have arrived, Philippa surmised, so she was happy to be waylaid by a group of admirers in the passageway where she still had a good view of the front door.

"Hey, Philippa, when are you going to go out with Tommy and put him out of his misery?" asked John, the resident clown, handing her a glass of fizz, which she downed in one go for Dutch courage.

Tommy, who was going to be a nuclear physicist, sent

her a panicked look through coke-bottle horn-rimmed glasses as he flushed to the roots of his oily dark hair and disappeared into the crowd.

John roared with laughter. Brains didn't count for much in their circles. John was popular because he made people laugh, while Matthew enjoyed star billing because not only was he Adonis-handsome, and the heir to a diamond dynasty, he was their best rugby hope. Philippa knew the reason she had any sort of cachet was because she'd been Cape Town University's Rag Queen earlier that year.

And because she was Matthew's girlfriend.

"Tommy is a darling, but I can't risk breaking Matthew's heart!" Philippa responded with mock regret as John peered owlishly at her, brandishing the champagne bottle once more.

"I don't understand why you insist..." he pointed an accusing finger at her, "on going out with no-hoper Matthew Myburgh when you could have me!" He grinned as he carelessly emptied champagne into the various upturned glasses held out towards him, unperturbed by the shrieks of those whose feet got wet in the process.

"Talking of no-hoper Matthew Myburgh, he's certainly taking his time in getting here," Philippa remarked with a pointed look at the door.

Some time later, she was shocked to hear the clock strike ten. How long had she been talking? "Matthew was only going home to change. I knew he'd fall asleep!"

"Matthew? He got here ages ago," said Tommy, re-emerging from the direction of the kitchen.

"He did?" Philippa looked about her but could see no sign of him in the press of bodies.

A few couples were jitterbugging on the Chinese rug

that occupied a tiny rectangle of space amongst the party-goers and the furniture that had been pushed against the walls.

"I saw him upstairs a little while ago." He stabbed a finger in that general direction.

"Philippa... your hair! You look just like Audrey Hepburn!" came an enthusiastic voice after Philippa excused herself to weave through the throng. "And I love your dress!" Marcia Didcott, lounging upon the arm of a comfortable chair as she ruffled the curls of a young man who appeared to be asleep, raked her with an admiring look. "Where did you get it?"

"My mother made it," Philippa didn't mind confessing. Despite her father's position in the Colonial Service, there wasn't a lot of money to splash around, but her mother, who'd always liked to cut a dash, had sewed most of their evening wear. "You haven't seen Matthew, have you?"

Marcia pointed to the ceiling. "He was up there half an hour ago."

Half an hour ago?

Philippa pushed through the crowded sitting room as she made for the stairs. On the first floor, a couple with their arms wrapped about each other swayed to the mellifluous tones of a scratched Bobby Darin record someone had put on for the third time.

It was quieter up here. Philippa leaned against the wall and closed her eyes. She wished she hadn't drunk so much. The walls seemed to throb with sound, and her head spun.

"Somewhere Beyond the Sea" was the song playing.

Philippa swayed to the lyrics and felt the same longing for reunion as sung by her favourite rock 'n roll artist.

Where was Matthew? She missed him. How could he

not have come looking for her? Was he punishing her for not letting him kiss her and for being cross when he was late?

Oh, why had she let Susan get into her ear? Matthew needed gentle nurturing if he was to properly appreciate Philippa and consider her for the role she so desperately wanted. She needed to remember what she was working toward—a place in society that would make her mother's family regret having cast them aside.

That's what her grandmother had said in the letter Philippa had seen in her mother's desk drawer: that Eleanor shouldn't be surprised at being cast aside by her family if she insisted on being so selfish by marrying a nobody and living like a gypsy.

A gypsy! Even two years after reading that old letter, Philippa still burned with indignation.

When the song ended, she returned to the present and opened her eyes. It was time to resume her search, the Persian runner muting her kitten-heeled pumps as she trailed from room to room.

The first door she tried was locked.

The second bedroom was unoccupied.

Frustrated, she retraced her footsteps. Surely Matthew wouldn't have left the party without her?

Outside, a car hooted its horn. Looking towards the window behind her, Philippa noticed an alcove that hid the door to another room. The cottage was like a rabbit warren, bigger than it looked from the outside.

She knocked.

No answer. Perhaps he'd gone to sleep in here. The poor darling must be exhausted after rugby practice. Philippa shouldn't have insisted he come to the party.

"Hello?" she whispered, pushing open the door.

The room was in darkness, but the half-open curtains let in enough light from the street for her to make out movement on the bed.

"Matthew?"

There was a muffled shriek and, in the dim light, some furtive scrambling and smoothing of skirts.

It wasn't Matthew. "Sorry!" Hot with embarrassment, Philippa began to back out of the room. She was just closing the door when a familiar defensive feminine wail, "It's not what you think, Philippa!" made her flick the light switch by the door.

"Susan?"

The guilty lovers on the bed blinked owlishly, Susan smoothing her passion-spoiled chignon and straightening her blue chiffon skirts; Matthew, straightening his tie and adjusting his trousers, his gaze sliding guiltily away from Philippa's shocked face as he slid off the bed and came towards her.

"We weren't doing anything," Susan gabbled. "Really!"

"It's not what it looks like, Philippa—"

Philippa jerked her arm back as Matthew reached forward, his aftershave enveloping her like a cloud of betrayal. Tears stung the back of her eyes as she wrenched open the door behind her once more, trying to make sense of the scene.

Susan? Her best friend?

And Matthew? Her boyfriend?

"It's not what you think." Matthew pleaded innocence now, but in the harsh light, there was no mistaking the lipstick on his shirt collar and around his mouth, nor the guilt on both of their faces.

Without waiting to hear another word, Philippa spun round and ran from the room. Her careful plans, her dreams of a life with Matthew, her path back to her mother's world —all of it crumbling around her as she fled.

Get it HERE

ALSO WRITING AS BEVERLEY OAKLEY

A LONDON LADIES IN PERIL MYSTERY
Murder and mystery in a high-class London brothel in the 1870s.
A Fatal Rendezvous in Mayfair
Murder at Madame Chambon's
The Governess of Everleigh Manor

FAIR CYPRIANS OF LONDON Series
Saving Grace
Forsaking Hope
Keeping Faith
Wedding Violet
Christmas Charity
Loving Lily
Books 1-3
Books 1-5

HEARTS IN HIDING Series
The Duchess and the Highwayman
The Bluestocking and the Rake

Duchess of Seduction
The Countess and the Cavalier

SCANDALOUS MISS BRIGHTWELLS Series
Rake's Honour
Rake's Redemption
Rogue's Kiss
The Wedding Wager
The Accidental Elopement
The Honourable Fortune Hunter
The Courtship Caper
The Wilful Widow
The Gypsy and the Gentleman
Books 1-3
Books 4-7

DAUGHTERS OF SIN Series
Her Gilded Prison
Dangerous Gentlemen
The Mysterious Governess
Beyond Rubies
Lady Unveiled: The Cuckold's Conspiracy
Books 1-3
Box Set: Books 1-5

GEORGIAN MYSTERY ROMANCE Series
Wicked Wager
Her Valentine's Secret

The Daughters of Sin series follows the intertwining lives and sibling rivalry of Lord Partington's two nobly born - and two illegitimate - daughters as they compete for love during several London Seasons.

With Hetty and Araminta both falling for men on opposing sides of a dastardly plot that is being investigated by Stephen Cranborne, a secret agent in the Foreign Office, there's lashings of skulduggery and intrigue bound up in the central romance.

What Readers are Saying About the Series:

"...lies, misdeeds, treachery, and romance. What an impressive story! Ms. Oakley has a unique way of telling her stories, bringing unknown heroes/ heroines into the spotlight, as they navigate a world of espionage, and intrigue, all while trying to survive and find their HEA. Magnificent and mesmerizing!" ~ **Amazon reader**

"Full of secrets, murders, intrigues. You feel you know the characters and want to strangle some of them, especially Araminta!!! I have since read all in the series and can't wait for Book 5... This is a series I will read again and again." ~ **Amazon reader**

Below is the order of the books:

Book 1: Her Gilded Prison

Book 2: Dangerous Gentlemen

Book 3: The Mysterious Governess

Book 4: Beyond Rubies

Book 5: Lady Unveiled: The Cuckold Conspiracy

Buy the complete series as a Box set and save.

Enjoy - sizzling romance with passion and intrigue!

THE DUCHESS AND THE HIGHWAYMAN

A duchess disguised as a lady's maid; a gentleman parading as a highwayman.

She's on the run from a murderer, he's in pursuit of one.

Married off at a young age to a brutal nobleman, Phoebe, Lady Cavanaugh, longs for love—and enters into a risky affair. Framed for her husband's murder, she flees wearing only a blood-stained chemise and is rescued by a handsome 'highwayman' who believes she's Lady Cavanaugh's maidservant.

Hugh Redding has his own reasons for hunting the man whose mission is to see the infamous and elusive Murdering Duchess hanged for murder. And Phoebe, the 'maidservant with aspirations above her station' might prove the very weapon he needs—once he teaches her how to behave like a lady.

Only when Phoebe mysteriously disappears does Hugh realise the real identity of the spirited wench he'd set out to tame—and the danger she's in.

Burdened by the knowledge of his unwitting role in placing Phoebe in mortal peril, Hugh must now polish his skills as a gentleman, not only to save Phoebe from the gallows, but to win back her heart.

What the readers say:

"This love story has so much going for it - strong characters, friendship, "building of trust, a common enemy and of course, a beautiful second chances rómance." ~ **Amazon reader.**

"A heart pounding read!" ~ **Amazon reader.**

"I loved how the author gave us an exciting opening scenario and then smoothly and effortlessly built the story up to an exciting and riveting climax. Wow!" ~ **Amazon reader.**

Read for Free in KU here.

About the Author

Born into a family of adventurers, Beverley (B.G.) Nettelton spent her earliest years in Lesotho's remote, mountainous terrain, drawing inspiration from the African kingdom's craggy peaks and far-flung valleys to shape her *Wings over Africa* series.

Under her other pen names - Beverley Eikli and Beverley Oakley —she writes historical romance with mystery and suspense, and Regency Romantic Comedies.

Beverley's dashing bush pilot characters are based on the handsome Norwegian aviator who swept her off her feet when Beverley ran safari lodges in Botswana's pristine, game-rich Okavango Delta.

She began her writing career as a journalist, but it was during long aerial survey contracts around the world—often as the sole woman among the crew—that she began to write romance novels.

Beverley lives just north of Melbourne with the same wonderful husband she whisked away from Botswana thirty years ago, together with their youngest daughter (the oldest lives in Norway), and a gorgeous, dopey Rhodesian Ridgeback.

When she's not writing, she runs a bed & breakfast & Farmstay business (called *Wuthering Heights*) in South

Australia's beautiful wine growing Clare Valley with her two sisters, and teaches Writing.

You can connect with her at:
Beverley (at) beverleysbooks.com
www.beverleysbooks.com
facebook.com/BGNettelton
https://www.instagram.com/bgnettelton_author

www.ingramcontent.com/pod-product-compliance
Lightning Source LLC
Chambersburg PA
CBHW050106120726
47904CB00004B/1242